WHEN THE WIND BLOWS

WHEN THE WIND BLOWS

By

MARGUERITE STEEN

KAYE & WARD LTD
LONDON

First published by
Cassell & Company Ltd
1931
Reprinted by
Kaye & Ward Ltd
21 New Street, London EC2M 4NT
1975
Copyright Marguerite Steen 1931

ISBN 0 7182 1108 1

Printed in Great Britain by
REDWOOD BURN LIMITED
Trowbridge & Esher

WHEN THE WIND BLOWS

CHAPTER I

For two days storm had raged on the island, and there was
said to be more to come. Along the ragged line of beach
the breakers piled themselves in hummocks of grey glass, or
forced themselves with the violence of waterspouts up the
long, narrow gulches, filling them brimful of churned white
water and spray. The savage undertow sucked back from
the black lava reefs, leaving them exposed like the vertebræ
of some prehistoric monster, and returned laden with kelp,
which it piled against cliff and embankment. Turbulence in
a hundred little pools and crevasses, left stagnant at low
tide; small, terrified crustaceans scrambling into rock fis-
sures to escape annihilation from the element that threatened
their strongholds; quivering rock things, half torn from
their moorings, resisted with all their pliant force the onslaught of the sea that laid bare their foundations at one
moment, only to bury them the next in the flurry of shingle
and sea-wrack carried in the heart of a mountainous wave.

Gallinules and sulmers, wheeling through the fountains
of spray, opened wide their beaks, and were strangled by
the brutal wind, which, coming into being in the long night
about the Pole, bore down on the island, avid to rend and
to destroy.

The island has two names: one it owes to the grim
religious inspiration of an early settler, Jebusa Horne, who,
being one day at sea in his canvas coracle, and looking back
upon the island, is supposed, according to legend, to have

seen, shaping itself in a column of pale fire on the top of that
sharp basaltic peak that crowns the rock, a gigantic cross. He
may really have seen it; strange apparitions come, between
night mist and setting sun, upon the islands of the south
Atlantic.   Between fear and religious ecstasy, Jebusa Horne
is said to have fallen upon his knees in the coracle—a
miraculous act in itself, but vouched for by his companions
—and, crying out upon the Lord in a loud voice, christened
the island Calvary.   As Calvary it figures upon a few large
scale maps of the southern seas; as Calvary it lingers in the
minds of the few who have looked upon its sharp and bitter
outline. A place of martyrdom: a place accursed: a meeting
place of the winds that have played their part in its existence since the days when some convulsion of the ocean flung
up the volcanic group of which Calvary is one. When the
wind dies, death sinks upon Calvary: an unnatural stillness,
like an ashy veil, falls over the whole island: bird, beast and
man are alike uneasy, and can take no pleasure of the lull,
because of the deep apprehension which takes possession of
them. They are all children of the wind; when the wind dies,
they are fatherless and motherless.

The second name of the island survives among the
islanders themselves. Old Jebusa—a natural tyrant—had
done his best to eradicate its pagan syllables, but when his
vision took place, the days of his autocracy were drawing to a
close; to put it plainly, he was senile. His seed, growing up
about him with incredible virility, considering the unpromising soil he had chosen for its sowing—not that you will get
present-day Hornes to admit that their great-great-grandmother was a creole—dismissed the vision as another signal
of old age. Jebusa must have been pathetic in those days;
his frame had grown altogether too feeble to support the
blustering authority with which he strove to quell three
strapping sullen sons and a buxom daughter. He had his
recompense, however, when the Burrows-Holbrooke Expedition visited the island, somewhere in the beginning of
the century, deferring to Jebusa in every particular regard-

ing established names and customs. As Calvary the island was entered upon the maps of the Expedition, and Jebusa, sighing with relief, felt that he had done something to erase the old impious traditions of the place.

So the island, which remained El Secredo to most of its inhabitants, became Calvary to the world in general—or at any rate to that limited section which had heard of its existence.

"The Secret of the Atlantic": that was the full name bestowed upon it by those Spanish pirates who had found there a convenient *cache* for their plunder. A bloody—and irrelevant—record they left behind them; a few hazy legends survive of rolls of moidores, bullion, pearls, diamonds and so forth—doubtless much exaggerated—which were commandeered on behalf of the British Government in the latter part of the eighteenth century.

Only the descendants of the pirates remained to resent this appropriation of their perquisites; the poor, effete remnant of a stock that had worn itself out with violence, and left a clutch of half-breeds, imbeciles and degenerates to welcome the British garrison on their landing. No written records survive of these early peoples; knowing the climatic conditions of El Secredo, one wonders how they managed to support life at all in such inimical surroundings, for both animal and vegetable forms take poorly to the barren soil. One hears vaguely that one was a Circassian; an extremely unlikely story drags in the name of a Manchu princess; a Roman courtesan seems to have had something to do with it. The pirates appear to have ranged far for their women, and, when tired of them, apparently dumped them on El Secredo. Marriage within the prohibited degrees seems to have been a recognized thing: with rare confusion of offspring, and all the concomitant results, as deduced by modern psychopathists.

Beyond a little distracted gibbering, and a few choreatic attempts at resistance, we may assume that the inhabitants put up a poor defence of the treasure which conveyed little to their diseased minds. As no contemporary historians make mention of any notable addition to the country's revenue in 1797, or thereabouts, it seems likely that the reputed treasure had dwindled to a few handsful of coin, a string or two of pearls, and perhaps a little bag of those small yellowish diamonds, of no lapidary value, which are still to be found in the agglomerate and scorral layers of the island itself. If the pirates had a *cache* on El Secredo the invaders did not discover it, and after a month of search among the sea-bird haunted caves, took out their disappointment in witticisms at the expense of the helpless islanders, before settling down to make the best of the pirates' leavings.

In the same way that every American lays claim to ancestors who came over in the *Mayflower*, so it will be found that no present-day islander will acknowledge descent from any island-dweller previous to Jebusa Horne. According to them the descendants of the pirates faded out from sheer effeteness, within months of Jebusa's landing. Yet to the thoughtful, it must appear a little curious that twenty-five lusty British lads jettisoned on El Secredo by order of their government, and not recalled until a year after Horne had made his forced landing, from a ship jury-rigged after a fifteen days' encounter with the roaring trade winds, should have left no more tangible trace of their occupation than a few obsolete fire-arms, a ship's bugle and the rag of the British flag, jealously preserved in the mission. A number of Jebusa's shipmates returned to England when the cruiser came to pick up the garrison, and a little nucleus of hardly a dozen remained, from whom, according to that carefully bowdlerized Calvary history which is circularized in home quarters, the present population of just over a hundred sprang. There are, however, long memories among the islanders, and now and again, set free by some act hardly in accordance with the stern present-day morality, old legends revive, and are circulated in whispers among such of the community who are sure of their own family trees. The people of El Secredo have their own methods of enforcing law and order; and, to put it plainly, some of these derive more from a Manchu or Roman type of legislation than from Western standards of law-giving.

To these whispers the Reverend Smith Prudhomme turns a deliberately deaf ear. For the sake of his own peace of mind, the Reverend Smith denies that the vice-haunted corpuscles which circulated in the veins of Circassian slave, Manchu princess or—most horrid thought—Roman courtesan, could survive to pollute the blood of his little flock, who have been under the protective wing of British Protestantism ever since old Jebusa Horne, with tears in his rheumy eyes, dispatched an appeal to the government to send a spiritual shepherd to Calvary. With "tushes," with "pooh-poohs," and with hearty recapitulations of the historic landing of old Jebusa from his wind-battered sailing ship, when, according to the Reverend Smith—who was indifferent about his facts, but, like a good many other people, grew more certain the less data he had to go upon —the last of the pirates' descendants was a bedridden old woman, he refuted legend. He was the kind of man who obstinately refuses to see what he does not wish to see; and when the islanders broke into one of their sporadic attacks of whispering, when the name of Spidhorodellis went chiming on the wind—how the dickens had they got hold of its strange syllables?—when fingers began to be pointed and conjectures hatched for the departure of one of their flock from the accepted normal, the Reverend Smith Prudhomme sallied forth, full of sturdy purpose, spiritual heartiness and healthy righteousness, to call the attention of men already dog-tired with their endless struggle against the elements to the fact that the mission roof needed repairing, or a portion of the allotments refencing. And as they toiled he led them in song; for according to the Reverend Smith, a cheerful spirit was a short cut to godliness. Following a missionary named Simpson, known for the gloominess of his spiritual outlook, the Reverend Smith felt it incumbent

upon him to exaggerate the sprightliness of his naturally
sanguine temperament, until, in a more sensitive community, it is probable he would have gone in danger of his
life. Upon the El Secredo people, however, his determined
"Ha-ha's," his really frightful bonhomie, had as little effect
as a pebble flung against granite. They humoured him so
far as to grunt the choruses to his songs, and when the task
was ended, the Reverend Smith, feeling that he had won a
battle for the Lord against the powers of unrighteousness,
as typified by the ghosts of El Secredo, would tramp back
to his wife with *Onward Christian Soldiers* on his lips.

"I think I've fixed *that*," said he, on the second day of the
storm, as he annexed the kettle in which Mrs. Prudhomme
had been heating a little water, and proceeded to wash his
hands. "Look at those, Mary! More like a navvy's than a
clergyman's, eh? Ha!"

"Fixed what, Smith?" asked Mrs. Prudhomme, who
never missed her cues. The Reverend Smith, still humming
about his soldiers, fixed upon her a bright and Christian
smile, as he passed his two wet hands over the high and
conical scalp whose baldness he continually endeavoured to
conceal—although El Secredo is not critical of tonsorial
adornments—with a streaky disposal of his somewhat sandy
locks.

"They've been whispering again," he announced, por-
tentously. "I've fixed the men; nothing like horny-handed
toil"—Mrs. Prudhomme winced; she had literary sensitiveness, although fifteen years of the Reverend Smith had
toughened most of her fibres—"for chasing away un-
healthiness. It's the storm, of course. I always notice they
get particularly unsettled just before a storm. I'd like you
to have a little sing-song to-night for the women."

"Very well, Smith," said Mrs. Prudhomme; nor, to her
credit, did she sigh for the hour she had planned to spend
in writing up the diary which was her substitute for a letter
home. A ship was overdue; Mrs. Prudhomme was living
for the mail, for the letters from her own people that would

serve for a while to transplant her, in imagination, from El Secredo to the Sussex village she had left three years ago.

Night was falling, and the oil-lamp flickered in the draughts which crossed and recrossed the narrow room. Where did they come from? No one ever knew; the walls were like patchwork, with pieces of tarpaulin, bullock hides and odd garments hung up to exclude the winds that seemed everywhere to have right of entry. Three feet thick the walls were, built of basalt rock; and the Atlantic winds made grass of them. The familiar whoop and sob under the low-cut eaves no longer troubled the Prudhommes; they were used to it—as to most of the other privations of the island.

"By the way, Mary"—a slight frown creased the smooth brow of the Reverend Smith; his wife interpreted this as a sign that he was about to become official—"I'd like you to make sure that Sanchia is there to-night."

Mrs. Prudhomme looked meekly towards her husband; she had a bad cold in the head, with which, and a large, unlaundered pocket-handkerchief, she struggled before replying.

"I'll make a point of seeing Sanchia," she assured him.

"You'd better take her along with you, Mary." The Reverend Smith searched querulously for fleas, then looked up so suddenly that Mrs. Prudhomme realized with a start that for once in her life she had missed her cue.

"It's this wretched cold," she apologized, incoherently. "I really think I shall have to take some aspirin; how many are left? What is it about Sanchia, Smith?"

The Reverend Smith, contented as an angler who, after patient waiting, had at last landed his fish, leaned back in his chair, the only comfortable one in the room. Wide and deep, with slung seat and back of cowhide, from which the hair had been worn in shiny patches, it was originally the possession of old Jebusa Horne, whose grandson had presented it, in token of respect, to a predecessor of the Reverend Smith.

Smoke belched down into the room, as the wind slapped
the chimneys with the flat of a giant hand; the Reverend
Smith, with lungs like leather, made little of it, and continued his flea-hunting; Mrs. Prudhomme struggled with a
fit of coughing, and finally gave in. . . .

"You have got a cold," he remarked, judicially.   "We
must take care I don't get it.   The drug chest is getting
pretty low, and there won't be any hope of a ship while this
weather continues.   It is difficult to remember that one's
duty is to be bright, when one has a cold; but I know you
will do your best.   Oh, yes, Sanchia.   By the way, I have
often meant to ask Sophia Mullyon how she came to christen
her daughter Sanchia.   A strange, foreign note—not—
hrrum—quite the thing, one feels, in a community so
essentially British as ours.   Unfortunate, too, in a way.
One is inclined to fancy—these things just flash into one's
head—that it gives the girl ideas about herself—ideas——"

"What kind of ideas?"

"Oh—just *ideas*," said the Reverend Smith; and Mrs.
Prudhomme sighed.   Somehow, whenever he was beginning
to say something interesting, it tailed off, like that.   She
never quite got used to the disappointment of it.

"I'm afraid she's taking very badly to this idea of marriage with Gregory Jodrell."

"Perhaps they won't get married after all," suggested
Mrs. Prudhomme, for something to say.

"Don't be silly," said the Reverend Smith.   "Sanchia's
got to marry, and so has Gregory Jodrell.   Old Jodrell was
talking very seriously to me about it the other day."

"But surely, if they aren't in love with one another——"

"Counsel of perfection, my dear Mary.   How many
times am I to remind you that things don't work out like
that on Calvary?"

"But supposing she were in love with someone else?"

"In that case," said the Reverend Smith, piously, "the
course of true affection"—he rarely spoke of love, save in
connexion with holy matters—"would no doubt have to—

hrrum—take its own course. What a peculiar sentence—
ha! But I don't need to pick and choose my words with you,
my dear. To return to Sanchia: both she and her mother
inform me that she has no preference whatever. She only
knows that she does not particularly want to marry Gregory
Jodrell. I must say that it strikes me as rather unnatural that
a comely and—hrrum—ripe young female like Sanchia
Mullyon should not, with—hrrum—the material at her disposal, have developed preferences by now. By Jupiter,
Mary, there's a Goliath for you!"

Mrs. Prudhomme regarded sympathetically the insect
her husband had just captured. Even for El Secredo, which
produces them in millions, the flea in question was a
pontifical specimen of its kind.

"Some girls develop later than others in that respect,"
she said. "Sanchia is a very unusual girl—a very intelligent
girl—quite different from the others. I sometimes think
there must be something in that old tale after all."

"*Mary!*" bellowed the Reverend Smith, "I will not have
you bringing up that regrettable and disgraceful story—do
you hear me? Sanchia Mullyon is Sanchia Mullyon; to
regard her as anything else is to revive a whole lot of
undesirable matters that are a menace to the community at
large."

"I'm so sorry, Smith. I can't help being interested in
the old island stories."

"So long as you regard them as stories and do not begin
to associate them with living people, it doesn't worry me
what you are interested in. But kindly remember, Mary,
that the whole solidarity of Calvary rests upon its disassociation from those earlier pagans.

"When I first came to Calvary," stated the Reverend
Smith, in the voice in which he was accustomed to rehearse
the lectures he hoped to deliver on his return to civilization,
"I was, I will frankly own, shocked by the business-like
spirit which the inhabitants brought to bear upon the holy
sacrament of marriage. Affection—hrrum—in its deepest

form, in fact one might say, *love*"—Mr. Prudhomme dropped
his voice to the note which genteel people use for words
like adultery, lavatories and vomiting—"had always seemed
to me the only basis upon which one could contract matrimony. Practical experience has given me, by the grace of
God, a wider outlook, a deeper appreciation of the funda-
mental needs of mankind. Affection for the people of Calvary
has given me a better understanding of their motives.

"Calvary," said the Reverend Smith, raising his voice
and his head simultaneously, as though he addressed a
distant gallery, "is probably the only British colony of
to-day with an overpowering male majority. Unique indeed
are the social problems of this outpost of our——"

"Empire!" gasped Mrs. Prudhomme, who, seeing the
noxious adjective hovering between his top teeth and his
lower lip, could not for her life help the interruption.

"The old question of the survival of the fittest becomes,
on Calvary, a problem of the sharpest significance," resumed
the Reverend Smith, unchecked. "The women, for some
reason known only to Providence, have, during the last two
generations, produced male children in a proportion of
forty to one. Calvary is, in fact, fair field for the sexual
experimentalist." Here the Reverend Smith coughed,
feeling that his broad-mindedness had carried him, perhaps,
a little far. He was not naturally broad-minded: with the
result that any statement transcending the bounds of the
purely conventional burst from him with the effect of an
oath from the lips of a less discreet individual. As Mrs.
Prudhomme showed no signs of distaste, he coughed once
more, before resuming the thread of his discourse. "The
obvious problem is the provision of means by which the
finer stock may propagate itself."

"In other words," said Mrs. Prudhomme, who, being a
little feverish with her cold, was less in sympathy than usual
with her husband's prolixity, "it doesn't matter so much
about the Hawkinses and the Robertsons and the Martyns
and the Barkers, but Gregory Jodrell must have children."

"The rest can wait," pronounced the Reverend Smith, not quite approving of the bluntness of this statement. "One never knows what a ship may bring—and in three or four years the younger girls will be growing up——"

"But surely they will belong to their own contemporaries?" put in Mrs. Prudhomme. "It seems rather foolish to rob one generation to furnish another, doesn't it?"

"Always the pessimist, eh, my dear? Ha!" said the Reverend Smith, "what does R. L. S. say about the sin of depression?"

"Really, I'm not at all depressed, Smith——"

"Even if the worst happens, and, say, the Barkers die out, Calvary will not suffer to any notable degree. *Most* unsatisfactory, the Barkers: you will remember what a bad report Simpson left of them. An account which I am bound to say was in no way overdrawn. Something—hrrum—unhealthy in that stock somewhere. Morally all right, I suppose—they're always at the services; but from the social standpoint a dead-weight. Calvary," said the Reverend Smith, with a temporary return to his platform manner, "can't afford dead-weights. Each man must pull his stroke or the boat capsizes. Think of those potato crops last summer: not more than a few hundredweight in all from Job Barker's land. Which section of the allotment wall fell in first? The section in charge of Solomon Barker. Ineffectual, inert," summarized the Reverend Smith—and paused to recollect what they were really talking about.

"And now the curious situation has arisen that, with seven or eight young men of marriageable age on the island, of whom, by virtue both of breeding and character, Gregory Jodrell takes precedence, there is only one young woman who, having reached years of discretion, can suitably be named as his future wife."

"What's the hurry?" asked Mrs. Prudhomme, half absently. "Why can't Gregory wait, with the others, until Martha and Betty Robertson and little Machita have grown up?"

"Those are matters, my dear," said the Reverend Smith modestly, "that cannot becomingly be discussed between a man and a woman."

"I wonder why," said Mrs. Prudhomme simply. "When Bulger goes wandering out at night you always tell me that I needn't worry, that it just means he's on heat and must gratify his instincts. I suppose it's like that?"

"A little," admitted the Reverend Smith, awkwardly. "By the grace of God, and through the stern discipline which nature metes out in these parts to those who struggle for their daily bread, the young men of Calvary have learnt to control their baser natures. It is a lovely thought—indeed a very lovely thought, Mary," he amended, rising, and going to draw aside the window-curtain, to look out into the whirling night, "that since the days when Jebusa Horne first set foot on Calvary no sin has polluted our little community. I sometimes think that his stern old spirit has become our guardian angel; I feel in a way accountable to Jebusa Horne."

Mrs. Prudhomme looked up from her darning, and let the hand with a sock on it fall into her lap. When he said things like this, she felt that she was very fond of Smith. The pity was he did not say them more often. Like many women, she found the touch of humility very endearing—the more so because it was so rare.

"The free Atlantic breezes," he continued, lyrically, "have purified our hearts! How strange it is to think that here, where grass grows unwillingly, where every tree is a challenge to the destructive forces of nature, where the potato——" he broke off: the potato fell short, somehow, of poetic requirement—"where the seed material falls from generation to generation upon stony ground, the seed spiritual burgeons and brings forth the sweet fruits of faith, hope, charity, purity and trust in the benevolence of an all-wise God!"

Mrs. Prudhomme glanced at the clock. If she was really to collect the women for the singing practice, it was time she

was on her way. In a little over an hour they would be preparing supper—a scanty meal, in these days when the boat
was expected, and provisions of every kind running low.
She cast an inquiring glance at the Reverend Smith. If only
he would change his mind! It seemed so thoughtless, at the
end of a day's work, when some of them had not seen their
husbands since daybreak, and on such a night, to expect
them to leave their firesides and stagger through the windy
dark to the mission-house.

Unfortunately, the Reverend Smith misinterpreted her
ocular question.

"That's right, my dear; you had better be setting out.
There is more gossip goes on between now and bedtime
than at any other hour of the day, and they must be taken
out of themselves."

Why? thought Mrs. Prudhomme, as she drew over head
and shoulders the storm-cloak which three years of sea-spray
had turned from its original navy to a streaky bice-green.
Why shouldn't they gossip? In the name of goodness, what
had they to talk about, on Calvary, save each other; and what
harm was done by it? Once, at her husband's request, she
had tried getting them together and reading to them; but,
worn out with their hard day's work, and lulled by the sound
of her voice, they had fallen asleep, and Janet Hawkins, who
was very stout, had rolled off her chair and broken a blood-
vessel. It did not seem worth while repeating the experiment. They could not sleep in singing time, for she kept
them on their feet, save for short rests between the songs;
but she felt a brute for doing it, and was always weakly
apologetic in her manner towards them. It would have surprised Mrs. Prudhomme very much if she had known that
they were fond of her.

She found and lit the lantern, and stood with one hand on
the latch of the door.

"I'm sorry for poor Sanchia, all the same," she stated, as
though something had obliged her to say it.

"Dear me, I don't see why you need be, Mary," answered

her husband, a trifle fretfully; Mary was trying in these moods of mild disagreement. He would almost have preferred it if she had given fierce battle to his pronouncements. "You must not let your naturally sympathetic nature run away with you, my dear. Gregory Jodrell is an excellent fellow, and will make her a good husband—probably better than she deserves," he added, with that touch of spite which Sanchia sometimes roused in him; she was so independent—there was something almost lacking in respect in her bearing, and she spoke as though she were one's equal. Impelled by his religion to be, theoretically at least, a socialist, the Reverend Smith Prudhomme acknowledged a weakness for people who paid tribute to his standing as a gentleman.

"But he is so dull—and Sanchia is not like the rest of the girls," said Mrs. Prudhomme hurriedly; and, having launched her little dart in Sanchia's defence, passed out into the wind, feeling she had been a little foolish; for surely no one was more capable of looking after herself than Sanchia Mullyon!

The wind spun her round before she found her balance; breathlessly she clung for a moment to the side of the mission-house, before rallying her forces to plunge, in its very teeth, along the rough stony road—scarcely more than a cart-track—which led to the settlement. The lantern fell clattering from her hand, and rolled to extinction in a pool. The wind robbed her of her breath and the thunder of the Atlantic throbbed in her ear-drums; she could see the white crests of the breakers as they plunged along the foreshore, like a procession of ghosts sketched on the blackness of the night. The ghosts of Calvary! She felt like a leaf spinning in the blasts of eternity. A sudden wave of desperate homesickness tightened her throat; she fought against it with all her might, telling herself there was no time for homesickness on Calvary. She had got to be bright and cheerful, for the women's sake. If only she did not feel so ill, so hot and cold in turns, and her throat so horribly sore. She had a pain between her shoulders, too. . . .

She shook herself angrily, determining to give no more thought to her own insignificant ills. In another year she would be back in England, and this would all be like a bad dream; she might even enjoy looking back on it.

Resolutely she turned her mind to the subject they had just been discussing.

Even if one was not fond of Sanchia Mullyon—and how, indeed, could one be fond of anything so arrogant, so contemptuous?—one could not help being interested in her. She was so much the most unaccountable of all the unaccountable things on the island. Sometimes it seemed to Mrs. Prudhomme—who struggled, vainly, against imaginative tendencies—that Sanchia was the spirit of the island; the lava and basalt of its conformation seemed to have gone to her making, the turbulent grey of the Atlantic was in her eyes, and the alkaline quality of her resembled the springs on Calvary, only one of which was available for drinking purposes. Twice a week, during the summer droughts, ox-wagons fitted with vast wooden drums set out for the farther side of the island and returned with the water-supply, which even then had to be boiled before it was fit for human consumption.

At all times the girl seemed completely alien; her spirit, withdrawn to an immense distance, stood exteriorly and surveyed the conditions to which she was condemned. At least, this was how it struck Mrs. Prudhomme. "She is the only one who has the wit to be cynical about life," thought Mrs. Prudhomme—and was immensely shocked at herself; for surely cynicism is not wit.

The Mullyons were of the earliest among the settlers: the first Mullyons had come with old Jebusa—they and the Jodrells. The Hornes had become extinct with the last generation, when Stephen Horne met his end in the cloud-burst which sucked him over the gulch called Steaming Creek, and dashed him to death upon the rocks below. But they had left their seed behind them; there were few island families that could not boast a strain of Horne blood.

Stephen had just been married, and mourning for his death was modified by the fact that his untimely withdrawal had left another woman at the disposal of the community. Within a few months Sophia Horne, born a Robertson, was married to Thomas Mullyon, and became the mother of Sanchia, and, in due time, of twin boys as well. Of these, one was born a cripple, and died in infancy; the other had married when but a lad of seventeen.

One may assume that Sophia Mullyon held her head high because she had managed to produce a daughter. From childhood matrimonial plans circulated about the cradle of the young Sanchia. There could have been no more fuss about it if she had been born the daughter of a reigning king. It was generally accepted that Samson Jodrell would have first say in the matter of her disposal. It is said that he went by night to the Mullyon's house, and looked upon the infant Sanchia, dozing and dribbling in her crib.

"Gregory, my son, is a fine fellow," was all he said; but the Mullyons understood, and were satisfied. A Mullyon and a Jodrell; that was as it should be. Two of the oldest island families joining. No one criticized the mute decision, save, when Sanchia was nine or so, and a wild, headstrong creature, old Betsy Barker, who, having passed her hundredth birthday, was exempt from the formalities which bound other folk. Betsy's mother had accompanied her husband, who was Jebusa Horne's first mate, and Betsy's memory at a hundred and one, though freakish, had a way of retaining matters which—in the opinion of the Reverend Smith Prudhomme—were better forgotten.

"You looking Mullyon-way for Gregory!" she snickered one night, in the Jodrells' kitchen. "You might ha' done better than that, surelee, Samson Jodrell! Mullyon blood bain't like Barker blood"—family pride prompted this side-long reference to two weedy nieces, one already stricken with tuberculosis, but both affianced, and with their weddings in sight. "Nor like Jodrell blood neether. Queer folk, is Mullyons. Mullyons isn't Mullyons all through."

They let her drivel on; they had heard it all before, old
Betsy's apocryphal tale of the first Mullyon and his wife,
whose child, born dead within an hour or two of landing,
was replaced, unknown to the mother, by a baby of dubious
parentage. Betsy swore that her mother had been a party to
the act of exchange; but the singular thing was that no one
seemed to know of it. Apparently there had been chaos on
the night of landing: Flora Mullyon was delivered almost
untended, within a hundred yards of Atlantic rollers, upon
the beach. At any rate, all had been confusion, and William
Mullyon, together with his wife, seems to have accepted the
child as their own.

"They say there was no women on El Secredo," wickered
old Betsy. "Well I mind her; she looked like a fairy—that
thin the wind would blow her away; an' hair on her like flax
on a spindle, all hung wi' shells savage-like, and stones as
worn't shells neither. She couldn't speak naught but her
own heathen tongue, and poor crittur, her wits was astray.
But she was pretty—eh! I can see her like 'twas yesterday.
Some said as she was young an' some said as she was old, but
I can't tell ye which was right. The sea took her."

So much for the pirates' leavings—if one accepts Betsy's
story. Flora Mullyon died of her exposure, and the child
called Mullyon was reared by devious means, and, in his
turn, married and begat children who survived him. From
this questionable stock, therefore, according to old Betsy,
sprang Thomas, the father of Sanchia. Against her version
one has to set the stout persistence of the first Mullyon that
the child was his own. In El Secredo records one may read
the entrance of the baptism of Ralph, the son of William and
Flora Mullyon, both of Charmouth in the county of Dorset;
born on El Secredo the first day of March, 1829, baptized
July 6th, 1851, a date coinciding with the baptism of his own
first son, James.

Those who affect to accept the Barker version of the tale
adduce this as additional evidence that Ralph Mullyon was
not entitled to the name he bore. William Mullyon's piety

was part of the island tradition; he and old Jebusa are said to have led the islanders in prayer long before Jebusa's prayer for a missionary was answered by the British Government. It is known that the first missionary was sent out in 1840, and the doubting Thomases declare it is unthinkable that William should have neglected for eleven years to have his son received into the church. His carelessness in this respect is put down to indifference, since the youth was not his son; others say that Ralph Mullyon was a rebellious and frowardly fellow who refused baptism, but was eventually brought into the way of righteousness by his marriage with Anna Horne. Either way it appears, according to these disputants, that Ralph was no Mullyon.

However that may have been, William Mullyon bestowed his name upon the lad, and no Mullyon of the present generation has ever showed, by so much as the flicker of an eyelash, that he accepts the blot painted upon his escutcheon by the grimy finger of old Betsy Barker.

Yet, if her tale were true, what fearful fluid ran in the veins of the young Sanchia?

Samson Jodrell, a man incapable of prevarication and slow to believe in it, vetoed the Barker history. Thomas Mullyon was his friend, a staunch, narrow-minded Puritan, whose virtues were enhanced by the Horne stock in his blood. Sanchia was a fine girl; whose coyness, where Gregory was concerned, was proof to old Samson of her self-respect. Not that El Secredo women had any call to pursue their men. Samson glimpsed the devil behind her apparent coyness which promised surprises for the somewhat lethargic Gregory, when he should have her for his own. Samson was all for hastening the wedding; Sanchia had been coy long enough. It was time Gregory was settling down, turning his attention to the land—as no doubt he would do, when once the mating maggot in his blood was appeased. Sanchia would become Gregory's domestic beast, bearing his children, caring for his house and his health, merging herself as time went on into the replica of those other island women, from whom, at a very early age, the rigours of existence stamped the fugitive bloom of their youth. It was as well that the wives of El Secredo men lost their powers of attraction soon after marriage; it consolidated a contract beside which, on El Secredo, the laws of the Medes and Persians were feeble and fleeting.

Sanchia Mullyon was to become Gregory Jodrell's domestic beast. An attractive and suitable programme—from Samson Jodrell's point of view.

CHAPTER II

As Mrs. Prudhomme plunged along the track towards the settlement, the lights towards which she struggled were suddenly effaced, and before she had time to wonder at this phenomenon, she found herself crashing full-tilt into an object moving in the opposite direction to herself. Mrs. Prudhomme disengaged her front teeth from the gritty surface of serge, and a faint cry escaped her. Three years of El Secredo had enhanced, rather than diminished, her fear of the dark—a small shameful fear which she kept locked up from herself and, above all, from the Reverend Smith. Her cry was torn to ribbons in the gale, it assuredly never reached other ears than her own. Mrs. Prudhomme shrieked above the wind.

"Who is that?"

The answer came after an appreciable pause, as though the speaker was not accustomed to making use of his tongue hurriedly.

"It is me, ma'am; Gregory Jodrell."

"What are you doing?" screamed Mrs. Prudhomme; her heart still hammered against her side.

"I was going," he began slowly, "to have a look at the embankment. I thought it might ha' gone in the wind."

"Haven't you a lantern?"

"Ay; I was saving the candle until I got there."

She was reminded that, until the arrival of the ship, every candle-end they possessed was precious, and hoped guiltily that no one would discover, before morning, the lantern she had carelessly dropped in the pool. The roar of the sea gathered itself into a huge inimical trumpet-blast. Mrs.

Prudhomme staggered in the effort to maintain her balance against the wind. Suddenly her courage went. Ordinarily Mrs. Prudhomme had the courage of the very timorous; it must have been her cold which weakened her, for it suddenly seemed to her impossible to traverse those few remaining yards without something to hold on to.

"Do you mind giving me your arm as far as the Robertsons?" she cried, fumbling in the dark for where she supposed his arm to be. He crooked it silently, and the two of them pressed together, steadying themselves now and again against the sidelong blast of the gale. They stood panting, at last, under the Robertsons' porch, a squat excrescence masking the doorway from the sea. Mrs. Prudhomme's knees suddenly grew very weak, it seemed impossible immediately to let go of the arm, impersonal and hard as rock, which had supported her tottering steps so far. To detain him she said hurriedly:

"I was going to get the women together for a little singing in the mission; but I'm not sure that it's fair to expect any of them to turn out."

"It's blowing," said Gregory Jodrell, laconically.

"I thought—at least Mr. Prudhomme thought" (she felt disloyal in refusing to accept the responsibility, but indeed the thing she had come to propose now seemed to her outrageous) "they might be glad of a little singing to-night. The wind's so—so sad!" She caught her lip in her upper teeth, feeling she had said something foolish.

"It never stops blowing on El Secredo."

"Do you think the women would like to come?"

"Ask them."

She understood by now that the islanders did not mean to be offensive when they spoke like that. It was simply that the wind, for ever snatching the words from their lips and whirling them into limbo, had taught them to economize in speech. Vaguely she felt that Gregory Jodrell was well-intentioned towards her.

"Will you go to the Mullyons', and ask Sanchia for me?"

Smith or no Smith, she could not face the struggle round the corner of the bluff which separated the Mullyons' cottage from the rest of the settlement. "Will you tell her that Mr. Prudhomme *particularly* hopes that she will come?"

"If you like." None of the enthusiasm of the lover was in his voice, but she felt, or imagined she felt, him stir at her suggestion.

"Perhaps you will bring her yourself? It's a horrid night for a girl to be out—alone."

"I'll fetch her—if she will come," he answered, heavily. After a moment he added: "Not as Sanchia fears the wind."

She thought of saying: "When are you and Sanchia thinking of getting married?" Her position as the missionary's wife gave her the right to say this kind of impertinent thing. But somehow she found it difficult, even one thousand five hundred miles from social niceties, to exert her prerogative upon the islanders. "I never was cut out for a clergyman's wife," she thought, ruefully; "I can't bear prying into people's business." Smith never seemed to mind; a wave of genuine admiration beat up in her for the assurance with which, at the end of three years on the island, he went about among the people, probing their secrets, compelling their confidences—or what passed for such. With a shamed feeling of disloyalty she found herself wondering if they really did tell Smith things?—not the commonplaces of their daily lives, but the real things: the things in their innermost: their secret thoughts and aspirations. Once, very tactfully, she had hinted as much to her husband, and earned a superior smile. "My dear Mary, you don't understand the simplicity of these people. They have no secret thoughts, as you term it. Their lives are just work and sleep. They have no time to think. And by the way, Mary, I'd like you to get a little more into the women's confidence."

"They're so dreadfully dignified," she sighed. Lovely to believe, like Smith, that everyone confided in you; why, he even thought he knew Sanchia. Mrs. Prudhomme gasped to

think how that would make Sanchia laugh. There was something uncanny in the girl's laughter; one always felt that she
was not laughing with you, but at a secret, bitter joke of her
own.

Mrs. Prudhomme raised the latch and went in. At first
she had been in the habit of knocking; but on finding that
her timid tap was productive of nothing but mute astonishment on the part of the householders, she had mastered her
timidity to the extent of walking in unheralded.

The room, like the one she had left, was thick with smoke,
and impregnated with the strong smell of fish. John Robertson, whose house it was, was master of the fishing fleet; for
weeks now he had been unable to put to sea, and the nets,
bone dry, were festooned from the beams of the low ceiling,
so that one had to stoop in passing under them; the two
Robertson children sat at the table, mending one of the nets
—short, stubby little girls with their heads tied up in shawls
of black wool; their cheeks shone like apples—"Early
Margarets"—hard and crimson as cherries; their small
chapped hands worked busily, under their mother's direction. By the light of several oil lamps Mrs. Prudhomme was
able to make out the figures of a group of women, gro-
tesquely anonymous in their bunchy black gowns, who sat
with their backs to her, in a whirl of flying feathers. She saw
that they were plucking birds—the "molly-mawks," whose
coarse, oily taste suited the palates of the menfolk. In the
gust from the opening door the feathers scudded across the
floor; some of them rose and fell softly on the knees of the
knot of men, sheepishly collected as far as possible from
their womenfolk. They raised their hands phlegmatically
and beat them away. Mrs. Prudhomme hastened to force
the door back in the teeth of the wind. As she turned, a
woman rose and curtsied, her squat, ungainly figure out-
lined against the lamp behind her; no one else stirred, save
that the men's scarred hands went up to their forelocks, and
the women turned and nodded their heads, then resumed
their work.

"You're all very busy," said Mrs. Prudhomme, regretfully. "I don't feel I ought to disturb you."

They made no disclaimer, but the women looked up again, and an El Secredo person would have recognized that there was friendliness in their glance.

As her eyes became accustomed to the smoke, she saw who, beside the Robertson family, was there. Janet Hawkins, Rose Sanguinetti and the small crooked Barker woman —a Martyn by birth. With the exception of Rose Sanguinetti, who was expecting her first child—and praying it might be a girl—the rest of the women were in their early forties; but forty on El Secredo is as good as sixty elsewhere. The lamplight shone on their lined faces, battered brown by the weather, and lined as deeply as withered figs. Each was impassive as a thing carved in wood; child-bearing and household labour, with few opportunities for relaxation, and these at long intervals, had crushed any spontaneity or animation from the bearing of these women of El Secredo. Patient like oxen, and with some of the stupidity of beasts, lightened now and again with a flash of cunning—the nearest the female population of the island comes to intelligence— they sat dumbly, listening to the conversation of the men, which was stilled at Mrs. Prudhomme's entrance. "These people are kindly, are grateful, are friendly," said Mrs. Prudhomme to herself: but she said it in the spirit of those followers of Coué, who, in hopes of growing "better and better," repeat daily the charm which is to lead to their regeneration.

"Give Mrs. Prudhomme a chair, Martha," directed Maggie Robertson, before resuming her occupation.

"I thought we might sing a little," confessed Mrs. Prudhomme. "The wind *is* bad to-night, isn't it?" Her tone apologized, begged for understanding. There was a short silence before she was answered.

"I'd ha' thought you'd ha' got used to the wind by now, ma'am," said Janet Hawkins, not unkindly, just as one who states a fact.

"It's very foolish," owned Mrs. Prudhomme, and added,

with a longing to justify herself: "You see, we never have it like this at home. Perhaps you don't feel like singing to-night."

"Maybe the children do," offered Maggie Robertson, after another silence. "Martha and Betty?—you'd like to sing, wouldn't you?" A hint of maternal authority was in Maggie Robertson's voice; one gathered that Martha and Betty had better find it expedient to like singing. They lifted round eyes from their work; Mrs. Prudhomme knew from the expression in them that they were interested in what they were doing, unwilling to be torn away. But children do not rebel against their parents on El Secredo. "And maybe your sister's little Machita, Rose? Did ye come alone, ma'am?" Her eyes twinkled over Mrs. Prudhomme's figure with kindly depreciation. "I'd ha' thought the wind would ha' carried ye away."

"I met Gregory Jodrell," said Mrs. Prudhomme, "and he gave me his arm."

From the glances which passed she knew immediately that before her coming they had been talking of Gregory Jodrell. "I asked him to go along to the Mullyons' to see if Sanchia would come."

"Sanchia won't come if Gregory asks her," giggled Rose Sanguinetti, nudging Janet Hawkins, who sat next to her.

"Oh, dear!" cried Mrs. Prudhomme.

"Sanchia'd not come if an angel from heaven was to ask her!" cried the little Barker woman, shrilly. "She's that con- rairy these days. Sophia says it's the storm. She's always excusing Sanchia. But we know what we think, eh, Maggie?"

"Hold your tongue, Charlotte," snapped Maggie Robert- son. "I don't mind if I come for an hour, ma'am, so long's I'm back in time to boil the potatoes for Jack's supper. I suppose, ma'am, you couldn't let us have a little salt? We've been as careful as could be, but wi' six mouths to feed, and Jack such a one for having his meals tasty——"

"I dare say I could spare a little," answered Mrs. Prudhomme; "but I'm afraid the sack's nearly empty by now."

Maggie Robertson rose and went to the food cupboard, from which she took a bowl of eggs.

"We've all we want in eggs just now; these will just go bad afore we've time to eat them," she asserted.

Mrs. Prudhomme took two penguin's eggs with a word of thanks. Exchange was the law of the settlement; to offer the salt free of barter would have been mortally to offend the recipient. She threw a glance at the men, who sat mutely, huddled together, with their shadows flung on the whitewashed wall behind them like hump-backed beasts; John Robertson and his two grown-up sons, his brother-in-law, Peter Hawkins, and two fellows who sat with their faces hidden, their heads sunk on their breasts in sleep; their hands hung down between their knees. Mrs. Prudhomme knew that for the greater part of the day they had been fighting the sea, strengthening with boulders the embankment which had been newly built to afford some protection to their narrow strip of arable land, until the Reverend Smith burst upon them with relentless energy, to enlist their services in the reinforcement of the mission wall. They must be worn out. A most tender sentiment of pity welled up in the heart of Mrs. Prudhomme for this lonely people, to whom, apparently, so little was given to compensate for their pain of living. She began to wonder why they were made at all: a metaphysical problem which seemed so little likely to be solved that she hastily rose and made signs of going.

"I don't suppose you will feel like coming to the mission," she said nervously. The men looked at each other, as if unwilling, each one, to assume the responsibility of refusal. "That's all right," said Mrs. Prudhomme, with a gaiety she felt sure rang false. "My husband is ever so grateful for all the help you gave him this afternoon."

She wondered, as she made her escape, why she never could help saying these things: they were neither appreciated nor understood. The women were more gracious, but even

from them thanks came painfully, and they were discountenanced utterly by any gratitude which was offered to them.

The Martyns' house; the Sanguinettis'; the Barkers'; thank
goodness she need not struggle on to the Jodrells'—there
were no women there. Lucky that Janet Hawkins had been
with Maggie Robertson. The row of little stone cottages
that went by the name of Atlantic View, where the younger
married couples lived until the time came for them to move
into their parents' houses. Ought she to go to the Mullyons',
after all? Supposing Sanchia would not come with Gregory?

Bracing herself, she went breathlessly upon her errand; all
seemed quite willing to come—she was thankful of that.
Barbara Martyn even went so far as to say she would slip
round the bluff to Sanchia's, and bring her along with her.
Bruised with the times the wind had dashed her against the
walls and boulders, but triumphant, and foolishly grateful
to them for coming to support her, Mrs. Prudhomme turned
her back at last on the wind, and was hurled along the track
to the mission. She must get there first, light the lamps,
open the harmonium, see that the stove was drawing properly. Again the weakness of homesickness almost mastered
her. Mrs. Prudhomme was the kind of woman who idolizes
her home; the shabbier it is the more she loves it. The little
home in Sussex had been very shabby, but not a thread in the
worn-out carpets, not a leaf in the hedgerow escaped the
benediction of her memory. Painfully she yearned for
the tiny drawing-room that looked so cosy at night when
the curtains were drawn; for the old Broadwood piano on
which she had practised as a girl. Who was looking after it
now? They had let the vicarage when they came out to the
Cape; the locum who had taken the Reverend Smith's place
was a bachelor who preferred to take rooms in the village.
Was someone heartlessly pounding out jazz on the frail
yellow keys that responded so tenderly to her timorous
accompaniments? Tears started to her eyes; the boom of the
Atlantic sounded like a threat.

She was playing the harmonium as the women stumbled

in—"The March of the Troubadours," which she had played
for her schoolfellows—oh, a century or more ago, it seemed; a
tuppenny challenge to the storm, a call to gaiety all were far
from feeling. The mission roof was low, and buttressed
against the cliff itself; sometimes during service the goats
scrambled up on it, and made such odd noises sliding about
that the children were convulsed with giggles.

Dumbly the women unwound their shawls and stood
about in groups, their work-scarred hands folded over their
waist-belts. The oil-lamps were reflected in the black win-
dow-panes against which the night pressed jealously, as
though it only waited to pour in through the glass and
quench the lamps that defied its supremacy.

Mrs. Prudhomme jumped up from the harmonium.

"I think we ought to practise the new part-song," she
said brightly, because no brightness was in her. The
Reverend Smith had impressed upon her the duty of being
cheerful, and she was very dutiful by nature. "But first—
shall we have 'Eternal Father'—because it really *is* such
a bad night?"

One thousand five hundred miles from civilization their
voices rose, puny against the storm. There came a sound like
a peppering of small stones; they rang on the zinc roofing.
A few of the women looked up; the rest were too inured, or
too occupied with their singing. For a few minutes the
mission echoed with the downpour; the bellow of the sea
was pierced with the sharper, nearer sound; lightning played
for an instant across the windows, giving a fearful glimpse
of boiling ocean.

"You will have to come nearer the harmonium," shrieked
Mrs. Prudhomme. They drew in obediently, like sheep
towards the shepherd. Suddenly she felt tender, protective
towards them; a ridiculous feeling, because of them all, she,
probably, was the only one who feared the storm. But it
gave her a foolish kind of courage, to pretend that these
people were dependent upon her. All the women had come
—except Sanchia. If Sanchia had been there, it would have

been to her that they would have turned for protection: Mrs. Prudhomme was sure of that, and glad, for once, that Sanchia had stayed away. But Smith would be annoyed, if he remembered to ask about her. She should have gone to the Mullyons' herself. There was Sophia Mullyon's long, sheep-like face; but Sanchia was not by her side. Sophia had muttered that Sanchia had stayed behind to look after the supper.

She had shirked her duty in sending Gregory Jodrell. But anyhow, the rest were there; they had all come to her —towards the example of her courage and tranquillity as towards a light.

She threw up her head and sang more loudly, not caring whether or not her voice carried through the storm.

Next day a curious white light lay upon the island. It lingered eerily in rock pools, in every crevice that would hold water, filling them with milk. The kelp was shifting about like sargasso in the currents that raced about the island, the sodden bodies of fowls that had been lifted over the embankment bobbed in piteous feathery abandonment on the ebb and flow of the sea; a surly sea, whose surface suggested treachery. In the curious clarity of the light every rib and vein of the rocks stood out as though magnified; torrents gushed down the carven furrows of the peak, and every inch of the cliffs was white with sea-birds. Never had El Secredo looked more stark, more naked, more worthy of its wicked legends.

Barns and outhouses were reduced in many cases to a pile of refuse and timber. Most of the morning the men were employed in repairing damage. A bunch of the square-shouldered, broad-built lads of the island clambered along the foreshore, collecting driftwood which had come down in great quantity during the night; at their approach the sea-birds rose in swarms, with shrill cries of resentment at being disturbed at their feast—the million fishy bodies which had been thrown up and stranded among the rocks. An albatross

rose with majestic defiance, clutching in its huge claws a
half-eaten conger. Some children came screaming from the
inlet known as The Rescue, with news of a whale that was
stranded there. A party of men set off to secure the oil and
blubber which should replenish their lamps; and the sea
continued to race before a whimpering wind that seemed
exhausted by its excesses of the night before.

All were aware that the storm had not spent its force. A
sober anxiety was in every face, but none of the desperation
that might have been expected. They had lived so long with
the wind that it had ceased to appal them; its worst excesses
were, to the people of El Secredo, no more than the blustering of a schoolboy bully. Self-protection had taught them
most of the tricks necessary to defend their lives and property. Much more vital was the shortage of the food supply,
which, following on a poor harvest and worse vegetable
season, had left the islanders with little save fish and sea-
birds to support existence until the arrival of the overdue
ship. There were empty stomachs and heavy hearts on the
island. The last of the flour had gone a fortnight before, and
they had reached the bad end of their potato store. Potatoes
can only take the place of bread when they are fresh and
sweet; hardened as were their stomachs, few of the islanders
could make much of pudding made with sour tubers, which
only a liberal application of salt would have made palatable.
But salt also was at a discount; fats of all kinds had nearly
gone, and stewed fish and molly-mawks had lost the power
to stay their hunger.

From the earliest light of dawn a look-out was kept over
the sea; in school the children were almost unmanageable—
for ever making excuses to jump up and look out of the
windows, or lethargic for want of proper nourishment.

While the storm lasted there could be no question of a
landing. For over a mile from Calvary the treacherous lava
ribs run out into the sea; their serrate edges would rip open
a ship from bows to stern. The few ships that come to
Calvary—scarcely ever more than one in twelve months—

cast cable a couple of miles out, and their boats are guided to the beach by the fishermen's coracles, which, fashioned from driftwood and covered with painted canvas, draw so little water that they can navigate the shallows in safety.

Although the wind had fallen, labour was a painful matter. Backs ached and the sweat ran down between the beetling brows of the men who struggled with ox-cart and a primitive crane to replace the boulders which had been hurled from the newly-built embankment. A lump of basalt, weighing a hundredweight or more, crashed downwards, losing its precarious balance, and fell on the hand of John Robertson, who, unable to pursue his usual occupation—beyond laying a few shore-lines—had volunteered to help. The men—including the victim—stared at the crimson pulp that showed when the stone was rolled away. Pain was such an everyday matter that none offered sympathy, or even thought it worth while to comment on the accident, when Robertson went staggering towards his own house, leaving a trail of scarlet behind him on the rocks. Gregory Jodrell, in charge of the business, motioned to have the stone re-hoisted; three men threw their weight on the handle of the crane, which rose jerkily, creaking and swaying. For a moment the wicked black mass swung perilously over their heads; then, by the efforts of the other three it was levered into its place and wedged with narrower strips of slag, so that it ceased to rock. The gang stood back and looked at Gregory; it was past their eating time, but none would cease labour until he gave the sign.

There was an odd similarity about the group—the similarity which results from inbreeding. Allowing for differences in colouring, each man might have been the brother of the rest. None overtopped the mark of five feet six inches, and some looked shorter for that breadth of shoulder characteristic of the islander. It seemed as though Nature, having stunted every tree and shrub, had turned her attention to the human beings and moulded them into grim uniformity with their surroundings. Gregory himself barely

reached the five-feet-five mark; his head was large in proportion to his height, the features reproducing those of old
Samson Jodrell, his father. It sometimes gave people a
shock to behold that noble head on the short, squat frame;
like the rest of them, Gregory was long in the body and
short in the leg—a construction which does not make for
grace.

There was something almost apostolic in the aspect of
these young men, all of whom were bearded like the
mariners of old, with harsh curling hair that clung about
their throats and crawled towards the high cheek-bones.
Gregory Jodrell wore his beard shorter than the rest, clipped
with the scissors close to the long jutting chin that distinguished his family. Job Barker was the slightest of the
family, and tuberculosis showed in the stoop of his narrower
shoulders; the tallest was Samson Hawkins—christened
after his godfather, old Jodrell—twelve months' Gregory's
senior, and with something choleric in his ruddy colouring.
His eye challenged the sober one of Gregory; one could feel
that he did not take kindly to the authority of a younger
man, even with the Jodrell tradition behind him. He spoke,
since Gregory was slow in giving the permission to stop
work.

"Eating time, Gregory?" The inflection showed a conventional deference, but the attitude of the man was more
that of one who issues a command than of one who awaits
an order.

Gregory Jodrell nodded, and the men tramped back to
where they had left their food-baskets. Each could easily
have gone home for his meal, but it is an island custom that
at midday the women and children eat alone. Even if a man
is not working, he will take his eggs and his slice of potato
pudding and eat it on the shore opposite his own dwelling,
rather than sit down to table with his family.

They climbed over to leeward of the embankment, and
began to eat their food in silence. Each man, before dropping
down out of sight of the water, had cast a glance across the

sea, in hopes of seeing the trail of smoke that should tell them that their long vigil and fast were over. To the first man who raised the "Sail ho!" a special reward was offered—first choice from among the crates as they were brought ashore. But the horizon showed wide and blank as a sheet of grey canvas; they fell hungrily upon their food—such as it was.

"There's a thing I was wanting to say to ye, Gregory Jodrell," rumbled Samson Hawkins, unexpectedly.

Gregory looked up, nodding his head. He had been lost in dreams of the embankment; he was proud of this, the first piece of constructive work for which he had been responsible. Men age rapidly on El Secredo; already, at sixty, men spoke of Samson Jodrell, his father, as "old Jodrell." At one time the master-builder, Samson had delegated the erection of the embankment to his son. It had suddenly become necessary because of the extensive erosions made by recent storms; upon it depended the salvation of the only arable land the island possessed—the narrow strip which runs like a circle of dull jade round the base of the rock, gashed here and there by the gulches that slowly and inevitably gain a few inches each year. Samson had felt himself unequal to a task of such magnitude. It meant the erection, along nearly ten miles of uneven ground, of a barrier at least six feet in thickness. In some places it was almost impossible to find a purchase for the stones; when a certain height was reached, the whole structure slid like a pack of cards, the steep gradient of the ground and the rocky surface on which the wall was built—for not a yard of pasture could be spared—forming a chute down which would plunge boulders large enough to kill a man if he should be caught in their track. The task had not been without danger to life and limb—and Gregory had accomplished it without damage. The accident to John Robertson's hand, and young Hawkins's broken leg—his own fault, the young fool, for neglecting orders—were the only mishaps since they started building. Two years it had taken Gregory to complete it, for the work was subject to long interruption through the bad weather, and often the men had come back to find the work of six or eight days swept away in a single night. In his sluggish way Gregory was proud that last night's damage was no greater; it was a tribute to his workmanship. The wall was his masterpiece; he loved it, as the mother loves the child she has brought forth in pain, because each boulder which went to its making bore the history of straining sinew, of toil under sun and rain, of careful planning and calculation. "Your ugly old wall!" Sanchia had called it. "If you had planted trees now——!" Was not that a foolish thing to say? As though trees would have been of any use. They would have been uprooted in the first storm, or dwarfed into scrubbiness, and, anyhow, what use would they have been against the sea and the wind? The embankment was to protect the trees—such as they were: the apple orchard which old Sanguinetti had planted fifty years ago, which had miraculously survived, and which provided the island with fruit in season; and the weeping willows which were the sentimental fancy of one of the missionary's wives—she had actually brought them out from Stratford-on-Avon with her: "A trophy of the Swan," she called them—no one knew why. A tiresome woman, who insisted upon reading Shakespeare's plays to them, and she didn't half get mad if anyone fell asleep!—as one was bound to do, with the wind, and the flat voice of the missionary's wife reading stuff no one understood. There were no other trees on the island; the last one had been cut down when Sanchia was a baby, to provide firewood for the mission. What did Sanchia know about trees?

With all these things in his mind, Gregory turned a lacklustre eye upon Samson Hawkins.

"Ay, Samson?"

Samson cast a glance towards their companions; Gregory, quick-witted after a fashion, guessed that they had already been discussing the matter, whatever it might be.

"We want to know if Sanchia Mullyon is bespoke to you, or not," said Samson Hawkins, and a rumble of assent went up from all save Job Barker, who feared to commit himself. Since John Robertson had left them, those who remained were all young, single men, of the marriageable age.

Gregory Jodrell tilted his head back against the wall, and his eyes followed a thrush as it shot rapidly across the pasture, flying low, almost, as a martin; it is a trick the birds learn on El Secredo—all save the cliff-dwellers, who take the wind for their cradle.

"I'm wedding Sanchia Mullyon if she'll take me."

"You've asked her?" pressed Samson.

"Ay."

"And she's given ye no answer?"

"Nay."

"You'll ask her once again, Gregory Jodrell," said Samson in a low voice, "an' then——"

"Ay; and then——?"

"Then," said Samson Hawkins, with a swelling of the veins on his broad forehead from which the hair grew far back, showing a tendency to premature baldness on the temples, "then, Gregory Jodrell, if she still flouts ye, ye can stand aside and let others take their turn. The other lads an' me—we've made up our minds to draw lots and take it in turn to ask Sanchia Mullyon—if she'll none of ye."

Again Job Barker was silent in the chorus of agreement. His own plan was different. Once let Gregory Jodrell be out of the way, and he was waiting for no lottery; he'd go in and take his chances. There were ways—and Job Barker believed he knew them. But with a Jodrell it was not safe to take risks.

Gregory continued silent. Samson smote his fist upon his knee and thrust his face towards Gregory's.

"Ye've h'ard, lad? There's others of us wanting a wife besides you, and there's bin too much shilly-shallying about this to suit the rest of us. If you're not man enough to drive her to the Yea, let someone else try."

"Maybe she's waiting for the Lord to direct her heart," said Gregory simply.

"If that be all," said Samson Hawkins, in whom, as in the rest of the islanders, the religious instinct slumbered lightly, ready to be aroused at a moment's notice, "what can we do better than pray to the Lord *now* that the heart of Sanchia Mullyon be turned i' the right way?"

He was on his feet; the wind had divided his red beard and was blowing it in two ruddy streamers across his shoulders. The white light from sky and sea filled his pale eyes, as they stared with an almost fanatical eagerness at Gregory Jodrell. A short silence fell upon the men; not in any sense a silence of embarrassment, for the people of El Secredo had the habit of praying together before ever the missionaries came to relieve them of the responsibility. The patriarchal custom of evening prayer still lingered in the older homes, although some of the young married couples had ceased to practise it. When limbs are weary the lure of sleep is strong, and the farther one departs from the fortitude of the patriarchs, the less spiritual stamina one has to resist the claims of nature.

At last Gregory Jodrell lifted his head and looked Samson in the face.

"I'm not against it," he answered, in the island's idiom of assent.

The men came to their feet, looking now to Samson as their guide. With a deliberate movement he threw down his cap to kneel upon, and the rest followed his example. Each closed his eyes so tightly that the rest of his features were wrinkled up, and clasped together work-scarred hands at the level of the breast. For a while there was silence: El Secredo silence, which is filled with the noise of wind and water and the crying of the birds.

"O Lord," said Samson Hawkins, "Who hast led our forefathers to this lonely place, and hast preserved us from the stormy blast and amid all the perils of the deep, and hast blessed our homes and given us the means to live: we beseech Thee for the sake of the quick blood Thou hast put in all men to look upon our afflictions and give us happy issue from all our tribulation. Thou knowest, O heavenly

Father, the sin that Adam and Eve committed in the garden, and how according to Thy holy law its punishment has passed from generation to generation, so that we are sore oppressed and need the grace of Thy holy Spirit to keep us in the right way. O Lord, Thou hast thought fit in Thy providence to ordain that we seven, and Peter Martyn, who is not here, should come to manhood and desire woman. Grant, O God, that our seed may not pass away, and since but one of us can take a wife, put into the heart of Sanchia Mullyon which one it shall be; so that she shall, if it be Thy will, choose Gregory Jodrell, or another. And send Thy grace upon the unchosen, that they may continue to live without sin, not doubting the wisdom of Thy providence, but trusting that Thou wilt send the sign of Thy pardon upon this island and bless us with girl-children, for the sake of Thy only son, our Lord. Amen. Amen."

The seven boys—they were but little more, for Samson, the eldest, had only just passed his twenty-first birthday— knelt as though reluctant to rise, to pass out from the Presence in which each of them devoutly believed.

It must have been the devil that brought Sanchia Mullyon upon the scene at such a moment: Sanchia, whose strange-syllabled name was in each of their hearts, who was loved by two and desired by all the rest of them. She had come silently across the pasture, her cloak blown out like the mainsail of a ship, her slimness moulding the clumsy garments of the island into a kind of elegance upon her young body.

Unacccountable, I think we named Sanchia, a little while ago. In other surroundings, perhaps, she might not have been remarkable; there were few qualities of positive colouring or demeanour to single her out among a crowd of girls in a civilization where good looks are easily come by, and it may have been merely the contrast with so much that was stark and hideous that made one turn to Sanchia as to beauty. Beauty is, after all, a relative matter; and there are a few people who maintain that Helen of Troy was a small, mousy woman with demure eyes and a knack of getting her own way. If so, she had little in common with Sanchia Mullyon. Sanchia, although small, was decidedly not mousy. Force seemed pent in that lightly built body of hers. One might, perhaps, evolve some giantess of the Atlantic from the crags of El Secredo; if so, that was not Sanchia Mullyon. A discreet Italian madonna comes nearer the type; one of those innocent-seeming madonnas who look sideways from their lowered lids, to which the painter's brush has given a quirk of malice. Her eyes, we have admitted, were like the Atlantic; a sullen grey, set in under lashes black as Calvary nights; but she seldom troubled to employ them on her fellow men. Her hair, an indefinite brown, slipped smoothly like satin from its centre parting, and was netted behind in a heavy knob. She had the vanity to find and polish long shells, which her brother cut into prongs, to support the weight of her hair. She had a fastidious way of handling things, and, since coming to womanhood, a knack of keeping herself very clean. And she always had that look as if she *knew* that she was not Mullyon at all: as if she could remember the night when great-great-grandmother Mullyon was delivered of a dead child on El Secredo beach, and they substituted—*what?*

So Sanchia, taking the short cut from The Rescue, where she had been to have a look at the whale, came across the pasture, the wind carrying the sound of her footsteps away from the men who knelt in the shadow of the embankment, so still that, at first, she had not perceived them; for it was Sanchia's custom to walk with her eyes cast down, their sight turned darkly inward upon the secrets of her own soul. So walking, she might at times have been mistaken for a young witch, there was something so withdrawn, so secretive about her. One might pass her within touching distance, and she would give no sign, unless it suited her.

Her eyelids flashed up in surprise as she came upon the kneeling group of young men, as still, as reverent in their attitude as though they awaited the coming of the Lord. Sanchia experienced a prickling sensation, such as she got

sometimes when listening to the Reverend Smith Prudhomme's sermons. She detested having to attend the
mission services, which, to her, were no more than play-
acting performances at which the Reverend Smith, as principal, made the most of his opportunities. She hated the
kneeling, the forced humility, the obedient chorus of
"Amens," the diffidence her father and mother displayed
to the missionary. She could not explain why religion was
so distasteful to her, but experienced a savage independence
of spirit when she heard the Calvary people—she always
spoke of the island as El Secredo—petitioning the Lord for
this, that, or the other. She had to bite her tongue and
clench her hands until the nails left little crimson brackets
on her palms, to prevent herself rising up and crying out:
"What's the good? What's the good?"

She had prayed a prayer of her own, from the time when
she was ten years old, up till a few months ago. Her prayer
grew out of the dreams which came with her development
into womanhood; dreams which nearly drove Sanchia out
of her mind, they were so intangible, so full of fiery and
undisciplined colour. Once she had tried to describe one
of these dreams to her mother, and Sophia Mullyon, crying
out in horror, had declared that her child had had a vision
of hell, and calling up her relations, had made Thomas
Mullyon pray aloud that his daughter Sanchia might be
delivered from the temptations of the devil; which made
Sanchia feel a fool. She had no desire to have her dreams
exorcised, and resolved in future to keep them to herself.
Her own prayer ran: "O God, if Thou art God, deliver me
from El Secredo." She still muttered it fiercely to herself,
against the prayers of the congregation, but merely from
habit. She had ceased to believe in a God who was such a
personal friend of the Reverend Smith Prudhomme that He
would assuredly find some plausible reason for refusing
Sanchia Mullyon her harmless request.

Prayer had become transmuted into fixed determination;
one may imagine Sanchia, one thousand five hundred miles

from regions where such ideas were in currency, practising thought force on her own, until the very sinews of her body contracted with it. Her mind was so focused upon this matter of escape from El Secredo that she had literally nothing to spare for the sexual preoccupations natural to a young woman of her age.

It was an island scandal, some five years old, that Sanchia Mullyon had had to be thrashed into being confirmed, by her father, as determined in his way as Sanchia was in hers. Think of a red-faced Sanchia, all stiff, starched cotton frock, the pleated bosom of which creaked with her heaving breath as she knelt before the Bishop, hiccuping into sobs at the critical moment; an indiscretion which covered her parents with shame, and led to a very uncomfortable conversation between the Bishop and the Reverend Mr. Simpson. The Bishop was interested in Sanchia, whom he recognized as a being apart from her fellows; tactfully he suggested preferential treatment. Sanchia, he declared, could be a great force for good in the community. Unfortunately, to the Reverend Mr. Simpson she stood for nothing but an unmitigated nuisance, to be avoided as much as possible. Sanchia was confirmed; but among the secrets locked in that inscrutable bosom was the fact that she had never received the Sacrament. Refusal to attend Communion would surely have been met by physical compulsion; parental discipline is still primitive on El Secredo. So no one save Sanchia knew that her lips were closed tightly against the holy wine, and the wafer slipped into her pocket for later disposal. She looked so quiet that no one would have suspected her of such impieties; in fact, the attitude of the Reverend Smith Prudhomme became notably more fatherly as he bent over the kneeling Sanchia, whose soul, seemingly so humble, was so fiercely set on reserving its independence.

The youths looked up, startled, as she stood among them; for a moment, Samson Hawkins, who, like most of the families, had Horne blood in him, believed he was vouchsafed a vision, in which Sanchia revealed herself to him as his own. But no vision could have appeared so mocking as the small, neat Sanchia, with a bunch of sea-thrift clasped in her hand.

"What are you about?" she asked, briefly.

They scrambled to their feet, Gregory Jodrell feeling the most foolish of the lot.

"'Tis time we were at work," he said, turning to his companions.

Sanchia, snubbed, stood and smiled. Her arms hung by her sides: naked from the elbow downwards, and white as milk, until they reached the brown gauntlet of her wrists and hands. She had wanted to feel the wind upon her arms, and, not dreaming of encountering anyone in her solitary walk from The Rescue, had rolled her sleeves back. On El Secredo the women do not show their flesh, save those limited areas which must, for practical purposes, be left uncovered. Samson Hawkins, feverishly conscious of those white arms of Sanchia, and stung to resentment by the knowledge that others were sharing the privilege, took a step towards her.

"Cover yourself, Sanchia! 'Tis unseemly to go about like that."

Sanchia's smile broadened; she made no movement to obey. Instead she lifted her two arms sideways, like the wings of a gull, and looked along them consideringly, as though they interested her.

"Some folks likes to see a girl's arms uncovered," she replied, thoughtfully.

"Ay! Fornicators and whoremongers, in Sodom and Gomorrah, belike!" thrust Samson roundly. The crimson had risen through the dark tan of his face.

Gregory Jodrell stepped forward, so that he stood between Sanchia and her opponent; the rough, almost insensitive palm of his hand closed harshly on one of her wrists, and as he forced that arm to her side, the other dropped slowly, gently, in time with it. She looked steadily at Gregory.

"I want to talk with ye, Sanchia. We'll be on the embankment maybe another couple o' hours yet. Will ye meet me then?"

She frowned, chewing her lower lip.

"Oh, maybe; if I've nothing better to do," she returned, ungraciously.

Unexpectedly the voice of the younger Hawkins boy spoke up from behind Gregory. He was a smaller, more springy fellow than Samson, and dark as his brother was ruddy; the black hairs of his beard had crawled over his face until there was only the space of an inch between them and his deep-set eyes.

"You'd better meet Gregory, Sanchia Mullyon; else—maybe—someone'll find a way to make ye."

The veiled threat in the speaker's tone cut short Sanchia's breath for an instant. Her glance flashed round the circle. In the seven pairs of eyes fixed upon her she read the message that no woman—be she reared on an Atlantic island or in the heart of Western civilization—can fail to recognize. There was none of the diffidence of wooing in that look, but the raw mating instinct. Long ago she had estimated the precariousness of her own position, but she was determined not to marry. To marry an El Secredo man was to remain bound for ever. Sooner than that she had determined to fling herself into Steaming Creek. She realized now that they were trying to force her into a decision, and all her native stubbornness took flame. She tossed her head.

"I'd like to see the man as would make me do anything I didn't want to do," she challenged. A cracked laugh broke from young Jim Hawkins.

"Has ta forgotten thy father, Sanchia Mullyon? Surely he can govern thee right enough!"

The clumsy jeer whitened her cheek; she turned on her heel and would have left them, but that Gregory cried:

"Hold thy tongue, Jim! Sanchia, you'll meet me?"

"I'll maybe take a walk as far as Sail Point," she flung

across her shoulder. "If you are going that way, Gregory Jodrell, you can give me a hand across the rocks."

"'Tis stormy for Sail Point, Sanchia," he answered, gently. "The wind's rising already—and look at the water!" The sea, which had flowed sullenly since daybreak, was racing past, crisped with white foam as far as eye could see. "'Twill be a hurricane in an hour or two."

She deigned no reply, but went on her way with bent head, as though she would shut out all but her thoughts.

As she went Samson Hawkins spoke solemnly:

"Before the Lord, if there were another woman on Calvary I'd see Sanchia Mullyon dead afore I'd wed wi' her! She'll take some taming, Gregory Jodrell—an' I misdoubt you're the man to do it. As God's my judge, I'll thrash her if she comes to me!"

"Better take a lesson or two o' Tom Mullyon!" laughed his brother. Their eyes met, with a deep defiance in their depths. Samson Hawkins wondered what he would do, if his brother Jim should turn out to be the fortunate man. There had always been amity and goodwill between the brothers, until the last few months; when he had known sometimes that Jim was avoiding his company, and he found himself sparking into anger over matters that would normally have left him unruffled.

Gregory's prophecy about the hurricane was fulfilled before dusk fell on the island. Work on the embankment had to be abandoned; it had become dangerous, tampering with stones the weight of a man, when, at any moment, the wind might carry one off one's feet, hurling one to destruction with one's burden.

The party returned from The Rescue, butting head downwards into the gale; the ox-cart was loaded with the grey lumps of dripping blubber, to be dumped in the shed on Samson Jodrell's land, preparatory to the malodorous business of melting it down.

The Reverend Smith Prudhomme, who had insisted upon joining the expedition, had just reached home, and in the intervals of trying to remove from his clothing the glutinous traces of his recent occupation, addressed his wife rather pettishly.

"Of course, it may simply be the effect of the wind—I have noticed that a hurricane always makes the people irritable. You remember, Mary—it was just before the last one that Ben Robertson had his fight with the youngest Martyn boy."

"Yes, Smith?" said Mrs. Prudhomme, who, having reached the point in her cold when death seems a simple and satisfactory solution to all things, had given in so far as to stretch herself on the connubial bed, and was shivering violently under all the clothing she could heap upon herself.

"Have you taken some aspirin?" asked the Reverend Smith, absently. "I hope they are not all gone, for it is almost certain I shall catch your cold. There is no getting away from the fact that there is a very bad spirit abroad. I never remember things being quite so disquieting since my arrival on Calvary. Sullenness. I really cannot endure sullenness, Mary. Moreover—one cannot be certain—without practical experience, of course, but——"

Mrs. Prudhomme moaned, but managed to turn her moan into an expression of attention and sympathy for the Reverend Smith.

"I certainly *thought*," said the Reverend Smith, cautiously but impressively, "that the breath of Peter Martyn smelt very peculiar as I was speaking to him just now. *Calvary beer!*"

For all her physical discomfort, Mrs. Prudhomme started.

Calvary beer stands for the sole rebellion of the islanders against the authority of the missionaries. Of the six clergymen who had followed each other to Calvary, each one had vowed himself to the discovery of the illicit still and the stamping out of the manufacture of this inflammatory liquor. Each had failed; each left to his successor an exhortation to carry on the good work, with an extensive history of his own attempts, and some indication of quarters that might repay watching. Each had left with the firm conviction that, given another six months, he would have tracked the brewer down; and the first question of former Calvary missionaries, on meeting each other, is: "Well, did you find the still?" Each was obliged to report failure.

The trying part was that, on the face of things, each man was above suspicion. During the singing of the temperance hymn, the missionary's eyes would dart suspiciously from man to man, trying to deduce from some lapse of enthusiasm a personal interest in the forbidden produce; but each sang lustily, and with an earnest face, the old-time denunciation of spirituous liquors. In a community of little over a hundred, on an island whose total circumference amounts to less than twenty miles, it would seem impossible to conduct an illicit manufacture. Mouth-to-mouth catechism only brought home to those who tried it the uncomfortable conviction that Calvary men, so honest and so upright, could lie when it suited their purpose to do so. "This still," wrote the Reverend Thomas Berkeley, some time in 1893, "is the one stronghold of the devil in this little community of righteousness."

The Reverend Smith Prudhomme, when he set forth for Calvary, had been informed of the still. Mr. Simpson, in clutching his belongings and making a rush for the ship which conveyed the Reverend Smith thither, pressed into his successor's hand a bulky envelope containing explicit information as to the taste, smell and colour of Calvary beer, with an exhortation to keep an eye on Job Barker.

At the end of six months, the Reverend Smith came to the conclusion that Mr. Simpson had weakly followed precedent in making Job responsible for the sins of the community. Some fellows seem born to be black sheep, and Job was emphatically one of them. After thinking matters over, the Reverend Smith decided to follow his favourite course of pretending that undesirable things had no existence, save in men's minds. He prayed quite sincerely that nothing should occur which might make it necessary for him to take steps only too likely to result in a humiliating failure; and so far his prayers had been answered. In his three years on the island, the Reverend Smith could truly say that he had never so much as caught a whiff of Calvary beer. The men, he reported, were sober and God-fearing. He earned some sort of negative popularity for departing from the custom of his predecessors by showing no kind of interest in the sharper, apparently more inaccessible part of the island. The joke of seeing their pastor spread-eagled upon a bluff, from which, sooner or later, he was bound to need rescuing, had begun to pall on the islanders.

CHAPTER III

ONE may, in passing, take a glimpse of that stormy youth of Sanchia Mullyon's, since in childhood lies the germ of all that the human being later achieves. In adolescence she learned, with the natural secretiveness of the islander—exaggerated in Sanchia's case, because all that she felt and did was prone to exaggeration—to draw a veil of curious stillness before that inner turbulence which so vexed and irritated her parents. At the age of nineteen we make acquaintance of a suppressed and wary character, perpetually on guard; behind that locked exterior there dwelt the angel of her pride and the devil of her contempt—the familiars with whom in her helpless silence she held her sole communion.

Sanchia, a stranger. Among the lethargic island children one may figure her: perverse as quicksilver, with a frame narrow, brittle and fragile-seeming as the bleached skeletons of sea-creatures cast up by the Atlantic on El Secredo beach, yet live with a whip-thong-like strength and pliability that could bend and bend and never break. Some such quality enforced the child's mind, that might else have given under the constant chastisements, the secret snake-like whispers that impugned her sanity and hinted at her heredity, a matter that, for all her acquaintance with old Betty Barker's legend, affected her not at all at that period. The mocking face of an elf and medusa-locks of salt-stiffened hair, blown behind her little nocturnal countenance like a witch's web. Too unkempt and unclean to earn her due of commendation for the childish good looks that were hers: too vicious and deceptive in glance to get credit for innocence in

47

her motives, even when these—as rarely happened—were innocent. A constant wonder, a constant question, a stubborn rebellion in those Atlantic-grey eyes; a child tormented by itself, lacking the interpretation of those wiser and older, who might have unravelled mystery and simplified the fearsome act of living.

Strange terrors informed Sanchia's childhood, together with strange, inexplicable moods of courage. There were days when she was almost insanely brave: days when she felt that she could actually toss herself off a ridge like one of the gulls and float down, down through the silken air to rest upon the beach, days when her body seemed like a fragile horn through which the wind, setting its lips to hers, could blow a piercing music. And she would open her mouth and try to reproduce the sound, and at once the light and exquisite feeling would vanish: Sanchia, Sanchia, Calvary clod—heavy thing, helpless thing, foolish thing. The light died in her eyes; grey-faced, a half-wit, she crouched, in impenetrable abstraction through the lessons that fed so poorly a mind avid for richer fare. The Reverend Mr. Simpson was a brilliant mathematical scholar; he granted Sanchia Mullyon her ability, but perhaps one cannot blame him for refusing, on strictly ethical grounds, the *pons asinorum* to her adventurous spirit. It might have become her bridge of vision. But what has Euclid to say to an island woman whose simple duty is to couple and produce young? He laughed lazily over Sanchia's eagerness, frowned upon her abstractions, and, when she was fourteen, hinted to Sophia Mullyon that the girl had learnt as much as was good for her. Sophia reluctantly kept her at home; Sanchia was a problem, and, to put it bluntly, Mr. Simpson felt that it was time Sophia took the brunt of her responsibilities.

Her fears were as intangible as her moods of courage. Physical fear she had none; pain—the pain of a scarred shin, of a stinging jellyfish, of her frequent thrashings—she bore with an unchildlike fortitude. Her physical punishments filled her with a savage loathing for those who humiliated her, but acted as no deterrent. But she would lie awake in terror at the sound of the beating of her own heart; a fear, senseless as that of an animal, would seize her in listening to the soughing of the wind in the rock crannies of the island, and—returning at sunset from egg-gathering expeditions— she would avert her face from the rock, for fear of seeing —*things:* for fear of hearing a call: for fear of the light touch on her shoulder which should claim her, bewitch her, gather her into the shadow company that, in the legends of Betsy Barker, haunted the Peak itself. A wild and ungovernable imagination, incapable of describing or clearly visualizing its own impressions, tormented Sanchia in certain phases of the moon, and ebbed and flowed with the tides about El Secredo shores.

Once, out of bravado, she announced to a ring of gaping schoolchildren, that she would take them up the Peak and conjure a devil for them. They went there at sundown, in a high wind; the sun climbed up and down the rock face, the shadows of birds passed slowly like sickles across the steep surface, the sky was lighted with wan, waterish copper. She climbed to a ledge above the huddled children, who stood below, terrified into silence. She spread out her arms, facing the rock, and licked her lips. And courage suddenly deserted her. Of all the company present she alone believed in her ability to raise the ghosts of El Secredo. She flung up her arms like windmill sails, gave a screech like a gull, and plunged across their heads on to the shale: staggered, regained her balance, and fled, at the head of the stumbling, screaming pack.

But it was in stormy weather that she became most formidable. "Sanchia's queer—there's going to be a storm!" In the middle of Bible lesson or sewing class, she would throw back her head and laugh eerily: or she would fling her slate in the air, and allow it to fall and shatter in the middle of the schoolroom. And after this brief madness, she would sit like an idiot and suffer reprimand to fall upon her, unconscious as a stone, with glazing eyes. She feared no storm; the elements but raised in her some obscure reaction, set her nerves a-shimmer with a kind of sensual ecstasy. "She ain't afraid," said the children. "'Tis the thunder inside her, like; Sanchia Mullyon be mad in thunder." The charge of madness was woven through the web of her childhood; an easy explanation of the inexplicable. Beside the stolid, unimaginative Robertsons, the Barkers and the Jodrells, she appeared mad indeed. The Reverend Simpson, with a touch of melancholy philosophy, subscribed to the charge, but noted, for private communication to the society which had placed him there, that the results of inbreeding showed startlingly in the younger generation. What about the Barker boys, who, at the end of seven years' schooling, could barely shape the letters of their own names? With Sanchia one sensed excess; with the majority of her contemporaries it was a matter of lack. Excess and lack of what? Intellectual virility? Hardly that; one could not call Sanchia's a virile mind—that hairsprung organ that controlled her actions. One man's meat: El Secredo: the island itself: mandragora to the majority, to Sanchia an irritant. The girl was alien in every breath she drew.

What emotions had Sanchia Mullyon, at the age of twelve, or thereabouts? Fear she knew, intimately: hatred and rage had graven an infinitesimal line between her young brows. In every islander she sensed a natural enemy, a malicious critic. She had not learnt to despise her traducers, that latter-born security of secret knowledge and power had not come to her rescue. She took an elfin and diabolical pleasure in feeding their malice. She was devoid of the average child's sense of attachment and affection towards its parents. To Sanchia her mother and father stood for the symbols of anger, punishment, continual nagging, petty interference and—most distasteful of all—religious exhortation. She would escape from Thomas Mullyon's prayers and stand alone, clenching her hands and biting her lips until the blood started; "Damn God—oh, *damn* God!" she would mutter, in a transport of half-terrified rage.

It was shortly after her twelfth birthday that consciousness of her sex began to trouble Sanchia. "She'll be worse'n ever now," the women muttered among themselves, gloating over a pale, farouche and elusive Sanchia, who drove her playmates from her with chattering rage, and disappeared into the mountain. She played truant from school, was missing from dawn till dusk. For once, Sophia did not punish her; perhaps she felt the prickings of sexual sympathy. The girl was marriageable—at twelve years old. The news sped through the island, the men gleaned it from their womenfolk, and Sanchia, pitched into unwilling maturity at an age when more fortunate children are playing with their dolls, felt their eyes crawl over her like palpitant fingers, shuddered in premature understanding of their desire. For the first time in her life she went to Sophia for protection; mutely, like a stricken animal, she hid in her mother's shadow, and Sophia, understanding, yet not understanding, for every physical process was simple and natural to her, nor had her own ripening been attended by such shadows as brooded upon Sanchia's, gave her a rough and voiceless sympathy. It would be three years, at least, before the girl could marry; as well leave her in peace. Sophia dispatched her husband to Samson Jodrell's; here, through the medium of nods and monosyllables, mainly, the cradle pact was ratified. When the time came, Gregory would be ready; so much was understood. Sophia nodded her head when Thomas returned, and rallied the moping Sanchia with mimic scoldings, her only coinage of affection.

And, for a space of time, Sanchia was wretched. The giggles and nudges of the children stuck in her soul like barbs. The loathly reminders of some of the women: "You're a woman now"—filled her with a morbid dislike of her own young ripening body. She felt them gloating

over her, as captives gloat when another is added to their
number. They no longer guarded their tongues in her presence; she slunk away from their obscene whisperings and
nudgings and innuendoes. She might, so far as physical
functions went, be a woman now, but she took such
reminders like an urchin, sticking out her tongue at her
tormentors and running away. She also developed a habit
of shrugging her shoulders forward, in the attempt to conceal the now apparent thrust of her bosom. Rose Banks, a
year her junior, and in every way less developed than
Sanchia, thrust out her chest like a pouter pigeon, and was
suspected of padding the front of her Sunday blouse. She
came creeping to Sanchia, seeking to force confidences. At
last Sanchia brought her ten sharp finger-nails down the
length of Rose's cheek. Goaded to it by Rose's mother,
Sophia Mullyon was obliged to thrash her daughter
for this last savagery; Sanchia swaggered away with
impudence on her lips and arms akimbo. She was
miserable, miserable; but she would not allow others to
guess it.

For that black first month she acted like a mad thing;
prancing and yelling one moment, slinking behind rocks
the next. Daring her schoolfellows to precarious climbs
about the mountain, slashing the fishing-nets with a knife
stolen from her mother's kitchen, creeping out at night to
set doors and gates ajar, so that the penned animals escaped
and scattered themselves far and wide over the island. She
was devilish; without pity or kindliness; unmanageable save
in the brief hours of schooling, when she seemed to crouch
and gather fresh inspiration for her cruelties. She knew she
was wicked, and she resigned herself to wickedness. She
built up an atmosphere of lawlessness, and steeped herself
in a criminal atmosphere of her own creation. She discovered in herself the power of making others fear her. She
was like the wind itself, changeable, keen and cruel, uncertain, dangerous and destructive in all her moods. She took
a craze for tormenting the smaller children, who scattered

like chickens at the hovering of a hawk. She seemed to get some cold satisfaction from inflicting physical pain; even the big lads hesitated to tackle her, for she would use indifferently feet, hands and teeth in the defence of her person, and, fresh from some bullying attack on one or other, would stroll away with buccaneering gait, a gibbering triumph on her lips. She was small and lightly built, but so powerful! Her thin brown fingers were like steel, her body like whip-thong; no one could master her.

Sometimes the boys shot sea-birds to supplement the household diet; Sanchia had a better way. She would catch them in her hands, pouncing on them suddenly, from behind, as they stood preening themselves in feathery unconsciousness in the sun. Her lithe body crawled over the rocks like an octopus: one swoop, and her fingers closed round the feet of the wretched bird, which fought with whirring wings against the bright-eyed death that threatened it. She would let it struggle for a little, until the wild and tortured thing smote at her hand with its gaping beak, and then—crick: one sharp twist, and the soft warm bundle would sag in her hand, with lolling neck.

Then, with the second month, came a change: swift, inexplicable, one of nature's imponderable tricks which she reserves for female nature. Sophia felt it first— like that brooding lull which ushers in the wind's worst excesses: the lull which sets people a-fidget about unnecessary tasks, and jerks their heads spasmodically across their shoulders, as though in apprehension of an unseen enemy.

It was Sunday; the islanders had been to church. The prim procession of scholars in their starched Sabbath garments moved across the shingle in a ripple of morning sunlight. The waters danced along the outer edge of the kelp; peace and Sabbath calm infused the air. Sanchia Mullyon, as prim, seemingly, as any, stalked solitary a little

ahead of her parents, her hair pushed away under the
battered rush hat she wore. In a few moments smoke
belched from all the chimneys: while the women set about
preparation of the midday meal, the men stood about in
clumps, smoking their pipes and exchanging the grunts
which pass for conversation among the islanders. But when
Sophia Mullyon called her daughter to eat, Sanchia was
missing.

She was not hungry: or, at any rate, the fare provided by
her mother did not tempt her. The morning was lovely; the
birds basked in thousands on Sail Point, and her fingers
twitched with the predatory desire. She stripped herself of
the white frock, dragged her ragged everyday dress over her
head, and stole away unobserved, the secret huntress on the
trail of her quarry.

The sunbaked rocks struck warm through her serge
frock; motionless, her stomach pressed to the stony ledge
on which she lay, Sanchia waited; below her, on a narrow
sliver of rock, two gallinules puffed out their feathers and
settled softly in the sun. Out shot an arm; a cloud
of gulls rose screaming into the air, and in Sanchia's
clutch the victim struggled like a mad thing to join its
fellows.

She laughed; her laughter tinkled down the rock face with
the soulless sound of crystal. She drew herself upright,
looked for a moment into the terrified eyes of the bird, and
—wrung its neck.

Softly the feathers settled down against her hand. As
though the murderous deed had shocked them, the cloud of
birds swept silently away, and Sanchia was left alone, with
death. A chill ran through her body. She looked down upon
the creature spread fanwise across her knee; the beauty and
symmetry of it penetrated her consciousness for the first
time. For the first time she was shocked by the wanton
destruction of beauty. And as she raised her head, and her
small face down which the tears, not of pity for the bird, but
of regret for its loveliness, were cascading, the conception

of beauty in the general was abruptly born. Like every islander, she had taken grandeur for granted. Now, in all that lay about her, she could observe but one uncomely thing—Sanchia Mullyon. The exquisite spotlessness of nature revealed to her her own unkempt condition; in the immaculate plumage of the dead bird she read reproof of her disarray. For several weeks she had gone unwashed, unkempt; she had fought off Sophia's attempt to strip her and force her into the steaming tub that served them all on Saturday nights. She had scrambled on her Sunday dress over her unbathed body, and concealed beneath her hat the hair, stringy with sea-salt, which had so matted itself that no comb would separate the formidable silky tangle. And now in the aerial dance of the distant birds, in the silvery elegance of the soft dead thing in her lap, she felt reproach. Supposing it had been she, Sanchia, who had met her end, whose body had been picked up on the beach below; a bundle of dirty rags and unclean flesh for people to stare at! Physical pride flamed up in her, the blood beat up in her cheeks. Through the death of a bird Sanchia Mullyon had entered into her heritage of femininity. No longer a soulless elf, but a woman in embryo crouched upon the Point, and when at last, clasping the dead bird, she started to descend the cliff, it was with movements of decorum.

Her first act was to bury the bird; in a circle of rocks she scraped out a hollow sufficiently deep, and, folding the wings around the still-warm body, laid it softly down, trampling the sand above it.

To the unsophisticated islanders, Sanchia's change of demeanour was no less sinister than her previous condition. They watched her, as cats watch a clockwork mouse: mistrusting it, suspecting the supernatural. In place of active rebellion, they gapingly beheld a cynical acquiescence, much more disturbing than former defiance; and when, without prompting from Sophia, Sanchia let down her skirts and pinned up her hair, although still a scholar, they gaped even wider and whispered among themselves.

On Calvary, as elsewhere, the lengthening of dresses and the pinning up of hair is taken as a signal that the maiden in question is prepared to entertain aspirants. In Sanchia's case, the fact of her betrothal to Gregory Jodrell was a matter so generally accepted that, apart from grins and winks, furtive snatches at the hand and cat-calls when she went out walking, no one took active steps to woo her. Tutored by Samson Jodrell, however, young Gregory developed the habit of dropping in at the Mullyons' o' nights, was received formally by the old people—and totally ignored by Sanchia. She, bending over her lesson-books, plodding through the arithmetic primer for the second time, had no time to spare for Gregory's attentions. Sophia tried to make up, with winks and nods, for her daughter's shortcomings: Gregory, undaunted, went stolidly on with his wooing. When she had left school, Sophia promised. . . .

And when, at fourteen, Sanchia left school, her mother, anxious—perhaps over-anxious—to anticipate the problem of Sanchia's unoccupied time, delayed no longer, but told her bluntly that there was no sense in putting off the question of her marriage to Samson Jodrell's son.

The dark, secretive look of the girl deepened, as she listened in silence to her mother's statement. In former years Sanchia would have flown into a passion, and flounced out of doors. She had learnt a different and much more difficult method of resistance latterly. She heard Sophia to an end: Sophia, who, anxious perhaps to avoid the unreassuring expression of her daughter's face, had jerked out the information between the spasms of her housekeeping occupations. Sanchia, between indolent efforts at polishing the pans her mother had scoured, allowed her eyes to rest on the horizon, and there was something ironic in their depths.

"So ye can just set to work an' get your things ready," ended Sophia, breathlessly. "Ye can have the taffety gown to be wed in, an' there's a heap o' white stuff for ye to make your shifts from i' the old chest yonder."

"I'm not wedding," said Sanchia.

"Eh?" gaped Sophia, suspending her work to glare at her child.

"'Tis o'ersoon," declared Sanchia reasonably. "I'll take my time an' look about me."

"Ay, ye can look," retorted Sophia viciously; "but ye'll not be finding a better nor Gregory Jodrell as ye're promised to, so a-done wi' your rubbidge an' settle down like a decent Calvary maid."

"I've not promised myself to Gregory Jodrell," she returned, with a toss of the head. "I'm not an ox or an ass, am I, to be gi'en away wi'out a will o' my own? Maybe I'll not wed a Calvary youth at all; I'm not drawed to 'em, an' the world's a big place, wi' a mighty power o' men in it."

"Ye're mad," whispered Sophia Mullyon. "Don't let yer father get wind o' yer notions. Calvary ye're born an' Calvary ye'll wed; what else, forsooth?"

"Maybe, maybe," she answered, with false imperturbability. "But I'll wed in my own time, an' ye can bide till I say I'm ready."

The news that Sanchia was not "settled" sped round the island in the voiceless way that such things became known. Thomas Mullyon, coming in from work, found his kitchen full of young men: dour, uneasy and silent, sitting with their shoulders hunched and their faces dropped shamefacedly towards their chests; for an hour or more they had sat there —it was the recognized method of Calvary wooing. By their presence there each signified that he was suitor for the hand of Sanchia. A little apart from the rest, dumbfounded, red-faced, sat Gregory Jodrell, not knowing what to make of this challenge to his own footing in the house. Sophia, nervous, flushed, acidly voluble, bustled about, scolding Sanchia who sat, as cool as though the room had been empty, sewing on the shifts to which her mother had recommended her. Cool, insolent and speechless, she might have been deaf, dumb and blind—to the wretched youths and to her mother. Her needle slipped silently in and out by candlelight; otherwise she might have been a small statue of ivory, diabolically demure.

"What's this?" demanded Thomas Mullyon, striking his stick upon the stone floor. The youths shuffled their feet, Sanchia raised her head for a moment, and allowed a smile to slant one corner of her mouth, before she resumed her needlework; Sophia made a noise like "Tscha!" and vanished. "Get out o' here, the pack o' ye!" bellowed Thomas Mullyon; and, when they had gone, turned upon his daughter like a lion.

But when she slid out of his hold, trembling and scarlet, chewing her lips to restrain the shrieks which her new-born pride would not allow her to utter, the angry man felt a lack of the satisfaction which such previous chastisements had brought him. As he knelt on the stones, shouting his customary prayer that the Almighty might chasten his frowardly child, his voice grew sharper in the attempt to drown the small creeping doubt that threatened his triumph. For the first time Thomas Mullyon questioned his own supremacy over his flesh and blood. He felt as though he had been beating the empty body of Sanchia, which her soul had sloughed and left in his hands for mockery; and in all the subsequent thrashings he gave her, he had this same disconcerting sense of thrashing an empty thing. Never again did she vouchsafe a sound in response to her father's punishments, and, in time, these lost their savour for Thomas Mullyon, although he continued, mechanically, as people continue to pray after the spirit of prayer has departed from them. He believed that thrashing Sanchia was a duty he owed to her and to his God.

Others beside he were conscious of the ominous change in the girl. Although the youths continued to hang about her there was fear in their attitude towards her. She seemed so secret, so locked away, so strangely quiet. Gone were her antic outbursts of rage and of hooliganism. Her voice grew lower, and she spoke little; a faint cloud of disdain hung about her; she let it be seen that she despised the boys of Calvary—and none more than Gregory Jodrell, her affianced husband—not that she would admit the betrothal. She spoke of herself, always, as free, and repeated that she would make her choice in her own good time—a piquing situation for Calvary lads, who had little notion of wooing. There was no romance about marriage on the island; boys and girls were paired in their cradles, and grew up aware of it. The act of coupling was regarded prosaically enough as a means of keeping up the island population.

The years went on; Rose and the rest of Sanchia's school-fellows were married. She held to her virginity, seeing no shame in it, stubborn in her resolve to have her own way. She grew slightly acrid, as old maids are said to do; was cool and aloof with her mother and alienated from her father. Their authority she shook lightly from her as a duck shakes the drops of water off its wings. No young man was allowed to enter the Mullyon house save Gregory Jodrell, and, as often as he entered, Sanchia would rise, coolly take her hat down from its peg, and go out for a long solitary walk along the shore.

"Ye should follow her, Gregory," muttered Sophia Mullyon, one day when Gregory stood there, looking abashed, seeking to take his departure, since the object of his visit was removed.

"Nay, I'm not for pushing where I'm not wanted," he answered.

"A maid don't know what she's wanting."

"Sanchia knows, right enough."

Samson Jodrell roared with laughter at his son's ill-starred wooing.

"She's leading ye on, Gregory! Don't ye let her see ye're caring. Ye'll have a rare time wi' such a one when ye wed her!"

In the opinion of the women she was hard: hard as nails, and proud as though the devil were in her. She had no little easy ways of sympathy or interest about her; she would sit in an ironic silence while they gossiped or indulged in the little excitements of the island—excitements that usually centred about the birth of one of the cows, or a Sunday dress someone had fashioned from oddments: "'Tis gay an' fine an' a rare credit to ye, Janet Hawkins," someone would say, and the proud Janet would turn and twist her portly body in gratification—until Sanchia's cold, scornful eye stripped half the pleasure from her. She had no natural kindliness: at least that was what they said of her, until she puzzled the lot of them by bursting into tears when Thomas Mullyon killed an old gander whose cantankerous ways had been a menace to passers-by for a month or more. He came clumping into the room where Sophia sat sewing with Sanchia and three or four others—the limp feathery body of the bird swinging by its neck from his hand. Sanchia rose with a cry, stabbing her needle into her finger and not noticing it.

"What are ye about, Sanchia?" cried Sophia Mullyon, snatching the material from her, as her blood reddened a corner.

"Ye've killed the gander!" choked Sanchia. "Ye've murdered the poor thing!"

"Hold yer daft tongue!" muttered Thomas, and she hid her face in her hands and ran from the room, leaving them agape upon her folly. For whoever heard of such a fuss being made about a dead bird? The girl was losing her wits.

She ran behind the house, and, leaning against the wall, hid her face in the crook of her arm, while tears soaked her cotton sleeve. The hideous helplessness of feathered things against mankind swept over her: she prayed aloud, hardly conscious that she was praying: "O God, forgive me, because I once killed birds!" The air seemed charged with murder; all day and every day on Calvary it was kill to live, but the death of the old gander, who had been a sort of domestic pet before he turned cranky: who ran waddling after her when she set out on her lonely walks along the shore—this seemed an outrage. Flinty towards most human beings, Sanchia had a secret kindliness towards animals that was utterly inexplicable to the islanders. To them the island creatures represented food; to Sanchia, denied human friendliness through the idiosyncrasy of her own character, they were something more. She hated to see the molly-mawks brought in, their feathers splathered with blood and mud, and had refused to help her mother to prepare them for table. She no longer went to the sheep-killings, which provided the youth of Calvary with a seemingly tireless spectacle; she shuddered away from the warm dead things that men were always to be seen carrying to their houses: she shuddered inwardly, for she was too proud to betray her feelings to them. She preferred that they should think her heartless; it was part of her secret, of the wilful mystery which she drew between herself and the Calvary folk she despised.

She took a perverse pleasure in seeming indifferent to the ailments of the men and women, to her father's rheumatism and her mother's frequently recurring Calvary fever. "That Sanchia—she's as much heart as a stone." Let them think it!—and leave her free to spill the balm of love and pity upon the animals, the poor, uncared-for, half-starved things that fulfilled uncomplainingly their destiny of providing food for the stomachs of the human beings.

She went sneakingly about her errands of kindliness; did a few ridiculous things, like attempting to put the broken leg of one of the sheep into a splint, took fresh armfuls of dried kelp to the wretched horses whose beds were seldom renewed by Job Barker, and coaxed the wild, thin, nervous cattle into something approaching friendliness. Then Samson Jodrell owned a dog—one of the half dozen on the island; an emaciated mongrel, existing somehow on the results of its own hunting, but disabled by age and blindness from catching enough to fill its ravenous stomach. She fed the dog, surreptitiously, on scraps filched from her mother's larder; but Sophia was watchful, and knew to an inch of cheese the provisions she had in hand; sometimes days would elapse before Sanchia could steal anything.

Sneaking into the outhouse where Samson tethered it, when it was not needed for helping with the sheep, she found the animal lying on its side, panting for breath. She saw blood clotted on its side and stooped to examine the wound. So accustomed was she to such horrors, that she hardly sickened when she beheld the flesh laid back to the bone. At once she understood what had happened; one of the rams—a brute with a broken horn—had charged the dog, which had been left to creep away in its agony, because the people of Calvary, in their own fortitude, saw little reason why trouble and time should be wasted on a dog— one, moreover, that had finished its span of usefulness, and might as well die that way as any other.

She sat for a while with her hand on the head of the dying animal. There seemed little she could do; the wound was too deep for the creature to recover—the entrails bulged at the edges of the wound. It came to her, however, that the poor wretch was likely to linger on, even for hours, in its agony. That at least she could prevent.

She rose and went boldly to Samson Jodrell's door; and it seemed like kindly fate when Gregory himself opened to her. Gregory would at least understand better than Samson.

"There's Neptune dying in yon shed," she said, shortly. She held her breath to control her tears.

"Ay," said Gregory, kindly enough; "my father told me as the old ram had charged him."

"And did ye not bother to go and look at him?"

"I've been busy wi' the sea-wall all day, Sanchia," he answered, humbly. The glitter in her eyes—a glitter of unshed tears—disturbed him profoundly.

"Ye must shoot him! 'Tis not right to let a creature suffer so!"

"He'll be gone soon enough, poor beast."

"Was animals meant to suffer like that?" cried Sanchia. "Ye know right well they was not! Go an' look at him yersen! See how ye'd like to be lying on hard stone, gaspin' yer life out, wi' a great tear in yer side!"

He followed her reluctantly to the shed; he was the same as the other islanders in not believing in making a fuss of animals, but the innate kindliness of his nature cost him a pang as the dying beast rolled up its glazing eye at him as though in a mute plea for pity.

"My father'd got no business to leave him that way," muttered Gregory.

"Get yer gun, now, Gregory, an' put an end to it!"

"My father'll be mad if I waste cartridges; we've gotten but a few left."

"Damn yer father an' his cartridges! If ye don't do as I tell ye, Gregory, I'll search the house through till I find 'em an' do the job mysen!"

The idea appalled him more than the thought of his father's wrath; as he went to fetch the gun he remembered with a sense of shock that Sanchia had used an oath in speaking of his father; it was a fearful thing to the stern-minded Gregory.

He found her kneeling, no longer attempting to conceal her tears.

"All things in pain ought to be killed," she sobbed. "Ay, an' folks too. 'Tis just devilment, pain is. Go on, Gregory; do it now, while my hand's on him."

Gregory placed the nozzle of the gun to the dog's temple and drew the trigger. The report sounded frightfully in the narrow shed; when the smoke had cleared away, Sanchia still crouched there, with her hand on the poor tormented body which had ceased to feel pain.

She lifted her head and looked at him dimly.

"If I believed in a God, Gregory," she said, with her faint, ironical smile, "I'd ask Him to bless ye for that."

Gregory Jodrell stood with his feet apart and the gun under his arm, looking down at her steadfastly.

"I'll ask Him to forgive yer unbelief, Sanchia, an' the way ye spoke o' my father, an' bring ye into His Holy Tabernacle, for Jesus' sake!"

She seemed about to make some bitter answer; pressed her hand to her lips and, springing to her feet, whirled past him and out of sight.

CHAPTER IV

"If there is an outbreak of intemperance among the people," cried the Reverend Smith Prudhomme, smiting the clenched fist of one hand into the palm of the other, "I shall unhesitatingly lay the blame at Sanchia Mullyon's door!"

"Poor Sanchia," whispered Mrs. Prudhomme; "they are making her responsible for everything."

"She is shirking her responsibilities," pronounced the Reverend Smith, dogmatically. "By her vacillations she is plunging the community into a ferment of discontent. Until she is married to Gregory Jodrell, there is no hope of our settling down to the daily——"

"But surely," said Mrs. Prudhomme, desperately, "Sanchia's marrying Gregory won't make as much difference as all that? The others will still want to get married—and I'm so sorry for poor little Martha and Betty, who will certainly be married long before they are ready for it."

"I don't agree with you," said the Reverend Smith, stiffly. "With Sanchia's wedding the element of uncertainty will be removed from the situation. When the others know that their—hrrum—aspirations are useless, they will settle down and turn their minds to vital matters once more, until—hrrum—some means of settlement presents itself."

"What means?" persisted Mrs. Prudhomme, who was rapidly approaching the fretful stage of her fever.

"I really don't know," confessed the Reverend Smith. "I *don't* see what I'm expected to do in the matter. It now rests with the Jodrells and the Mullyons. I can hardly—hrrum—put the matter plainly to Sanchia herself, but really it seems imperative that something should be done quickly."

Mrs. Prudhomme, closing her eyes, wished that she could not so distinctly visualize Smith as a distracted guinea-fowl, flapping about a farmyard.

"I catch glances passing from one to another—snatches of conversation are hushed as I come along. It is all very unsuitable. The pastor of such a community as this should be in the confidence of every man. I have lived among them as one of themselves——"

"Perhaps when the storm is over things will be better," said Mrs. Prudhomme, in a loud voice, with which she hoped to scare away the guinea-fowl.

"I doubt it," said the Reverend Smith gravely; "it really looks almost as if I shall have to take up the question of immigration once again. A great risk. A great risk—I do wish," said the Reverend Smith, dolefully, "that this problem had not arisen during my ministry, for I feel utterly incapable of dealing with it; yet it is clearly my duty to do so."

"The only obvious course," murmured Mrs. Prudhomme, "is to sanction polygamy. The men will have to go shares with their wives——"

"You had better try to get a little sleep," said the Reverend Smith, kindly. A shout drew him to the outer door, and having opened it, he called across to the bedroom where his wife lay: "Do you know where the iodine bottle is, Mary? Tom Mullyon has laid his hand open."

As Mrs. Prudhomme passed into a convenient swoon, she just had time to wonder why Smith could not have said: "Tom Mullyon has cut his hand:" it would have made all the difference. . . .

When the bandaging was over, the missionary and the islander stood looking each other in the eye. The Reverend Smith liked Thomas Mullyon; he was one of the most respectful of the congregation, and it certainly was a hard cross to lay on a man—to give him a daughter like Sanchia.

"Sit down and smoke a pipe, Tom," said the Reverend Smith, and pushed him into the corner of the settle by the fire. Closing the bedroom door, he moved fussily about, lighting the lamp and placing the tobacco jar at the elbow of his visitor.

"I've been wanting a chat with you for several days."

Thomas Mullyon looked up attentively. One saw where Sanchia had got her Atlantic-grey eyes; the same eyes looked watchfully from beneath Tom Mullyon's shaggy brows. He had the dour look of the early Puritans, but one felt instinctively that here was a man jealous for the right, one who would deliver himself to martyrdom rather than resign his principles of right and wrong.

"There seems to be a great deal of uneasiness in the settlement just now," said the Reverend Smith, seating himself in Jebusa Horne's chair, and crossing his knees in token of preparation for a long talk.

"Ay, there is," agreed Tom Mullyon.

"Now, Tom, I daresay that most of it concerns your daughter."

A puff of smoke obscured the features of the man opposite from his interlocutor. He sat silent, with that formidable silence of the islander who is resolved to give no inch until he is assured of his ground.

The Reverend Smith waited; he had learned to do that, although it went against the grain.

"The matter is, minister," said Thomas Mullyon at last, "that human instincts go bad in a man, unless they are let go their own way—subject to the provision of the Lord. Things look black for Calvary unless grace is given to us to restrain our appetites. Sanchia has naught to do wi' all that. It's right enough for us wedded men; but Calvary lads have been lusty since the beginning of time. 'Tis by their lustiness that Calvary has stood and witnessed to the glory of the Lord. There ha'n't been no sin on Calvary since the days of Jebusa Horne: leastways, what sin there's been has been stamped out through the blessing of righteousness bestowed on Calvary folk."

Suddenly the Reverend Smith Prudhomme thought of

the illicit still, and yearned to ask Thomas Mullyon what he knew of that; but his good angel prevailed, and he nodded his head gravely. Yes, according to the records, Calvary folk had a summary way of dealing with their sinners.

"What we want to know," went on Tom Mullyon, slowly, "is how to preserve the island's grace. It canna be done by prayer alone."

"That's true, certainly," said the Reverend Smith, who, for all his profession, was a practical man. "But what do you think we should do, Tom?"

"The ship's overdue," said Thomas. "'Twill be a twelve-month or more afore we get another; but maybe the older fellows like me and Samson Jodrell can hold the fort for the Lord until His answer comes—if so be the others know it is coming."

"Oh, yes," agreed the Reverend Smith, his mind darting off at a tangent, and missing the latter part of Mullyon's speech, "and no doubt the cricket and football teams are of great value——"

"Minister," said Thomas Mullyon, "did ye ever hear tell that kicking a ball was any use to a lad, when he'd got the woman fever in his blood? Women must be brought to Calvary."

"I was just speaking of immigration to my wife," admitted the Reverend Smith. "It's a very difficult matter, you know, Mullyon. Selection—hrrum. I fear that not one girl in a hundred would make a success of life on the island. The—hrrum—tendency of modern times is rather to weaken the powers of resistance of the human frame than—hrrum—to encourage that sturdiness of physical and moral fibre essential to life in such a place as Calvary. To put it plainly, Tom, Calvary has not much to offer the young women of to-day."

"They say there are over many women in Britain now," persisted Thomas Mullyon. "Women have the mating instinct, same as men; male and female, the spirit of the Lord stings them to procreation. Maybe the prospect of motherhood would make up to some of these young females for the hardship of life on the island."

The Reverend Smith Prudhomme, who had been recently enough employed in a parish teeming with young females, had his doubts. Motherhood, in their opinion, was a much exaggerated pleasure, and a heavy price to pay for the wedding-ring on one's finger. If there had even been a picture-house on Calvary! The nearest approach they owned to the "movies" was an antique magic-lantern, left behind by the Reverend Mr. Simpson in his flight. An appeal for a cinematograph plant had been dismissed by the Society for the Propagation of the Gospel as "liable to induce discontent among the natives." As far as entertainments went, they were dependent upon their own efforts, and worse off than many an African settlement.

"It will be very difficult," he repeated; and returned to his point about Sanchia. "Don't you feel, Tom, that if Sanchia was settled, things would quieten down—for the present at any rate? You will admit it is very disquieting for the young men to have a girl as—hrrum—attractive as Sanchia, continually before their eyes."

"She would still be before their eyes," said Thomas Mullyon gloomily. "The Lord has thought fit to chasten me by giving me a daughter who is a temptation to my fellow men." It struck the Reverend Smith that his sister, who was blessed with four daughters, none of whom was liable to tempt a blind man, would find Tom's point of view an original one. "It is the Lord's will, and I must bear with it. But it is hardly a week since I thrashed her with my own hands," added Thomas, severely.

The Reverend Smith started. It was disconcerting to imagine any young woman of marriageable age submitting to corporal punishment from her own father; how much more startling when the young woman in question was Sanchia Mullyon! To his horror he found himself visualizing the scene: Sanchia in the humiliating attitude. His childhood's experience made it impossible for him to imagine a thrashing taking place otherwise than across the knee. He saw Sanchia's white flesh exposed . . . and just managed to check a cry. There must indeed be something devilish in the girl that she could call up these ungodly thoughts in the mind of a minister of the church.

His glance at Thomas Mullyon showed him that the father saw nothing incongruous in the proceeding. One could not, of course, interfere with the domestic discipline of these people; but Sanchia——! It occurred to the Reverend Smith that in moments of irritation he would dearly have liked to have slapped Sanchia Mullyon, and his horror turned to a sort of grudging admiration for the intrepidity of Thomas.

The wind hurled a shower of pebbles against the windows.

"It is going to be a bad night," said Thomas Mullyon.

Sail Point bears the oldest surviving name on El Secredo; it is the outcrop pointing due west from which the remains of the garrison first sighted Jebusa Horne. The rocks there bear some resemblance to pumice, their surfaces eroded into hummocks which are at odds with the jagged conformation of the rest of the island. If one is sufficiently surefooted, one may make one's way to its extremity, and thence look upon the whole of the island; mark how its steep sides climb, shedding the sparse vegetation as they go, to the summit. Here, if one ventures to climb it, the feet sink into the crust of decayed lava, and a cup-like ridge of basalt conceals the crater lake of the extinct volcano. The thin, wild Calvary sheep graze upon the lower reaches of the slope, indistinguishable among the boulders; and the arable region terminates sharply at Sail Point, where the cliff soars up almost perpendicular to the height of a hundred or more feet, and is penetrated by many caves, in which probably the pirates dwelt. They are now haunted with birds that provide the islanders with an important part of their food. Parties go birds'-egging there in the proper season, and the slipperiness of the rocks makes it difficult to return with one's harvest intact; as though the birds know it, they build in the most impudently accessible places, only safeguarded by the difficulty—for human beings—of obtaining foothold on the rocks.

"I thought I'd ha' met you on your way back."

Gregory Jodrell had crawled, plunging and panting, up to the mouth of the lowest of the caves, where, from the beach below, he had seen Sanchia sitting, so still that black eaglet, sea-hen and petrel—shyest of birds—remained like statues in her vicinity. She affected not to hear his shout, and Gregory, who had brought a lantern for safety, was forced to make the awkward climb, in the teeth of the freshening gale and handicapped by the strange sulphurous light of sunset, that sent curious shapes of clouds racing so swiftly over the cliff-face that one had almost the sense of moving in a kaleidoscope. The birds, which had been so still for Sanchia, rushed in a wheeling cloud about his head, so close that he could feel the fanning of their wings, and was half-deafened by their shrill outcry.

He stood at last by Sanchia's side, dodging the drippings from the roof, getting his breath after the scramble. The place was littered with birds' offal and with eerie bone refuse; Sanchia half-sat, half-leaned against the rock, her hands clasped behind her waist, her eyes fixed as steadfastly upon the far horizon as though Gregory were not there. Very still she was; yet to Gregory it seemed that her stillness was not that of repose. Rather was it like the moment when the runner poises, ready to shoot like an arrow at the word of command. She seemed as if she might suddenly slip away—anywhere.

"Come; it's high time we were getting back; it'll be dark in half an hour."

"Let it be dark," said Sanchia Mullyon, sombrely. "If it grows too dark to walk, I shall spend the night here with the birds. It won't be the first time," she added, in reference to an incident that had set the island by the ears, when fourteen-year-old Sanchia had vanished for twenty-four hours, returning cool as a cucumber to take her expected thrashing. "I was tired of folk," had been her brief explanation, when called upon to account for herself, and she smiled when they called her "fond."

The water broke into lather against the Point, climbing the rocks in dense white fringe, and falling back, lovely as lace, upon the surface of the waves. Elsewhere about the island the kelp kept the waves in subjection, save on the stormiest days; but from Sail Point the currents swirled it away. That was one reason why Sanchia liked Sail Point; she hated the kelp, lying always like a dead thing on the top of the quick water.

"The storm's coming up quickly. Come—or I'll have to carry you!"

She turned her head, and smiled up at him with her dim little face, like one of those pale flowers that lie in the depths of rock pools.

"Sit down, Gregory Jodrell," she said, deeply; and although he knew it was madness to linger, he found himself obeying her. "Why make a to-do about the storm? If it comes we shall be better here than in our houses."

"You know right well, Sanchia," he muttered, "we cannot spend the night here together."

She laughed, with the eerie gurgle of a sea-bird. A petrel swept almost across their faces, staring at them for an instant with its strange mad eyes; and, as a light in a theatre suddenly seems to shift, so the light on the horizon shifted, darkened several degrees, and wrapped the pair of them in a deeper gloom.

"You've come here to pester me about wedding you, Gregory Jodrell. Are ye fond, that ye let yourself be driven to tormenting me, with naught to come of it?"

"I love you," said Gregory, desperately; "when will you marry me?"

"I'd sooner marry a dead man than you, Gregory Jodrell!" she retorted, cruelly. "Ye're only half alive your-

self! Marry you! I'll tell you what you want me to marry
you for. You want to father your children on me, and make
a servant of me, and have me baking your meals and mending your clothes till I'm an old woman and I die and you
bury me up yonder, in the cemetery. By an' by we'd stop
talking to each other, because we'd said all there is to say;
and then we'd go on being together until we hated each
other—like Maggie Robertson and John."

"What are you saying?" said Gregory sharply, for John
Robertson was his cousin. "Take care of your tongue,
Sanchia. Maggie's going to have a child in January."

"Fancy sleeping with a man you hate! Fancy bearing
children to him. I'd sooner be light, an' sleep with who I
please, when I please to do it——"

"Father, forgive her!" cried Gregory Jodrell, for her
words cut into his heart.

"You and your religion!" Her voice rang with contempt.
He made a little pleading movement, as though he wanted
to take her hand.

"Sanchia, you don't mean what you say."

She ignored him, and presently, to his great confusion,
bent her head, and covered her face with her hands.

"Sanchia!" cried Gregory; "what is it you want?—and,
by God, I'll try to give it you."

She answered, in a voice so steady that she could not
have been weeping, but so faint that it was nearly lost in
the gale, and he had to crouch at her side to catch her
words:

"Somewhere—when all is dark—there are lights, and
people sing and dance and are gay."

"Why, Sanchia, we have good times on the island, don't
we? Think o' Rose's wedding, and how Timothy played
his fiddle an' you danced the lancers with me! All the lads
envied me that night, Sanchia! You were a bonny sight, the
way you went tripping up an' down in that blue gown o'
yours——"

"'Twas pink," said Sanchia, with feminine resentment.

"Maybe it was; I'd no eyes but for your face that night. Why, our wedding'll be even finer than Rose's, Sanchia! The ship will be in soon, an' it'll be the greatest wedding on the island. I've got a fine young calf and——"

"*Fool,*" said Sanchia Mullyon. Her hands dropped from her face. "What do you think I am, Gregory Jodrell, to part with myself for the sake of wedding feast and a night's dancing to the fiddle and the women all a-whispering to me and all the lads drunk with Calvary beer? What comes after? Work from morning till night: till my hands grow all shapeless and my hair starts coming out and my body's like a bolster wi' child-bearing! There's Maggie Robertson, just gone forty, and she might be twice as old; it fair hurts one to look at her and remember what a bonny girl she was."

"Looks are naught," grunted Gregory. "They're but vanity and temptation, anyhow. Who cares for looks? On Calvary there's no time for looks. Jack didn't marry Maggie for her looks."

"Do you believe that?" He was too simple to recognize the bitterness in her tone. "Maybe on El Secredo the men are blind. Maybe they don't care when a woman's eyes wrinkle up and her hair goes dead like the kelp and her body grows into an ugly lump. It's all part of the cruelty of El Secredo. Women aren't meant to be like that! A woman's meant to have a soft body, and——"

"That's enough," said Gregory, his ears reddening.

"You're scared of prettiness, aren't you, Gregory Jodrell? It fairly scares you out of your wits to think about it. Like all the rest of the men you'll try to stamp down prettiness when it comes your way. They say your mother was a rarely pretty woman when she was young; but not when Samson Jodrell had done with her—poor creature! But away from El Secredo the men aren't so cruel. They cherish a pretty thing when they see it."

"What do you know about other men?" whispered Gregory.

"Light the lantern, and I'll show you."

He cast a glance at the swiftly blackening sky, and obeyed. If they did not leave the cave within the next few minutes they might indeed spend the night there, and then——! His brow broke into sweat as he pictured being alone with Sanchia through the long hours of darkness. Without hypocrisy he prayed that he might be spared that temptation.

She had taken a folded slip of paper out of the bosom of her dress, and spread it out on her knee. Gregory could see, as he held the lantern towards her, a column of newspaper print; Sanchia had evidently cut it from one of the papers that found their way to the island in the crates, as packing. She began to read aloud, rather painstakingly and affectedly, as the children were taught to read in the mission:

> The craze for beauty-competitions has spread to the remoter villages of the industrial north. In the little town of Burnup, no fewer than fifty girls entered for the competition organized by the Mayor, to decide the Beauty Queen of Burnup. The honour fell to Miss Cissie Hoster, a charming eighteen-year-old blonde. The competitors were judged in bathing-suits by a committee which included several of the town councillors.

"'Tis an abomination!" cried Gregory. "For shame, Sanchia, to read such stuff."

Before she apprehended his action, he had snatched the piece of paper, torn it into fragments and flung them out upon the wind.

"There was a photograph," said Sanchia, mildly. "Some of the girls were very pretty; you would have thought so yourself. Don't be a fool, Gregory. It is not that I want to strip myself and walk before people so that they may judge if I am nice to look at; but I do want to live among people who *count* such things; who don't think it ungodly to tell a woman she is pretty and good-looking. I want to find people who think about that sort of thing as if it was quite as important as building an oven, or killing a sheep, or making an embankment."

"But it isn't!" said Gregory, half stunned by the comparison.

"But it is!" cried Sanchia. "Only not here, on El Secredo, where people are so busy just *living* that they haven't time to spare for prettiness or anything that isn't bound up with their eating and drinking. Why, to El Secredo men, a woman is just something to sleep with, an extra pair of hands to do the work."

"I have always liked looking at you, Sanchia," said Gregory, heavily.

"Well, what else had you to look at?" she cried, with youthful arrogance. "You don't know anything else. There's no other girl on the island—since Rose married—to take your eyes away from me. I won't be married because I'm the only ripe woman on the island. When I marry, 'twill be to someone who has seen other women, and chooses me because he likes me better than any of them."

"How can you say that kind of thing, Sanchia?" asked Gregory, wonderingly. "How can you marry like that—on Calvary?"

"Don't ships come? One day some man will come off a ship, and I shall go away with him, and no one will ever see me again."

Gregory sighed heavily, casting an anxious look at the sky, which pressed down upon the heaving water like a leaden cup. In contrast with the pale yellowish light of the lantern, all outside seemed suddenly to have slipped into darkness. Looking cautiously over the lip of the cave, slimy with the birds' droppings, he found to his dismay that the beach was nearly indistinguishable. He could hear the soft sound of Sanchia's breathing and the rustle of her serge skirt on the rock, behind him.

"Come; we must go quickly," he said abruptly, and started as his outstretched hand fell on her shoulder. He felt a thrill go through it. It was a thin little shoulder, like a child's. It filled him with the same sense of tenderness that he felt for lambs and young birds. At that moment he almost choked with his tenderness for Sanchia, and his hand tightened on her shoulder in the lantern-light.

"Before God, I do love thee, Sanchia Mullyon!" he said, hoarsely.

"You can kiss me if you want to, Gregory Jodrell," came her disconcerting answer. "I would not mind being kissed by you."

His hand fell away as though something had burned him; all his inherited Puritanism was up in arms.

"If you will tell me when you will wed me, I will kiss ye, Sanchia." His voice softened despite himself as he added: "I will do all you ask me to make you happy, if you will wed me."

Her laughter was echoed by some bird which broke into a long ghostly giggle against the roof of the cave.

"'Tis too heavy a price to pay for one kiss," she demurred. "Maybe I could find someone who would kiss me cheaper than that!"

The mocking echo of her words brought a sudden terror to his heart. He put up his hand to his throat to loosen the muffler before he could choke out the words:

"Have ye been kissed, Sanchia Mullyon?"

"If I have, Gregory Jodrell, 'tis no business of yours."

"Have ye no respect for yourself?" he groaned, wildly.

Again she laughed; and somehow, he found his hands clutching her; she seemed soft, small, incredibly yielding. He hardly knew what he was about to do: hurl her from the mouth of the cave, or bind her to him in a dreadful embrace from which the two of them would emerge, damned— damned to eternity! As he hesitated, the wind screamed, and at the same moment something warm and feathery was dashed into his face. A bird, broken in the storm; he felt it flop at his feet as they started apart. To Gregory Jodrell it was the very hand of God that had saved his soul in the critical moment from destruction.

He became aware that she had vanished from his side.

"Sanchia!" roared Gregory, terrified that she would slip

and be dashed to atoms as she ventured into the force of the gale which now came screaming round Sail Point as though a thousand devils were behind it. It hit Gregory full in the face, robbing him of his breath. Fools that they had been, to linger so long! He slung the lantern on a string across his shoulder, and waited a moment, clutching the rock, to remember the principal footholds that the cliff face offered at this point. Fortunately they were not high up; this, the lowest of the caves, was not more than fifteen or twenty feet above the rocks, but to misjudge by an inch was enough to plunge one to destruction. Not so very long ago one of the Martyn boys had broken his spine at this very place, and in broad daylight too.

"Sanchia!" roared Gregory again; and this time her voice came faintly to him from below. She seemed to be safe; she rode the wind as a witch rides her broomstick.

He let himself down into a sitting position, and, groping and clutching, twice slipping dreadfully, at last felt the shingle grate beneath his feet.

She was waiting for him. There, in the wind's jaws, there was but one thing to do: to cling together, arm in arm, and batter their way towards the distant lights of the settlement. As they started to do so, a roar came over the sea, like the thunder of the gods.

From time immemorial, the instinct of fear has driven mankind to seek each other's society, as though, united, they could withstand the thing that seems so formidable in solitude.

Mrs. Prudhomme was perhaps the only person on El Secredo who knew no fear on that night which stands out in the records as one of the most frightful the island has ever known. Mrs. Prudhomme was not afraid because the fever of her cold had merged into delirium. She lay smiling, with a scarlet patch on either cheek, and babbling quietly about the tulips in the large crescent bed at Fiveoaks, which, it appears, she thought should have been replaced by wallflowers. The Reverend Smith, who had sent for Maggie Robertson, paced about the living-room, magisterially positive that this was just one of Mrs. Prudhomme's heavy colds that she had always managed to have in the winters at home. All conversation had to be carried on in a loud key, and between them, the Reverend Smith and Maggie Robertson, with the roar of the sea and the lashing of the rain, missed most of Mrs. Prudhomme's little monologue on tulips.

A knock came, and Samson Jodrell entered, the water running from his oilskins in streams. He dashed the rime from his beard and eyelashes before touching his cap to the Reverend Smith.

"It seems the people would like to get together in the mission and beseech the Lord," he stated, simply.

The Reverend Smith beamed, reaching towards his own sou'-wester. Such calls as these were unction to his soul, for he had come out to Calvary with the fixed determination to be a hero, and in justice to him it must be said that he had not neglected his opportunities. It may seem a petty sort of heroism to walk three hundred yards from your own door to the mission on a stormy night, but none knew better than the man who had brought the call that death lurked in every step. Nothing easier than to be whirled off one's feet into the sea. Ordinarily a length of hawser formed a kind of hand-rail along the weather side of the track between the missionary's house and the mission; but the Reverend Smith had parted with his hawser twenty-four hours before, when the roof of the young Sanguinettis' recently-erected house showed signs of being unable to withstand the storm, and threatening to break away with another night's wind. At any moment, too, one might be stunned by a blow on the head from timbers, slates, and odd implements, or even the body of some unfortunate animal, which the wind was hurling about as though they were leaves.

"I will go and get the room lit up," he said cheerily, as he tied the tapes of his sou'-wester beneath his chin. "I'm afraid we have Mrs. Prudhomme very poorly—she will not be able to come. But let the people know I am on the way—and look out for yourself, Samson."

He tip-toed into Mrs. Prudhomme's bedroom—an unnecessary piece of thoughtfulness, for if he had gone in with a policeman's rattle the sound of it would hardly have risen above the gale. The Reverend Smith suddenly realized this, and addressed his unconscious wife in a bellow.

"The people want me in the mission, my dear. Take care of yourself."

"I always think the yellow wallflowers look so beautiful with those clumps of forget-me-not," murmured Mrs. Prudhomme.

"Thank you, my dear; God bless you," said the Reverend Smith, not to give her the trouble of repeating herself. "You'll see she has plenty of barley-water, Maggie," and so saying, he plunged out into the storm, like the Happy Warrior.

CHAPTER V

No one would have guessed that they were frightened, the
people of Calvary, as they stood up straight, their hymn-
books in their hands, to sing the first hymn given out by the
Reverend Smith.   The only sign of their fear was their
presence there; they had wanted to get near to God, and
here, in God's house, was the best place to do it.   Their
minds were simple and logical as the minds of children, and
the faith of their fathers persisted in the same simple forms
as it had followed for the last four generations.

The windows of the Hawkins's house had been blown in;
they had hastily hung up tarpaulins before coming to the
mission.   Ralph Martyn, the youngest child on the settlement, had been flung against an ox-wagon, and stood up
proudly with a bandage round his head and his arm in a
sling.   The other children eyed him enviously.   Lack of
imagination or the calmness of their parents may have
accounted for their quietude.   Only little Machita Sanguinetti, clinging to her mother's skirts with a hand
like a bird's claw, while her black eyes almost darted
from her head, whimpered faintly, and the thread of
sound she made was swallowed up in the singing and
the wind.

From *Abide with Me* they went to *Lead, Kindly Light*,
while the babel without swelled so that each man
could barely hear his neighbour's voice.   The Reverend
Smith, glancing at the stove, tried to estimate whether the
amount of fuel available would serve them until morning.
It was plain that no one could leave the mission until the
storm abated.

As the people sat down in the pews for a brief rest, during which the Reverend Smith passed up and down the narrow aisle, leaning over to shout a word of cheer to some child or woman who seemed about to collapse under the strain, the door of the mission burst open, and Gregory Jodrell and Sanchia Mullyon were swept in on the force of the gale. As Gregory turned and flung the full weight of his body at the door to close it, the Reverend Smith realized with a start that in the excitement of the situation he had not missed either of them. He glanced frowningly about the mission, finding self-justification in the fact that the place was crowded. Sanchia seldom sat with her parents, and the Mullyons had their pew crowded with their grandchildren; it was easy enough to overlook a couple in the dim and wavering light of the lamps.

The pair of them were dripping, and Sanchia's cloak was rent from shoulder to hem; it fell in two sodden strips behind her, mingling with her hair. But her face was pale and calm; it seemed, in fact, almost indecent that she should preserve so sincere an indifference to conditions which might indeed have daunted any other woman. Gregory's trousers were tattered, and his head was bleeding. In contrast to Sanchia's his face was almost wild. Samson Jodrell lumbered from his seat and went towards his son; the watchers saw their lips move, but could catch no words. Gregory's eyes fell, he appeared to answer reluctantly.

Sophia Mullyon, thrusting her way in front of a gaping grandson, got hold of her daughter and dragged her towards the stove. With anxious movements she spread out Sanchia's skirts to the heat, and steam began to rise from them. Sanchia stood, looking down at the steam and smiling, as if she was amused. All could see that Sophia Mullyon was questioning her daughter; Sanchia held her lips closed, and shook her head, smiling. All eyes were on the girl; none looked at Gregory, who slipped into a seat at the back of the room and seemed to evade attention. His shoulders hunched themselves together, as if he were shivering.

The Reverend Smith went down and shouted at him:

"Come up to the stove, Gregory—and dry yourself, with Sanchia."

At first he shook his head; then, yielding to the compulsion of a hand on his shoulder, rose once more and shambled up the aisle. Sanchia greeted him with a smile. It was the most beautiful, most impudent smile. Everyone saw it, and knew that Sanchia intended them to see it. The women nudged each other, and their eyes spoke eloquently.

"She's betrothed to him! She's given him his answer!"

The glance of Janet Hawkins sped sympathetically to her two grim-faced sons. Personally, she was not sorry to be spared having Sanchia Mullyon as daughter-in-law, but her mother's heart yearned over her two lads, who had, surely, as much right to consideration as Samson Jodrell's son.

Someone sobbed; hysteria was not far away. An ear-splitting crash of thunder broke, seemingly, right overhead, and even the older women cowered; a child screamed, and Rose Sanguinetti hid her face on her husband's shoulder.

"Shall we sing again?" roared the Reverend Smith, with his hands funnelled on either side his mouth. They gave signs of assent. In a stentorian voice, Peter Hawkins, who was the precentor of the services, struck up *Eternal Father*. The people came again to their feet, with knees, perhaps, a little less steady. An ominous bumping upon the zinc warned them that something had broken loose and was being carried by the wind. It crashed and slid; something dropped heavily outside the window near which Samson Jodrell was standing. He paused for a moment in his singing to cry in Thomas Mullyon's ear: "'Tis one of the cows!" The poor beast had been carried over the cliff top in the storm; they found it at daybreak, groaning its life out with a couple of broken legs.

Someone took a hymn-book to Sanchia—which she held as though it were a curiosity, not attempting to use it or to sing. She still stood by the stove, where all could see her, but the calm had departed from her face. Here, under shelter, the storm sounded much more awful than it had done when she and Gregory struggled along the foreshore, crawling from boulder to boulder on hands and knees during the latter part of their journey. Watching her across their hymn-books, they saw—some of them with satisfaction—that the girl was deadly white, her lips half-open, as though she struggled for breath, and her eyes strained wide with fear in their depths. Once she put her hand up to her throat, as though she had pain there; suddenly she began to tremble. They could all see the tremors that convulsed her as she stood there, yet none moved to support her. Her mother, who might have done so, was standing stiffly, red-faced, with her eyes on the print; she knew that Sanchia had shamed her once again before the community. Thomas Mullyon sang grimly, with his eyes on the little altar; and Gregory Jodrell stood as mum as Sanchia, with eyes cast down and his hands clasped before him. He seemed almost to be in a trance.

Then an incredible thing happened. From the heart of a brief lull there emerged a mighty roar: the roar of a ravaging wild beast set loose; and the wind tore its way in through the wall of the mission, knocking a nine-foot gap in the stones as though with a battering ram.

By a miracle, no one was caught beneath the wreckage, although a boulder caught Job Barker on the shoulder, breaking it as though the bone were china, and a child let out a rending shriek as its little foot was ground to pulp beneath another. Before the cries had died down, the kerosene from a lamp that had been knocked over caught the matchboarding, and ran up in a streak of flame, which spread before the wretched congregation had time fully to realize its danger. There was a stampede to the door, which they found was jammed by the sudden sideways cant of the building. They turned like animals in a trap. Few there were that remembered afterwards how Sanchia Mullyon stood with her arms locked round Gregory Jodrell's neck, while scream after scream issued from her lips. "Gregory! Gregory! Save me! If you save me I will marry you!—for I will not die a virgin!"

Few, I say, remembered this thing; for it was then that the Reverend Smith Prudhomme had his supreme chance of being a hero, and acted upon it as a man should. Snatching the altar cloth from the table, and tying it across his mouth, he picked up the injured child and another, and, butting his way through the frenzied people, plunged, with the children in his arms, through the gap in the wall. It sounds a simple thing to have done; but one must remember that on El Secredo the houses are built without mortar; that the displacement of a keystone may result in the collapse of an entire building, and as the Reverend Smith made his exit he was in mortal danger from toppling stones, falling joists and the like.

His example saved a panic. Seizing their womenkind, the rest of the men took the dangerous means of exit, and, placing the children in their mothers' arms, the Reverend Smith dashed back into the blazing building. He might never have known fear in his life. Always with an intense admiration for deeds of derring-do, he had never, before his arrival on Calvary, had the opportunity to prove his own calibre, and the danger of the situation was quite lost, so far as he was concerned, in the pleasure of the discovery that the qualities he had so admired in others were incorporated in his own moral make-up. Coughing with the smoke, he made sure that no one had been trapped, or had fallen unconscious between pews and benches, most of which were smouldering by now. His energies were now directed towards the salving of the communion vessels, which were kept in the little cupboard he used as a vestry at the farther end of the building. But as he struggled through smoke and sparks towards it, a hand jerked him backwards and dragged him unceremoniously through the gap in the wall. To this day the Reverend Smith, ignorant of the futility of his aim, cherishes a grudge against Thomas Mullyon for cheating him of a part of his coveted heroism.

The wind, as though in compunction for its act of brutality, had died down somewhat, as they stood on the beach, watching the fire burn itself out. A few hopeful spirits had insisted upon flinging buckets of water at the doomed mission, but one might as well have expected Vesuvius to be put out by a shower of rain. The wind was still strong enough to beat the flames upwards, the downpour which might have saved them had stopped an hour before, and the building was soon gutted. The zinc roof grew red-hot, then slid over sideways in a great curl of molten metal.

As the Reverend Smith stood, wiping the sweat from his brow, a hand was thrust into his. By the light of the sinking flames he saw Sanchia at his elbow, and, behind her, Gregory Jodrell.

"We want to be married," said Sanchia, shortly. "You must marry us now."

Perplexity creased the moist brow of the Reverend Smith, as he stood looking down upon Sanchia. Gregory was frowning at his feet; plainly he did not like this. Only the girl looked positive, as though she meant her outrageous demand to be granted.

Although there is no law on Calvary which prevents the celebration, at any hour of the day or night, of the marriage ceremony, the Reverend Smith recoiled before this startling disregard for convention. He was, moreover, genuinely revolted by the egotism which could intrude personal matters upon an occasion such as this, when the hearts of all properly constituted individuals should surely have been uplifted in gratitude for their deliverance from death. Above all, the Reverend Smith Prudhomme was a thoroughly con-

ventional man, whose every instinct rebelled against con-
ducting important services at unorthodox hours. Although
his parish lay one thousand five hundred miles from regions
where people trouble themselves about such matters, he
always liked weddings to be arranged to take place between
eleven and twelve in the morning.

He cleared his throat, and looked sternly upon Sanchia;
then it struck him that probably the girl was unstrung with
the experience she had just been through, and his expression
softened. It was difficult, however, in looking at Sanchia,
to believe her unstrung. Her moment of nervous collapse
forgotten, her face was as serene as the young May moon,
and even the disarray of her clothing did not seem to affect
her customary air of scrupulous neatness. The Reverend
Smith was sorely tempted, for a matter of seconds, to take
Sanchia at her word and hurry her into matrimony while she
was in a mood to be hurried; who knew what the morning
might bring forth? Almost immediately he mutely prayed
forgiveness for the thought. To rush a girl into marriage on
the high wind of an emotional experience would be an act
without principle, an act to which no clergyman worthy of
the cloth would lend his sanction. Gregory Jodrell, too,
was to be considered. He, at any rate, did not look eager.
Not that Sanchia's expression was eager, either; there
was just a kind of cold certainty upon her face, which
had the odd effect of chilling the Reverend Smith's
blood.

"Surely there can be no hurry, can there, Sanchia?" he
asked, in a low, embarrassed voice.

"I told Gregory I would marry him if he saved me from
the fire," said Sanchia, clearly. "I'm afraid of changing my
mind if we wait till morning."

The Reverend Smith was afraid—very much afraid, too!
It weakened his proper resistance to her preposterous
suggestion, and caused him to mutter, in a very half-hearted
way:

"But surely, my child, the—hrrum—solemn estate of

marriage must be approached with more thought than this?"

"What is there to think about?" said Sanchia, bluntly. "You know I've got to get married; and I've told you how it is I am marrying Gregory Jodrell. That doesn't take much thinking about, does it? You know it's what you have all been waiting for me to do; and if I start thinking about it, I'll very likely not do it at all—and then what will happen to El Secredo?"

The Reverend Smith looked desperately about him, seeking the Mullyons or Samson Jodrell. A little group of the older people were withdrawn to a short distance, and were kneeling with bent heads upon the shingle. The Reverend Smith was uncomfortably reminded of his duty; of course he should now be leading the people in prayer, whereas he stood in conversation upon utterly irrelevant matters with Sanchia Mullyon. The girl's very existence was antagonistic to the spirit of religion! More than once, catching her eye when he was in the pulpit, she had made him feel silly: a most improper state of things between a minister and a member of his congregation.

No help was forthcoming from Gregory, who continued to stand, as though stricken mute, with drooping head and his hands clenched in front of him.

John Robertson, who had stood close enough to overhear part of the conversation, here touched the missionary on the shoulder.

"You'd best come to my house; it's nearest," he offered, "and maybe this thing had best be talked out now, when the time's ripe for it."

"But the Mullyons?—Samson Jodrell?" cried the Reverend Smith, loath to take the responsibility of any move in the matter.

"I'll fetch them along, minister," said John Robertson, and turned away.

Mutely the Reverend Smith found himself walking between Gregory and Sanchia towards the Robertsons' house. Wretchedly he knew that this was the opportunity for a grave exhortation, for an appeal to both of them to postpone the fatal act until they had had time to consider it and its implications. Yet his mind was a blank; not a phrase, not a line from the scriptures came to his aid. He seemed only able to think of the pettiest things: of the unseemliness of celebrating a marriage with his face and hands black and sweaty from his struggle with the flames, of the inconvenience of not having a prayer-book at hand—was his memory absolutely to be trusted? There had been so few weddings since he came to Calvary. Of his own disappointment in the fact that the burning of the mission was liable to be eclipsed by an event of far greater importance to the majority of the community. Of his own overwhelming weariness, that naturally succeeded his being cheerful for some five hours on end, followed by the affair of the fire. He had a right to be weary; it was, after all, little wonder that as he staggered up the Robertsons' path with Gregory and Sanchia his mind spun into a misty blankness.

Vaguely he heard the voices of those who followed; great heaven, had John Robertson invited the whole island? He stumbled against a table, and half-sat, half-leaned upon it, while people pushed past him. The room was full of the buzz of voices—very far-away they seemed to the Reverend Smith, until John Robertson had found and lit the lamp, and, blinking his eyes, he saw that the whole of the population of El Secredo—or as many as it would hold—was packed into the low-ceiled room. With the lighting of the lamp, conversation had ceased; packed together like sardines, and silent as death, the assembly flowed out into the night. One could see their pale faces pressed against the windows, an eerie gathering for a wedding—if wedding it was to be. Surely the Mullyons would not stand by to see their only daughter disposed of, like a creature of shame, at dead of night?

Sanchia stood close to his elbow; at first glance he could

not locate Gregory, but found him at last, thrust into a corner, with burning, half-shamed eyes that sought the missionary and seemed to convey some sort of appeal, or warning. The Reverend Smith passed his hand wearily over his brow. If only he could read the message of Gregory Jodrell's eyes. He was trying to say something.

The two Mullyons and Samson Jodrell stood together, as though taking comfort from each other's proximity. Their heads were proud, as befitted the aristocracy of the island, but Sophia's fingers plucked nervously at the fringe of her shawl.

"This is a very unusual occasion," began the Reverend Smith, desperately. "A very unusual occasion indeed. I suggest that before going further we pray for guidance."

"Amen," came deeply from many parts of the room, and even from the crowded darkness outside. Sanchia seemed about to say something, but the look on her father's face checked her.

The Reverend Smith prayed, shortly and confusedly. Outwardly calm, inwardly he was in a very agony of humility and despair. He knew that he was up against a situation too big for him to handle. His prayers for Sanchia and Gregory were all mixed up with silent appeals on his own account, that he might be shown some way out of this devious coil, and granted wisdom to act as a priest should. The Amens followed, in varying keys. The Reverend Smith drew a deep breath, and looked over the intervening heads to Gregory Jodrell.

"Your mind is fully made up, Gregory?" he asked, trying to sound assured. The silence that followed was broken by Sanchia, who cried, contemptuously:

"Well, Gregory Jodrell! Speak up; do you want me or not?"

Old Samson took up the cudgels for his son.

"Ye have no call to speak that way, Sanchia. Right well we know Gregory has loved ye sin' the pair o' ye were babes."

"That's true," said Gregory, at last; the words came painfully. "But I could ha' wished it had not ended—this way."

A murmur of sympathy followed his speech. Gregory was a favourite among men and women, and, much as they desired to have the matter settled, many of the islanders thought poorly of Sanchia for her manner of capitulation.

She gave her little laugh, and, lifting her arms, began to twist her hair into its knob at the back of her head. Negligently she held out a hand to Rose Sanguinetti for a hairpin to secure it in its place, and Rose hastily robbed her own shining coil to provide Sanchia with what she wanted; retiring thereafter to her husband's side, as though she wished to be acquitted of any partisanship in her act.

"Maybe if Gregory is not eager," said Sanchia, busy with her hair-dressing as though she were alone in her bedroom, "there's others as are."

A sort of sigh hissed in the air; the Hawkins boys and Job Barker were wedged in the doorway. Sanchia regarded them as indifferently as though she were a slave, destined for the highest bidder.

"I forbid ye to speak so, Sanchia!" cried out Sophia Mullyon.

"It does not seem to me," said the Reverend Smith, "that Sanchia is looking upon this grave, this—hrrum—very grave matter in the right way."

"The right way? What is the right way?" said Sanchia, with a terrible quietness. "I have got to get married—eh? Somebody has got to have me for a wife. . . ."

A conversation with his wife recurred rather uncomfortably to the Reverend Smith's memory.

"It seems so sad that there shouldn't be a bit of romance about Sanchia's wedding," Mrs. Prudhomme had said, in her regrettably sentimental way.

"A good many young women would think it very

romantic indeed, to be the only girl among seven young men, each of whom is anxious to marry her," he had retorted.

"You know it's not a bit like that really," reproved Mrs. Prudhomme. "It's just a question of being a brood mare, mated with the best stock. And Sanchia knows it. She's the first woman on the island who has realized it. The others accepted it meekly; the excitement of getting married made up for everything to them. But Sanchia's eyes are on the future. As a matter of fact, the brood mare comes off better than Sanchia; she has a chance of variety at any rate."

The Reverend Smith had looked uneasily at his wife. She was such a mild, submissive-looking thing to come out with these anarchical statements. He was not a man who appreciated originality of outlook. But his good narrow mind had stored his wife's remarks, and all unconsciously they coloured his outlook upon Sanchia, in a crisis when, it must be admitted, she was behaving very badly indeed. He was a little shocked to find himself thinking quite gently of Sanchia, in a situation which surely called for stiff clerical authority. "It is partly the storm, of course," murmured the Reverend Smith to himself; he was grateful to the storm for providing an explanation not too atrocious for Sanchia's conduct. And suddenly his lips were opened; in after years he spoke of that moment as an hour of revelation. For twenty minutes he addressed the awed and silent people; all his hesitancy gone, he seemed, as he humbly expressed it later, to become a channel for the Holy Ghost. He could never recollect what words came into his mind; but some of the base materialness, some of the sordidness of the scene vanished, and each man became aware of a Presence that he could not name. Prying curiosity gave way to a more delicate feeling; indeed, there were three or four who withdrew from the scene, and in those who remained the spirit of reverence stirred, albeit sluggishly, leavening the coarse motives which had drawn them there.

Sophia Mullyon suddenly broke into a little whimper of crying; she mopped the tears out of the furrows in her cheeks with the edge of her black apron.

"Mullyons has never been wed this way," she sobbed. "'Tis downright wicked of ye, Sanchia, disgracing the lot of us. Wedding i' the night, as if ye was ashamed o' what ye're doing!"

"Maybe I am ashamed," answered Sanchia, softly. "But what's it matter? You know right well I'm not Mullyon, Mother, for all I'm your daughter. I am just myself."

A look sped among the Barker supporters, the flush grew purple on Thomas Mullyon's face.

"You are the child of God, Sanchia," said the Reverend Smith gently, and somehow, although he had doubted it on occasions, there was no doubt in his heart now.

"Cease thy arguing, girl; an' wed her, minister, d'ye hear me? Maybe 'tis a sign o' grace entering into her; the Lord comes in strange ways. Come forward, Gregory Jodrell, an' stand where the minister can get at ye."

Gregory pushed his way from the back of the room; he was deathly pale. A deep misery of shame overwhelmed him, that things should be settled in this fashion between himself and Sanchia. He had striven to prevent her carrying out her purpose, knowing well that it would grieve Samson Jodrell—whose eyes had not once met those of his son since they came into the Robertsons' house. There is an elaborate formality attached to weddings on the island; to dispense with these would be regarded as an insult by the old people, and he had nothing ready for Sanchia. The house which he had started to build had not risen to more than the height of its eaves from the ground, for bad weather, setting in earlier than usual, had checked them in the work of thatching. Of course, there was room for him and Sanchia in the Jodrell house, built half a century ago to accommodate the offspring of his prolific grandfather. But the notion of a Jodrell-

Mullyon marriage being conducted in this haphazard fashion
struck at the roots of Gregory's family pride; and reminded
him, too, that he had not made that spiritual preparation
which, to his honest and sober mind, was as indispensable
a part of the wedding ceremony as the killing of the
calf, the cranberry tarts and sweetmeats which, from time
immemorial, have accompanied such festivities on the
island.

To be wed at midnight!—within a stone's throw of the
destroyed mission: when, to Gregory's mind, they should
all have been down on their knees giving thanks for a safe
delivery from their danger; in sodden garments, whose
unseemliness insulted the occasion. . . . Would Sanchia
always display this callousness to the feelings of simpler
people? wondered Gregory. He saw—or thought he saw—
on the faces of the younger men expressions which showed
that they were glad not to be in his situation. Convention is
a matter of iron bonds on El Secredo, and there was not one
in the gathering who was not, in some degree, shocked by
Sanchia's handling of the affair.

Once again old Samson Jodrell came to his son's relief,
heaving himself suddenly upright from the chair, which he,
by virtue of his years and standing, had commandeered.
Leaning on the two-inch stick that supported his stiffening
limbs, his figure stood out, patriarchal, against the smoky
lamplight. The fire had been raked out, because of the
danger of red-hot ashes blowing into the room, while the
family was at the mission, and the air was charnel; foggy
with men's breaths and sour with the stench of sea-wrack
which hung about the nets.

"Maybe, in all this business over my son's wedding," he
pronounced, through the snow-white beard that covered his
face, "we are forgetting the mercy of the Lord which He
has vouchsafed us. 'Tis a grief to me, as 'twill be to you,
Thomas and Sophia Mullyon, that our children will not be
wed in the church which, as punishment for our sins, has
been taken away from us. 'Twas the hand of the Lord,

which chasteneth them whom He loves. All of ye know right well that there has been sinful thought abroad in Calvary these many months, and this blow which the Lord hath sent is to remind us of His watchful providence, and to call our hearts to repentance. Let us prepare our hearts with a hymn; and while we are singing it, I charge ye, Gregory Jodrell and Sanchia Mullyon, to think solemnly upon this thing ye are about to do, and pray that ye may be blessed, and given increase and prosperity, according to the will of the Lord."

It struck the Reverend Smith Prudhomme, as it struck many of those present, that here was an old man bearing his sorrow finely. All knew of his love for his son Gregory; a few had heard him talk with pride of the fine doings that there would be when Gregory got married. An axe was laid to the roots of his pride by the pale girl who stood there with set face; and not by the quiver of a muscle was he betraying his pangs.

Suddenly Sanchia moved; lifted a hand a little way, as though she wished to draw the attention of them all to what she was about to say.

"I want to say something," she began in a low voice. "You are insisting on *marrying* me to Gregory. I would just as lief ha' lived with him, unwed. Nay, hush, Mother! I know how you feel, and you too, Sanson Jodrell; maybe Gregory feels the same. But I want you to understand. There's no call for prayers and hymns, really; they won't make this wedding o' mine a bit more holy than if Gregory and I just lay down in a field and mated like the cattle do. There's no blessing for our sort of a marriage. But I'll do my best for ye, Gregory."

For an instant the Reverend Smith Prudhomme was impelled to throw up his hands and cry:

"Before God, this marriage shall not take place!"

It seemed to him, suddenly, the most hideous thing he had ever done. But the agonized faces of the Mullyons and old Samson Jodrell, stirred from his proud serenity by

Sanchia's cruel words strained through the shadows towards him as though beseeching his aid; and he knew that he lacked the courage of his convictions. He laid a hand restrainingly on Sanchia's shoulder, and the girl turned her head—and smiled at him. Hardly knowing what he did, the Reverend Smith gave out the first line of "Recessional:"
"*God of our fathers, known of old.*"

As the tune swelled gravely forth, Gregory Jodrell gave one miserable, loving look at Sanchia, dropped on his knees, and covered his face with his hands. She stood upright, proudly, her pale face turned towards them all, as though she would hide nothing from them, her eyes wide open, and the ghost of her smile to the Reverend Smith Prudhomme hovering on her lips. So far as she was concerned, all was over. Her parents and Samson Jodrell had triumphed—or believed that they had. They had sacrificed her to the Jodrell line; but never was sacrifice so calm.

Gregory scrambled to his feet, and whispered something in his father's ear. The last Amen had been sung, and the Reverend Smith solemnly motioned Sanchia and Gregory nearer his side.

"Which woman will provide a ring?" asked Samson Jodrell, turning towards the onlookers.

As a dozen hands tugged at the thin metal bands embedded in their gnarled fingers, Sophia Mullyon wrenched her own off, and passed it to her daughter.

"'Tis Gregory should have it," smiled Sanchia, and handed it over. She was as cool as though the matter did not concern her at all.

"Dearly beloved," said the missionary, "we are gathered together here in the sight of God and in the face of this congregation, to join together this Man and this Woman in holy Matrimony."

The words, he was relieved to find, came easily to his lips. He spoke quietly, simply, with more feeling than he usually brought to a ceremony a little staled by repetition. Suddenly he remembered his feelings, when, as a young priest, newly

ordained, he first read the office of marriage: what a sacred
and wonderful thing it had appeared, how reverently he had
regarded the young couple about to embark on the greatest
of human adventures, how earnestly he had prayed, in
silence, that they might be happy and blessed. It seemed to
be that same earnest young priest who now spoke the con-
secrated words over Gregory Jodrell and Sanchia Mullyon,
in a voice low and charged with solemnity:

"First: It was ordained for the procreation of children——"

"Amen," uttered Samson Jodrell. Sanchia's eyes met his
like bright steel. The Reverend Smith paused for a moment,
and went on. . . .

It was over. Sanchia Mullyon had become Sanchia
Jodrell. She and Gregory stood looking at each other—he
with a kind of shamefaced triumph, through which broke
the radiance of his joy; she consideringly, as if a little uncertain what to do next.

It was a moment of anticlimax, a moment usually filled in
by Mrs. Prudhomme and the harmonium with the *Wedding March*. People began to shuffle their feet, as though
anxious to depart. A few came shyly forward to shake hands
with Samson Jodrell and the Mullyons. The air was full of
the sweaty reek of their clothes; some few, released from
the solemnity of the past hour, broke into broad grins,
and cracked jests more broad than delicate. Weddings,
after all, were an excuse for such things, and they were
not to be cheated of their rare opportunity of jesting
by the fact that this one had taken place at an unheard-
of hour, between two extraordinarily unfestive young
people, who looked, now all was over, more dead than
alive.

"Maybe we'll be having the feast when the ship comes
in, ma'am?" someone, determined not to be done out
of the expected merry-making, said to Sophia Mullyon.
She flung her apron over her head and burst into loud
weeping.

The Reverend Smith Prudhomme, now rocking on his feet with exhaustion, offered his hand to Gregory and to Sanchia. She whispered, "Thank you:" and then, as though her mind was suddenly made up, linked her arm in Gregory's, and the pair of them walked through the opening that was made for them, out under the ragged sky, where actually a few stars now twinkled.

CHAPTER VI

ONE might have thought that with the storm, the burning of the mission, and Sanchia Mullyon's wedding, the cup of Calvary's social excitements was full. People question the records sometimes: "But did all these things happen in a single night?"—and they bend a little pitifully over the curt line which sets forth the death of Mrs. Prudhomme, to be followed, at much greater length, by the account of the wreck. On Calvary, as in other parts of the world, events rarely come singly. For long months on end, stagnation: and then—hey, presto! hurly-burly, a maelstrom of happenings into which is drawn every living soul on the island.

It is to be feared that in the excitement of the fire and of Sanchia's wedding, most people—including her husband—forgot Mrs. Prudhomme. One does not pay much attention to sickness on the island, and a cold is such a trivial and unheard-of matter that it passes unnoticed, save by the sufferer, who copes as well as he or she can with the splitting head and aching throat which accompany the disease. No islander ever "catches cold," and even Maggie Robertson who, to her lasting credit, had not been drawn from her vigil by the flames which lit every room in the missionary's house, took no particular heed of Mrs. Prudhomme's ramblings. Kindly woman as she was, she felt her duty to be accomplished when she held the cup of barley-water to Mrs. Prudhomme's lips at intervals, or replaced the coverings which were thrown aside in her growing restlessness. She was fairly used to the "island fever," a very mild form of malaria which takes the islanders occasionally, and had never seen pneumonia in her life. No, Maggie Robertson was not to blame. She met the missionary on his return with an anxiety which was all for the effects of the fire and the safety of her family.

"Oh, sir! Has all passed safely?"

The Reverend Smith dropped into a chair.

"Yes. She's married. It's a great relief, a great relief," he answered vaguely. Maggie Robertson stared at him as though she thought he was wandering.

"*Married?* But the fire, sir! The fire! Are the children safe?"

"Oh, yes. The fire." He passed his hand over his forehead, trying to remember. "Nothing was harmed—I mean no one was hurt—except one of the little ones—a foot crushed, I think. It's all for the best," he concluded, with his voice trailing away. His glance wandered about the room. Where was Mary? She, surely, should be here, to welcome him, to hear the tale of the night's adventures.

"Thank God," said Maggie Robertson, wiping the back of her hand across her eyes. "You'll be wanting to get to bed, sir. I'm afraid the mistress is very restless—maybe you'd like me to make you up a bed on them boxes there? She's right poorly, I dare say—but fever's always worse in the night."

"What? She's got a fever?" The Reverend Smith was across the room and at his wife's bedside as he spoke. Mrs. Prudhomme lay breathing noisily; her eyes were half-closed, and only the whites showed between the lids. The flush had faded from her cheeks, leaving a greenish pallor. The Reverend Smith, more accustomed than Maggie Robertson to the illnesses of civilization, recognized that she was very ill indeed, and his heart gave a painful tick.

"Put some pans on and get the water hot. She must be sponged down at once." But, as he said it, instinct told him that it was too late to sponge down Mrs. Prudhomme, and fear, which all night had deserted him, crawled in through window and door. The gulf between El Secredo and the safe shores of England yawned wide as eternity. . . .

In the settlement, people were crawling into their chilly beds. Physically exhausted, inarticulate as they always were, each knew that the thought in his neighbour's mind was the thought of Sanchia and Gregory Jodrell, locked in each other's arms. An interest less morbid than friendly wondered what Gregory was getting of his bargain. Poor lad! He'd not looked as if he thought much of it; but Jodrells must have heirs. Would the first child be born at the end of the nine months, and would it be girl or boy? 'Twas to be hoped that Sanchia would get on with her childbearing quickly; there didn't look to be much guts in the lass. Little she was, and inclined to be weedy. Jodrells should be stalwart; Jodrell children were born big and heavy, and kicked their way out of the womb, giving their mothers a rare time in the process. Three, or perhaps four, was the utmost a woman could manage of such obstreperous offspring: Ellen Jodrell had died with her third—Gregory's youngest brother, a boy still in school: the second had drowned with the fishing fleet when he was but sixteen—and, on the face of it, Sanchia did not look as though she could manage three. So long as one was a girl all would be well.

These thoughts they communicated to each other, in their dumb fashion, by nods, half-spoken phrases and grunts of assent and dissent. The two Robertson girls, rolled up in their wooden bunk that hung like a martin's nest to the wall, whispered and giggled.

"I'd never be married at night, would you, Martha? I'd feel that stupid, just walking out an' goin' to bed in front o' everybody."

"I'd not ha' been wed in my old shabby gown, if I'd been Sanchia. Did ye see? Her cape was all split up behind and her skirt dangling loose, as if someone'd pulled it. I'll have a clean white frock wi' plenty o' starch when I get wed, won't you?"

"Ay; and I'm going to wed Timothy Jodrell, I am; so then I'll be Sanchia's sister-in-law, and she won't have to tease me an' go on at me for having a dirty face, like she does now."

"Has Timmy as't ye?"

"Nay; I as't him, because I didn't mean to be left to that Simeon Barker. 'Is nose is always runnin'. Fancy kissing someone that 'as a runny nose!"

"An't there going to be a feast? 'Tis downright mean o' Sanchia if there an't no feast, because she gets wed in the middle o' night 'stead o' daytime, like ornery folks."

"I don't know. It's a funny-like wedding. I liked Rose Hawkins's wedding. I was as sick as a cat after I done eatin'—do you remember? Hers was a fine wedding, it *was*. Do you remember us making a wreath wi' marigolds as minister's wife gave, for Rose to wear on her head, because Sue Barker's hat that she was going to wear blew over the Point the night before?"

Samson Hawkins stood by the window, staring out into the blackness; there was nothing to be seen but blackness—there and in his own soul. On the great square bed his two brothers lay snoring. He could not make up his mind to join them. A profound despair had mastered him, in which, as his fathers had done before him, he cried to heaven for help, and none was forthcoming. The fear and horror of sin was heavy upon him, and he did not see how, in the years to come, he was not to sin. For it was sin to lust after another man's wife. Half consciously he dropped on his knees, but he could not seek God, for his mind was full of Sanchia and of Gregory. He hated Gregory for the laggard way in which he had accepted his heaven-sent gift. Had he been in Gregory's place, there would have been no need to summon him forward to stand at his bride's side. He would have taken her before them all—when and where she would. Sanchia: not any woman—but just Sanchia! Hot tears gathered in his eyes and ran down into the red crop of his beard. Sanchia. Not children to carry on his name—but just Sanchia. As Samson Hawkins knelt there, a light ripped across the heavens, like a falling star.

For a moment he knelt aghast, wondering what fresh phenomenon was in store on this fearful night: when another light joined it, and this time Samson Hawkins had the wit to see that the star was not falling, but mounting, mounting, climbing heaven: and a faint delayed reverberation caught his ears. A ship's rocket! The long overdue ship was out there, in peril—the ship that carried all their hopes, their food supply, their means of communication with home.

"Sail ho!" roared Samson Hawkins, and made a plunge at the bed, rolling his brother Jim out upon the floor, hitting George clumsily across the face with the flat of his hand. "Sail ho, ye sluggards! Ship's here—please God she'll not founder before our very eyes!"

While the others, wide awake instantly, scrambled for their clothing, he flung himself across the living-room and seized the old ship's bugle which hung above the fireplace. With the full of his lungs he blew the blast that was to call the settlement.

In a moment the deserted beach was alive with bobbing lanterns, with folks who, having just fallen into their first heavy sleep, were half-dazed by the summons which meant so much to them all.

"She's sent up two rockets, I tell ye!" shouted Samson Hawkins. "She's in trouble, sure enough."

A wail went up from the assembled islanders. Clustered together, there was little they could do, save stand helplessly while the stores they so desperately needed were swallowed by the Atlantic. A score of youths rushed wildly at the wood-pile, dragging it from its storage place and stacking it upon the beach; someone staggered past, bearing the tussocks of dried grass they use for thatching on the island, and Henry Martyn came running with a tin of kerosene.

"For God's sake, are yer wits gone?" screamed an old

woman. "Will ye destroy all our firing and leave us wi' naught to boil a pot?"

Her cry was carried away on the wind; the light was laid to the pile, and it flamed up, sixty feet or more, filling the beach with a red glare that danced on the pale faces of the watchers. A noise of sobbing, of scattered shouts, of prayer and cursing rose. Into the midst of it strode the Reverend Smith Prudhomme, hatless, with the sandy streaks of hair blowing about his wild face.

"Before God," said Samson Jodrell, turning to him as he approached the bonfire, "the ship's lost, and we are all to starve."

"Starve?" said the Reverend Smith, dully. "What does it matter if we all starve? My wife has passed away."

For a moment they thought him mad. Few had heard of Mrs. Prudhomme's sickness. Then, looking upon his face, they knew he was not mad, and there was a slow movement towards him. Their individual distress was forgotten for a moment in sympathy for his own. They had liked Mrs. Prudhomme, while agreeing among themselves that she should never have come to a place like El Secredo. So small and slight she was—no sort of woman to stand up to the island and its savage enmity towards mankind. They began to remember her queer shy ways; the way the children took to her; how good she was in illness. Janet Hawkins had taught her how to use the primitive Calvary stoves: three of the men had built a special kitchen for her. Last time the ship had been late, she had gone without almost everything for herself in order that they might have as much as possible. The younger women remembered how interested she had been in helping them to make pretty things, how she had torn off the ribbon from her hat to give to one, and unpicked the lace from her petticoat for another. And she had given Mrs. Sanguinetti all her chemises for Rose's trousseau.

They clustered about the missionary, without words to voice their sorrow, but expressing it in the mute respect of their bearing. And suddenly the Reverend Smith lifted one clenched fist and shook it at the black sky.

The flames dodged here and there, the smoke whirled downwards, and sparks settled on the watchers' clothing, as they stood in silence, dedicating their regrets to one more victim of El Secredo who had led so gentle, so harmless a life that it seemed the jealous forces of nature might have forborne to crush so weak a thing.

At eleven of the next morning, much of the salvaging was over. The tide, running strongly towards Calvary shores, had carried to the island a portion of the wreckage. Since the first streak of dawn men had been rushing waist-deep into the water, hauling on floating objects as they came in sight, disentangling them from the kelp, which formed a vast draw-net round the foreshore; tugging to the beach a battered crate, an oar, a body lashed to a spar or floating aimlessly, spread-eagled in the heart of a wave. Once a raft came in sight; they could see the figures on it, sodden with the sea: an arm or a leg was washing backwards and forwards with the tide. They must have been secured by ropes, or the waves would have carried them away.

The Reverend Smith, who had worked with the rest, as though the fierceness of his grief had given him a strength beyond his own, cried out for a hawser, and, with a loop of it about his middle, and three of the heaviest fellows on the end of it, insisted upon going out of his depth in the attempt to salve the victims. But the hawser impeded his swimming, and time and again he was battered against the lava reefs, until he flung up a hand and they towed him in, unconscious, with a couple of his ribs stove in and his stomach swelling with the sea-water he had swallowed. Samson Hawkins, who alike had ceased to value his life, clutched the hawser and flung himself into the surf. They watched him battling with the sea like a dog: his head bobbing in the trough of the waves or submerged beneath a breaker that rushed in like a maddened horse from the outer seas. He was a stronger swimmer than the Reverend Smith, and succeeded in reaching the raft, to which he clung for a little while, catching his breath painfully. But when he found he was in the company of the dead, he let go and plunged again towards the shore. A little later the raft was washed up, and they unbound the bodies of four dead sailors and laid them side by side on the beach.

There were fourteen bodies there before noon, only one of which showed any signs of life. The Reverend Smith, with his ribs bandaged, stood directing the men who were applying artificial respiration, when the fifteenth body came bobbing in on the tide.

One of the Hawkins boys rushed in to receive it, and as it sagged in his hands, water-logged and helpless, he turned a startled face across his shoulders, and yelled to the watchers:

"By Christ!   A woman!"

There was a rush towards him. A dozen hands helped to pull young Jim Hawkins and his burden from the undertow of the waves. He staggered a few steps up the beach and let it slip, suddenly. The clothes—what remained of them—dragged it down: it lay face downwards on the shingle—the little, narrow body of a woman, with seaweed-coloured hair, cut short like a man's, which was smeared across her eyes. Instantly a corps of men used to life-saving got to work; there was no sign of life in the body, but efforts would not be relinquished until the last hope was gone. Meanwhile, the other survivor, being rolled and pummelled and shaken, until, between the stones of the beach and his rescuers' hands, his body had begun to resemble a piece of liver, had opened his eyes and gulped twice.

A light-built fellow, with sharp features and clean-shaven, save for the stubble on his chin; the women pressed curiously forward to look upon this *rara avis*. Beyond the Reverend Smith Prudhomme, no man shaved on the island. It may have been that to do so was thought a mark of effeminacy, or it may have been for more practical reasons that they guarded the stiff fleece which acted as protection to their necks and throats.

The stranger was slimmer than El Secredo men, and taller, though not, as Western standards go, a tall man; thin-wristed and thin-ankled, with bones that stood out like knobs. He was not in sailor's clothes, but in a suit of which the eyes of the Reverend Smith alone were able to judge the value. A reach-me-down, of provincial cut; the sea-water had already played havoc with the shoddy material of which it was made.

Presently this castaway had recovered sufficiently to be helped up the beach by a couple of the men. Indeed, Gregory Jodrell, who had been foremost among the life-savers, could have carried him easily. There was no weight in the fellow. He sobbed and whimpered as they lifted him, evidently unable to control himself. Janet Hawkins hurried indoors, to see to the fire and provide some food for her family, and for the stranger, who seemed mutely to have been adopted by them. They could get no word from him that would help to identify him. With shock, maybe, he had lost the use of his tongue.

The Reverend Smith went back to the group about the woman, from which, with some delicacy, he had withdrawn, feeling that a woman, even a shipwrecked one, might not care to have more witnesses than necessary to the very unsightly process of recovering from drowning. He found that, so far as her sensitiveness was concerned, he might have spared his tact and satisfied his curiosity, for she was lying exactly as he had left her, except that they had got her flat on her back, and brushed the hair out of her eyes.

"She's breathing," panted one of the life-savers, looking up from his task.

The Reverend Smith looked down upon the small, tired features of the woman who lay at his feet. A narrow little face, with blunt nose and chin; bones much in evidence, and

skin a greyish tan—with plenty of wrinkles. The Reverend
Smith, who prided himself on guessing ages, decided that
she was between forty and fifty; probably nearer fifty, of the
two; there was plenty of grey in the hair above the brow. A
long, dogmatic upper lip, and crows'-feet at the corners of
the eyes. It did not strike the Reverend Smith that there was
something brutal in thus summarizing a defenceless woman
under the cold glare of an ironic sun, which had thought fit
to tear its way through the cloud-banks for a brief glimpse
of the destruction wrought overnight. Her figure was
youthful, indeed; but that was characteristic of the times.
Undeveloped as a girl of fifteen, it lay almost as flatly and
limply as a worn-out garment, on the shingle.

"She had better be got into a bed," said the Reverend
Smith, shortly. He was a little disappointed. The unknown
woman did not seem likely, on the face of things, to help to
solve the problem of Calvary.

"Maggie'll take her," stated John Robertson, who, with
his bandaged hand, had been able to do little in the salvaging,
and had stood by rather awkwardly.

"She's had a bad night," frowned the Reverend Smith.
"She was up—with my wife." It did not strike him immediately that everyone on the island had had the same kind of a
night, from one cause or another.

A movement of recollection bent Robertson's head, and
the heads of the men who still laboured on the unknown
woman. So quickly had one event followed on the heels of
another that there had been no time to pay proper reverence
to the dead. Rose Sanguinetti made an eager movement,
putting her head against her husband's shoulder, but was
frowned into silence. Precedence on El Secredo is as
strictly observed as in any London drawing-room: Jodrells
first, then Mullyons, then Robertsons—all, be it understood,
of the older generation. The younger couples, whether
they be Jodrell or Mullyon, must wait their turn. The
Jodrell household was out of the question; Samson, with
the orphan children of his brother Joshua, as well as

Gregory and Timothy under his roof, had as much as he could handle. Sophia Mullyon, it was thought, might have offered Sanchia's vacated room, but the thought did not seem to strike her. Hospitable as are the islanders, and jealous of their hospitality, the night's events had befogged poor Sophia's mind to the dulling of the keen edge of her natural kindliness. It was in answer to a nod from Tom Mullyon that Robertson had spoken, offering, in the absence of his Maggie—who, it is presumed, was about her sad task of laying out Mrs. Prudhomme—the shelter of his roof to this friendless female waif cast up on Calvary shore.

Among the women who stood looking down on her was Sanchia—Sanchia Jodrell, with her hands planted on her slim hips. A few sidelong glances were stolen at her, pitying her for the interruption of her wedding night—a matter which seemed to affect Sanchia not at all. Her calm face looked down at the unknown woman with a kind of cool, pitiless curiosity. She was interested in the appearance of the stranger; would have liked to have housed her on her own authority, but lacking accommodation to offer, was constrained to silence.

It is to be feared that hopes which ran high when the sex of the castaway was discovered, sank again when her age became apparent. Not that any save the Reverend Smith guessed aright in the delicate matter; Calvary women look like that when they are twenty-eight or thirty. But a spinster of that age is unheard of on the island, and sly glances at the left hand had shown it guiltless of wedding-ring, a suspicious circumstance.

While John Robertson marshalled his dancing Martha and Betty to do their duty in their mother's absence, and Henry Martyn carried the still unconscious figure of the stranger up the beach, the rest of the men busied themselves in examining the crates which had been washed up, spreading their contents to dry, and estimating the extent of the loss and damage. More would come, borne in from time to time, probably over a space of several weeks; but whatever that might be, the water would have got at it and rendered it useless. With a grinding anxiety they set to work to split open the crates and disperse the goods along the shingle, where the sun would get at them.

A heterogeneous collection of mission clothing fell out of one crate, in soaked condition; the kind of thing people fling into rummage sales, with a vague idea it will do for the heathen. Fortunately the people of El Secredo have no standards of comparison; a small section of the beach took on the appearance of a corner of the Berwick Market, stones weighting down the garments to keep them from flying away. The butter was safe, mercifully—and there was a little lard; the rest had gone down, or drifted away from the island. No soap or cleaning materials, the women saw with a groan. *No flour :* this was a hideous blow to the poor, hopeful community—although the flour would have been useless if it had reached them in that way. A number of crates of oranges and dried fruits; scores of floating fragments that had once been crates, and contained—what? A big consignment of salt pork and bacon. A groan burst from the Reverend Smith Prudhomme, as they opened before his eyes a small sealed packing-case containing innumerable tubes of aspirin and homœopathic drugs. So far as he was concerned, it had come too late.

The children were splashing in and out of the waves, snatching at driftwood, dodging the stinging jelly-fish and catching with shouts the big sea-snails which are regarded as a delicacy on El Secredo; one had to keep a sharp eye on them, or they would have stolen the raisins and dried figs spread out on the shingle. Presently the division of the stores would take place—as much as there was to divide. As a rule this ceremony took the better part of a morning; Samson Jodrell, who had charge of proceedings, computed that it would be over in an hour. Thomas Mullyon and he stood apart from the rest with watchful eyes, to see that there was no pilfering, talking of a system of rationing which might tide the island over the interval which must pass before another ship reached El Secredo. No doubt when hope was abandoned she must have wirelessed, and her message would have been picked up by other ships; the plight of the islanders would soon be known, but six weeks might elapse before another ship was sent to their rescue.

The sharing-out took place always under conditions of the strictest equity, a blindfolded man calling out the names haphazard, as the unknown articles were taken in the distributor's hand. Afterwards they went round among themselves, and some bargaining and exchange took place: for what use were a pair of jack-boots to Jim Hawkins when he wanted wire-fencing?—and what could Janet do with an umbrella (yes, there were people mad enough to send umbrellas to Calvary) when she was crying out for another boiling-pan? Rose Sanguinetti was vain enough to like having the umbrella, and careless enough in her housekeeping not to mind whether she went short of a pot or two.

It was evening before the guest in the Robertsons' house opened her eyes, looked round, and remarked:

"Oh—I've got here, have I? I meant to come."

She then rolled over on her side, tucked her nose into the pillow and fell asleep. The Reverend Smith, calling later to inquire after the visitor, was slightly disconcerted when summoned by an imperious voice to the inner room.

The unknown woman, sitting bolt upright in bed, wearing a nightgown of Maggie Robertson's, which resembled a blanket, gathered round her throat, addressed the Reverend Smith briskly and without any apparent embarrassment:

"Did they save my typewriter?"

The Reverend Smith, rather shocked by this preoccupation with secular matters on the part of one with whom he had been prepared to render thanks where they were due for her miraculous preservation from drowning, returned stiffly:

"They saved your *life*," and frowned reproachfully upon his interlocutor.

"What the dickens is the good of my life without my typewriter?" snapped the lady, and informed the Reverend Smith, in short sentences of considerable pungency, that she was a novelist, by name Lenox Robbins, and that she had undertaken the voyage to El Secredo in order to obtain material for a fresh book.

"By the way," said she, briskly, "you haven't a cigarette anywhere about you, have you? I'm fairly pining for a smoke."

"I dare say there are a few over at my house," rejoined the Reverend Smith, doubtfully.

"I'll come and get them to-morrow," said Miss Robbins. "Well, here we are. I'm glad I'm not drowned. This *is* a go, isn't it?"

On consideration of the matter, the Reverend Smith found that he agreed with her.

"While I think of it," said Miss Robbins, hunching her knees up under the bedclothes, "you're a married man, aren't you? They told me on the way out that your wife was with you—you might ask her if she'd mind letting me have a nightdress. There's a bit too much of the hair-shirt about this one for my undisciplined flesh."

The Reverend Smith found himself telling her, dully, of the death of Mrs. Prudhomme. There was a short silence; then she thrust out towards him a fist as small and hard as a boy's.

"Hard luck," said Miss Robbins, but her voice was noticeably softer. "I say—what about going and getting those cigarettes? We might have a chat, but I'm no good at talking unless I've got a gasper in my mouth."

He wondered, as he stumbled back to the mission house, how in the world El Secredo would take to this strange specimen of the female sex; and a hard suspicion smote him that there were squalls ahead. It seemed too bad, reflected the Reverend Smith, as he hunted among cartons and empty tins for the remains of his cigarette store, that, having got Sanchia Mullyon off his hands, he should now be landed with a problem likely to be quite as acute as Sanchia herself.

"Oh, well," sighed the Reverend Smith, "they'll send us another boat in a month or two—at latest; and meanwhile—one can only do one's best, and put one's trust in the Lord!"

CHAPTER VII

SANCHIA JODRELL sat sewing; long, languid stitches that she looped carelessly into the material, in time with her long, languid thoughts. The bleakness of the Jodrell house yawned about her, in a succession of whitewashed rooms, sparsely furnished. A woman interested in home-making might have done something to mitigate their barn-like emptiness; but Sanchia had no gift in that direction and, moreover, had not learned to look upon it as her home.

She felt as one may feel caught in the lull between a storm and a storm; a sense of waiting obsessed her, made it impossible for her to settle to anything. The fact of her marriage was a dream, from which she must presently awaken. The routine of her own home, similar in all externals, differed—she could not say how—from the lifeless procession of the days which she passed alone, from the dawn which took Gregory from her side, to the night which brought him back to her again. She was not sure that she welcomed his presence; sometimes she found herself dreading it. With her hands pressed against her bosom she would sweep wildly from room to room, praying: "Don't let him come back, don't let Gregory come back." In these moods his company was worse than the solitude. Her heart leapt sickeningly when she heard his boots and Samson's clatter on the cobbles. Their presence brought her no companionship, but a deeper, more hopeless aloneness. Sometimes it seemed as though they spoke a different language from her own. Dumbly, and with a joyless mechanism, she would set their food on the table and, sitting down with her hands in her lap, listen while they talked—always of the same things: of the wall, of the rebuilding of the mission, of the day's catch, of the calving of the cattle, until her head dropped on her bosom, and she slept. Or she would sit, strung taut like a violin, trembling and rebellious, determined not to let herself become as the other El Secredo wives, resentful because they thought it not worth while to include her in their conversations; hating Gregory for the mute, affectionate looks he threw at her when Samson's eyes were turned away; bracing herself to withstand his nightly importunities; stubborn in her resolve to reserve herself. For what? She could not have told.

The days were interminable. She had plenty to do, for the two Jodrell nephews were in the house, as well as Timothy, Gregory's younger brother. She had their food to prepare, to see to their cleanliness, to chase them to school at the proper hour, and to mend their clothes—always, boy-like, in need of repair. She performed such tasks morosely, with slovenly inattention to detail, hating young Seth and Barnabas for the trouble they gave her, Gregory for subjecting her to it, and Samson because he took her labours for granted. Marriage was as she had said: a long round of household drudgery, with never a word or look of thanks for one's pains.

At first she had gone to her mother's; but she found Sophia impossible. A gulf had widened between them since her marriage. No doubt Sophia continued to resent Sanchia's behaviour, and their conversations were stiff and grudging, full of bitter upbraiding on Sophia's part, of chill self-justification on Sanchia's. "You wanted me to marry Gregory Jodrell; I've done it. What are you grumbling about?" Gradually Sanchia ceased to visit her mother; since her marriage neither her father nor her brother had deigned to notice her existence. The girl was lonely and miserable—although no one guessed it, she held her head so high. She had taken to the black woollen shawl which is a kind of insignia among the married women of El Secredo: pulled tightly over her head, and knotted behind her waist.

She went about little, and had nothing to say to those who, from curiosity, or perhaps even an obscure kind of pity, addressed her.

"Ye shall have your little home, Sanchia, the minute the mission's done," Gregory would whisper, feeling for her hand in bed, where she lay, still as though she were sleeping, by his side, but alert to every movement on the part of her bedfellow. The slightest motion on his part to entwine her, to exercise his rights upon the woman whom he had married, and she stiffened into resistance. One gets no pleasure of a woman that way. Gregory set his teeth; there was no weakness in him, he was fully aware of his rights and intended to make full use of them, if he had to struggle with her to do it; but their sleeping-room was separated from his father's by no more than a thin wooden planking; every sound they made was audible to the wakeful old man on the other side of the partition. Gregory knew that Samson was listening; every morning he turned away from the look, half-anxious, half-mocking, in his father's eyes. A rough sense of delicacy, of consideration for Sanchia, whom he loved, caused Gregory to restrain the nature which boiled within him. Only he reminded her of what was due to him, of what she was withholding, by that oft-repeated whisper in the dark: "Ye shall have your little home, Sanchia—soon."

Her teeth gritted as she answered:

"I don't care if I do."

"'Tis hard work for ye, looking after us all."

"I've naught else to do."

His mouth sought hers, which remained hard as marble beneath his demanding kisses.

So her needle went wearily in and out, to the accompaniment of her drear thoughts, until one day she tired of it abruptly. The wind was singing under the eaves, the sea looked almost blue; out beyond the further ring of the islands a monster berg had come down from the Antarctic circle, like a pale ghost of Spring; the air was white with sea-birds, and their screams mingled with the shouts of children on the beach. She flung her sewing aside, and came to the door, where she stood for a moment, closing her eyes to the caress of the breeze. With a sudden gesture of abandon she plucked the shawl away from her bosom; the air slid cool fingers down to her breasts. A tremor ran through her, a tremor like the stirring of the sap within the trees. She gave one glance behind her at the cheerless house, and ran out upon the shingle, not caring where her steps should lead her.

As she turned towards The Rescue she felt as though she had escaped from some element that sought to hold her. She was Sanchia, just Sanchia: not Mullyon or Jodrell, but a free soul, carving its way in freedom.

As she reached The Rescue, that small, curved bay on the western side of the island, where the kelp is so dense that it almost appears as though one could walk on it like the sea-birds, were it not for the occasional throb of its surface when the water struggles to throw off its deadly pall, another figure came slowly towards her, with as solitary an air as her own.

Sanchia knew that this was the stranger, "The Man without a Tongue," as the islanders had christened him: for the gift of speech had never returned to his lips since the waves threw him up on El Secredo shore. Familiar as was his figure to the rest of the community, she had looked upon it but from a distance, and it was with a lively sense of curiosity and adventure that she now sped forward, her eyes fixed on the unknown man, who, seeing her, seemed also to quicken his step until they stood face to face.

She found herself almost touching him, looking upwards with the blunt interest of a child into a pair of hollow and clouded eyes that stared at her over high cheek-bones, beneath which the flesh fell inwards with a hollow sweep towards the stubble of a somewhat weak chin. The sprouting beard gave an air of uncouthness and wildness to features refined almost to the point of femininity. The stranger over-topped her by several inches; he was the

tallest man that Sanchia had ever seen, despite the slouching
way in which he carried his shoulders. Lightly built, too.
The white hairlessness of his chest, from which the ragged
shirt fell away, the way the bones stared under the thin
masking of flesh, fascinated her.

It did not occur to Sanchia to speak; she stood there, so
close that each was aware of the radiated warmth of the
other's body, her eyes wide, every sentient part of her alert,
as though through her very pores she would assimilate,
would communicate with him.

Suddenly he stepped back, making a strange sound in his
throat. The glance he cast about him was wild and despairing, as though he were conscious of being in a trap; she
understood that. More expressive in her gestures than he,
she clasped her hands to her breast and threw them wide, as
though she, too, would escape. The gesture, for all its
subtlety, conveyed something to him; he whimpered like a
dog and clasped his hands over his head; she saw from the
trembling of his garments that he was shivering.

In that strange moment all her being flowed towards him.
She felt, in spite of his dumbness, a line of communication
open between herself and this hapless wretch; her look
bathed him as in light, she became translucent, standing
there. No impulse to speak, to clothe the intimacy of the
situation in the clumsiness of words, marred the exquisite
delicacy of her emotion towards him. She began to move
away, looking across her shoulder as she went. She made no
sign of invitation, yet he followed her, and she moderated
the swiftness of her step to accommodate the clumsiness of his own. There is sand at The Rescue, but it
is broken up by stony eruptions that are traps for the
unwary.

She led him back towards the house, cutting across the
pasture to avoid passing the men who were at work on the
mission—Gregory among them. He followed her like a
dog—limpingly; she saw that one of his feet was bound up
roughly in a piece of cloth; either he had lost a boot, or had

injured himself in some way. The uneven sound of his step behind excited her; as they reached Samson Jodrell's house she ran up the cobbled path and flung open the door; within its shadow she waited for the stranger.

He came timidly, bending his head to pass the low lintel. She held her breath as his shadow flung itself across the stone floor, even to the hearth.

He looked about him for a moment, as though seeking something. His eyes darkened, looked puzzled; suddenly he made a movement as though to withdraw. She understood, in the current that passed between them, that the bare emptiness shocked him. Without the slightest conception of what household decoration might mean, the ugliness of her surroundings leapt out at her; the grimy walls, that needed whitewashing; the uncurtained windows, the muddle of men's clothing that lay here and there among her shiftless attempt at housekeeping. Since no woman ever visited her, she never troubled to keep order; she had come into a house man-tended—or, rather, man-neglected, and had seen no reason for altering matters. She had not wedded Gregory Jodrell to become his father's housekeeper; when she and Gregory went into their own cottage no doubt she would bestir herself, for the sake of her personal pride. But she was ashamed that the stranger's eyes should now light on the signs of her negligence; she had a fierce longing to explain herself, a desire to obscure with *herself* the graceless details of her surroundings.

She caught his hands suddenly; the softness of the palms astonished her, even as she held them; the dark hairs that ran along the back were coarser than the thin, fine flesh; she held them, looking down on them with curiosity, while she drew him towards the fire.

She pushed him gently into Samson Jodrell's arm-chair, and stood close, looking down upon him. There was autocracy in her bearing, a sense of possession. He looked up at her frowningly, as though less willing to be possessed than she was to possess. She studied him as impersonally as one

might study a picture, without embarrassment, or acknowledgment of his power to return the scrutiny.

The only sounds were of their breathing and the crackle
of the fire. But she could feel herself flowing towards him,
entering into him, making herself a part of his mystery, of
all the unknown that lay behind his inscrutable brow. Her
imagination seized upon his dumbness; if he had power to
speak, what might he say to her? What might he tell her of
the things she longed to know? What thoughts in which she
had no part fulminated behind those high and narrow
temples? What was his voice like, when he could speak?—
and how did its accents differ from those of Sanchia and her
fellow islanders? His dumbness tantalized her, whipped her
into a strange excitement, as though someone had brought
to her a key to mysteries she had yearned all her life to penetrate, and she could not find the way to turn it. Her lips
parted, and the breath came pantingly; her fingers twisted
themselves together, yet she stood still, gazing down upon
him, absorbing him through every nerve.

It occurred to her that if she were to question him, he
might be able to write the answers, but she was unwilling to
break the strange bond of silence, which seemed rather to
bind him to her than to separate them. The clumsiness of
words might bring disillusionment, would surely shatter the
fineness of their curious intercourse. She found nothing
awkward in pretending dumbness, like his own. She waited
for some gesture that would give her a clue to his thoughts,
and it came slowly, stiffly, as from one unaccustomed to
using his hands in self-expression. A shrug of the shoulders,
a restless movement of the head from side to side, and the
eyes fixed on hers with inquiry. He was asking her if she
lived there. Sanchia nodded her head once or twice, gravely,
and waited for the next.

He got up, and went to the table, to finger a coat of
Gregory's which lay flung among unwashed crockery and
the remnants of the last meal. It occurred to Sanchia that she
had given back her mother's wedding ring. For an instant

she hesitated, and then clasped the finger and thumb of her right hand round the fourth finger of the left. He understood, but his eyes still strained with inquiry. Suddenly he made a gesture with both hands that followed the periphery of her whole body. He did not touch her, but she shivered as though his fingers had traced their passage on her naked flesh. The question puzzled her; it was clearly related to herself. What could he want to know about her? How old was she? She laid a hand on her bosom, and took his own hand in hers; one after another she counted off the fingers; ten, and then five, and then four and touched her own bosom again. He smiled, shaking his head—that was not what he had wanted to know: and then nodded, to show that he had understood. Her eyebrows cocked themselves in inquiry; but he shrugged his shoulders. He could not remember his own age.

They stood still once more, close, within touching distance; and the air quivered between them.

The step of Samson Jodrell clumped upon the cobbles. Without seeming haste or furtiveness, Sanchia stepped apart from the stranger, as the old man came in. He stood, leaning on his stick and surveying them both. She felt the fine tendrils of their communication swamped in a murkiness of dubious thought. She turned a cool, expressionless face to her father-in-law.

"What's to do here?" asked Samson Jodrell, harshly.

"I found him at The Rescue," began Sanchia, and it struck her that this failed to explain his presence there.

"Ay? And why didn't ye leave him at The Rescue?"

She shrugged her shoulders and pointed to the dumb man's foot.

"He's gone lame; I'm going to bind his foot for him."

"Yon's Janet Hawkins's business."

"Maybe Janet's busy." She moved towards the kettle, aloof and undisturbed.

Samson Jodrell hesitated; but his pride would not allow him to turn the stranger from his door.

"Set ye down," he muttered, and lowered himself stiffly into his arm-chair.

None of them spoke a word while Sanchia filled a bowl with warm water, found some clean rag, and unrolled the sand-caked bandage from the stranger's foot. There was a cut there, long and deep; it was full of grit and matter, and the dumb man winced as she bathed it. Her small body curved itself to the action, and the shawl which had slipped from her head left exposed a tender patch of white flesh at the back of her neck. The stranger's eyes, oblivious of Samson, fastened upon the little patch; with a growl and a hitching forward of his chair, Samson bent and jerked the shawl higher. The stranger looked up, his eyes puzzled, to meet the fiery glare of the old man.

"Now," said Samson Jodrell, "ye can go back to yer own place, my lad."

The stranger rose; Sanchia leading the way, he limped towards the door, which she opened for him. As he crossed the threshold his hand brushed her own; she knew it to be an accident, yet the tremor which ran through her sent the blood mounting towards her temples. Watching him limping away, she held her hot cheeks to the breeze. A feeling of triumph and excitement lightened her limbs and elucidated life for her. Ay! Gregory and his father might imprison her, but the house could never be the same again. The shadow of the stranger lay upon their hearth. She almost felt as though, turning, she still must see its dark silhouette, flung across the grey stones; she could set her feet there, where the shadow had lain, and feel them stirred to dancing.

"Sanchia!"

She turned calmly to meet the yellowish glare of Samson's eyes, fixed upon her like the eyes of an old tiger.

"Sanchia Jodrell, for all ye've no ring, ye're my son Gregory's wife."

"Would ye have me deny common kindliness to a lame man?" she retorted, carelessly.

"He lives wi' Janet Hawkins. Her kindliness is enough

for him, I'm thinking," answered Samson. "Ye were mightily close together when I come in, the pair o' ye, Sanchia Jodrell."

"Have ye naught better to do nor spying?" she asked, bitterly.

"Beware, Sanchia Jodrell! The eye o' man may fail, but the eye o' God sees all, even to the sins o' the human heart."

"Maybe it takes no count o' the good o' the human heart," retorted Sanchia, irreverently.

"Take heed o' blasphemy," said Samson, heaving himself upright. He came so close to Sanchia that her nostrils were offended by the sweaty reek of his clothing. "Ye are my son Gregory's wife, an' he wed ye to have children by ye. The Lord punishes them as forsake His ordinances."

"Maybe that's so," cried Sanchia, stung to open resentment. "I've naught to say to that, eh, Samson Jodrell? A woman must do as her man bids—is that it? 'Tis time you men o' Calvary l'arned that a woman can please herself, even if she be sold, like an ox, to highest bidder. Say me another word o' my duty to Gregory an' I'll quit him an' do as I please."

She saw the formidable fist of Samson raised to strike her, and stiffened to receive the blow. At that moment Gregory returned; he stood in the doorway, half-dazed by the tableau which presented itself within. Sanchia, scorning to cry for protection, dropped her eyes to the ground; she looked the picture of a meek, obedient schoolgirl, receiving her punishment for some fault of which she was not guilty.

"Father!"

The old man lowered his fist and flung his stick clattering to the ground.

"Will ye leave it to me to teach yer wife her duty?" he roared, and stumped from the room.

"Sanchia," said Gregory, "the mission's near done, and it'll take no more'n a week to get our house ready. Ye'll be glad to go, Sanchia?"

"Glad? Is one glad o' anything on El Secredo?" she retorted cruelly, and shook herself free of his detaining arm. She flung the clothing on the floor as she cleared the table, and threw the pots and knives on it for the evening meal. The shadow still lay there; Gregory had his feet in another man's shadow. It lay there still as a crouching animal; when night fell it would rise and come up the stairs and draw her from Gregory's side to walk the moonlit beach. And when dawn came it would shrink and return, to lie quietly across the hearth until night informed it with life again.

The boys came shouting in for their supper; she thrust them out of her way, snapping at them, as she went about her task of preparing the food. They ate in silence; the cloud of Samson's wrath brooding upon them and quelling the riotous spirits of the younger ones: saddening Gregory, who loved his father, and leaving Sanchia chill and untouched as an ice maiden. She sat at the side of the table, ignoring her food, her eyes cast down, busy with her own thoughts.

The next day, when the men had gone to work, she set to and scoured the house from floor to ceiling. Catching her brother as he went to work, she got him to mix her a pail of whitewash, and dashed it over the walls until they glared at her. Years of grime were disturbed by Sanchia in her savage labour; at noon she flung chunks of bread and dried cheese at the boys when they came from school, and cleared them out of the way of her activities. Tables and chairs were scrubbed, using odds and ends of soap she had discovered among the muddle of Samson Jodrell's attempts at house-keeping. Since Ellen's death women had crossed the threshold but rarely; now and again Samson's married daughter had come in to give the place a superficial cleaning, but she was too busy with her own housework to spare much time for her father's. By nightfall Sanchia was as tired and irritated as any suburban housewife after her spring-cleaning. She had folded away or hung up the collection of odd garments which had collected behind doors and in every unoccupied corner; the house looked emptier than ever, but so scrupulously clean that her heart rejoiced at it.

But she was tired; so tired that when the boys had gone to bed and old Samson had shuffled away to his own room, she remained with her hands in her lap, as she had sat throughout the evening, her small face pinched and peevish with her exhaustion. Gregory rose heavily, putting his hand on her shoulder.

"Coming to bed, lass?"

She looked up at him shrewishly.

"I suppose ye've not noticed all I've been doing, Gregory?"

He looked about him, with the stupid expression of a man just waking from sleep.

"Ye've been putten things away, haven't ye?"

"Ay! An' I've cleared a dozen years o' muck, an' whitened the walls."

"I thought they looked something different," said Gregory, contentedly. "'Tis a rare fine thing to have a woman about the house agen."

She made an impatient movement.

"An' I'm too tired to sleep wi' ye, Gregory. Ye can take yourself to bed. I'm lyin' i' the shed next the boys; I've shaken up the old hay mattress ye left i' the outhouse, an' I've got some blankets. I'll lie alone to-night."

He stared at her, utterly taken aback.

"Nay, ye can't do that, Sanchia," he began, nonplussed. "What 'ud my father say if he knowed o' it? 'Tisn't seemly for a man an' his wife to lie apart."

"Do ye think I care what your father says? Are we children, to do all he bids? If I'm old enough to wed, I'm old enough to choose my bedding, maybe!"

"Nay—but I'll never sleep a wink for thinking o' ye, Sanchia."

"Then lie awake," said she tersely; and, getting up, left him, barring the door behind her.

She heard his footsteps, irresolute upon the cobbles; she

took off her clothes and wrapped the blankets about her to protect her flesh from the prickliness of the hay mattress, which rustled as her body pressed it. Alert for all her weariness, she heard the stairs creak; heard Samson's voice:

"What's ado, Gregory?"

Gregory's mumbled reply was inaudible.

There was a pause, then a single blow on the door behind which she lay. She took no heed, pulling up the bedclothes to her ears. The blow was repeated, and still she gave no sign.

"What are ye up to, ye frowardly woman?" came Samson's voice, roaring through the gaping timbers.

"Let me alone—let me alone; let me sleep," she answered.

"Ye've no call to be sleeping there. Unbolt the door and get to your proper bed."

She heard titters from the boys' room next door; stubbornness and anger reddened her ears. She made no reply, but lay as still as a mouse. She heard Gregory say:

"That'll do, Father; the lass is tired. She's been working hard all day."

"Ye fool!" growled Samson Jodrell. "Will ye be o'erridden by a woman? Will ye be shamed under your own roof by the woman ye've wed? Is the man in ye dead? Before God, Gregory Jodrell, no son o' mine shall be thwarted by a woman. 'Tis a trick she's playing on ye and ye lack the wit to see it." Like a maddened bull he was now charging at the door, which creaked and trembled before his onslaught. She heard a smothered imprecation from Gregory, a shuffle on the stone floor, and the dull thud of a heavy body flung aside. To her straining ears then came the sound of heavy breathing, and a sound more terrible still: the sound of Samson Jodrell solemnly cursing his elder son.

For all her indifference to religious matters, Sanchia found herself shuddering as the slow Biblical thunder of his words rolled out. Gregory had struck his father—a sin for which she was responsible. In spite of herself she began to weep;

an overwhelming conception of the loneliness and misery of her life broke down the superficial hardness which had gathered like a crust above the feminine tenderness of her nature. She felt herself a thing accursed. She wept herself to sleep.

Next day she resumed her cleaning. She polished the windows until their panes caught every flash of sunlight and sent it streaming in rays of gold across the beach. While so occupied she was aware of groups that passed her, staring and whispering. The women and girls were electrified by her activity; they made excuses to pass and repass the house, nudging each other, and tittering at the back of her high-held head. She affected to ignore them, returned indifferent "good days" to such as addressed her. All the while her eyes were alert for the stranger, but he did not put in appearance.

The bareness of the windows struck her so overwhelmingly that she determined to go to Maggie Robertson and find out if she had any stuff that would serve for curtains. From childhood Sanchia had learnt to rely upon the good nature of Maggie, her aunt by marriage; so rich in kindliness was Maggie Robertson that she had found some to spare even for the reserved, insolent girl who was so indifferent to advances from her own sex. Sanchia would not ask her mother, well knowing what to expect—the sarcastic comment on her new-born house-pride. Maggie would likely have some odd scraps she could sew together, patchwork fashion. She thought longingly of things cherished by Sophia in an old sea-chest; shawls and dress materials, hoarded from generation to generation, that were borrowed whenever there were junketings on the island. The most beautiful of all, a gown of maroon taffetas, embroidered from hem to knee, and all a-dance with minute fringes and ruffling, had been intended for Sanchia's own wedding; no other girl had ever worn it, and she was to have covered it with a Paisley shawl the colour of old wine. For the first time she thought of these things with longing and jealousy;

a desire to beautify herself as she was beautifying the house
stirred in her heart, and filled her with a painful hatred for
the coarse gown of brown serge and the black woollen
shawl which was all she had to serve her until the ship came
in. Some cotton dresses she owned, but these were too
cold for such weather, and she had outgrown many of
them.

She stepped sedately from her doorway, and it so happened that Miss Robbins also was taking exercise, in a
direction which brought her across Sanchia's path.

Sanchia thought she liked Miss Robbins; she was very shy
of her, conscious of her own ignorance and the limitations
of her vocabulary, but drawn, almost against her will, by
the personality of the elder woman: who strode along man-
like, in a way Sanchia found very peculiar, with her hands in
the pockets of the same knitted suit in which she had been
thrown up on Calvary shore: with a cigarette gummed to
her lower lip, and her grey hair blown up tuftily by the
wind.

Sanchia curtsied primly.

"Hello," remarked Miss Robbins, and stopped to tap the
ash from her cigarette on Samson Jodrell's fence. "I haven't
seen you about for some days. What have you been doing?"

"I've been cleaning my house," answered Sanchia.

"My God!" said Miss Robbins, "if there was one place
on earth where one might have expected to have escaped
spring-cleaning, I should have thought that place might
have been El Secredo. I like dirt. It's so friendly."

Sanchia decided that Miss Robbins, although pleasant,
was mad; but she smiled, and waited.

"Come and take a walk with me," invited Miss Robbins.

"I was going to ask Maggie Robertson for some stuff for
curtains," hesitated Sanchia.

"You won't be popular," advised Miss Robbins.
"Maggie is up to her eyes in cleaning, too; that's why I
have come out. I always clear out when people insist on
cleaning things; can't concentrate, you know, when people

are working round me. I like company, but I do prefer it supine. What do you want curtains for?"

"I haven't got any," said Sanchia, simply.

"Why don't you show me your house?" suggested Miss Robbins.

"It's not mine. It belongs to Samson Jodrell."

"Oh! The father of the tribe. You're his daughter-in-law, aren't you?"

"Ay."

"Well, where is the house?"

Sanchia was glad that Miss Robbins had not insisted on paying a visit before; she flung the door open with a thrill of pride in the spotlessness of floor and walls.

"H'm. Definitely *not* luxurious," commented Miss Robbins. "Is there any law against material comfort in this place?"

This was beyond Sanchia, who remained silent.

"I see what you mean by curtains," said Miss Robbins. "They would make a difference, wouldn't they? A hearth-rug as well; I've felt like tying my feet round my neck ever since I came. Come along to the vicarage—I dare say we'll find something that will do for you."

Sanchia hung back, so obviously that Miss Robbins turned to look at her.

"Oh, I see. You're the black sheep of the community, aren't you? I wonder why? You don't look much like it, Never mind; I'll ask the parson for you. He's not really so foolish as you think him; got points, but they take some finding, I admit. He gives me anything I ask for, just to keep me quiet, I fancy. I'm a bit of a cross to him too, you know. I fancy he'll be glad when the ship comes to take me off. I'm not sure whether I'll go, yet; I'm beginning to like this place."

"Like the island!" repeated Sanchia; by now it appeared to her that Miss Robbins was very mad indeed.

"Why not? One generally likes something entirely new, doesn't one? I'm rather glutted with civilization at present," said Miss Robbins. "It's so awfully limited, really. One doesn't seem to get any further. You might like it—we'll talk about that, one day."

When they returned from the mission house, which Sanchia had refused to enter, loitering on the shingle while Miss Robbins interviewed the Reverend Smith who, busy correcting the exercises of the senior class, would have given Miss Robbins the half of his kingdom to get rid of her, they carried between them a gay patchwork counterpane, once the property of Mrs. Prudhomme's mother, which Miss Robbins declared to be the very thing for Sanchia's curtains. Sanchia herself was a little doubtful; modern ideas of decoration had not reached the island, and, accustomed to her mother's imitation Nottingham lace, she doubted the effect of the patchwork at her windows. The opinions of her neighbours weighed lightly with her; her habit of mind towards them was too scornful to admit of her allowing them to influence her judgments: but to Sanchia herself the gay octagons and squares seemed bizarre adornment. Miss Robbins was enthusiastic.

"That's gorgeous!" she declared, holding up an armful of the counterpane against the whitewash. "Pulls the whole place together at once. Let's cut them out now—where are your scissors?"

Not so easy to find; Sanchia's tidying had been drastic, and Miss Robbins, seated in Samson's rocker, had lit a fresh cigarette before they were discovered.

The two women bent eagerly to the task. Miss Robbins's tongue was seldom still, her conversation, if erratic, picturesque. Sanchia had the sensation of being whirled through elements strange and exciting. Miss Robbins rarely stopped to explain; she assumed Sanchia's understanding, while acknowledging her intelligence. The questions, often clumsily framed, began to fall from the girl's lips like autumn leaves. To have met someone who took travel by aeroplane for granted! As the sewing proceeded she learned how one gets into and out of an aeroplane; how the machine is made to rise in the air; the words volplane and nose-dive, illustrated by the flight of the gulls, became poetry upon her lips—her first acquaintance with the poetry of life.

Miss Robbins's sewing was like her speech: loose and erratic; but it was less than an hour before the curtains unfolded their banners upon the walls. Miss Robbins stood back to get the effect.

"Your neighbours will very likely say they're awful. You don't mind that?"

"There's naught but fools on El Secredo," returned Sanchia, scornfully.

Miss Robbins turned to look on her with unconcealed surprise.

"What on earth makes you different?" she asked, curiously.

"Nay, I don't know. I wish sometimes," said Sanchia, covering her face with her hands, "that I was the same as the rest o' them. I might be more contented like."

"They say discontent is a gift of the gods," said Miss Robbins, slowly. Her trained imagination caught at the idea of the torment of life on the island for such a one as Sanchia, and her heart warmed towards the girl. She patted her awkwardly on the shoulder. "Go on being discontented; it will take you somewhere—some day."

But where? In heaven's name, where, on such a desert as El Secredo? The conjecture interested her, drove her to seek her own society, to leave Sanchia to clear up the bits and clippings. She strode off along the beach, with a word of warning to herself: "One must be careful what one says to that girl. No sense in making her life more of a hell than it is already." The next moment a thrill caught her breath and lent speed to her feet. Here, surely, to hand, was the prettiest plot that ever novelist drew from an existence whose ends are—from a writer's point of view—woefully limited by nature's fondness for repeating herself, and the editorial aversion to coincidence. With a little manipula-

tion, Sanchia Jodrell might afford her a subject richly
worthy of her pen.

Sanchia, left alone, looked joyfully round the room. Miss
Robbins had insisted upon opening the windows, which had
remained sealed for many years; creaking and groaning, the
stiff sashes had relaxed their grip of paint and dust and
warped wood; the boom of the sea filled the echoing space,
the wind caught the heavy folds of the patchwork and
bellied them into the room. It had ceased to resemble a
prison; to Sanchia, growing accustomed to their rebellious
blazonry, the curtains seemed like the imprint of her own
personality, which had triumphed over some obscure
oppression.

"They look *gay* like!" she whispered, rapturously. There
were Rose Sanguinetti and Nell Barker, peeping and
giggling. Let them giggle! Colour meant naught to them.

She caught her shawl about her and sped out; she must
find him—must show him the result of her handiwork, the
metamorphosis that had taken place since his first visit.
Her steps led her straight to The Rescue. As if they had had
an assignation, she found him waiting for her, sitting on a
rock; she felt that he had waited there many days.

They returned, hand in hand, careless of observation,
heedless of caution, she dragging him after her into the
altered house. No need to bid him "Look!" she flung out
a hand, that included the spotless walls and the bravely
blowing curtains. As she did so, she saw once again, and
caught her breath in seeing, that his shadow lay across the
hearth, almost as it had lain before.

At first he stared, scarcely understanding; the male mind
does not readily grasp the details of a room's arrangement.
The brilliance, the glow about her gave him the cue to the
situation; she saw a faint, reluctant smile creep about the
corners of his lips. With a gesture spontaneous as a child's
she clapped her hands, looking at him for approval. His
glance bathed her as in light; she blushed like the dawn,

painfully conscious of her stained and shabby gown, wishing she had a new one, that it might have been summer, that she might have worn a flower in her breast.

Then she became dignified, as a châtelaine. She led him from room to room, watching the progress of his shadow, jealously, as it shortened and elongated itself about the walls. Everywhere, everywhere; there must not be a corner into which it had not penetrated. Following the obscure promptings of her soul, she led him even to the little cabin, where she had passed the night alone. . . .

CHAPTER VIII

"WE are up against many difficulties—many *peculiar* difficulties," said the Reverend Smith, adding the qualification as an afterthought, since, from his companion's expression, he gathered that he had failed to make the desired effect.

Miss Robbins, among whose qualities diffidence was hardly to be named, had grown into the habit of dropping in at nights to chat with the missionary. Why she did it she could hardly have explained. The idea of charity she would have scouted; the Reverend Smith Prudhomme was, in her opinion, a fool, and she did not take kindly to fools. But the truth was that even less than the society of fools could Miss Robbins support the taciturnity of the Robertson family, and she came to the Reverend Smith, as she said, to oil her jaws.

The Reverend Smith, who was no more addicted to silence than she, found Miss Robbins a trial. First, because she seemed to have no conception of the deference due to himself, and secondly because she did not give him nearly enough opportunity to air his own views, and thirdly, in a minor degree, because he disliked her unfeminine habit of smoking. This he looked upon as a bad example to the women and children of El Secredo, and had ventured upon a mild hint to that effect—a hint which, it is hardly necessary to remark, Miss Robbins high-handedly ignored.

She now sat opposite to him, in Jebusa Horne's chair—for he was constrained, against his will, to make this concession to a feminine visitor, even one so dubiously feminine as Miss Robbins—with her feet stuck out in front

134

of her and her hands in her pockets. The Reverend Smith, uncomfortably propped in the corner of the very hard settle, had opportunity to reflect upon the many nights that Mrs. Prudhomme must have sat there, with stiffness creeping up her spine and a numbness settling in her buttocks; the reflection did not contribute to his ease, either of body or mind.

Looking up, he saw with apprehension a fold appearing between the brows of Miss Robbins; this fold he had begun to know as the sign that she was about to disagree with him, and beside her disagreements those of Mrs. Prudhomme were very mild indeed. She appeared to have a genius for criticism in its narrower sense, and he had a fretful kind of feeling that she had him at a disadvantage. Whatever might be Miss Robbins's lapses from the standards laid down for a guest, the Reverend Smith, so far, had not been able to rid himself of a sense of responsibility as her host. So he drew himself up very stiffly, laid the tips of his fingers together, and prepared, not for the first time, to give battle, so far as the limits of hospitality allowed him to do it.

"We can take all that for granted," said Miss Robbins; "but what I don't understand is your not making better use of the opportunities which come your way."

"My dear lady, do you think—if you will excuse my putting it so—that you, as a recent, and, I may say, welcome arrival"—he hoped that she would catch the irony in his tone, and was rewarded by the grimace she threw at him—"can judge of the magnitude of our accomplishment in this distant corner of our—hrrum—far-flung Empire?" (A sense of disloyalty to Mrs. Prudhomme teased him as he employed the adjective, but it seemed as though it would not be denied. Mary, of course, had been eccentric about such matters; she had no feeling for the rounding of a sentence.)

"Who flung it, and why?" murmured Miss Robbins, trivially. "Anyone can see what you've *done*," she agreed, kindly. "What beats me is the things you have missed.

With everything in your favour, you don't seem to have got anywhere in the last fifty years."

She got up, and the Reverend Smith, half-dazed, saw her ferreting about in the bookshelves in the corner of the room. He had, as a matter of course, and in the best tradition of island hospitality, given Miss Robbins *carte blanche* to make herself at home, but he had never come across anyone who availed himself so wholeheartedly of the permission, and wondered sometimes how far Maggie Robertson's eager kindliness was holding out. Miss Robbins had grasped the principles of communal living in all its implications. He was a little anxious, sometimes, when he observed the extent of her undoubted popularity, for Miss Robbins did not strike him as a person likely to be chosen by the Church Missionary Society to be turned loose in a community like Calvary.

Miss Robbins strode back from the bookshelves, bearing in one hand one of those large, useless volumes, full of antiquated letter-press and steel engravings which people think suitable to send out to mission settlements, evidently under the impression that the settlers' minds can stand more than their own of this kind of thing.

The steel plates were protected by sheets of thin tissue paper, which Miss Robbins, in the calmest possible way, proceeded to tear out.

"My dear lady! Really!" cried the Reverend Smith. "Excuse me—but, really! Those books are the property of the mission, you know!"

"And a fat lot of use they are to the mission," replied Miss Robbins, with a friendly smile. "Look at it: "Haunts of Ancient Peace in Great Britain," published by Crosse and Blackwell—I beg your pardon, Swan and Blackwell, 1863! Now, I ask you, Mr. Prudhomme! What good is that to these wretched people, who have as much peace, ancient or otherwise, as is good for them? When I get home I'll send a parcel of *real* books to you——"

"It's very generous of you," said the Reverend Smith,

stiffly. "I hope I may be permitted to see the list, other-wise——"

"Otherwise you'll censor them when they arrive, eh? Well, you shan't have the chance. I shall address them to Sanchia Jodrell!"

"That will be quite unnecessary," pronounced the Reverend Smith. "*All* parcels that are received on the island are communal, and are divided among the people at large."

"Dear me. If that isn't tyranny, what is?" murmured Miss Robbins, still busily tearing out sheets of tissue paper. "It just occurred to me," she condescended to explain, "that I might make some more cigarettes, if we rub the tobacco fine. If you don't behave nicely you shan't have one."

"Thank you, I prefer my pipe; and in any case I should not like to think that I had used mission property for such a purpose."

"Oh, rats to that. It's the first time in its life it's been useful. Well, to return to what we were saying: Why have you done so little?"

"Perhaps, if you will explain yourself further, I may be able to draw your attention to matters which have escaped your notice."

"Well, I came out to Calvary—why Calvary, by the way? It's such a mournful kind of a name; El Secredo is much prettier, and people haven't any business to go altering names like that."

"You know the name Calvary was bestowed upon the island by the first settler, Jebusa Horne, after he had seen a vision——"

"Everybody has visions, some time or another. I think of much worse names than that when I see a vision—generally after my third cocktail." Miss Robbins was now deliberately flippant, because the Reverend Smith always, sooner or later, got on her nerves. "But I don't go about trying to rechristen Piccadilly Circus and Hyde Park Corner."

"I think, Miss Robbins, this levity——"

"Is highly unsuitable on the lips of a woman of forty-eight. Of course it is. But it's your fault. You're altogether too serious; it makes me hysterical at times. You really ought to have a sense of humour, you know; no parson can do without one. Well, I came out to El Secredo, expecting —I don't know what; marvellous things. And I'm thoroughly disappointed. There; I've said it at last. I always wanted to get one up on Oscar Wilde. He said he was disappointed with Niagara, didn't he? Well, if I can be disappointed with a shipwreck and a desert island, there's something really remarkable about me."

The Reverend Smith's glance mutely reproached her with the introduction of the name of Oscar Wilde into the conversation.

"To have lost the ability to marvel," he rebuked, "is surely to separate oneself from the angels."

"Perhaps. I never was particularly en rapport with the angels," said Miss Robbins, with continued flippancy. "Well, here you are—and by 'you' I mean every one of the six or seven missionaries who have come to El Secredo in the last few years; years during which thought has been revolutionized throughout the civilized world, years of mental and moral progress——"

"I beg leave to question the latter," interpolated the Reverend Smith.

"Don't interrupt. They were at least *years of progress*," stated Miss Robbins. "And how much of it have you brought out here? You have got the most wonderful material in the world to your hand; you've got a community with absolutely virgin minds—at least, you had, until you polluted them."

"My dear lady!"

"You come from a world of courage, of new thought, of formulated ideals, which intelligent people all over the face of the earth are trying to put into practice against the old standards of sin and error that have taken root in all centres of civilization. What a chance of creating Utopia!"

"I do not feel that Utopia could geographically exist within a thousand miles of the South Pole," replied the Reverend Smith.

"Fiddlesticks to geographical position. Utopia is a mental state, not a matter of latitude. There could be Utopia in Lapland, if the right man were found to create it."

"I feel that your novels must indeed be remarkable, Miss Robbins," said the Reverend Smith, silkily. "It mortifies me extremely not to be acquainted with them."

The lady reddened; with this thrust the Reverend Smith had indeed drawn blood, for the truth was that an exceedingly small public was acquainted with her work. By no stretch of the imagination could Miss Robbins be described as a successful novelist. She was neither good enough nor bad enough to single herself out from the ruck of British women flooding the markets with a novel a year. None of the famous slashers among the reviewers had found her worthy of his steel; nor had Arnold Bennett or Lord Beaverbrook been fired to gratuitous advertisement through the "accidental" falling into their hands of a review copy. Influence and high social connexion were alike denied her, and if, by seven months' hard work, she could make two hundred pounds on a novel, she felt she had not done badly.

Miss Robbins was one of those unhappy writers who aspire to first-class work with a slightly second-class mentality. Her aspirations would never allow her to be satisfied with what she had written, nor could she scale the Olympic heights with her mutilated muse. At intervals she made up her mind to write trash, in order to make money; and then the disquieting fact forced itself upon her, that trash, in order to succeed, must be written with conviction, and for her life Miss Robbins could not help writing it with her tongue in her cheek. The British public is quick to suspect mockery and, turning sullen, refuses to buy. Swinging back to her old style, she would produce a book about which her small circle of supporters would wax enthusiastic, and her publishers say: "I think we have a winner this time, Miss Robbins!" She had learnt by now not to allow herself to be stirred to foolish optimism by such prophecies; for lo, on its appearance, Gerald Gould or St. John Ervine would dispose of it with such airy nonchalance that it was practically stillborn on the bookstalls. Miss Robbins was, to put it plainly, sick of this kind of treatment, and her trip to El Secredo, an expensive gamble to a woman whose means were by no means adapted to such, represented her final attempt to find a subject that should command the respect of the reading public. No one, she was certain, had ever written about El Secredo; hardly anyone had heard of it. It offered a fair scope to her somewhat mordant pen, and she had seen it establishing her reputation as a serious novelist.

But, for the present, she was totally obscure, and knowing this, she mentally registered a point to the score of the Reverend Smith Prudhomme.

"You have come out here, bringing these people the dry bones of an outworn religion," she struck.

"Pardon me," said the Reverend Smith, "you cannot expect me to turn the other cheek to blasphemy."

"Who's blaspheming?" asked Miss Robbins. "I don't mind betting that I could teach these people more about Christianity in five minutes than you missionaries have succeeded in cramming into them in fifty years."

"I am surprised, with those views, that you have not taken up mission work," said the Reverend Smith, dryly.

"Not in my line. I would rather practise my religion—such as it is—than preach it."

"We try to do both on Calvary."

"Look here," said Miss Robbins, suddenly. She stretched out her arm for the Reverend Smith's tobacco jar, and extracted a pinch of the mixture which she began thoughtfully to roll between the palms of her hands. At her elbow, on the arm of the chair, lay a number of little roughly torn squares of tissue paper. "I like the Calvary people—most of them; they've got all sorts of possibilities. That's why it annoys me to find them all done up in parcels and pigeon-holed away by you missionaries. If you had to come here and take charge of their lives, why on earth didn't you help them to develop themselves, instead of cramming them into a whole lot of little moulds devised centuries ago, and rejected in the present day by everyone with two penn'orth of original thought? You've brought them religion—of a sort: the ugliest sort you could get hold of; reach-me-down religion, like the reach-me-down clothes people send to rummage sales; out-of-date religion that people at home have done with, and, like the old-fashioned coats they throw out of their wardrobes, pass on, thinking it will 'do' for someone less fashionable than themselves. It's a damned shabby way of treating them, if you ask my opinion."

The Reverend Smith rose and made a totally unconscious movement towards the door.

"Come back," said Miss Robbins; "I'm not trying to insult you, I'm just trying to make you think. Come back and sit down; you can't go out on the beach, because it's blowing a thousand miles an hour, and you may as well listen to me. I may say something quite intelligent by and by. It's a way I have. A lot of rubbish first, and then a solid chunk of good sense. I write like that, too; that's what annoys people about my books."

"I should think many people find your books very annoying indeed," snapped the Reverend Smith, pettishly.

"Oh, not so many as all that, worse luck; I'd have better sales if they did. Do sit down; this is just getting interesting. There's a cigarette for you—it may taste a bit fishy—I had to put a tiny dab of glue on to hold the paper together; but we're used to fish, aren't we?"

The Reverend Smith accepted with reluctance the little bundle of loosely rolled tissue paper and tobacco which Miss Robbins passed to him.

"I dislike your way of referring to religion as—hrrum— a matter liable to be influenced by the caprices of fashion," he said stiffly. "Christianity remains Christianity from age to age."

"If the intellectual discoveries of the past centuries have not taught us to put fresh interpretation on the Gospels, among other matters, what good are they?" riposted Miss Robbins. "Not that I think it takes much intellectualism to get at the Christian principle, if you once set about it. What is Christianity, anyhow? Obviously, following the teaching of Christ—a much more understanding and broad-minded person than you parsons make out. I've always been interested in Christ; a fine character—only lacking in humour."

"My dear Miss Robbins!" said the Reverend Smith, genuinely pained. "You speak as though our Lord were a common individual like ourselves."

"I've never been able to swallow the immaculate conception," confessed Miss Robbins. "By the way, have you ever read 'My First Hundred Thousand Years'?—written by a German, of course. The Germans aren't afraid of subjects like that. Just a jeu d'esprit, perhaps. Never mind. I find it much easier from my own point of view to look on Jesus of Nazareth as a human being, with, if you like, more divine attributes than the average man. I can get on that way. I'm a materialist, you know. Of course, it's just a point of view."

"It is the difference between faith and unfaith," pronounced the Reverend Smith, pontifically.

"Rubbish," said Miss Robbins, busy on her own cigarette. "I'm nearly as old as you are, and I've thought things out for myself. I know what works in my own case and, I believe, in the case of a number of other people similarly constituted to myself. I'm a religious woman, although you may not think it. I'm willing to admit that your sort of religion may fit some people; what I grumble at is your trying to make a Procrustean bed of it. Do you expect a suit of clothes cut for Timmy Jodrell t · fit Tom Mullyon's back?"

The Reverend Smith grunted, and the next moment spat violently and cast his cigarette into the fire.

"Abominable!" he ejaculated.

"Was it?" she asked, innocently. "Well, well! As I was saying just now, I have the greatest reverence for Jesus as a man; his only shortcoming, as I pointed out, is his lack of humour."

"My good woman," said the Reverend Smith, in an awful voice, "do you expect God to be funny?"

"God," said Miss Robbins, "is at the back of every laugh that lightens the heart of man. He is the Greatest Humorist of all. Why, good gracious, man, can you look upon a penguin and deny that God has a sense of humour? Could you have listened to the soldiers jesting in the mire of Flanders, and denied that God was doing His best to make up for the tragedy of life?"

The Reverend Smith's thoughts lay too deep for words.

"Here, on El Secredo, one thousand five hundred miles from the nastiness which so-called civilization has grafted upon the human race," said Miss Robbins, "one might expect to find the true Christianity put into daily practice; a community of people living tenderly, lovingly at peace with each other, in mutual tolerance and charity. What does one find? A hard, Calvinistic morality, based on Mosaic law rather than on the teachings of Jesus; expressing itself in petty prejudice, in suspicion and jealousy. And what beats me," said Miss Robbins, waving a hand as though the whole matter were beyond her, "is that I find you revelling in it! Priding yourself upon it! Why, good heavens, man, you make as much fuss about it as though you'd achieved marvels, when you've really only taken the easiest way. Any modern school teacher will tell you how easy it is to maintain order on the old lines of discipline and punishment; it takes something more than common ability to give freedom, and see that it is used to the best advantage."

"You are advocating Free Thought?" said the Reverend Smith, astutely.

"How I hate labels," sighed Miss Robbins. "I don't advocate anything, in a general way. How on earth could standards that satisfy the old Mullyons do for Sanchia Jodrell, for instance?"

"Sanchia Jodrell is the least satisfactory member of the settlement."

"By which you mean that she won't allow herself to be standardized quite as easily as the others. And how do you know Sanchia isn't right and the others wrong? On the face of things that seems more likely, doesn't it? She's got a hundred-per-cent. better brain than any other on El Secredo. I should have thought that Sanchia might have been allowed to go her own way, without the continual penalization of criticism which is levelled at her from every quarter, with, I imagine, your knowledge and sanction? Where's the Christianity in that—eh? Christ didn't nag and He didn't scandalize. There's as much nagging and whispering on El Secredo as in any mothers' meeting. You know what they're on about now? That Sanchia's been seen walking with the dumb man, over at The Rescue. Their minds are so nasty and so evil that they won't even grant innocence in a case like that!"

"Human nature is the same all the world over," said the Reverend Smith, sententiously. "Sanchia has not—hrrum—been reliable, in the past, and you must remember that the islanders are very jealous of their good name."

"If humanity is the same all the world over, what's Christianity been about, in the last thousand years? And a dumb man——!"

"Even as an unmarried woman, Miss Robbins," the Reverend Smith was stung to retort, "you cannot contend that dumbness is any barrier to conduct—hrrum—reprehensible in the extreme."

"Pshaw!" said Miss Robbins—or a syllable to that effect. "You parsons are all alike. How on earth you have the impudence to get up in your own pulpits and preach charity passes my understanding. Sanchia's conduct is her own affair, and I must say that she seems admirably able to look after herself, if people would only allow her to do it. Of course, if I were in her position, I'd 'go wrong' just to spite that prying old father-in-law of hers!

"Another thing. Do you know what I came across the other day? A round half-dozen of small boys, peeping in and giggling at Maggie Robertson's window when she was giving the girls their bath. She'd left a corner of the blind looped up. Now, the sight of each other's naked bodies should be as great a commonplace to these children as the rising and the setting of the sun. What is unnatural about the human body? What's all the fuss about nudity? I told Maggie, and she agreed that it was 'nasty' of the boys to peep; but she couldn't see my point at all when I told her that it wasn't the boys' faults, but their parents', for making all this mystery about sex. Maggie Robertson couldn't see it; nor could the other women—any of them, except Sanchia Jodrell."

"You would oblige me very much," said the Reverend Smith, "if you would refrain from discussing such matters with Sanchia Jodrell. Her point of view is already sufficiently unorthodox——"

"Don't bother about that," said Miss Robbins. "I haven't any ideas to give Sanchia which she hasn't already thought out for herself; all I can do is to help her to articulate them. That girl has a remarkable mind—one might even call it a cultivated mind. So far as I can see, she is the only person on the island who had ever so much as glimpsed the possibilities of her mental make-up; who hasn't just been content to live like a beast of burden. It can't have been easy—keeping one's soul alive in surroundings like these. There's where you make me mad!" said Miss Robbins, frankly. "You've all—the whole lot of you—neglected the one rare thing set in your midst; it's as if you'd taken an orchid and tried to treat it like a potato. An orchid isn't utilitarian, you may say; what if it isn't? Is all life bound up in utilitarian ends? And, while I think of it—can you let me have another writing-block? I've finished the last one."

The Reverend Smith went to the store cupboard, whither the sound of her voice pursued him.

"You see what I mean, don't you? Here, where one might expect to escape all that, one is up against all the dirty little vices of a small town."

"No!" thundered the Reverend Smith; "you will not find gambling, theft or adultery on Calvary!"

"I wonder why there is so much fuss made about adultery," mused Miss Robbins. "What is it, after all, but the sin of loving too much? As love is the chief doctrine of Christianity, one might think it should be treated, not lightly, but at least with sympathy by people who were truly loving. After all, that Nazarene prophet I so much admire was very nice to the woman taken in adultery."

"Miss Robbins," said the Reverend Smith, solemnly approaching, without the writing-block in his hand: "you are talking very dangerously. I will tell you a thing which we never speak of on the island; a thing which is locked in our hearts as a warning for all time. Sixty years ago, a Calvary woman fell into the sin of which you have just spoken. The people of Calvary, jealous for their purity, took the punishment into their own hands. The wretched woman and her paramour were bound face to face and flung into the sea at Sail Point."

"Barbarous," commented Miss Robbins.

"Exactly; but the incident—which I must beg you never to refer to in the hearing of any islander—will serve to show how Calvary people cherish their good name."

"And murder?" asked Miss Robbins, interestedly. "Have you ever had murder on the island?"

"Never, thank God," uttered the Reverend Smith, earnestly. "Through His grace we have been preserved from the sin of taking life."

"Only spiritual life," corrected Miss Robbins.

The Reverend Smith stared.

"You see, from my peculiar angle of vision, it is rather more wicked to deprive a person of his spiritual existence than to destroy his body. Life, after all, is a fleeting matter—as a lot of your hymns take pains to tell us—which we are bound to lose sooner or later. But the soul! My God, can't you see that by nagging, slandering and backbiting one can maim, or even destroy, the immortal soul which is surely of much more importance than a man's body?"

"There is no need for such advanced metaphysics on Calvary," said the Reverend Smith, after prolonged silence. "The islanders are simple folk. Each man is given the grace of the Holy Spirit to withstand false accusation; conscience, the dweller in the innermost, is man's supreme judge between himself and those who falsely accuse him."

"I have always wondered," said Miss Robbins, rising, "how the Church has managed to hang together so long. I now know it's by virtue of the sheer wall-headed refusal of its ministers to pay attention to any argument which departs from the lines laid down five hundred years ago. That block, please. Sorry you don't like my cigarettes. They *are* fishy. Good night."

The Reverend Smith, kneeling beside his bed, prayed with more than usual fervour that the ship might come soon and relieve Calvary of its anarchical visitor.

The first sight that met his eyes on waking was that of the figures of Sanchia and the dumb man vanishing round the corner of the bluff, towards The Rescue. The Reverend Smith, peering through his window, with his rug clutched tightly round his pyjamaed-legs, had strong temptation to say "Damn:" especially when he realized that the couple had been observed, not only by himself but by most of the occupants of the row of cottages known as Atlantic View, who, it being washing day, were early astir, lighting their boiler fires and carrying water from their butts. Why was not Sanchia similarly employed? The Reverend Smith jerked down his window-blind fretfully. It was Gregory

Jodrell's business, not his; but the reflection did not lay much unction to his soul, for he knew too well that whatever concerned a member of the community was bound, sooner or later, to concern him as well.   He would have to speak to Sanchia, whose innocence, despite Miss Robbins's eloquence, he was inclined to doubt.

He heard the outer door clash; it was Maggie Robertson, come to prepare his breakfast, a duty she had assumed since Mrs. Prudhomme's death. He heard her clattering about the hearth, and braced himself to cry a cheerful "good morning" to her.

He clothed himself sufficiently to join her presently in the living-room, where Maggie, on her stout knees, was occupied in kindling the fire. The Reverend Smith, busy as usual with the fleas which seemed to find a strange attraction in his person, nodded genially and went to fill the kettle for his shaving water.

"Well, Maggie?"   He was never averse to a little gossip with Maggie Robertson. She represented to him the ideal type of islander, discreet, deferential, yet friendly; she reminded him of an old parlourmaid of his father's; he enjoyed patronizing her, and felt that she equally enjoyed his patronage. She lifted her red, lined face and indulged in that relaxation of the muscles which is the island woman's interpretation of a smile.

"Good morning, sir," she responded, in her toneless voice.

"We seem in for a little better weather," he chatted, as he returned from the water-butt. "If this continues, we may look for the ship any day. By the way, Maggie, how are you getting on with your visitor?"

"With who, sir?"

"With Miss Robbins, of course," answered the Reverend Smith, with a touch of asperity. He felt that Maggie should have known better than to have forced him into specification; but the temptation to pump Maggie was too strong to be resisted.

"Nicely, thank you, sir," answered Maggie, and fell to scouring the hearth. The Reverend Smith frowned.

"I hope that she gives you a hand with your housework; an extra individual to look after increases one's labours."

Maggie sat back on her heels, looking up at him.

"I don't think Miss Robbins is used to much housework, sir. It seems easier, like, when she just keeps out o' the way. But we'll be right sorry when she goes. It's lively-like, having her there—though she do talk a deal we don't rightly understand. The children has took to her properly; I never h'ard Martha an' Betty laugh the way she makes 'em since they was born; light-headed they sounds, at times; but 'tis good for 'em."

"Ah, yes; an entertaining woman; with—hrrum—peculiar views. I hope you fully understand her views are peculiar, Maggie."

"Maybe, sir," said Maggie, falling to work again.

The Reverend Smith scratched vigorously, in a frowning silence.

"She seems to be friendly with Sanchia Jodrell."

"Ay, sir?"

Now, by rights, thought the Reverend Smith, there should not have been that questioning inflection in Maggie's voice. Who should know but she if Miss Robbins and Sanchia were friendly? Surely she was not seeking to conceal anything from him?

"I am a trifle uneasy about the friendship. Miss Robbins is—hrrum—a very interesting woman, with—hrrum—perhaps a little too much freedom of thought. I do not feel it is good for Sanchia to see too much of her."

"Maybe not, sir."

The Reverend Smith had the most unseemly longing to seize Maggie by the shoulders and shake the discretion out of her. He stood, looking down on her with exasperation.

"I saw Sanchia Jodrell this morning," he exploded.

"Going to The Rescue," supplemented Maggie, with her eyes on her work.

"Yes; look here, Maggie—I think one of you elder women should say a word to her."

Maggie's expression respectfully accused the Reverend Smith of folly.

"Sanchia don't take kindly to advice, sir."

"Unfortunately I know that," responded the Reverend Smith, and lashed himself into a puerile anger. "Her conduct is most unseemly. I don't know what Gregory is about."

"Seems like Gregory were afeerd of her," said Maggie. "He's not the man his father was. But 'tis none o' our business. I'm right sorry for Janet Hawkins."

"For Janet Hawkins?"

"Samson Jodrell went to Hawkinses' last night, and when he come away Janet were crying sorely. She's said what she can; but 'tis main hard talking wi' a dumb man; and there seems times when he's nigh half-witted. Janet'll be glad when the ship comes in."

"It is a sad thing for the Mullyons."

"Ay. Seems like as if——" Maggie hesitated, scrambling to her feet and looking doubtfully at the Reverend Smith for permission to continue.

"Well?"

"I've never given no heed—neither me nor Jack—to the tales as they tell; but Mullyons is decent folk, and 'tis queer Sanchia should act so——"

"Now, Maggie!"

"'Tis like a germ i' the blood," she ended, apologetically. "Wickedness is like consumption, haply. It lets one generation go an' then—'twas the half-sister o' Tom Mullyon's father as forsook the way o' the Lord afore."

The Reverend Smith, instead of scouting the suggestion, stood very still; an eerie sense possessed him, as of contact with forces beyond the narrow bounds of his spiritual influence.

"I'll get your breakfast, sir," said Maggie, dutifully.

Sanchia and the dumb man walked on, round the bluff. The wind was keen in their faces, the exquisite freshness of morning tasted sweetly on their lips, the air was full of salt and spray. Sanchia walked a little apart, her head held high; there was a gay elasticity in her step, adventure in the carriage of her shoulders. In every fibre of her body she was aware of the stranger; in his silence she found a stimulation to which she could not put a name. Always she was tantalized by his mystery, by the things he held away from her; his barrier of silence, instead of repelling her, led her on.

He too walked lightly; his foot had partly healed. The long lightness of his body seemed to balance against the wind, which tossed the long dark tuft of his hair about his brow. The stubble about his chin was developing into a short beard, yet there was nothing of the islander about him. A slim visitant from another sphere; it was thus she thought of him. The word "fairy" shaped itself uncertainly in her mind; she knew it was wrong, and deplored the poverty of her own vocabulary to clothe the strange situation. He was akin to her; that was the thing she felt. She waited eagerly for the moment when his returning strength should allow her to lead him into curious fastnesses of which she alone knew the secret. She wanted to lead him on the perilous climb up the rock, into that crunching area of decayed lava, into that desert of the imagination which the crater enclosed; in all strange things, in all poignant experiences he seemed to have a part. Up there, alone with the ice-cold, unfathomable water and the sky, she could possess him more fully, could launch herself and him upon the liquid currents of spiritual freedom, in which his mystery would dissolve itself and become comprehensible to her own equally enfranchised spirit.

Suddenly she stood still, and, watching her as he had grown accustomed to doing, he saw her make a strange, slow gesture, which suggested the ascent of the rock. He nodded, several times; she knew that he had understood that he was willing to allow her to lead him. She pointed to the sun, and brought her arm slowly down to the horizon, and repeated this movement twice; the day after the morrow, she meant, but he was slow in taking her meaning. She did it several times, each time pausing to raise her brows in query, but the cloud of incomprehension did not lift from his eyes. She let her arm fall to her side, defeated, not disheartened; her look bade him follow her farther.

They came at last to the beach of The Rescue, where the rocks divide like two long arms upon a narrow slope of sand; the kelp was white with sea-birds, and a faint haze of green spread itself upon the sour tufts of yellowed grass; in summer these would blossom with the faint lilac of sea-thrift. She saw the pledge of coming beauty in the shy, reluctant green, and bent to touch it. An Aladdin's treasury of shells lay about their feet; romantic sculptures of the deep sea, piled in drifts against the rocks in bewildering conglomeration of curve and spiral. He picked up a fragment red as the heart of a rose, and held it wonderingly in his hand; her attention sprang to him greedily. Her own mind yearned towards his thoughts, and as he raised his head their eyes caught and held one another. Once again she had that intimate sensation as though he had touched her, and her knees trembled. A slow smile dawned on the stranger's face; it reminded Sanchia of the reluctant sunshine which breaks from the depths of a cloud and strikes upon the greyness of the ocean. Slowly he raised the shell, and held it against her lips. She felt its coolness, and understood what he meant; her lips and the shell glowed together in a fusion of rose colour, his eyes lingered upon them, and then he moved, and at arm's length dropped the shell upon the sand. She could hardly restrain a little cry as she swooped upon the shell and put it in her pocket.

It was time for her to return; to make up for these stolen moments she would have to work doubly hard at the pile of men's clothing which awaited the wash-tub. With no gesture of farewell she turned and left him; as she sped back towards the settlement the shell in her pocket seemed to burn like a little hot coal, of which the pain was sweet. She climbed the escarpment, because she knew that she could travel more swiftly along the grass of the pasture; scrambled over the embankment, and ran towards the houses. It was as though she had left the sun behind her; her body felt shiveringly cold, save for that small area warmed by the little shell. She hoped that she would meet no one; a disconcerting development of recent days had been the breakdown of her stony indifference towards her neighbours. Was it her imagination, or had their attitude to her altered? It seemed sometimes as though they were almost inimical. Their mockery she was hardened to; she had borne it since she was a child; but it seemed to her as though a deeper element of malice had stolen into their attitude towards her. She despised herself for being affected by it. She was innocent! No act of hers gave them the right to treat her so. She guessed that the Jodrell boys had gossiped about the night she had spent apart from Gregory, and hated them for it. What right had these people to concern themselves with matters between Gregory and herself? And Samson Jodrell's hatred of her was spread about the house like a thundercloud; he could accept her labours, and yet insult her by his hatred.

Wherever she went, whispers followed her. Not the women alone were guilty of gossiping about her, but she had seen the boys' heads together, and had caught such looks upon their faces as no woman can endure to read, unless she be dead to shame: a sort of leer, a hatred tinged with lasciviousness, as though they envied the thing that made them angry. She was no fool; she knew that these detestable looks had to do with her friendship with the stranger, but she also attributed them to her having elected to marry Gregory Jodrell. In satisfying one man she had disappointed six, and they hated her for it.

As she approached the end of the embankment, where it finishes just at the first houses of the settlement, a shower of small stones came over the wall, and struck her stingingly on bosom and cheek.

"Have a care!" cried Sanchia, and sprang on the wall to see who was responsible. The pebbles could only have been flung by a human hand. There was no one in sight; there was no sound, save the booming of the sea, the mournful cry of the birds, and the distant hammering over at the mission. Sanchia Jodrell, standing flushed and irate on her husband's embankment, realized that she had been stoned.

CHAPTER IX

THE shadow was lengthening. It seemed sometimes as though it took in the whole house. Sanchia was aware of it pursuing her from room to room; it seemed incredible that no one saw it but herself. It was her companion, it was the Mute Critic, for whom she now kept the house scrupulously clean. She had taken with indifference Samson's crude ironies at the expense of her decorative efforts, and had begun to polish things, so that chairs and tables glowed with a winy light, the windows mirrored her passage. It did not matter to her that Gregory was blind to her activities, that Samson sought peevishly for objects she had thrust into drawer and cupboard—for, like most people to whom housewifery is a new experience, Sanchia's ideas of orderliness extended only to those things which met the eye. It irritated her, on an occasion when, her mother coming for the first time since her marriage to visit her (Sanchia bitterly felt that the whispers of the neighbours had worked upon Sophia's curiosity, rather than on her motherly feelings), Sophia looked about her with an air of gratification and some wonder, saying: " Ye've got the place rarely, Sanchia!" Praise from her mother had always embarrassed her. Perhaps it was Sophia's fault; perhaps, when Sanchia was at home, her mother had been too ready to seek some ulterior motive in the girl's good deeds. In justice to Sophia let it be said that her daughter's brief bursts of virtue had too often coincided with her requests for some favour. But in the present instance it seemed as though there was little to be gained, and Sophia took the signs of Sanchia's housewifely activities as evidence of a change of heart, and departed to peacock the news abroad among her neighbours, who, looking askance at each other, thinking their own thoughts—which were not in favour of Sanchia Jodrell.

Samson Jodrell returned, weary from his day's labour, seeking the clay pipe which Sanchia, hating its ugliness and rank smell, had stuck in a drawer. In its place he found a small rosy shell. The impudent exchange kindled his ill-temper, and he threw the poor, pretty thing on the ground, grinding his heel upon it, until no more remained than a pile of rosy dust.

"Sanchia," he shouted, "what have ye done wi' my pipe?"

She came, leisurely, from the outer kitchen.

"What call have ye to go shifting my pipe, an' cluttering the place up wi' yon rubbidge?"

Her eyes widened as she saw what he had done; one hand went to her throat, as though something tightened there.

"Ye've broke my shell!"

"Fetching muck into th' house! Where have ye putten my pipe?"

"Ye can seek your pipe!" cried Sanchia, with a sob strangling in her throat, and fled, slamming the door behind her. It was as though some live, feeling part of her had been destroyed. She was in the grip of her misery when the boys came clamouring in for their food.

It was a wet day; the marks of their boots fouled her spotless floor, which, on the suggestion of Miss Robbins, she had sanded. She had done more; fired by Miss Robbins's descriptions of the decoration of her flat in Chelsea, she had gone out and gathered shells; with a child's delight in creation she had sat for an hour arranging them in a creditable pattern around the swept hearth. She had known that Samson would mock at them, but, coming in stonily to prepare the meal, she looked upon the ruin of her pathetic attempt at adornment. With no malicious attempt, with the

careless boorishness of their age and upbringing, Seth and
Barnabas had trampled the shells into the ground. Her lips
whitened, the upper teeth setting into the lower one, and,
swinging round, she caught Seth a stinging blow on the ear.
The boy cried out, more in surprise than in pain, and asked
sulkily:

"What's that for?"

"Ye should live in a pig-sty, all the lot o' ye," sobbed
Sanchia. "Don't ye see what I done wi' the floor?"

"What's the good o' doing that?" asked Seth, with
some reason on his side. Barnabas broke into a horse-
laugh and deliberately kicked a little row of shells
aside.

"She's gone babby-like," he scoffed. "Her—wi' her
curtains an' to-do! Who's coming to see ye, Sanchia? Are
ye giving a feast an' expecting the Bishop?"

"Hold your tongue, or I'll clout ye again!"

"Better have a try!" invited Seth, squaring in readi-
ness.

The cloud of her wretchedness darkened through the
evening. Gregory could get no word from her. He had had
a hard day, and on the morrow was starting his own house:
his and Sanchia's. He wanted to talk to her about it; but she
was stony. Her small, shut face and the tightness of her lips
forbade communication. There was tartness in her very
movements, as she whisked the dishes from the table and
went about some mysterious business of her own in the
kitchen. Gregory heaved a deep sigh, drawing his chair
up to the fire, beside which sat Samson. The glumness
of their elders had reacted upon the boys, who vanished,
whispering.

Samson sat still, his eyes fixed upon his son; Gregory was
painfully aware of those eyes, which begged for confidence,
while they accused him of folly. In the last weeks the whole
structure of his home life had tumbled about him. His love
for his father suffered continually under the blight of his dis-
pleasure; the ugly memory of the night when, for Sanchia's

sake, he had laid hands of violence upon the old man, although, apparently dismissed by them both, was lively in their memories. His love for Sanchia, cheated of its means of expression, tortured him. His fellowship with the other men suffered too; he felt that they despised him. Samson Hawkins, for one, was at no pains to conceal his contempt; the failure of Gregory's marriage was in every curt sentence he flung at his one-time friend. It was a thing too plain to be ignored. What other Calvary man would suffer his wife to go stravaging about the island with a stranger? What other man would allow himself to be deprived of his conjugal rights at the caprice of the woman he had a right to call his own? Gregory felt that they knew about this, too, inwardly reproaching his father with the divulgence of the secret. Family pride might have sealed old Samson's lips, but the tale had leaked out, was common property in the island, exposed him to the mockery of them all. It might be Seth or Barnabas, of course; he felt his brother Timothy to be above suspicion.

"Gregory."

"Ay, Father."

"Ye had as well stayed unwed, I'm thinking."

Gregory stiffened to opposition.

"Ye have no call to think it."

"Have ye made that woman your wife?" pursued Samson, relentlessly.

"Sanchia is my wife," said Gregory.

"Ye lie," said Samson Jodrell. Gregory held his tongue; the old man made a movement of impatience.

"I never thought but ye had it in ye to play the man," he muttered.

"Ay, I can play the man; but I canna play the brute," answered Gregory, red to the ear-tips. "Father, can ye not see as this concerns Sanchia an' me? 'Tis not a matter for other folks to handle."

"Gregory, I want to see myself grandfather to your son."

"Ay, Father; but meantime there's Barny an' young Seth; ye've gotten enough young 'uns about ye, surely, to wait a bit?"

"The sons of the brothers are not like the sons of the sons," pronounced Samson Jodrell. "Gregory—I'm i' mortal fear she'll cheat ye yet. Maybe we did wrong forcing the pair o' ye to it; but 'twas her own doing at the last, an' there was none else. I was fain ye should be a man. She's wanton at heart, Gregory."

"Thou lies, Father!"

"Are yer eyes blind? How often has she bin wi' yon stranger, when ye've bin at yer work? Can ye answer me that? Have ye forgot the day I come in here, an' found 'em standing so's ye'd scarcely slip a sheet o' paper atween them? She's ripe for a man, an' if ye don't take heed to it another'll rob yer orchard. All lasses are same, lad; ye've gotten to master 'em afore ye win 'em. 'Tis a woman's way o' folly. I tell ye she thinks ye simple for not knowing it."

"I will force no woman agin her will," said Gregory, in a loud voice; the sweat dewed his forehead, and his hands were clenched. "Till she comes to me an' shows me in her own way she's ready, I'll not treat her as my wedded wife. Ask her I shall, an' keep on askin'; but there must be her will as well as mine, afore a child is born o' our two bodies."

"Ye're mad," whispered Samson Jodrell. "'Tis the will o' the Lord, I tell ye, that a wife shall rear seed to her husband; the undutiful woman must be led i' the way o' the Lord by the man as weds her. 'For the procreation o' children': 'tis writ. An' wi'out the act marriage is a sin an' a thwarting o' God's commandments." He came stoopingly to his feet, and laid a hand with a gesture of yearning on the shoulder of his son. "Master her, my son; master her this night. For by another comes ye may regret it sorely."

"Father," said Gregory, desperately, "ye canna understand. I canna take that way wi' Sanchia. She's not like the rest o' us."

At this moment Sanchia came through the room; the two men, starting apart, were included in the cold, intelligent flash of her eye. Her arms were loaded with blankets.

"What are ye after?" came like a pistol shot from Gregory; for all his partisanship, his father's presence, the old man's ironic eye, drove him to exhibit his own powers of autocracy—powers which almost every soul on the island, save Sanchia, had sampled from time to time.

"I'm shifting my bed again," said Sanchia, coolly.

With a noise like a growl Samson lunged at her; the bedding was snatched from her arms, one gnarled hand pointed tremblingly towards the narrow flight of stairs—little better than a ladder—that led to the room she shared with Gregory.

"Get back where ye belong, ye false woman. Lie wi' the man as wed ye."

"I will not," she answered, simply.

He snatched for his stick, dropping the blankets from his arm. Before Gregory could prevent it, the first stroke had fallen across her proud, unyielding shoulders. A cry broke from Gregory and, leaping clumsily forward, he wrenched the stick from the old man's hand.

"By God, ye shall not beat the woman as is mine!" he grunted, wrestling with the old man whose one-time strength leapt to resist his own: he prayed that it might not be necessary to hurt Samson. "Sanchia," he panted, while his fingers still bit into his father's shoulder, "ye had better go. This house is no place for ye. Get back to your home, till I've gotten our place fit."

With one hand on the place where the weal was already rising, she answered, defiantly:

"Will I be driven here an' there by such as *him?*

Gi'e me yon blankets, Gregory, an' let me bide my own way."

"Let go o' me, Gregory!"

"Not till ye're sane, ye old villain! Sanchia, for pity's sake do as I ask ye. Can ye not see he's out o' his mind? He'll do ye an injury if ye stay."

For answer she stooped, wincing, and picked up the bedding. The door of the shed clanged behind her, they heard her thrust the wooden bolt into place.

"Will ye believe me now?" Samson was bellowing. "I tell ye she's cheating ye because her heart's full o' the other man."

"'Tis wi' him I'll have my reckoning," answered Gregory, and let his father go. His heart cried for pardon; he felt that he, and not his father, was humiliated, as the old man crawled back to his chair, and sat there, muttering and chewing the white hairs of his beard.

The night passed hideously for all three. Gregory rose with the first streaks of light and went out, breakfastless and red-eyed, to his labour. Sanchia came from her retreat, chill as ice, ignoring all that had gone before, to be met by Samson and held in a vicious grip.

"Take heed o' this: if so be ye cuckold my son, I'll strangle ye wi' these hands as hold ye, an' my soul may go to hell for it."

She stared back defiantly, deigning no answer. After they had made pretence at eating, she set about her household work and, when the beds were made, returned to the living-room, to find Samson sitting in his rocker by the fire. She wondered a little, but would not lower her pride to ask why he had not gone out to his work.

As the morning wore on she realized that he was remaining to watch her. A cold and helpless frenzy almost mastered her, but she preserved her silence, and worked the harder, as in defiance of those rheumy, watchful eyes. "Out o' my way," she muttered, tersely, as she swilled a bucket of water across the flagstones, from which she had swept the sand. The clock ticked on towards nine; she returned from feeding the geese to find him closing all the windows. She stood still to watch him, and he paid as little attention to her as to a piece of furniture. She saw him fumbling in drawers and cupboards for some mislaid object; his bent figure was sinister as a dwarf's; there was malice in the hunch of his shoulders. Presently he found that which he sought, and Sanchia, still obstinately silent, watched him nailing up the windows: fixing sash to frame with three-inch nails, driven in with vicious and purposeful blows of the hammer. At first she supposed that he was doing this to spite her; he often complained that she had the house as cold as a shed.

He finished his task, and laid the hammer on the sill. Still he ignored the girl's presence. She was standing with hands folded, in the doorway which led to the kitchen; her small face was ironical, had he but glanced at it. He struggled clumsily into his coat, and then, with a sly movement, slipped towards the door. Suddenly she grasped his intent, and flung herself forward to intercept him. The thrust of his arm sent her staggering against the table; she felt its corner stamp a bruise into her flesh, and before she could regain her balance he was gone; she heard the key grate in the lock. She was a prisoner! He had locked her in.

She made no foolish attempts at escape, but went slowly back to the hearth and stood there, looking downwards. A strange sense of triumph, of having outwitted his malice, dawned in her mind. The shadow! He knew nothing about the shadow. Powerless were locks and bolts against that strange companionship which was hers night and day. She dropped on her knees, and with her forefinger traced its outline, where it had lain, slanting away from the window, since the first day when the dumb man had entered the house. It was there now; she saw it growing inside the invisible line traced by her finger. Giving free rein to her imagination, she saw it rise, flit before her, everywhere,

everywhere, from room to room. Now it was coming down the stairs, now its curious passage led it into the shed where she had passed the night, but always it returned to her, where she sat on the hearth, as though it came to her for reanimation, within the cabalistic outline drawn by her finger.

How long she sat there she had no idea; she presently heard a knock at the door. Without rising, she listened, and when it was repeated, called out:

"Who is there?"

"I—Miss Robbins. What are you doing?"

"I'm locked in," answered Sanchia, laughing.

"Locked in!"

"Samson Jodrell locked me in."

"The old devil! Can't you get out? Can't I get in?"

"Nay, there is but one door."

"What's he locked you in for?"

No answer; Sanchia's finger continued to trace the pattern on the floor.

"Does your mother know?"

"Nay—unless Samson's told her."

"Had I better go and tell her—or what about Gregory?"

"They can't do naught; he's gotten the key."

Miss Robbins's head appeared at the window, her features flattened against the glass to escape the reflection.

"Why are you sitting on the floor?"

"'Tis as good a place as any," shouted Sanchia, beginning to enjoy herself. "He'll have to open the door at dinner time; the boys have to have their food."

"Aren't you furious?"

"'Tis foolish like," conceded Sanchia.

"Come here; I can't shout to you over there without everyone listening."

Sanchia rose and approached the window, crossing her arms on the sill; her lips still curved in their elfin smile.

"It's disgraceful," asserted Miss Robbins. "No one has

any business to treat a woman so. Old Jodrell ought to be—shaken."

"He'd not take much heed o' that!"

"Gregory should be ashamed of himself."

"Nay, 'tis naught to do wi' him. He doesn't know."

"Shall I break the window?" asked Miss Robbins, valiantly.

"Nay, 'twould be a daft-like thing to do," said Sanchia, in an elderly fashion. "Gregory's gotten the last piece o' glass for his house, an' maybe the ship won't fetch any this time."

"But what's it about?" persisted Miss Robbins.

"Because I slept by myself last night," answered Sanchia, shortly. She a little wondered what this would convey to an unmarried woman of Miss Robbins's uncertain age.

"Upon my soul! It's barbarous!" Miss Robbins clenched a fist. "I'll go and tell that ass Prudhomme about it."

"He can't do aught!"

"Of course, it's your own fault, in the first place. I mean, all your faults—you women of the island. You haven't got any solidarity. You don't stand up for your rights."

"Have women any rights?" asked Sanchia, innocently.

"Good God!—and this is the twentieth century. My good girl, do you know that women have been sitting in Parliament for the last four or five years? Women are actually helping to make the laws of the land which govern yours—and you ask if women have any rights. Women are the owners of their own bodies; that's the first of their rights. The old chattel idea is dead—exploded; you don't become a possession of your husband's, because he happens to have put a ring on your finger—by the way, you don't wear one?"

"I was wed wi' my mother's; I had to give it back to her."

"Good. Don't you do it. It's just a survival of the chattel era."

"I'd like a ring," confessed Sanchia.

"Oh, I dare say; as an ornament. But not as a sign that some man thinks he owns you. You've started well—independently, I mean; go on. I want to see what happens. We'll have to plan reprisals, you know. Why don't you leave Gregory?"

"Leave him?"

"Go back home—anywhere."

"I'd be no better off; an' it won't be so bad when he's done wi' building our house. Gregory's not bad; he doesn't mean to be bad to me."

Miss Robbins started to say something; then apparently thought better of it.

"I'll come round again later," she announced, and walked rapidly away, her hands in her pockets. Her feminism was stirred to its profoundest depths. As behoved one who had taken part in many suffrage demonstrations, who had gone on hunger strikes for pouring tar in letter-boxes, smashing windows and otherwise making herself a nuisance to a body of orderly gentlemen bent on saving the country from ruin by reserving the suffrage for themselves, she resented Sanchia's pusillanimity. Her indignation boiled over in little disjointed ejaculations, as she stumbled across the foreshore, which was deserted at this hour of the day. As she turned the bluff she saw ahead of her the figure of the dumb man, sauntering among the rock pools, pausing now and again to peer into their depths.

Miss Robbins was interested in the dumb man; like Sanchia, but in a more articulate fashion, she sensed the strangeness, almost the fantasy of this nameless creature, whose dumbness was the least part of his mystery. Frequently she cursed the sea-sickness which, holding her in her cabin throughout the length of the voyage from Cape Town, accounted for her ignorance of his identity. The boats which sail to El Secredo rarely carry passengers; it would have been impossible, had she been up and about, to remain ignorant of the name and business of her fellow adventurer. Not a gentleman, thought Miss Robbins—not even of that anomalous class known as "gentlemen by education," but an *individual* : one who must, in the days before shock deprived him of his speech, have had qualities distinguishing him from his fellow men.

She had never attempted to hold much converse with him, although one might have thought that the opportunity for uninterrupted monologue would have been hailed by a lady so fond of the sound of her own voice; but she had an odd feeling that he did not like her. She had once offered him pencil and paper, suggesting that he might write the answers to her questions, but this had failed. He took and held the things awkwardly, and his efforts to write only resulted in a few formless scrawls on the paper. He gave them back to her, shrugging his shoulders; either he had never known how to write, or he had forgotten the art.

However, bubbling over with indignation as she was, Miss Robbins rapidly approached him; he raised his head and nodded, but a faint frown creased itself between his brows, as though he had not wished to be disturbed in his solitary musings.

"They've locked her in," began Miss Robbins, explosively. It was only afterwards that she remembered that he had understood of whom she spoke, without Sanchia's name passing between them. "Mediæval tyranny, I call it. She won't let me break a window. These islanders want a charge of gunpowder laying under some of them."

The dumb man looked at her with that singular intentness of gaze which sometimes exasperated her. It was like the attentiveness of a dog, that struggles to understand what its master is saying. "How annoying if he doesn't understand me: he mayn't even speak English," she thought, fleetingly but mere lack of comprehension was powerless to check her then.

"Of course, she ought never to be here at all; they aren't fit associates for her. They're like children—stupid children. Malicious, too. You're responsible for a lot of it," she flung at him carelessly. "Apparently a woman can't have any-thing to do with a man here, after she's married. Somebody ought to do something about it."

His eyes turned across her shoulder, in the direction of the settlement; she understood that he wished to go to Sanchia, and stepped aside.

"Go on, if you want to: you'll have to shout through the window—oh, I forgot; you can't shout. Well, she'll be glad to see you. But I should take care there's no one else about. It won't make it any better for Sanchia if you are seen talking to her."

As he went away from her, quickly, and without embar-rassment, she realized that she was responsible for his going, and what might come of it, and the knowledge gave her the same feeling of power and intoxication as she felt over the puppets whose actions she manœuvred on the pages of her books. Like many women, the direction of the action of others intrigued her, and it seemed to her that she held in her hands the strings of a promising situation, whose develop-ment might prove sufficiently dramatic to justify—from a literary point of view—her own intervention. Miss Robbins was not one of those writers who create their characters, and then give them *carte blanche* to follow their own inclina-tions; that may have accounted for a certain stiffness, a want of spontaneity in her published work. Very firmly she insisted upon retaining a grip on her protagonists, bending them neatly to demonstrate her own theories as to their actions.

Was the dumb man in love with Sanchia? Was Sanchia in love with the dumb man? If neither of them had, so far, succumbed to the erotic influence, how long would it take them to do so? Grimly Miss Robbins determined to delay her own departure from El Secredo, if necessary, but it hardly looked as if this need be. Resolved not to be cheated of her climax, she pondered upon the two, upon the antic situation. How would they react to their emotions? And what was likely to be the upshot? And how on earth was she to get a dumb man, who persisted in being an enigma, into her book?

She walked briskly, debating the ramifications of the plot, and clothing it instinctively in phrases like those which she put into her novels. The writer's delirium was upon her, and she walked so quickly that she was soon out of breath, for it was her habit to compose mentally, before sitting down to her typewriter, and, hating the physical action of writing, she had done little, since arriving on El Secredo, but to fling down disjointed paragraphs, which would set the stream of thought flowing freely when she returned to civilization once more.

The moral aspect of the case troubled her not at all; she prided herself upon an entirely objective attitude to humanity at large, and was as interested and detached in the present situation as though she were seated in the stalls of her favourite theatre, watching a play. What was more to the point, she felt tolerably sure that her publishers would be equally interested and delighted, and that even the reviewers would relax, for the nonce, their haughty insouciance and treat her seriously, if she could but capture and reproduce the fleeting aspects of this island drama.

She forgot her promise to return to Sanchia, but rested eventually in the cave which Sanchia had shown to her, at Sail Point, while she brooded upon her book.

When the failing light warned her that it was time to return, she fell in with a group of men, the returning fishing fleet, coming back after an unsatisfactory day. She hailed them with geniality; diffidence, as we have seen, was not among her virtues, and the dull reception of her bantering troubled her not a whit. But it struck her that night, for the first time, that there was something singular in the glances that some of the men threw at her. They gave her the unusual feeling that something was amiss with her personal appearance.

Miss Robbins was not self-conscious: neither had she the smallest illusion about her own looks. She had never been a handsome woman, and she realized, with an inward grimace, that life on a south Atlantic island is not calculated to improve the looks of a woman bordering on fifty, who has long been dependent on the kindly efforts of her hairdresser, manicurist and such people. She had managed to achieve a little amateur barbering with a pair of scissors, but was aware that this had not been attended with any noticeable measure of success. Her grey hair stood out in uneven tufts, and, since we are by way of being completely truthful, she had altogether failed to cope with a little tuft of hairs which sprang from a mole on her left cheek. Tweezers were necessary for the delicate operation, and occasional resort to electrolysis: and neither was available on El Secredo. Miss Robbins reflected, with some humour, that if her friends could see her now they would suffer a painful disillusionment; the stinging air had roughened her skin and reddened her eyelids; to put it mildly, she was not a thing of beauty. But it surprised her that the islanders, who might not be expected to be critical, should, apparently, have noticed it. They gazed at her very peculiarly: especially Henry Martyn, and the young man Job Barker, who had always struck Miss Robbins as a very unpleasant person indeed. She dropped behind, a little sheepishly. One of the men dropped behind, too.

She glanced up sideways; always capable of laughing at herself, Miss Robbins knew that she was behaving as coyly as a schoolgirl.

What hairy creatures these islanders were! She marked the tufts in Henry Martyn's ears, the thick growth on the back of his hands. He seemed to have no notion of addressing her, but continued to walk by her side, staring ahead of himself, saying nothing. For sheer devilment Miss Robbins refrained from opening a conversation; she plodded along by her companion's side, a little breathless from the wind: wondering at first whether he was shy, but coming to the conclusion, from the unruffled calm of his expression, that it simply did not occur to him to enliven the occasion with talk. If anyone felt shy, it was not Henry Martyn. Miss Robbins, choking with suppressed conversation, carried out the experiment to the moment of their parting.

"Good night," said she, gently ironic.

"Good night," said Henry Martyn, with no signs of observing her irony. They separated just before the stone wall running round the little empty garden of the mission house; the little garden where Mrs. Prudhomme had so assiduously cultivated marigolds and stout pink daisies the year before.

Miss Robbins's lively curiosity was awakened when Gregory Jodrell appeared, crossing the missionary's threshold, ushered forth by the Reverend Smith, whose hand lay upon the young man's shoulder with so clearly apostolic a blessing that Miss Robbins felt that she could have no peace until she knew what it was all about. Gregory's face was very red, the missionary's very pale, and the echo of their voices reached Miss Robbins, where she stood at a distance of twenty paces or more.

"You'll see what you can do, sir?"

"We must take it before the Lord," said the Reverend Smith, solemnly. At that moment he saw Miss Robbins, and his face clouded, because he felt that he could not bear Miss Robbins just then. She, however, not being hampered with sensitiveness, pushed open the iron gate before Gregory had reached it, and hailed the parting guest.

"Good night, Gregory. I hope you're not going to lock Sanchia up again."

He looked at her as though he had not heard her, touched his brow with his forefinger, and passed on. Miss Robbins

continued on her way to the door; she was much too interested to observe the marked lack of welcome on the
Reverend Smith's face.

"What's wrong?" she inquired, brightly.

The Reverend Smith compressed his lips and shook
his head. His physical resistance, however, gave way
when Miss Robbins took him gently by the shoulders
and pushed him into his own house, following him as he
went.

"There seems to be no end to the troubles of the
Jodrells," he muttered evasively. With anyone but Miss
Robbins he would have been rather glad to discuss the
situation; but he was a little weary of the way in which that
lady pounced upon his words, worried them, as a puppy
worries an old slipper, and tossed their remains gleefully to
the four winds of Calvary.

"You know old Samson locked Sanchia in to-day? It
really is a disgrace. Why do you let them carry on like
that?"

"Samson Jodrell knows what he is about," said the
Reverend Smith, with his lips set in a thin line. "I fear there
is very little grace in Sanchia. I must say I am sorry for
Gregory."

"And I'm sorry for Sanchia," asserted Miss Robbins,
stoutly. "Has Gregory been grumbling about her?"

The Reverend Smith turned and regarded his self-invited
guest for a moment in silence, before making his portentous
reply.

"Gregory Jodrell's wife has refused to have children."

"Well, why should she? I wouldn't have a child myself,
for anything on earth."

"My dear lady, the cases are not analogous."

"Perfectly. I've as good a right as any woman to bring a
child into the world. Better than some; for my child could
at any rate count upon a fair physique and a suitable proportion of wit."

"Heaven forbid," uttered the Reverend Smith, to whom

the idea of Miss Robbins propagating herself was a grim thought.

"If I were married, I mean, of course. Why should Sanchia have children? Heaps of women don't, nowadays —for all sorts of reasons: economic, physical or purely disinclination. Why should the love of two people be penalized with childbirth, when all that they really want is each other?"

"I really can't bear this," whispered the Reverend Smith.

"Oh, don't be weak-kneed, man! Why didn't you have children yourself?"

"God did not see fit to bless our union in that way," said the Reverend Smith, stiffly.

"Exactly. God doesn't intend every human being to reproduce itself. Why, the very idea evokes chaos! If Sanchia doesn't want to become a mother, no one has the right to force her to be one. Personally, I think she'd be no use at all as a mother," stated Miss Robbins. "She hasn't that kind of character."

"The wife who avoids her maternal obligations is no wife!" thundered the Reverend Smith. "She is no better than a kept woman!"

"Even they have children sometimes," said Miss Robbins, easily. The Reverend Smith swallowed.

"The women of Calvary must have children, or the race becomes extinct."

"Well, why shouldn't it? What justifies its persistence, anyhow? I can't for the life of me see anything particularly fine in these islanders. What has El Secredo got to offer the children who, willy nilly, are born here? What has it done to benefit the world by its existence? Why *should* it go on? It's self-centred; no good. It only exists because of the greediness of the British Government, which can't let go an opportunity of acquiring another scrap of territory, no matter how valueless. What right has the British Government to sacrifice human life to the acquisition of sterile territory? Sending men to die in the Polar regions, out of imperialistic vanity: colonizing an island as bare as hell, to gratify its lust of possession. Let El Secredo die out; Sanchia is perfectly right."

"You forget," said the Reverend Smith, wearily, "that this place has been home to its people for several generations. The British Government did not send Jebusa Horne."

"The British Government tacitly encourages colonization by the dispatch of provisions, and its missionary activities."

"That is merely the support given by the mother country to a courageous body of people who have chosen to live their lives here; if El Secredo were vacated, a garrison would, no doubt, be sent to take their place. The island is a port of call for Polar expeditions, and must be maintained."

"As a sort of jumping-off place for suicides! Oh, don't be so silly! Sanchia Jodrell is the only person with a grain of common sense on this island. She, at any rate, sees more than a couple of inches beyond the end of her nose."

"You do Sanchia too much credit, Miss Robbins. Her refusal is based on no more noble impulse than lack of personal inclination. I defy you to find any sense of racial obligation in her heart. The worst of women," said the Reverend Smith fretfully, "is that they will always insist on hunting for non-existent motives, in justification of actions which are really quite simple and instinctive. Mrs. Prudhomme used to do the same thing. It complicates life so unnecessarily. I wish I could impress on you how unsophisticated these people are."

"You can't help finding a formula, can you? But any intelligent person will tell you that a formula breaks down again and again, through the same thing: through the unintentional inclusion of the unknown quantity, x, which baffles the scientists. In psychology, you know, there is an almost unlimited x."

"Excuse me, I don't think I can quite stand psychology, Miss Robbins," said the Reverend Smith, rather pitifully. "I prefer to follow the instincts of the human heart. I am afraid I must ask you to leave me; I must have something to eat, and then I am going to try to get the Mullyons and Samson Jodrell to come in and talk over this—hrrum— distressing position."

"Surely," said Miss Robbins, staring, "the person with whom to talk it over is Sanchia herself? You can hardly treat her as if she were a child. Oh, come, come! How can you arrange a person's life in this overhead fashion, without consulting the individual it most concerns?"

"I always strive towards charity," said the Reverend Smith, with a reproachful look. "Sanchia *is* a child, as all the people here are children. Weddings on Calvary are always celebrated by a feast; in the minds of the people the feast is looked upon as part of the marriage ceremony itself. It is quite possible that, not having had her feast, Sanchia does not feel that she is properly married. I shall suggest that, whatever difficulties may present themselves owing to the failure of our sources of supply, it would be prudent to hasten on the preparations for the feast. I should not be at all surprised if, when this is over, Sanchia settles down and takes her position as Gregory Jodrell's wife in the serious spirit—hrrum—becoming to a young woman in her situation."

Miss Robbins stared once again.

"You're rather priceless, aren't you?" she said at last.

"Eh?" said the Reverend Smith, nonplussed.

"I suppose you daren't admit, even to yourself, that Sanchia's mind is about a century in advance of everyone's here—including your own. A child, indeed! *You're* the child, holding your dolls' tea-parties, trying to pat the turbulence of a volcano into quiescence with a battledore. All right, I'm not trying to be nasty. Go on."

"I have no more to say," rejoined the Reverend Smith, in

deep offence, "save that I intend to have a straight talk with this dumb fellow. It is very difficult to talk to him, because one cannot really be sure whether or not he understands. He really appears quite witless at times; a disconcerting person. But at any rate, we are agreed that Sanchia sees far too much of him, and he must be made to realize her position and his own obligation to the community."

"If he has any obligation to the community," said Miss Robbins, rebelliously—"a suggestion I beg leave to question—it's surely to give them a good shaking up; to disturb their self-satisfaction, their truly deadly righteousness. They're stiff with it! Their milk of human kindness is coagulated with it! Moral, you call them. Well, I don't call it moral to reduce a girl like Sanchia to the straits she now is in, to surround her with suspicion and malice, to——"

"Pardon me; if Sanchia is in the 'straits' you describe, she has herself to thank. I do not for a moment suggest that she has yet committed sin——"

"No thanks to you all if she hasn't," retorted Miss Robbins. "You've all bullied and blackballed her; you forced her into a marriage she had no inclination towards——"

"Miss Robbins! You have been told the circumstances of that marriage. It was Sanchia's own doing."

"In a moment of desperation, because she knew marriage was expected of her. Now, I ask you, Mr. Prudhomme: what could a man like Gregory Jodrell represent to Sanchia but the least of seven evils? His mentality is in its infancy; hers—by some freak of creation, heredity or what not—is ripe, avid, prepared to assimilate, to give forth. He's nothing better than a good dog, or a horse; she—well, she's a woman; and that's more than can be said for the female population on El Secredo. So far as physical functions are concerned, one presumes they're women; but apart from those, let me tell you, they're neuters, and Sanchia Jodrell is feminine to the tip of her little finger."

The Reverend Smith, closing the door behind Miss Robbins, mopped the perspiration from his brow. A violent woman! A woman without decent reticence in speech! How mild, beside her vitriolic pronouncements, sounded, in retrospect, the miniature rebellions of Mrs. Prudhomme. For a moment he stood, the good, narrow man, rendering himself to sorrow: then he pulled himself abruptly together and hunted for food.

CHAPTER X

GREGORY JODRELL stood face to face with the dumb man, looking up into his face. He had gone to Janet Hawkins's house to seek him out; there had been a sneering interest in the faces of Samson and his brothers as Gregory mounted the ladder leading to the loft where the stranger, when not abroad, spent most of his time lying on the pallet bed. So Gregory had found him, with his hands linked behind his head. At first he had hardly stirred; then when Gregory came to the side of the pallet, and, looking downwards with clenched fists, had muttered: "Get up; I've some'at to say to ye," he had risen, slowly, overtopping Gregory's height as his long, lean frame unfolded itself. The blank look complained of by Miss Robbins and the Reverend Smith was replaced by an almost disconcerting concentration; it was as though the fellow, deprived of the power of giving out, concentrated every particle of his physique in the act of hearing.

Gregory, his fists clenched at the end of his loosely hanging arms, wondered what it would be like to hit the fellow. He looked as though a single well-planted blow would smash every bone in his body. Gregory found himself hating him for qualities that he sensed but could not name. Good looks; he supposed the dumb man had that, for all his weediness. Tall he was; it was irritating to have to look up at him; but frail like grass, and thinly composed of bones and sparse flesh. His eyes were odd: one greyblue, the other with a blotch of brown extending from the pupil across the iris to its rim.

"Ye'll keep away from my wife," Gregory was saying.

He had said it a dozen times, at least; it seemed as though he could not stop saying it, nor think of words to supplement it. The eyes of the stranger held, imprisoned him; Gregory felt himself enmeshed in an intangible web, the web of the stranger's will to communicate with him. Once again Gregory paused to listen, expecting a voice to issue from those sealed lips. It seemed as though the fellow was mocking him; as though he could have spoken, if he would. Clumsy taunts sprang to Gregory's lips, his eyes swam in a red mist of anger. "Ye'll keep away from my wife!" It was weak to keep on saying it, but what else was there to say? One could not ask for explanation or justification from a dumb man. Gregory felt that a word, a sound would have set him free to drive his fist into that still face; as though he too felt it, the stranger maintained his strange, his diplomatic silence.

"If ye lay a finger on Sanchia, as God's above I'll smash ye on the rocks yonder!" said Gregory, pointing with his finger through the round eyelet of glass which afforded the single illumination of the room.

It was like talking to a statue; one could not even be sure that one's words were understood; one did not even know if the fellow was English. Elusive; had he known the word, Gregory must have applied it. He dropped his hands with a muttered imprecation, and descended the ladder. In the room below they watched him pass, silently; three men, debarred by the island's relentless law of hospitality from doing the thing they longed to do, and Janet Hawkins, who cursed the day the stranger had come to Calvary. He felt their scorn scorch him: he who might have done the thing, who had forborne, although his honour was at stake. He tramped back to the house, and, as fortune had it, found Sanchia alone.

"Sanchia. There is a thing I mun ask thee. Ye mun answer me, Sanchia."

The purity and pallor of her face, as she turned her head towards him, struck him with a powerful sense of having misjudged her; but his mind was made up, and his nature too stubborn to go back on his intention.

"Yon dumb fellow, Sanchia. Does thou love him?"

"Love," said Sanchia, wonderingly. "What is love?"

"Ye know right well what love is," retorted Gregory, hotly. "I ha'n't forgot, Sanchia, that afore we had a right to do it, ye asked me to kiss ye, over at Sail Point, on the night o' the storm."

"But kissing isn't love," she replied slowly. "A kiss is naught. Ye can kiss a person ye don't care a jot for."

He reddened, catching her hand.

"Have ye kissed yon fellow, Sanchia?"

"For dear sake, no," she cried, staring at him.

He loosed his grip, hanging his head.

"Ye'd never lie to me. It 'ud break my heart, Sanchia, if ye was to play me false wi' another man."

She moved away from him softly, with the free grace that singled her out from the other women.

"Are ye sorry ye wed me, Sanchia?"

"I had to wed," she replied, laconically.

"Would ye ha' been happier wi' another?" he persisted, bent on wounding himself.

"What other? Ye're all alike, you men o' the island. What are ye questioning me for?"

"Why will ye not be my wife?"

She became quietly and whitely angry.

"Has your father set ye on to badger me? Why aren't ye away yonder, wi' my parents an' Samson Jodrell, taking counsel how to master me? Ye'd be as well employed, as coaxing here at my side. I cannot tell ye why I will not wife ye. I cannot speak o' the things that are in my heart." She clasped her hands violently over her breast. "Gregory, I tell ye—I tell ye——" she struggled for expression. "I cannot tell ye! There's something here—it's like a bird; it cries to be free. I don't know how to set it free. It waits ——" She broke off, shaking her head in despair. "I've not the words," she ended, almost inaudibly.

"There's a plenty o' words, surely," said Gregory, stupidly kind; he ached to understand her.

"You'd say so," she answered, cruelly, "because ye never think o' things ye haven't words for. I tell ye, Gregory—I tell ye it's awful—sometimes—just to think things—an' not know how to talk about them—even to yourself. Just to feel a thing, an' not be able to lay hand on it, like. I feel's if I'm going mad wi' it now an' again." She finished with her head in her hands. "Words don't help; they hold back— the sort o' words I know. There must be other ways o' talking—things like Miss Robbins says. Somehow when she talks it's like listening to a foreigner; only it's English, an' we ought to know it—an' why *don't* we know it?"

She stopped as abrupt? as though a hand were laid upon her lips. Her eyes stared vacantly before her, as though she saw things not of this earth.

Gregory said, still feeling clumsily after the thing he was pursuing:

"But I don't want ye to *talk* to me, Sanchia."

"Nay," she replied, "I know that. Ye just want me to be a wife to ye, an' bear children for ye. I tell ye I will not do it. I wouldn't know what to do wi' 'em if we'd got 'em. I wouldn't know aught to teach 'em——"

"But there's the school, Sanchia."

"Ay! There's the school! It's done a lot for the rest o' us, hasn't it? It's given me naught. I'm teased an' teased wi' the things inside me—an' maybe the children 'ud be the same, an' everybody'd say they was wicked, like they said o' me——"

"But why did ye wed me, Sanchia, if these things was in your heart?"

"I wed ye because I'd vowed I'd do it," she answered, stubbornly. "I never wished to wed at all. I just wanted to be Sanchia Mullyon. I'm wild, Gregory; like one o' the gulls, like the island sheep—like the wind! I never was meant to be a wife to a man—leastways, not an El Secredo man. I want what ye cannot give me, an' because of it I cannot wife ye. An' I hate your father—I fair take pleasure in cheating him o' what he wants. Always prying an' listening to us when we're abed. Ye wondered why I gave over sleeping wi' ye, Gregory. It's just that I can't abide the thought o' him next door, listening for every rustle an' looking in my face next morning to see if it's done—the thing he's waiting for. I can't abide it! It makes me feel sick. It's nasty—like Seth and Barnabas peering in to see Maggie Robertson bathing the girls."

"It's not, Sanchia! An' ye're fancying things as aren't true——"

"Maybe I am, but they're my thoughts, an' I cannot help them."

"We'll be in our own house next week," he sighed. "'Twill be different then."

"Ye mustn't expect me to sleep wi' ye, Gregory."

"Why not? There'll be no one to hear."

"Nay, but——"

"Ye're keeping some'at back from me! Ye're deceiving me! 'Tis because ye love this other fellow! By God, I'll——"

"No, ye won't," she answered, coolly. "Love—I've told ye I don't know what love is. I reckon it's something that beautiful it can't come nigh Calvary."

"There's the love o' God," said Gregory, desperately. "Our lives bear witness to His everlasting mercy; wi'out it we'd all of us perish."

"If 'tis love sends folk to live in a place like this, I want naught to do wi' it. Love is comfort, an' being close to someone ye want to hold an' cherish, an' saving 'em pain, an' thinking 'em beautiful," she said slowly. "That's what love is; something tells me love's like that. An' I don't feel that way to ye, Gregory; it's o' no use saying I do. I'll keep your house clean an' cook your food for you; but I cannot give ye myself, for I don't love ye. I don't love anyone. I wish to God I did."

"What is it ye feel for the dumb man?" he asked, jealously.

"I haven't got words," she replied, after a little pause. "I feel—I just feel he's something like me—we're caged up, the pair o' us; but he can remember the days when he wasn't caged, an' I don't know aught but prison; an' it's like looking at a door, an' wondering what's behind it—an' fancying there's all kind o' lovely things—an' trying to find how to open it. An' because he feels like me I'm glad to be near him——"

"Ye're full up o' fancies," he said, angrily.

"Ay. 'Tis the way I was made."

"She come sneaking back, quiet like a mouse; I seed her myself. Oh, she's deep, is Sanchia Jodrell."

"Naught but a loose woman would carry on the way she does. 'Tis easy seen, to look at her, what she's up to, these days."

"An' do ye remember what she said at wedding? As she'd as lief live wi' Gregory unwed as be his wife? 'Twas a nice thing for Sophia Mullyon to stand by an' hear!"

"Judgment'll come on her yet, the hussy. Dumb man, forsooth! The loss o' a man's tongue don't make much odds to her like. You'd think for very shame she'd hang her head, but she shows herself all about, as brazen as though she was queen o' the island."

The bitter conversation passed in Maggie Robertson's living-room. Janet Hawkins, compressing her lips, had as little to say as any; she felt herself at a disadvantage, harbouring one of the causes of the strife. Others felt the same; the little Barker woman shot a malicious glance sidelong and her tongue was as sharp as her look.

"Ay, I'd not be you, Janet, for a ransom! Ye're lucky if ye know all as goes on under your own roof!"

"There's naught amiss in my house, Nell Barker!" retorted Janet, tartly. "I gotten a husband an' three sons to see as things is proper!"

The clack of women's tongues went on over the knitting needles; the men, for once, were not indoors. Young Martha and Betty, deprived of the favoured companionship of Miss Robbins, who also had taken herself into the moonlight for a solitary stroll, listened with open mouths and ears to the indictment of their cousin.

"'Tis a crazy-like notion o' Sophia Mullyon's, to have a wedding feast. 'Twill take a deal o' foodstuff, an' there's no heart in folks for junketing just now."

"A wedding feast'll maybe make Sanchia feel more settled like," put in Maggie Robertson, by nature a pacifist; her eyes, none the less, glinted brightly from woman to woman, inviting them to continue their chatter. "Leastways, that's what Mr. Prudhomme says."

"'Twould take more'n a feast to give Sanchia Jodrell a change o' heart," struck in Ellen Martyn, acidly. "Ye'd have thought more would ha' come o' all the to-do over at parson's house the other night. 'Twas all they could think o', seem'ly, to have a wedding feast! If she'd ha' been my girl I'd ha' given her her wedding feast—ay, wi' a birch rod in my hand! An' we're all to dress up an' rumti-tum round in Samson Jodrell's barn, on account o' a girl as shames us wi' her goings on."

"'Tis silly-like to have the feast now, so long after they're wed," put in Rose Sanguinetti, with the self-righteousness of a recently and elaborately wedded bride.

"There'd ha' been a deal more sense in waitin' for the ship to come. How's the cooking to be done wi'out a speck o' butter or salt? 'Twill be a queer-like sort o' feast."

"I'm glad my wedding wasn't like that," purred Rose, shaking out her knitting, which was obviously intended for the coming baby.

"Ay, yours was a rare fine wedding," praised Nell Barker, who had her reasons for keeping on the right side of the Sanguinetti family.

"I can't see how Miss Robbins makes such a to-do over Sanchia."

"Oh, well, she's a foreign body," said Maggie Robertson, not choosing that the flood of criticism should engulf her own guest. "Maybe she doesn't see things; an' anyhow there's queer things done in England now."

"These are unrighteous days," declared Janet Hawkins, solemnly.

"We'll ha' to be getting our clothes ready," said Rose, complacently; she had Mrs. Prudhomme's wardrobe to draw upon. On his wife's death, the Reverend Smith had recollected that Rose had been a protégée of Mrs. Prudhomme's, and had bestowed the scanty relics of the outfit which his wife brought to Calvary upon young Mrs. Sanguinetti, whom he judged worthy of the gift.

"I'll be borrowing the brown from Sophia Mullyon," put in Ellen Martyn, hastily. The wardrobe of El Secredo was as near communal as it might be, and at festival times a general pooling of resources took place.

"I cut the last o' the sheets up for frocks for Martha an' Betty," said Maggie Robertson, regretfully. "When they was confirmed, you know. Howsobe, they'll look rarely wi' a bit of starch an' happen I'll manage a sash for each o' them. Now hold your tongues!" she cried, irately, to the effervescent Martha and Betty, who made a great clattering with their boots at the prospect of future glory.

Miss Robbins had just turned homewards when she almost ran into Sanchia, who was making her smooth, inaudible way across the grass. The moon was shining brightly; it spread a sheet of silver over the island, and its pathway glittered right across the sea; a low, South Atlantic moon, lustrous as a shield in the sky. It was several days since she had seen Sanchia; her book absorbed her, her mind played continually about it, and the pile of notes in manuscript was growing on the floor beside her bed. She had the sense of lightness and elation which accompanies successful composition, in her receptive mood everything appeared vivid and clear to her, and coming upon Sanchia thus, suddenly, she was struck by the glowing quality of the girl's looks. The moon had brightly silvered her; she seemed to sparkle with moonlight. It emanated from her eyes, the pale surface of her skin, the folds of her garments. With one of those flashes of intuition which visit most people at times, Miss Robbins became certain that she was on her way to an assignation. The night grew more intense, more exciting; a vicarious thrill of excitement shot through Miss Robbins as she wondered how far the affair had progressed.

"Hello, Sanchia. They're going to give you a feast, I hear."

Sanchia's teeth flashed in the moonlight.

"Ay; so they say."

"Rather nonsense, isn't it?"

"'Twill be something to keep them busy," replied Sanchia, with a flash of humour, unexpected and delightful.

"And you? Does it interest you?"

"The house is ready," answered Sanchia, indirectly. "Gregory finished the thatching to-day, an' Samson Hawkins is fixing the windows to-morrow."

"You'll be more on your own," conceded Miss Robbins.

"Ay."

She became aware that the girl was restless. "I mustn't detain you," she remarked, standing aside.

Sanchia's smile flashed upon her once more. It struck Miss Robbins that there was something beautiful in her boldness, her lack of shame. She might be engaged upon a clandestine proceeding, but there was nothing clandestine in the carriage of her proud head, nothing furtive in her bearing. "You've got a fine courage of your own, Sanchia Jodrell," she thought, but did not say the words aloud. The girl was gone, swiftly, dipping from sight in a hollow; her small figure was swallowed in the earth, like Persephone's.

Miss Robbins was about to proceed on her own way, when, with that sixth sense which warns one of the presence of an unseen watcher, she became certain that her meeting with Sanchia had been observed. She stood perfectly still; the moonlight lay in silver patches about her, under the wall of the embankment ran a shadow black as ink, and in that shadow, she was convinced, lay the watcher. Presently she walked on, slowly; and went but a little way before she swung her head rapidly over her shoulder. What she saw made her stand still again. Five or six figures, bent, and obviously anxious to avoid observation, were gliding rapidly in the direction Sanchia had taken.

A sudden fear, not for herself, but for the girl, took Miss Robbins. The object of the watchers was clear; they intended to shadow Sanchia. Miss Robbins shivered to think of the possible outcome of their surprising the girl with her companion. How to warn her? She had not the slightest idea of Sanchia's destination; it might be The Rescue, a spot overlooked from a score of points: it might be Sail Point, where the caves would surely form a cul-de-sac, so far as escape was in question.

What were Sanchia's favourite haunts? Sail Point, of course; but something suggested to Miss Robbins that she was unlikely to have chosen this well-known spot as a rendezvous for her lover. To begin with, the caves offered a stiff climb for anyone with full use of his limbs, and the stranger was still weak and easily fatigued; she had often come upon him resting on a rock, or stretched full length upon the beach, and the signs of his exhaustion were patent to the view. No, Sanchia would not have chosen Sail Point; and The Rescue was equally unlikely; sometimes the men set night lines there, and at all hours the boys went trapping rabbits on the rough ground overlooking it.

She remembered a little path that ran upwards from the apple orchard, to lose itself among the crags of the peak; once or twice Sanchia had led her there, and pointed out difficult climbs and deep crevasses, where, said she, one could remain hidden for days without risk of being discovered.

Miss Robbins set to running across the pasture. She was in danger of observation, there in the moonlight, but once gain the shade of the apple trees and she would be screened from watchful eyes. She could at least make a noise to warn Sanchia; every sound would carry on so still a night, and the rattle of a handful of pebbles would be sufficient to scare the girl further into her hiding-place.

Miss Robbins found it difficult going; the ground was perilously uneven. She saw no sign of the watchers, so set off upon the upward climb. The path was precipitous, shaly and thick with shadow; Miss Robbins crouched, to afford less of a target for watchful eyes; she went slowly, with long pauses between her progresses. Once she was almost certain that she heard a whisper; it was like a particularly exciting game of hide-and-seek.

Every few yards she stopped to listen; but no sound came to her ears beyond the boom of the sea and the thin whistling call of the wind. She began to lose her breath, stumbled, and ricked her ankle rather sharply; as she bent to rub it she cursed Sanchia for leading her on a wild-goose chase. The silence began to irritate her nerves, the towering peak overhead took on a sinister black and whiteness, like an early Brangwyn, in the moonlight. Any one of the humped boulders might conceal the watchers who spied on Sanchia; what would their attitude be to herself? Miss Robbins did not apprehend violence; if it arose she had the unbounded confidence of small, wiry people in her ability to look after herself; but they would certainly prevent her carrying out her intention of warning Sanchia.

A low whistle came to her ears. She had already learned to distinguish the calls of most of the island's birds, and this resembled none of them. She looked cautiously about her, and it seemed that, at the edge of a narrow, inky cleft, a score or so of yards from the path, something moved. Sanchia— or her pursuers? She waited to make sure; and, the flicker of darkness—one could call it no more—being repeated, left the pathway and stumbled in the milky path of the moon

M

towards her objective. Her own shadow lay in an attenuated blotch of ink above her; she felt glad of its company.

As she reached the cleft, a hand caught her wrist and gave her a sharp tug forwards. Miss Robbins felt the ground slip from beneath her feet, and would have fallen, but for the support of a strong young arm which whipped itself like a coil of wire about her skinny little figure, lifting her for a moment clear of the ground.

"Damn you, Sanchia! What are you up to?" spluttered Miss Robbins. She could not see an inch before her, but they appeared to be in a narrow cranny, whose velvet blackness was slit by a silver streak of moonlight.

"Whisht!" whispered Sanchia. "What made ye follow me?" she asked, as she removed her steadying hand.

"Didn't you see? I thought you didn't. There are men out, watching you. I met them on the embankment as I left you"

"Ay, they're always after me," she answered, calmly. "I lead 'em a rare dance o' nights: 'Tis Robertson's lads, an' Job Barker an' Peter Martyn. I can go faster than the lot o' them, an' I coo-ee an' lead 'em on. 'Tis rare sport!"

Miss Robbins caught her breath. There was something almost diabolical about Sanchia at times, she was thinking; some sinister acquaintance with the powers of darkness. Was it thinkable that the girl had no realization of the grimness of the chase?

"But if they were to catch you, Sanchia?"

"They'd never do that," she replied, arrogantly. "I'm little, an' I can slip into places where they canna pass. 'Tis rare fun to be the fox, an' let them chase me."

"But Gregory? Doesn't he know——?"

"Nay, sure! He's down wi' Samson Hawkins in the carpenter's shop, helping him to get on wi' the woodwork for the house. They are at it till ten o'clock most nights; he's rare impatient, is Gregory."

"I thought you'd come out to meet——"

"Nay, now! How'd that be, wi' Jim Hawkins watch-
dogging as soon's the sun goes down?" she said, triumph-
antly. "It makes me laugh at times! Because they think I'm
his'n, they think I'm any man's! 'Tis four nights now I've
led 'em a dance, an' to see 'em in the morning, ye'd think
they'd never let the butter melt in their mouths! I was fair
overcome wi' laughter in church o' Sunday; seeing 'em all
setting so quiet an' godly, as no one 'ud think how they
turn into wild beasts when the moon is up!"

She fell to laughing silently; Miss Robbins could feel the
shaking of her shoulder. Primitive, sinister, yet completely
feminine, Sanchia's devilry appealed to her. Allowing for
the difference in hemisphere, what distinguished her actions
from those of her more civilized sisters, who decoyed their
men through the night clubs and tennis courts? Sanchia's
game was the more dangerous, but it was essentially the
same. Miss Robbins could not forbear a chuckle at the
thought of what the Reverend Smith Prudhomme would
make of this ungodly game. The lawlessness in her own
composition applauded Sanchia's idea of revenge upon her
tormentors, while a feeling of apprehension as to its outcome
rendered her uneasy. What, for instance, would be Samson
Jodrell's form of reprisal, if these night wanderings came to
his ears? There was a man capable of savagery in defence of
his family honour. "There has never been murder on the
island." No; but with that fanatic breed all things were
possible. It only needed the little more, thought Miss
Robbins, to precipitate a miniature Armageddon.

Sanchia thrust an apple into her hand; one of the small,
yellowish, withered apples of Calvary.

"We must wait here a little," she pronounced. "They'll
go round the other side soon, for it's there I led 'em the
night afore last."

"Who did you say they are?—the Robertson boys, and
Henry Martyn?"

"Nay, not *Henry* Martyn!" It seemed to Miss Robbins
that there was a peculiar emphasis in Sanchia's voice. "'Tis

Peter Martyn—the younger one." The sound of sharp teeth sinking into another apple reached Miss Robbins's sensitive ears. "But they're all alike, El Secredo men. . . . What do ye think *he* does, to earn his living, when he's at home?"

The question, coming suddenly, took Miss Robbins off her guard. She patted the rock behind her to find some place where she might sit, and let herself down upon a ridge whose chill struck through her clothing.

"It's hard to tell. His hands are pretty smooth, aren't they?"

"Ay," came deeply through the darkness.

"*She's felt them!*" thought Miss Robbins.

"A clerk, perhaps."

"What's a clerk?"

"Oh, someone who earns his living by writing."

"By writing?" The idea was a novel one to Sanchia; she asked simply: "Do you earn your living that way?"

"I try to; but it's not precisely the same thing as clerking," smiled Miss Robbins, in the dark.

"What does he write?" pursued Sanchia.

"Oh, rows of figures, probably, and adds them up."

"Sums," said Sanchia, succinctly. "I like sums; they make me feel strong——" she broke off, aware of that stifling inarticulateness once more.

"I don't," said Miss Robbins, tersely. "Of course, he mayn't be a clerk at all."

"A gentleman, perhaps?" inquired Sanchia; the esoteric word sounded strangely on her lips.

"What do you mean by a gentleman?" Miss Robbins spoke quizzically.

"They say Jesus Christ was the first gentleman," replied Sanchia, awkwardly, yet unwilling to plead ignorance. "An' lords an' so forth, they're gentlemen. But Jesus Christ was only a carpenter's son, like Samson Hawkins; I don't see——"

"The dictionary definition of a gentleman is a man of

good birth, a man of refined manners," replied Miss Robbins. "I don't know whether our young friend answers to either of those descriptions. On the whole I think not. He's too interesting to be a gentleman."

This line of reasoning was lost upon Sanchia.

"He's different," she said, helplessly.

"I'm inclined to agree with you on the whole." Miss Robbins wanted to ask the girl how much she had seen of him, but good taste prevented her giving free rein to her curiosity.

"'Twas queer, him coming like that; that night," said Sanchia, in a small voice.

"I'd just been wed," she supplemented; and stopped again.

"I always said I'd never wed an islander," said Sanchia.

"Why did you?" asked Miss Robbins, sharply.

"I'll tell ye," said Sanchia, suddenly. "I was afeerd. 'Twas the storm, an' the wind. 'Tis queer, the wind on El Secredo. It seems like as if it governs us. Ye don't mean to do a thing, an' the wind bids ye do it. Ye mean to do a thing, an' the wind says ye Nay. I was afeerd. The fire was burning up, an' all of a sudden I seemed to see myself burning up wi' it, and there seemed naught to burn. I hadn't begun to live! I wasn't ready to die! An' I thought if so be I escaped the fire, something else would come along. Ye don't know El Secredo; it hates human folk. It's always waiting to destroy 'em. 'Tis a poor thing to die a maid; an' Gregory Jodrell was the best o' the lot."

"Why on earth don't you all quit the island?"

"How?" said Sanchia, bluntly. "The men might do it, if they was to try; but it seems like as if El Secredo folk was frightened o' trying. Ye'd get so far, an' then the island 'ud reach out after ye and claw ye back, an' maybe punish ye for trying to get away."

"Wouldn't you be brave enough to try?"

Native prudence asserted itself, as Sanchia answered:

"It can't be, now I'm wed."

The devil of her experimentalism forced Miss Robbins to say:

"Marriage isn't eternal, you know, Sanchia." She had the grace to feel slightly apologetic to the absent Gregory as she said it, but the temptation of feeding fresh ideas to the fascinatingly receptive mind at her disposal mastered her decencies.

There was a short silence, followed by the pregnant question:

"What do folks do in England, when they are wed, an' they don't care for each other any more?"

"Get divorced, I think," said Miss Robbins, without stopping to think. The words echoed with all the strangeness of a foreign language in the confined darkness where they sat.

"What is divorce?"

"A sort of legal loophole for people who can't get on together. Hadn't we better be going?" asked Miss Robbins, beginning to regret her venturesomeness.

"That doesn't tell me aught," said Sanchia, stoutly. "How does one divorce?"

"It's a very troublesome, very unpleasant and very expensive process indeed," said Miss Robbins, firmly.

"Tell me about it.   Have you been divorced?"

"No.   I don't happen to have been married."

"Can ye just walk away from your husband, an' leave him?"

"Oh, dear me, no; it's not nearly as simple as that. You have to prove unfaithfulness, and all manner of things."

"Why?" asked Sanchia, simply.

"Well! I suppose they think it oughtn't to be made too easy. It wouldn't do to have people just 'walking away from each other' all over the place, would it?"

"But 'tis a foolish like idea; for if ye cease to love a man ye aren't wedded to him, an' if ye never loved him, ye weren't wedded at all," pronounced Sanchia.

"Those ideas are much too lucid for the administration of the law," returned Miss Robbins, smiling.

"And when ye are divorced, 'tis just as if ye'd never been wed?"

"Except for the trifle of your surname, which illogically remains the same as your former husband's—yes," said Miss Robbins.

"Tell me about it," commanded Sanchia.

She found herself, eventually, giving a graphic description of a scene in the divorce court. Literary enthusiasm carried her away; she had always had a peculiarly keen appreciation of the drama of the law, of the symbolism of the judge's robes, of the steely antagonism of counsel, of the ramifications of cross-examination, and the apathetic receptiveness of jury. By the time she had remembered to enumerate the grave disgrace and disadvantages attached to the status of divorcée, Sanchia's attention had apparently wandered elsewhere; Miss Robbins saw her small head and shoulders silhouetted against the silvery crack of the crevasse where they lay concealed.

"It seems as if we might be going," she said, softly.

Miss Robbins, accepting her companion's hand to aid her out of her stiffened position, reflected that at any rate Sanchia would have no opportunity of putting her new theories to the test on El Secredo.

They walked arm in arm back to the settlement. As they passed Atlantic View, Miss Robbins saw blinds being twitched aside. She wondered if Sanchia was conscious of the espionage, and assumed that she was, she held her head so high.

"I'll give ye a word o' warning," said Sanchia, suddenly. They stood still, outside the Jodrell house. "I'd not go walking alone o' nights, if I was you."

"Great heavens!" exclaimed Miss Robbins. "Who's likely to bother about me?"

"Ye don't know the island folk as I do," persisted

Sanchia; "and 'tis not wise, now, for a woman to go walking alone. Good night."

Miss Robbins chuckled as she swung on towards the Robertsons'. Quaint of Sanchia to assume that she, a jaded and unattractive woman of fifty—unlike most of her sex, Miss Robbins was fond of exaggerating her age; it gave her a sense of confidence—was subject to the same attentions as she! Quaint—but rather sweet. Not for the first time, her mind played with the project of taking Sanchia back to England as her companion, or perhaps her maid. There was something lovable about the girl. But, short of kidnapping, the project did not seem to hold forth much hope. Sanchia in England! Greedily Miss Robbins visualized an unlimited source of subject matter for future novels! She gave herself a shake.

"You're losing your principles," she told herself. "I wonder if that's necessary, in order to become a successful writer?"

CHAPTER XI

DURING the days preceding Sanchia's wedding feast it was as though a light danced over El Secredo: a fitful gleam that floated like a little lamp upon the dark surface of its discontent: that flickered up and died out, and seemed as though at any moment it might be utterly quenched in a rising of the dark and turbulent flood of the undercurrent. Like a lamp lashed to the topmast of a sinking ship, the Reverend Smith Prudhomme's geniality maintained its precarious glow. Confident of his own ability to outride the storm, he went about, radiating cheerfulness, steadfastly refusing to see signs which, to a more sensitive person, might have appeared ominous. He honestly believed that he had found a panacea for all their ills; he really thought that in the feast he had found a solution—temporary, but how gratifying!—of all their difficulties. His self-deception was so powerful that he had actually persuaded himself that with the formal installation of the young Jodrells among the well and truly wed of the community, dissatisfaction would smooth itself magically away.

According to the Reverend Smith, the islanders were "nervy." He did not use that expression; in fact, he had frequently reproved Mrs. Prudhomme with her rather frequent employment of it, as an excuse for certain temperamental exuberances which he considered morbid and unnatural; but his mind seized upon the excuse of the storm, the abnormal excitement through which all had passed, which had left its aftermath in their unsettlement; and he told himself—and others—that three days' merry-making would restore the balance of life. Even Miss Robbins, who prided herself upon seeing beyond the end of her nose, and who was not ordinarily to be prevented by any sentimental consideration from speaking her mind, had not the heart to blow upon his optimism. As a matter of fact she found the spectacle of such obstinate and impregnable purblindness fascinating, from a psychological point of view. Her idea was, crudely, to allow him his length of rope and be in at the hanging.

He became heavily jovial with one and all; at all hours of the day and night he urged the islanders to song—his favourite expression of lightness of heart. He fell upon the football club, reorganized it, and set thirty panting and insufficiently nourished men charging at each other's legs in a brisk wind all through a Saturday afternoon. He jollied the islanders—who bore it all with praiseworthy fortitude. They had their own way of being happy, apart from the Reverend Smith's forcible insistence upon it.

No details for the preparation of the feast were too insignificant to challenge his enthusiastic attention; he insisted upon assisting Maggie Robertson in her task of pounding potatoes into starch for the girls' finery—wasting much material in the process, and urging the breathless Maggie to join in the chorus of "Tipperary" as he smote the pestle into the mortar with resounding and dramatic thuds that sent the starch scattering in every direction. He behaved, in short, exactly like a large, tiresome puppy, that flings itself, barking, against everybody's legs, demanding to be played with when everyone's mood is the reverse of playful.

And beneath all his lightness rumbled the echoes of the coming storm. So far as the women were concerned, the Reverend Smith had, perhaps, some measure of success. For all Miss Robbins's pronouncements to the contrary, the women of Calvary were at least sufficiently feminine to welcome an excuse of donning their best and dancing in Samson Jodrell's barn; besides, the general preparation afforded rare opportunity for gossip. Not when Sophia Mullyon was about, of course; she, naturally, had charge of the arrangements: she passed with heavy autocracy from house to house, superintending preparations, and when she was gone gossip boiled over and tongues were as busy as hands. Sanchia herself took little part in the work; but this was usual. The prospective bride was expected to pass her days in needlework, in arranging her house, and, so far as one could see, she was doing something of the kind.

But this was the month for spading the land, for preparing the potato patches which are scattered all over the island, wherever an earth-pocket invites the plantation of crops. Apart from personal provision, much of the El Secredo trading is done in potatoes, and in the flocks of grey geese which each man rears. Digging leaves plenty of time for reflection; there was something threatening in the way spades were wielded, the innocent earth was flung over as though it covered a legion of corpses. Into his handiwork each man dug his discontent, his impatience, the restlessness of his blood, the torment of his uneasy nights.

Out beyond the ring of the islands a funnel of water rose glittering into the sunlight, blew sideways into invisible spray. A turbulence of waters, a curved silver shield which flung itself suddenly half out of the sea, left a trail of foam behind it, and rose a hundred yards farther on, travelling like a torpedo, blunt-snouted. A school of whales was off the islands, and the men of El Secredo knew that it was time to set about the most unpleasant of their yearly tasks.

Whalebone is the most valuable of the island's trading commodities; with whalebone and sperm oil the islanders pay for the more costly items of their provisions. Unfortunately, the great risk of hunting the whale in the canvas boats at their disposal limits the development of this, the most promising trade of El Secredo. Money and skill alike are lacking, and the islanders keep to a minimum their activities in this direction. Sperm and dolphin (which yield the oil and blubber), the "right" whale and the monarch rorqual, abound in their season about the islands, and, reluctantly, but with characteristic hardihood, the men take to the boats, which are loaded with their primitive and unreliable whaling tackle.

For several days, between the spells of their digging, the islanders had watched the waterspouts of the whales beyond the islands; less than a mile out from Sail Point, a huge old whale, hung with barnacles and sea-wrack, reared itself like some monster of the slime to scrape itself upon a sharp tooth of basalt projecting from the sea.

Janet Hawkins's husband, a man so small and insignificant that he lived like a shadow between the strapping sons he had begotten and his decent, bustling wife, roused from a habitual indolence at the prospect of the only task in which he took pleasure. Always, in the whaling season, Peter came to life, forsook his carpenter's bench, assumed leadership, startling people who had become used to overlooking his existence.

Like a muezzin he was seen upon his roof before dawn, clapping his hands, shouting and demanding volunteers for the adventure. They were a little slow in response; whale-fishing is no occupation for old men, and many of the young ones were constrained to deafness by the fearfulness of their wives. The Reverend Smith Prudhomme was the first to appear, chafing under enforced idleness. He had always longed to accompany the whalers, but the responsibility of his position forbade his risking his life unnecessarily, and the grim fact remained that never yet had the whalers returned in safety from their expedition. Last year it had been Harry Sanguinetti's brother, who, caught in the caudal frenzy of the infuriated rorqual, had been flung sky-high, his spine broken in two places. It had not been worth while picking up what was left of him. And another man had lost his forearm through the premature explosion of one of the small bombs used in harpooning, and bled to death before they could make the shore.

Gregory Jodrell sat, aware of his father's eye, while the summons went forth. He was no more afraid of obeying it than the rest, but he knew well the struggle that went on in the old man's heart. Both pride and duty urged Samson to dispatch his son upon the perilous enterprise, but all his bereaved fatherhood cried out to prevent the young man's going. The boys, intensely eager, watched one and the other, with occasional glances at Sanchia, who held herself aloof, as though the matter did not concern her. Outside the windows a knot of women gathered, chattering shrilly, their battered faces drawn into lines of anxiety; some of them had prevailed upon their men to stay at home; others, who had failed in their persuasions, stood with red-rimmed eyes, the tears chapping their cheeks in the chill wind. Silence in the Jodrell house: silence that waited upon Gregory's decision.

The two Robertsons came in each wearing his oilskins.

"Are ye coming, Gregory?" They touched their sou'-westers to Samson, and both sedulously avoided the mocking eyes of Sanchia, who waited, out of curiosity, to see what Gregory would do.

"Ay," said Gregory, heavily. He lumbered to his feet. "Reach me my boots, Sanchia."

She went calmly to get the long thigh-boots to which he referred. He was struggling into his jerkin of bullock-hide when she returned. Timothy, Seth and Barnabas ran out to help in the launching of the boats; from the doorway where she leaned, while Gregory got into his sea-boots, Sanchia could see them, up to the waist in water and kelp. The sea was grey and swift, but tolerably calm. Away on the horizon spouted the playful whales, a flash of silver coming now and then from their shining sides. Their bellow reached her like a muffled threat.

As she stood there, the stranger came down the track from the Hawkins's house. She looked sidelong at him; a sort of lightning passed between their two faces, which prudence darkened instantly to indifference.

Someone elbowed her aside; it was Gregory, coming to the door, followed by the Robertsons. Simultaneously the three men saw the stranger; Sanchia saw Jack Robertson nudge his brother, and an unpleasant smile curled their lips. She clenched her hands; what call had they to look like that? They passed her without a word, and her pride winced. Had they not, a little while ago, been eager for her favours, watchful for the frugal expression of her pleasure?

Gregory ignored the dumb man; he raised his arm in response to Samson Hawkins, who had hailed him, grudgingly, from the boats. Peter always took with him his eldest son, leaving the younger two to console their mother. Gregory turned to Sanchia, and laid both hands with a clumsy pressure on her shoulders. She returned his searching look with hardihood. She found it impossible to realize that they belonged to each other; always a little mocking voice sang in her head: "Sanchia *Mullyon*, Sanchia *Mullyon*." He was a stranger, whom she watched impersonally, yet with some appreciation of his bravery, embarking upon a quest so perilous that it might cost him his life. If Sanchia failed to realize the full implication of this, it must be remembered that danger is not taken seriously on the island. Death walks hand in hand with the islanders from childhood; by the time she was ten, Sanchia had seen a score of fatal accidents, and accepted, as a matter of course, that she might herself fall victim to one of the mischievous forces that rule the island. Had she cared for Gregory, her philosophy, like that of the other women, might have broken down. It struck her that if he did not return she would be a widow. How could this affect her? She remained, chained to this rock of the Atlantic, like a modern Andromeda; on the face of things, the dumb man was an unlikely Perseus. They would try to wed her again. That, to the last drop of blood in her body, she was determined to resist.

Seth came bellowing up the beach, stung by one of the "Portuguese men-of-war," as they call the stinging jellyfish. He was in great agony; Gregory loosed her, to attend to the boy's pain, and in view of the whole populace—and to the accompaniment of the thin and solitary cheering of the Reverend Smith Prudhomme—the boats set forth. So small and frail they appeared!—so monstrously incommensurate with the bulk and power of the monsters they set forth to capture!

"More suicide," commented Miss Robbins, tersely, as she turned away to assist the Reverend Smith in shepherding the wildly excited children towards the schoolhouse.

In Gregory's boat were Jed Robertson and Harry Sanguinetti—who might without loss of prestige have excused himself from the adventure; the Sanguinetti family had given their quota to the whaling industry, and Rose, whose time drew near, was hysterical and snivelled most of the day. But Harry had volunteered with the rest. Three others helped to man the boat, and Gregory was thankful that hard rowing gave them little opportunity of personal exchange. Once or twice he caught himself wishing that he might not return: then the impiety of the thought drove him mutely to pray for forgiveness.

Ordinarily the whalers kept their hearts up with jesting, with sea-chanties, and the heavy-handed chaff which passes as witticism upon the island; but a grim silence obtained in each of the boats, and each man knew that, besides his own, the eyes of his companions were set back upon the shore, upon the slight, desolate figure of the dumb man, who stood still, gazing after the retreating boats. They had half expected him to volunteer; he had, in fact, made some ineffectual gesture towards Peter Hawkins, when the boats were launched, and he understood, from the signs of the others, what business was afoot. Peter Hawkins, who had no axe to grind, shook his head, thrusting him aside; but a whisper of indrawn breath warned not a few that the same thought had been in all their minds: that there, on the tossing waters, El Secredo law does not hold good, that justice might be satisfied, without violating the rules of island hospitality.

They had begun by pitying, ended by cold-shouldering him; and the cold-shouldering had developed into a more intense and bitter feeling, a focusing of hatred which,

starting with Sanchia, speedily engulfed the one suspected
of sharing her guilt.

Suddenly, to larboard, shot up a spout of water, so close
that the men in Gregory's boat were caught in the sideways
blowing of the spray. All were taken by surprise, for they
had not expected to come so soon upon their quarry. Still,
at a distance of nearly half a mile, gambolled the young
whales, while within a hundred yards or less a giant
specimen—to judge from the height and force of the water-
spout—threatened their frail craft.

"Haul that main sheet, can't ye?" came the cry from Jed
Robertson; the boat came round with a terrifying slowness
into the wind, staggered, and shot abruptly away; in the
divide of a monster wave appeared a thing resembling a
smooth shoal of black india-rubber. The eyes of the men
were fixed upon it with fear and fascination; another tuft of
vapour rose in the clear air, a croon went up from the
assembled boats: "Ah, blow, blo-o-ow!"

"By James," muttered Peter Hawkins, "she's worth a
hundred an' twenty barrel, that one!" His thin wide mouth
was stretched in a kind of grin; by one of nature's anomalies,
this little, mean-statured man, timorous and self-effacing on
land, developed all the qualities of leadership when faced
with the perils of the sea. The dangers of whale-fishing
went to his head like wine; his insensate courage held the
fears of the others in check; one could not show the white
feather before a man old enough to be one's father.

The great black head of the whale rose slavering from the
trough, drove the waves before it like a destroyer. The
harpooners seized their implements: on came the monster,
towering. . . .

With a queer yelp, like a scared dog, Jed Robertson, with
his gun at his shoulder, pulled the trigger. The whale sank
immediately, and the backwash set the boats rocking so
violently that the attention of all was concentrated upon
maintaining their equilibrium. A growl of dissatisfaction

passed among the crews; it was like Jed Robertson to spoil
the chance of an easy catch by snatching at glory for himself.
As a matter of fact, none was so disconcerted as Jed himself;
he had yielded to a momentary panic, and crouching in the
bottom of the boat, tried now not to see Peter Hawkins
shaking his fist from the farther boat. A rifle-shot has been
known to disable a whale, but only when it hits the head, and
at close range. The utmost Jed had done had been to draw a
bubble of blood, and meanwhile the whale was off to spread
disorder among its companions. Anxious eyes beheld the
cessation of the antics of the more distant whales. Gregory
turned surlily upon Jed Robertson and spoke his mind.

"Thee'rt a fool, Jed! Why canna ye bide thy time like th'
rest on us?"

"Haud thy tongue," snarled Jed. "I can look arter mysen
as well as thou, Gregory Jodrell—I doesn't need telling by a
man as can't look arter his own business, let alone other
folks'!"

The taunt was flagrant. Gregory took it as an ox may
take a stone flung between its brows. Lowering, he
crouched over his oar, with his eyes burning at Jed Robertson.

"Thou'll swallow them words when we're ashore!"

"Yeh!" jeered Jed, "do ye think I be feered o' ye? Ye
canna make a woman feerd o' ye, let alone a man!"

Taunted beyond the limits of his self-control, Gregory
pulled the oar from its rowlocks and made as though to
strike Jed across the head with it. Harry Sanguinetti threw
up a hand and intercepted the oar's lethal descent.

"Take heed, ye pair o' fools! Will ye drown the lot o'
us?"

"We'd better drown," growled Jed, "then there'd be six
men less on Calvary. Then, maybe, yer wife could follow
her fancy wi' yon chap ye've left behind to look arter her!"

The boat rocked fearfully as Gregory made a snatch at the
harpooning tackle that lay almost within reach of his arm.
A heavy wave slapped them amidships, and he was toppled

from his seat, to wallow ignominiously in the water they had shipped. He brought his face, dripping and gasping, from the water, to curse Jed Robertson, who, separated from him by the bulk of Harry, laughed in response. A yell came from Peter Hawkins:

"Have a care, lads! They're coming!"

There was a rush for the various implements; not one of the men in Gregory's boat was an expert whaler, nor was there any practical organization in the distribution of the weapons. The whale-line, inexpertly coiled, engaged their ankles. They jostled and swore and thrust themselves into places.

Suddenly there leapt, almost entirely clear of the sea, a young cachalot; the watchers actually saw the horizon for an instant, between the curve of its body and the water. It dived with uncanny grace, considering its bulk. Harry Sanguinetti rose in the bows, the harpoon raised to his shoulders; in the other boats the harpooners did likewise, awaiting the moment to launch their weapons. To capture this fellow meant a rich yield of spermaceti, worth sufficient flour and potato seed to provision the island for six months.

The moment came: twin cachalots, racing each other like a pair of submarines, their square muzzles snapping sidelong at each other. The senseless heads and eyes of the whales were exposed, and the great livid caverns of their mouths, slavering sea-spume. Peter Hawkins shouted; Harry Sanguinetti plunged his harpoon up to the hitches, and over-balanced, falling overboard. No one had time to attend to him, as he scrambled his way back. Pandemonium raged on the boats, the bomb-guns were discharged and the faint sound of the detonations were drowned in the yells of the harpooners. As whaling, it was an exhibition which would have convulsed an experienced crew. The water boiled above the whales' frenzy; suddenly the lines ran out, and the boats sheered out to escape the wake of the monsters. Presently a tell-tale streak of blood appeared on the surface of the water, increased, spread like an enormous blot of red ink.

Jed Robertson, forgetful of his anger against Gregory, shouted triumph.

Black wrath had settled in Gregory's heart; his hands gripped the oars, as he reflected how easy a matter it would be to push Jed over the bulwarks, and manage the rest with a clumsy jab of an oar—ostensibly out-thrust to succour the capsized man. . . . Again his religion rose to scourge him with the sinfulness of the thought. *Sanchia.* She was responsible for his lapse from grace; Sanchia, who now—God, in heaven, what was she up to now, with the stranger, among the thousand hiding-places of Calvary? A haze like blood swam before his eyes, his whole body dripped with sweat. Dear as she had been to him, how could he set his love for her against his soul's righteousness? Inwardly he cursed her, for the sin she had brought upon him. Technically innocent, he knew himself to be, morally, a murderer; he desired the life of Jed Robertson, who mocked at him.

So lost was he in the blackness of his thoughts, that he heard the cry of Harry Sanguinetti, saw his frenzied bending to the oar, without realizing that it devolved on him as well to play his part in manœuvring the boat out of the danger zone. He caught, tardily, at the oars, a terrific blow caught the boat amidships, plunged her bows under with her stern almost vertically above them. In a chorus of cries, in a rain of flung tackle and cordage, Gregory found himself spinning through air. As he began to fall he saw the stupid, gaping faces of the men beneath him. . . .

They stood on the basalt ridge above the crater, Sanchia and the stranger; looking down at the black tarn, of unconjecturable depth, that lay beneath their feet. The wind curled itself whistling round the basin of rock, the atmosphere was gelid. Her hands and feet pinched with cold, Sanchia balanced, not at all unlike one of the sea-birds, upon a narrow shelf of rock, just beneath the razor-edge of the ridge itself. He, less courageous, crouched, clasping his knees, his eyes, half-horrified, half-fascinated, fixed upon the spectacle of desolation. Lozenged with wide cracks, the crater sloped greyly to the water's edge; across the level of the tarn the waves blew crisply; their ripples ran across the surface of the black shield like the march of a Lilliputian army. Here and there lay the bleaching skeleton of a sheep that had stumbled to death over the ridge; in pockets of the lava lingered snow patches.

Here, if ever, one tasted solitude. Overhead, the clouds piled themselves into the mighty arch of heaven, empty even of birds; they were above the birds, above even the thoughts of human kind. Not thrice in a decade do the islanders mount to the crater; they have enough walking to do in the exercise of their daily duties, without indulging it as a pastime.

She lowered herself to his level, turning upon him a deeply concentrated gaze. By this act of escape she had brought herself nearer to him than ever before; together they shared an experience she had never shared with any human being. Since the day she had discovered it, some strange motive had decoyed her back and back to the crater. Its silence, its sinister withdrawal, had lured her—but not too frequently, for she had the rare instinct of hoarding her pleasure—to seek it again. Her soul laved itself in the silence as her body laved itself in the transparent air. Once, assured of her solitude, she had slipped off all her clothes and stood up naked between water and sky. "Sanchia, Sanchia, Sanchia!" she had said; not quite understanding what she meant, yet sensing in that enfranchisement from all social forms her kinship with the mightier forces. Passionately she longed to tell the dumb man of that experiment; but she had pledged herself to a dumbness that matched his, and the time had not come to break her silence. Never yet had she suffered speech to enter into their intercourse; she took a queer, intellectual pride in discovering other means of surmounting their barrier of silence.

An eagle, perched upon the opposite ridge, surveyed them through a hooded and malignant eye. Instinctively Sanchia lifted her arms with a gesture like flight; as though taking the suggestion from her, the great bird rose and soared above the ridge, then swooped out of sight. She had not meant to scare it; only to show that she, too, longed to fly. She looked down upon her companion to see if he had understood, and found his gaze riveted upon her. Without any movement on his part she knew that his mind read hers. An almost sensual feeling of luxury overcame her, in the completeness of their understanding.

Abruptly she held out her hand and drew him to his feet; together, hand in hand, they began to cross the crackling and flaky surface of the decayed lava towards the water's edge. For the first time she was conscious of physical satisfaction in touching him; they had hardly done so before—a fleeting brush of fingers, perhaps: and she had bathed his foot. Always their communion had seemed too profound to require physical expression.

Chill struck from the water's surface towards their lightly clad bodies; she felt him shiver, but knew that he had no immediate desire to quit the crater. The solitude bound them closer together. Suddenly she was consumed by the desire to know his inner thoughts, to come by an exacter knowledge of his mind. She was jealous of what he withheld from her. For a little while she struggled against the wave which seemed to beat her against him; she stood stiffening beside the tarn, fighting an inclination as impossible as it was barbaric to seize him and shake silence from his lips.

A low cloud touched the opposite edge of the crater: tore like chiffon on the serrated ridge, and floated in little tatters of white against the black and grey of the cup. Sanchia's breath quickened and hung about her like a veil in the icy air.

Swiftly she turned to him, breast to breast; their bodies touching, bosom and thigh, the cloud of their breaths mingled, and his eyes, looking down into hers, sent a dizziness through her whole being. A fluttering like the wings of little birds took possession of her, and words broke from her lips—two words of which she was less than conscious, that summed the whole depth of her yearning:

"*Tell me*," said Sanchia, deeply.

She felt his hands take hers, and press them either side of his thighs; his mouth descended towards hers, and their lips met, held each other—for an infinitude of time. So still were their bodies that they might have been creatures petrified in the icy water of the tarn.

She began to tremble for the moment of withdrawal; never had she felt so complete identification with any human being. If he left her it would be like a rending of the flesh, just as painful, just as horrible.

They came apart, simultaneously, looking gently upon each other, illuminated by the same light which shone in each other's eyes. And she knew certain things that she had never known before. That she must quit Gregory; and that her soul and her body alike belonged to the dumb man; and that the bird which fluttered in her breast had folded its wings and was still. She felt tamed, gentle, compliant—she who since childhood had waged continual war with life. A woman's mind is almost always practical in such crises; she began instantly to plan the alteration of her scheme of existence. Everything must be different now: different and happy. When the ship came she would go away with her lover. She did not know how such a matter might be arranged, but she could ask Miss Robbins. Her whole mind strained towards Miss Robbins, as her body and soul turned to the stranger as a flower to the sun.

Hand in hand, as they had come—but how differently!— they recrossed the lava cracks and scrambled again to the ridge, where the wind met them with a rush that all but carried the stranger, unprepared, back into the crater again. Sanchia, used to it, steadied him with her arm. They crawled cautiously across the edge, and rested for a moment, looking down upon the slopes that lay beneath.

The islands hid the whaling party from them, but wherever Sanchia and her companion looked were the bent backs of the diggers at work on the potato patches. Old and young share the duty of preparing the land, and schooling hours are reduced to a minimum during this period, so that the elder lads may help their parents. Straggling up from the pens, where they had been imprisoned overnight, in order that the manure might be collected and folded into the freshly dug earth to fertilize it, came the sheep; from the heights above they appeared minute, like toys from a Noah's ark. Sunlight slipped shyly about the island, interspersed with cloud shadows, whose passing chill struck through the clothing to limbs sun-warmed. Away from the shadowy hollow of the crater it was much milder, although this was still the island's winter; but spring was at hand, coming across the Atlantic in the likeness of an ice-maiden; far out beyond the farthest island a mighty berg was calving: they could see the dark divisional scar seaming its pale side.

A few yards below where they rested Sanchia knew of a tiny cave, a favourite resort of her own; thither, from time to time, she had carried and strewn armfuls of hay-grass and dried moss, the same that the islanders use for thatching.

The short day was slipping noonwards; she knew that she should be preparing the midday meal for Samson and the boys. Her thoughts brought them to the mouth of the little cavern.

At last she knew that she must go. Lost she had been to the slipping of the sun seawards, to the gradual chilling of the air, to the shrill wind that sang about their hiding-place. Dusk had invaded the hollow; she remembered, quite calmly, that she had neglected her household duties, that the boys and Samson had doubtless had to find their food else-where. They would be searching for her. As she smoothed her gown and re-pinned her hair, she felt no fear, but a kind of calm triumph. It was as though she had begun to live, as though she had tasted immortality. The stranger's face was near and tender in the half-light. She delighted now in his gestures, which seemed to have acquired a new fluency, as though in the act of possessing her he had gained an eloquence that had been lacking before. She pointed downwards, smiling, and he nodded his head.

They descended together, walking weakly and carefully, each leaning on the other. She was conscious of him as a male; her erstwhile sense of protection was merged in her submission to his conquering power.

"The boats have come back," said Sanchia, suddenly, for she had forgotten to be dumb. She remembered, with her first touch of guilt, that Gregory had warned her to have the tubs ready, of potash-lye, for rinsing the spermaceti when the oil should have dripped off it. That was not done, nor had she remembered to go to the Martyns' for the tin baths to catch the priceless drippings. There was a strange quiet upon the beach; they must be getting on with their work, somewhere: very likely over at The Rescue, which was an easy place to land the whales.

Just as they approached the upper slope of the orchards, heads bobbed into sight over a hollow of the pasture beyond. Someone shouted.

"They have come to seek us," said Sanchia, calmly. No thought of fear possessed her. She walked towards the approaching people quietly, her head held high, and, at her side, the dumb man walked with an equal pride. The shout was repeated; her heart gave a sudden tick as she saw fists brandished, marked the savage and threatening aspect of the approaching group, men and women, whose shouts were carried backwards towards the sea, so that she could not hear what they were saying. Terror for her companion checked her advance; she pressed her two hands against his breast.

"Go! Go! They mean trouble. Janet Hawkins will see to you."

He shook his head decisively, removed her hands with his own. She cast a pitiful and apprehensive glance over his light and fragile-looking body; would strength be given her to defend him, as well as herself, if need arose?

Suddenly a figure broke ahead of the others: it seemed to

make some gesture of forbidding, of command, which the rest ignored. She now saw sticks in their hands, and as she took an involuntary step backwards, half minded to fly the way she had come, a stone flew through the air and fell within a yard of her foot. The leading figure became menacing, not to her, but to the crowd shouting at his heels; it was the Reverend Smith Prudhomme, and, for the first time in her life, Sanchia was thankful to see him. Yet what could he do against so many?—all of whom, it was only too clear, were inimically disposed towards her.

The wind shifted, carried the voices towards her.

"In the name of God!" the Reverend Smith was yelling, "I forbid you!"

"There she is—the strumpet! Let's at her! We'll l'arn her to mend her ways!"

Sanchia felt her spirit cower, while her body remained insolently erect before them.

"An' her fancy man! Let's hold o' him—we'll l'arn him to play tricks wi' Calvary wives!"

"Hold your tongue, Jim Hawkins! Stand back, I tell you! Sanchia—Sanchia, for God's sake——"

A stick was in the Reverend Smith's hand, but it was being used on her behalf; she recognized that. His staring eyes, his gaping mouth towards her, he struck backwards at the people pressing on his heels. Came a shower of stones, one caught her on the cheekbone, and she felt the blood spurt, even as the dumb man flung her behind him. She heard the dull crack of a stone on his skull, but would not, for pride's sake, cry aloud. He tottered, and once again it was her arm that suppported him.

"Stand aside, you!" cried the Reverend Smith. "Sanchia, we have come to fetch you home—Gregory——"

Before the words were out of his mouth, he was over-whelmed. She saw him go down, striking with his clenched fist upwards at the face of Jim Hawkins, in whom a devil seemed to have come to life. Gregory: what had he begun to say about Gregory? She felt herself seized, a swinging blow caught her under the ear, someone's hand clutched her dress and ripped it from the clumsy gathers at her waist. They were striking at her—with their sticks, with their fists. She dimly heard the Reverend Smith Prudhomme cursing— yes, cursing, as he struggled to rise from beneath the trampling feet that took no heed of his prostrate body.

Her terror was mostly for the dumb man; for herself she now felt an almost insolent indifference to life. Each blow fell distinctly upon her defenceless body, yet she hardly heeded them, thrusting away again and again the arms that obscured her view of the stranger, as he waged his pitifully unequal war against the incensed islanders. A moan escaped her lips as she saw him reel before a chest blow, delivered with the force of a sledge-hammer; the blood from a cut on her brow ran into her eye, she raised a hand to wipe it away, and a voice—a high, incisive soprano—rang through the bourdon of angry murmuring: "What on earth are you up to? Sanchia! Come to me."

It was Miss Robbins who, arriving breathlessly, caught Jim Hawkins a stinging slap on the ear, seized Nell Barker's wrist and twisted her aside, and ranged herself belligerently in front of Sanchia. The crowd fell back, resentful but non-plussed; none felt any desire to injure Miss Robbins, several among the men had a very good reason for not doing so. Harry Sanguinetti, still wearing his oilskins, his beard curled into little crisp ringlets with the sea-water, spoke on behalf of them all.

"We've gotten no ill-feeling towards ye, ma'am, but ye'd best keep out o' this."

"Ay—let's at her—at the hussy!" shrilled the little Barker woman; vicious as a witch and dancing with her passion. The women are worse than the men, thought Miss Robbins, glancing round the circle of faces. The Reverend Smith had struggled to his feet, and was groaning with the pain of his broken ribs; his white face, with the sweat rolling down it, turned wildly towards Miss Robbins. In their astonishment they had loosed their hold upon the dumb man, and he was gone like a hare, racing up into the mountain.

"Thank you, Miss Robbins," the Reverend Smith was gasping; she cut short further speech with a peremptory gesture.

"Are you all out of your senses?" she cried, sharply. "The only thing that matters is to get Sanchia to her husband. Sanchia, Gregory has had an accident—the whale-boat——"

Sanchia, half-dazed, felt her arm seized in a determined clasp; she was hurried, stumbling, down the stony path; the rest followed, growling, like dogs brought to heel by the lash. When they entered the house of Samson Jodrell the place seemed full of Gregory's groaning.

CHAPTER XII

FOR how long did the mournful echo of those groans ring
in the ears of Sanchia? It seemed as though there had been
no previous life to this: as though, as long as she had known
him, Gregory had lain there on his tumbled bed, resisting
attempts to make his rest easier, marking the hours with the
groans dragged up from those depths where life had ceased
to be. The injury was to his spine; so much the Reverend
Smith, who had studied medicine in preparation for his
"call" to Calvary, was able to pronounce with authority.
But how to treat it was another matter; one could only hope
that the paralysis would advance quickly. Meanwhile, drugs
were given; at first in cautious doses, then desperately, in
quantities that would have horrified the faculty, because it
was so terrible to watch the agony of a man like Gregory
Jodrell. It was possible, the Reverend Smith told Samson,
that Gregory felt nothing of his major injury; but the bones
of the upper arms were broken, and a splintered collar-bone
stuck through the flesh, until coaxed back by the minister's
primitive attempts at surgery; they had pulled a strip of the
shattered gunwale of the boat out of his chest, where it had
avoided the heart only by a hair's breadth. "Another six-
teenth of an inch, and Gregory would have been spared all
this," the Reverend Smith had confessed to Miss Robbins,
on whose arm, unwillingly, he was obliged to lean, as
he returned to the mission house, after accomplishing
what he could; he was sick and faint with the pain of
his own displaced ribs. "It is indeed difficult, in cases
like these, to trace out the providence of an all-wise
God."

214

"It seems to me very pretty proof of the existence of the devil," rejoined Miss Robbins, tersely.

"Why doesn't he die?" asked Sanchia, of one of those who stood with her beside the sick man's bed. Suspicious eyes flashed inquiry upon her, but she was unconscious of their scrutiny. The next few weeks were to prove how difficult it was to kill such a man as Gregory Jodrell.

The sympathy of the island turned towards Samson Jodrell, who acted as a man in a trance. He sat beside Gregory, refusing the food that Sanchia mechanically offered him. At the end of a week his daughter came.

"Ye mun come an' eat wi' us, Father; 'tis no manner o' good ye can do our Gregory wi' starvin' yoursen."

"An' leave my son to yon woman? Don't ye know"—the old man clutched her sleeve and brought his mouth close to her ear—"don't ye know she's naught but biding her chance to get rid o' him for good an' all?"

"Nay, now, Father; Sanchia's a bad woman, but she's not bad enough for that. Don't ye mind now how she used to cry when geese was killed? She can't abide death. Come away wi' us for a bit, an' maybe there'll be a change when ye come back again."

"I'd as lief kill her wi' my own hands first."

"Nay, ye don't know what ye're saying. Besides, Gregory wants her, an' ye canna gainsay him while he's sick."

The old man flushed with jealousy. Strange as it appeared, the name of Sanchia was the only intelligible word that crossed Gregory's lips. Day and night its syllables mingled with his groaning. She came, obedient as a dog to its master; one would have thought, to have seen her, that here was a meek, devoted wife, whose life-long endeavour was to obey her husband's command. If she was conscious of espionage, she did not show it. Silently, her whole being drawn to a sharp point of concentration, she went about her service, and, when her tasks were done, sat sewing, or idle, as the spirit moved her, on the opposite side of the bed to the bitter, resentful old man, whose presence she ignored.

Maggie Robertson, loyal as ever in her kindliness, had taken and added Seth, Barnabas and Timothy to her already overcrowded household. She was the only one among the women to show Sanchia any sympathy; Sophia Mullyon locked her house doors against her daughter, and passed long days in bitter weeping, not for Sanchia, but for Mullyon pride, that had been dragged in the dust. And the island, beneath its surface of quiet busyness, whispered and seethed and bubbled and waited.

When the Jodrell boys were taken under Maggie Robertson's roof, Miss Robbins offered to find herself other accommodation; she was not, in fact, sorry for the excuse to do so. The Robertson household was as Spartan as Samson Jodrell's, and she had an idea that she would be cosier, despite the slovenly housekeeping, with young Rose Sanguinetti. Rose had made overtures: had given Miss Robbins to understand that she would be very welcome. The baby would arrive any day, and she was willing to make herself useful. Even with the new-comer thrown in, she was likely to be more comfortable in the Sanguinettis' little cottage than at the Robertsons', which, to Miss Robbins's fancy, was growing more and more to resemble a very primitive and indifferently run hotel. It was impossible to find any quiet corner in which to elude the attentions of Betty and Martha; Maggie herself, taciturn at the beginning, had developed a confidential garrulity, for which, reflected Miss Robbins, she had only herself to blame. The literary sap was rising; at any moment it might overflow, and Miss Robbins was not minded to waste a single drop of the precious fluid.

Her suggestion was, however, taken as a personal affront by both the Robertsons; she spent the better part of a morning in appeasing the deeply injured Maggie.

"Don't you see," she cried, for the eleventh time, "it's

not that I want to leave you; I'm just trying to spare you a little trouble."

"Time enough to talk o' trouble when I start grumbling," sniffed Maggie. "What do ye think the neighbours 'ud find to say if ye quitted me now?"

Miss Robbins resigned with a sigh her hopes of escape to the Sanguinettis, and threw out her hands with a gesture of defeat.

"Oh, have it your own way. But I don't see where you're going to put us all. There isn't another inch of space in the boys' bedroom; you and your husband can't turn out, and you can't put Seth and Barnabas with the girls in the kitchen. You need my room—unless you're thinking of putting the boys in with me!—and there, I must say, I draw the line. One must preserve a little privacy—even on Calvary!"

"There's the shed down by the wood-pile: we can make the lads a bed down there-by," said Maggie, stoutly. "Gi'e them a blanket or two and they'll sleep sound as tops!"

Miss Robbins gave a little hop.

"Now, see here, Maggie. I've got an idea. Let me have the shed——"

"Never!" cried Maggie. "It wouldn't be seemly."

"Seemly be damned," cried Miss Robbins, heedlessly. "I *want* the shed. I'm going to start writing a book soon, and it's the very place for me. I can get on with my work without disturbing anyone, and I'll look after it myself——"

"That shed," declared Maggie, "isn't fit to put a horse in."

"Nonsense. You were going to put Seth and Barnabas and Timothy there. Now don't argue any more, there's a good soul. Let me have some bedding, and I'll go and fix it now."

Not so easily did Maggie yield to her guest's importunities; by the time she had carried her point, Miss Robbins felt as limp as a clout, and a burning hatred for humanity in general inflamed her mind. Seeking solitude and silence, she dashed away to Sail Point, waving vaguely in the direction of Sanchia's windows as she passed the Jodrell house. Twice she had offered to relieve Sanchia in her vigil, and each time her offer had been politely refused. Miss Robbins guessed, wrongly, that Sanchia was suffering from remorse, and decided to bide her time until this, the most fleeting of human emotions, had run its course. It annoyed her slightly, that Sanchia should indulge so feeble an emotion; she would have preferred, for the sake of her novel, that Sanchia should continue to treat life high-handedly; she promised herself to rally the girl, bring her to a more healthy frame of mind. It was, after all, no fault of hers that Gregory had come to grief in the whaling expedition. Sanchia was quite intelligent enough to have that pointed out to her, along with the weakness of regret.

And the stranger? Here she had come up against the formidable quality of the islanders' capacity for silence. To all her questionings they turned blandly ignorant faces.

"But he may be dead!" cried Miss Robbins. Impassivity expressed their profound indifference if this were so. They did not choose to share their curiosities, their heart-burnings with a stranger. She called on Janet Hawkins, and was received almost with hostility, when she discovered her mission. Janet Hawkins clearly felt that the matter was no concern of hers, and took no pains to conceal her own satisfaction at the disappearance of her lodger.

"But to starve to death, Janet——!" expostulated Miss Robbins. Janet Hawkins stared, and turned to her ironing.

"Far better to shoot him outright," said Miss Robbins, indiscreetly. Janet's face set in lines of disapproval; her lips wore the pinched, sanctimonious expression that the Calvary women assumed with their Sunday garments, as she replied:

"The sixth commandment is, 'Thou shalt do no murder.'"

"Nonsense," said Miss Robbins, crisply, and quitted the scene. She got as little satisfaction from the Reverend Smith Prudhomme, who refused, categorically, to discuss the matter.

"But are you going to let the man die?" she demanded.

"I dare say he will not die," answered the Reverend Smith, cryptically.

"You know something!"

"If I do," answered the Reverend Smith, "I must reserve my information for the present."

As she scrambled towards Sail Point, her sharp eyes scanned the rocks above for a glimpse of the stranger, who, she was convinced, was in hiding there.

The sky that evening elected to give one of its semi-tropical displays of colour at sunset. From west to east ran the flaming banners of the setting sun; little islands of emerald and blue floated briefly upon a golden flood, were submerged and glimmered for a moment before melting away. The Atlantic blazed; the bergs—daily more numerous on the far horizon—turned to the mauvish pink of strawberry ice; the farther seas were like a bed of tulips; even the rock caught in its sombre surface some warm reflection from the surrounding glow. Miss Robbins, lonely as a gull on the farthest limit of the Point, thought freakishly of Piccadilly Circus: of taxis skirmishing like ants, of the great swaying buses with *General* painted along their scarlet sides; of Bentleys and Minervas and Rolls Royces jostling each other for pride of place; of crowds disgorging themselves from the matinées; of an aeroplane writing *Daily Mail* in smoke upon the sky; of vanished Eros, and the desolate space where the flower-women now sit, like sirens cheated of their prey by the circular sweep of traffic which defeats all but the most determined pedestrians; of the photographs of "Mr. Cochran's young ladies," and the display of pyjamas, douillettes and boudoir caps in Swan and Edgar's windows.

All these things, once an essential part of her existence,

seemed to have retreated to a remoter world of fairyland,
that became translucent and dissolved in the green ridges of
the Atlantic, that piled themselves as far as eye could see.
Gilbert Murray's translation of Euripides sang in her mind
with a cadence rhythmical as the rise and fall of waves:
"Birds, birds everywhere. . . ." She was living in a world
created for winds and waves and birds. Above her climbed
the Peak, whereon Jebusa Horne had seen his vision of a
fiery cross. Its deeply striated sides veiled their blackness in
the thin glimmer of gold that seemed to cover every object;
the very wings of the sea-birds, as they floated from their
crannies in the rock, seemed gilded with that tenuous brightness; the surface of the kelp was minutely gemmed with
glittering drops of moisture, here and there merging into a
metallic sheet.

Miss Robbins, with a flash of most unusual humility, felt
herself to be an intruder; her small figure shrank, became
diffident, even humble. She lost—temporarily—the aggressiveness which is so often an attribute of small, insignificant
people, an aggressiveness which arises more often from the
fear of being overlooked, and, unintentionally, of course,
injured, by other more powerful beings. She looked at the
weed piled at her feet, and another tag floated into her mind:
"We are like seaweed, floating upon the dark tide of eternity." Who had said that? Not that it mattered; all that
mattered was that someone had had a beautiful thought, and
had taken the trouble to clothe it in words that lingered long
after the speaker was forgotten.

Never again could she leave El Secredo. It had made her
its own. Gradually it would take and mould her into its own
lava-like immortality. When she died she would become a
little pinch of El Secredo earth. "If I should die, think only
this of me. . . ." All her life Miss Robbins had gone about
priding herself upon her lack of patriotism. To inscribe
herself British on her passport had been a challenge to all
her deep-rooted objections to affixing the label to her
nationality. "I am a citizen of the world," she was wont to

say, proudly; then the little teasing onlooker in her inner-most would remind her that this was a fairly pretentious statement to make on the strength of a few visits to Paris, Oberammergau in 1920 (from which she returned super-ciliously, with a lot of opinions on commercialized Chris-tianity) and a trip under the auspices of Messrs. George Lunn (Tour UW, Twenty Days Round Italy with Naples and the Hill Towns—including Motor Tour from Perugia to Assisi). She disliked the companionships and the dis-illusionments of cheap travel and could not afford to travel luxuriously; equally she hated the heartiness and physical vigour of those enthusiasts who periodically exhorted her to join them on camping holidays. "The *only* way to see a country, my dear." "What does it matter?" she would cry. "In imagination I have visited Karnak; I have stood on every conceivable bridge at midnight; I have preceded Stella Benson through China and know every pagoda and lily-pond between Hong Kong and Pekin; I have talked with the kings of Mandalay and looked from the tomb of Nedjibeh Hanum across the Sweet Waters of the Bos-phorus." Insularity was her favourite windmill; against it she never ceased to tilt with the dexterity of a female Quixote. "Home is no matter of red or black earth; it is a state of the mind. I carry my home with me wherever I go."

She swayed on the slippery rocks, challenging El Secredo, with her hands in her pockets, to forbid her adopting it as her home. She felt with pride that she had succeeded in shedding the complexities of civilization more rapidly and more completely than most women would have done in her place; she took some mildly malicious pleasure in picturing one or two of her sister novelists in the same situation. Madge Bendysshe, for example, robbed of artificial aids to the famous "personality" exploited as assiduously as that of a film star by her photographer and publicity agents, would become—simply jelly. Violet Atholl—who admitted that she became vacuous outside a radius of thirty miles from

Hyde Park Corner! Ruth Corby—one could go on piling them up: all the literary Titanesses whose volumes elbowed hers off the bookstalls—with an occasional doubtful exception, Miss Robbins saw them being crushed out of their petty, padded existence by El Secredo.

"I want to die here!" she cried aloud, and almost believed she meant it. She stretched out her arms towards the Peak—and then the enormous indifference of Nature made her feel that she was being presumptuous, theatrical. What did it matter to El Secredo who died there? Antic imagination leapt out of bounds, gave her a grave like Stevenson's: "Under the wide and starry sky." Who on earth would care where Lenox Robbins, the obscure author of a few second-line novels, was buried? The Homeric laughter of the Atlantic thundered in her ears, there was mockery in the shriek of the sea-birds. Year by year these died, in their thousands; their feathery bodies decayed, the winds bleached their skeletons, these crumbled into dust, became part of El Secredo. Some day she would be one with the sea-birds, and her soul, if this survived, would squeak about the caverns, a small strange thing, alien in an alien company. It would be better, then, to be near something one had known.

The golden veil was wearing thin; shadows were pouring themselves into the rock crevices, a chill wind stole across the water, ruffling the waves, stirring the kelp. She stood very still, with her eyes fixed upon the rock. Like ink, the shadows, blotched in beneath overhanging bits of rock; almost immediately above her were the pirates' caves; in the mouth of one she saw a faint movement. Birds? How rapidly twilight fell! The rim of the sun glittered for a second on the horizon, then dipped, and in that odd, almost theatrical way, all the light shifted. Like iron grey now, the rock, its erstwhile sun-warmed surface chilling to the wind. That movement again, in the caves: she narrowed her eyes. Not birds; something larger. So intense was her gaze that she forgot to wink. With a sense of profound hallucination she began to see that the rock face was alive with moving shapes, human in proportion, but performing such antics as surely no human being could have achieved: running, leaping, posing in defiance of gravitation. Unclad, and in colour hardly less earthy than the rock itself. These were the ghosts of El Secredo! She caught her breath, wondering if any but herself had seen them; Sanchia, perhaps——? They writhed and melted, as though the wind had taken a handful of greyish dust and twisted it for a moment into human form, then scattered it again.

Miss Robbins shuddered slightly. Imagination, of course; there was nothing there. She became her normal self, a small, nervous woman, whose chief weapon against life was her self-assurance, which was largely a matter of bluff. Rather a tawdry and impertinent little person; yes, some kindly disposed individual might call her scheming "sheer femininity;" women were supposed to enjoy wire-pulling, but to do it "nicely" they were supposed to exert their wiles on behalf of someone else. She was working for her own ends; putting ideas into Sanchia's head, encouraging the girl to behave lawlessly—just for the sake of her wretched novel. Photographing the islanders with the persistence of a journalist, laying bare the privacy of their homes and minds—for a royalty of (how did her contract run?) fifteen per cent. on the first two thousand. . . . An ungraceful way of returning hospitality; but if one is less creative than photographic, what is one to do? In coming to El Secredo she had not expected it to be like this; she had not expected to find, for instance, that money had no currency. Her intention had been to pay for her lodgings in hard cash: a concession which surely allows one liberty of the pen?

"One must live," said Miss Robbins, as though in answer to some objection; and came slowly homewards.

Sanchia was standing in her doorway.

"How's Gregory?" called Miss Robbins.

"He's no different," replied Sanchia; she spoke half

absently, with her ear cocked to catch a summons from within. It came: Miss Robbins heard the loud, groaning "San-chia." The girl darted in, waiting for no second call. Miss Robbins thought: "She might never have set eyes on him!"—and her reference was not to Gregory Jodrell. For the first time she thought of Sanchia as the islanders thought of her: heartless. It seemed inhuman that she could so utterly dismiss her lover, without knowing of him whether he were alive or dead. The suspicion struck her that Sanchia had found some way of seeing or communicating with him; only to be dismissed as an impossibility. Samson Jodrell played watch-dog day and night over her actions, and his vigilance was enforced by every man and woman on the island. "Well," thought Miss Robbins, "I suppose death is a very unimportant thing on El Secredo: but I'd thought better of her."

Her annoyance with Sanchia abated when she came to inspect the new quarters which Maggie Robertson had prepared for her. The shed—built of stone, with a roof of planks and tarpaulin held down by boulders—had been swept and garnished; that is to say the floor, after scouring, had been sprinkled with clean sand, and round the inner walls hides were hung to exclude draughts as far as was possible. Lighting, beyond a narrow lancet, looking towards the bluff, there was none; a small oil-lamp smouldered in a niche, filling the place with smoke and stench, and the bed was an impromptu affair of planks and trestles; yet Miss Robbins, who had been so pernickety over the divan she had ordered from Waring's to replace the brassy four-poster of her landlady's choice, was enraptured. For the first time since her arrival on the island she was to enjoy privacy, and the prospect charmed her.

So impatient was she to enter into possession of her kingdom that she gulped her supper, and, on an impulse of hospitality, rushed round to the Reverend Smith Prudhomme, to bid him to a house-warming.

"Tea and cigarettes," she explained. "I'm really quite

good at them now. I found a heap of old church magazines
one day — the paper's exactly right — thin and tindery;
but you have to be careful it doesn't crack as you roll
it. Tastes a bit inky, perhaps, but you soon get used to
that."

"Many thanks," said the Reverend Smith. "I really
think I prefer my pipe."

"Do as you like, but come along. How are the ribs?"

"Mending nicely, I think; not perhaps in the pattern
intended, but——!" The Reverend Smith grimaced over
his mild joke.

A few minutes later Miss Robbins closed her door with an
air of triumph.

"Not so bad, do you think?"

"Hrrum — very cosy indeed," agreed the Reverend Smith,
trying hard not to look at the bed, which was indeed a
difficult object to avoid, for it occupied an important section
of the space in the little chamber. Miss Robbins, busy with
the oil-stove, commandeered from Maggie, did not observe
his embarrassment; even had she been less occupied, the
darkness would have covered it from her.

"Sit down. Where? On the bed, of course. I shall get
Samson Hawkins to make me a chair, eventually; Maggie
can't spare any."

"I hope you have a lock on this door," said the Reverend
Smith.

Miss Robbins lifted her head to stare, suppressed a giggle,
and asked: "Whatever for?"

"You certainly should not sleep here alone, without some
such precautions."

"I'll see to it some time. Do you have much house-
breaking on El Secredo?"

"Permit me to say," said the Reverend Smith who,
having looked about him vainly for a less compromising
resting-place, was obliged to lower himself gingerly upon
the extreme end of the bed, "that, as a woman, you are the
object of considerable interest on Calvary."

"I suppose you mean Henry Martyn," she replied, calmly. "He's rather a bore; can't you give him a hint about it?"

The Reverend Smith produced his pipe and looked thoughtfully at Miss Robbins.

"You understand these people much better than you pretend," he stated, and hesitated over striking a match. "It seems hardly suitable to smoke in a lady's—hrrum—bedroom."

"Call it a combined; I once went on tour with a theatrical company for a little while. We don't bother about that kind of thing. Light up and don't be suburban. I hope you like your tea strong, because I don't know how much got into the pot and how much I spilt. This will probably ruin your digestion," she added hospitably.

"Thank you, it will be delicious, I am sure," said the Reverend Smith, primly. He was a little uneasy in his present situation. Unconventional; and the populace of Calvary was not in a mood to overlook the conventions. Miss Robbins continued, however, in happy ignorance of her guest's embarrassment, to make herself very comfortable with a pillow wedged between the wall and her spine, at the head of the bed; the little oil-lamp continued to give its dubious light, which attracted the night-flying insects of El Secredo in hundreds through the little unglazed lancet, and, in spite of the lack of other illumination, there was an air of ease and intimacy about the little cabin that comforted them both, and sent their minds wandering back to England. Perhaps, thought Miss Robbins, she had not been quite sincere in wishing to live and die on El Secredo.

"It's like a forbidden feast in the dormitory after lights out," she said, sipping her tea too noisily for good manners.

"Ah—yes!" It was really excessively embarrassing to sit on this woman's bed in the dark, with her leg—positively her leg, which she had not had the modesty to cover with her skirt!—within reach of one's hand. It was teasing, to have a woman's leg within reach of one's hand. He would drink his tea as quickly as possible—she had made it confoundedly hot!—and go, trusting to heaven that neither Thomas Mullyon nor any of the elder folk of Calvary should observe his departure.

"When is Gregory Jodrell going to die?"

"Our lives are in God's hand," intoned the Reverend Smith. A sigh came out of the darkness, and an angry and impatient rustling of the straw mattress evinced the disagreement of his companion.

"How can you do the things you do, and mouth such shop-soiled twaddle?"

"I beg your pardon?"

"I suppose it hasn't occurred to you that the way you came to Sanchia's rescue the other day was a remarkably plucky act."

"My duty as a priest," said the Reverend Smith, simply.

"No doubt; but a priest with two broken ribs? Priests don't bear charmed lives, you know. They were all out of their senses with rage, and you might have been the victim, together with Sanchia."

"You forget that you shared—and no doubt mitigated—my danger." Privately he had considered Miss Robbins's intervention an act of officiousness; even as he lay beneath the feet of his aggressors he had been profoundly convinced that his authority could not fail to quell them. He had resented Miss Robbins's arrival as he had resented Tom Mullyon's rescue of him from the burning mission. He was inclined to be greedy over his heroisms.

"Nonsense; they wouldn't have touched me," boasted Miss Robbins. "I'm a stranger and a woman, and I haven't done them any harm. Why don't you give Gregory an overdose one day? You'd be benefiting both him and Sanchia."

"Rather a macabre form of jesting, don't you think, Miss Robbins?"

"Who's jesting? Excuse me—these fleas are really awful; they seem to find me irresistible."

"I caught the largest one I have ever seen the other day," said the Reverend Smith, who always became animated on the topic of fleas. "Fully an eighth of an inch in length. I heard it first—dropping on the writing pad I had left on my desk. I lit the lamp——"

"And for goodness' sake," said Miss Robbins, to whom fleas were a simple bore, "what has become of the dumb man? He can't just disappear in an island of this size. I suppose he's hiding somewhere—unless some of these barbarians have caught him and made away with him. Anyhow, the poor fellow'll soon starve to death, unless he puts in an appearance with the white flag, soon."

The Reverend Smith Prudhomme cleared his throat.

"I think it would be prudent for us to restrain our curiosity with regard to him."

"All very well for you to talk about restraining the curiosity. I believe you know where he is. If he's on the Peak, I don't envy him." She caught her breath, suddenly remembering her odd vision of the afternoon. "Oh, this is a grim place—a horrible place!" she heard herself crying, unexpectedly. Could it really be she who said the words? she who had longed with all her soul to merge herself in El Secredo earth for ever? "I suppose there are ghost stories here, the same as everywhere else?"

"The islanders are not, I am glad to say, imaginative."

"But, good heavens, man, you don't need an imagination to see what *is!*" She checked herself sharply; she had been about to tell him of the creatures—devils—whatever they were—that she had seen upon the rock at sunset.

"There are always odd shadow effects at night," said the Reverend Smith. She thought: "He has seen them himself, and won't admit it!"

"What would you do if you saw a devil?" she asked, curiously.

"Happily the powers of evil cannot assume material

form," he answered, with the pompousness she found so irritating. "One would, I suppose, pray."

"It's to be hoped the dumb man knows plenty of prayers," she said, flippantly. "I wonder if Sanchia——"

"One does not know, of course," he said, misunderstanding her, "what relations existed between her and the stranger."

"But one naturally assumes the worst!"

"Sanchia does not bear a good character," he rejoined, stiffly. "Hrrum——" said the Reverend Smith, and lowered his voice. "For his own sake, one does not wish to push inquiry too far, but—I have put a little food on a rock near The Rescue each night, and by morning it is always gone."

"Do you mean to say," said Miss Robbins, in an altered tone, "that you, with your broken ribs, have gone scrambling along the shore after nightfall, to do this thing for a man of whom you thoroughly disapprove?"

"Starvation," said the Reverend Smith, as though ashamed of himself, "is an ugly thing."

"Why do you let me be so rude to you?" cried Miss Robbins, impulsively. "You know you're *solid* all through, and I—well, I'm just a windbag which, now and again, mostly by accident, produces a bit of tune. I don't mean to throw the slightest shadow of doubt on your intelligence, but I suppose it hasn't escaped your notice that animals might have got the food, rather than the person for whom it is intended?"

"I put it in a pail with a very tight lid," answered the Reverend Smith, without offence. "You see, I remembered he used to be very much attached to that piece of beach, and it is relatively easy to gain it without observation—there being liberal cover of brush and rock for a man who needs to make use of them. Luckily we have had moonlight nights lately, and the pail could not fail to be noticed—Maggie Robertson keeps my household gods exceedingly bright."

"You've got to give up this nightly scramble," said Miss Robbins, abruptly. "Now don't argue, for pity's sake, there's a good man. You, with your broken ribs!—and I'll bet you're running a temperature each night."

The Reverend Smith did not find it necessary to mention that his temperature had not been normal for several weeks.

"Nonsense. I can manage it perfectly well." There was no doubt however, from the tone of the Reverend Smith's voice, that he was sensible of Miss Robbins's approval, and by no means indifferent to it. This woman, for all her ungraceful means of self-expression—could she possibly write as badly as she talked?—was not devoid of the saving grace of respect.

"I'll go," she said, stubbornly.

"You can't," said the Reverend Smith. "I have every reason to believe, Miss Robbins, that you are under close observation, for your—hrrum—if I may call it so, rather indiscreet sympathy with Sanchia Jodrell."

"Sympathy!" exploded Miss Robbins. "I have no sympathy with her! She's behaved like a fish over this. She doesn't care two hoots what has happened to the man she's supposed to love——"

"I sincerely trust," said the Reverend Smith, "that she does not love him. If Gregory's accident has been the means of bringing her to a sense of her duties—God moves in a mysterious way, His wonders to——"

"Whatever Gregory's accident has done for Sanchia," said Miss Robbins, "I'll freely wager the advance on my next book that *duty* doesn't enter into it. Sentiment—cloying sentiment, if you like; but never duty! Why, the word won't fit her! It's like a child's cap on a grown woman!"

"Now you're antagonistic again!" protested the Reverend Smith, fretfully.

"Sorry. When you keep your mouth shut I can admire

and respect you really extraordinarily; but you do say such
foolish things. Mr. Prudhomme, this fellow is in a really bad
way, in spite of your provisions. He must be. He has never
made a proper recovery from the wreck; it's bitter on the
Peak at night——"

"I dare say he has made a comfortable enough place for
himself in one of the farther caves. He must be very cunningly hidden, for the Barkers and Jim Hawkins have
scoured the island, and would, I fear, have meted out very
rough justice to him, in spite of my exhortations. These
people are very primitive; in spite of their perfectly sincere
religion, there appear to be certain aspects of the Christian
faith that elude their understanding. Mercy and forgiveness
are qualities hard to find on Calvary when once their pas-
sions are roused. I really cannot blame myself or the other
missionaries for it; we have done our best, but we are up
against inherited instincts. I confess I am relieved each
morning to know, from my empty pail, that he is still alive,
and, apparently, unharmed. And, by the way, the fellow has
plenty of common sense; the first and second times I left
the pail I was forced to place it rather conspicuously on a
ledge just above high tide mark; when I came the second
time to recover it, I could not find it. I was rather annoyed,
for the pail is very convenient, in many ways; but at last I
discovered it, wedged very cunningly into a niche where a
casual glance would certainly overlook it. I have always put
it in the same place since; I'm very glad, because I needn't
rise so early to make sure of getting it before someone
notices it. I showed it to Tom Mullyon the other morning,"
chuckled the Reverend Smith, "full of sea-snails! A harmless deception—ha!"

"But can't you get him to come down, nearer home?
Couldn't you hide him in your house?" pressed Miss
Robbins.

"My dear lady, quite impossible. The utmost we may
hope is to keep in touch with him until the ship arrives,
when we can arrange for protection and get him off the

island. Dear me," sighed the Reverend Smith, "what a relief that will be!"

"Supposing Sanchia wants to go with him?"

"Ha! She must reserve her taste for wandering until a suitable opportunity presents itself."

"You mean until she's a widow? Men with injured spines often live for years."

"Alas, yes. Sanchia must accept her punishment for her sin."

"Why is punishment so important?" asked Miss Robbins, pensively.

"It is part of God's ordained law," answered the Reverend Smith, with an unfortunate touch of pompousness which earned for him a threatening movement of Miss Robbins's nearer foot.

"It's a great pity he's dumb," she said, at a tangent. "What's Sanchia to do with a dumb man?"

"Sanchia has nothing whatever to do with a dumb man. When the boat has gone she will forget all about him."

"I envy you your optimism. How easy it all sounds! But just supposing that Gregory opportunely shuffled off this mortal coil, leaving Sanchia free to follow her inclinations? There isn't much doubt where they would lead. She hates El Secredo; has always wanted to escape from it. Civilization in itself is going to be a tough nut for her to crack; handicapped by a dumb husband——"

"Really, you are allowing your imagination to carry you too far. You have no authority for assuming that he would marry her."

"None," agreed Miss Robbins, cheerfully, "beyond that contemptible thing known as a woman's instinct."

"I don't say it wouldn't be a solution," conceded the Reverend Smith. "It would certainly remove a very turbulent element from our midst; but one learns to distrust easy solutions. I confess that in marrying Sanchia to Gregory I had hoped for an end to our difficulties. That seems to have failed. I should certainly have to give very grave consideration to the question before assuming the responsibility of uniting Sanchia with an unknown person whose qualifications for—hrrum—providing for her are extremely dubious."

"I shouldn't imagine that either of them would stick at the marriage ceremony," said Miss Robbins, bluntly. "Of course, I think Sanchia's a fool if she runs away with him. If she goes at all she ought to go a free woman. She is quite sure to fall in love with someone else, as soon as she gets away from the island. The whole attraction of the dumb man lies in the fact that he's not an islander. She's romantic—within her limits—about him. He's a mystery man, and she's—well, she's a very ordinary woman, although you've made a sensation out of her on El Secredo."

"May God preserve Gregory Jodrell," prayed the Reverend Smith, solemnly. He rose with difficulty, his left arm closed over his bandaged ribs. "I think I must be going. Many thanks for your hospitality."

"Oh, don't go yet. I'm feeling friendly."

"Let us hope the feeling will persist until morning! I really had better go," said the Reverend Smith, with a return of coyness. "The hour is—dear me! A quarter past ten. Very compromising—ha!" On the wings of the jest the Reverend Smith slipped into the night, glad to assure himself by a sharp glance to left and right that his movements had not been observed.

The blankety silence of El Secredo night settled upon Miss Robbins in her little cabin; the boom of the waves and the hum of the wind was part of the silence. Miss Robbins undressed, caught a few fleas, performed some primitive ablutions and got into bed. So strong was the air that, although her resting-place was far from luxurious, she fell almost instantly into dreamless sleep.

Oblivion gave way presently to the sound of a tiny tapping; just so much noise as a trail of ivy may make, blown against a window-pane by a gentle breeze. Miss Robbins, between sleeping and waking, thought she was in her sister's cottage in the Cotswolds; she generally passed a few weeks of the summer with Sylvia—or as long as it was possible for them to be together without quarrelling violently. Something crackled; something else which apparently was parading gently along her hip, bit her suddenly. She scratched; not Sylvia's cottage, of course; that was an El Secredo flea. Again the tiny tapping was repeated; she listened, with quickening senses, and it came to her that she was not in Maggie's well-guarded inner room, but in the little lonely shed by the wood-pile, far enough from the house to be sure that, with an adverse wind, her voice would not carry to its sleeping occupants. Rather apprehensively, she remembered the Reverend Smith's warning about a lock on her door. Who knew that she was sleeping there? Probably the whole island had been informed, during her walk to Sail Point.

"Who's there?" she called out. "You can't come in— the bolt's on the door——" which was a rash kind of a lie, for anyone could have found out, by testing the latch, that there was no such barrier between Miss Robbins and her nocturnal visitor.

No answer. Miss Robbins, by now highly nervous, spoke more loudly.

"If that's you, Henry Martyn, go away. I'll speak to Mr. Prudhomme in the morning!"

There was a long silence; then the tapping was repeated, very softly but persistently. She tried to think whether there was any brushwood near enough to account for the sound. The wood-pile was half a dozen yards from the shed, however, and the tapping itself, although light, too definite to be caused by a blown twig. The inevitable explanation of it came to her so suddenly that she had leapt from her bed and was half-way to the door before remembering to snatch the bed-covering about her. She opened cautiously; the night was windy, with a pale watery moon slipping in and out among the cloud banks; but the greyness of its veiled light was sufficient to show her the figure she had expected, of the dumb man, standing pressed against the wall of the shed, merging himself in its darkness. She knew he had come for news of Sanchia.

"Come in," she whispered.

He slipped past her, without hesitation, and she closed the door behind him. They were lost to each other in the blackness.

"Wait a moment. I'll light the lamp."

The supply of matches was long since exhausted, and she was clumsy with the flint and steel, but the spark clung at last to the oil wick, ran along it in a line of blue flame. She adjusted the globe, and turned to look at her visitor.

He had fallen across the end of the bed; for a moment she believed he had fainted, but his eyes were staring at her, with pin-points of light in them.

"How did you know how to find me?" asked Miss Robbins—it was so difficult to remember he was dumb.

"Gregory's dying. At least, he may be. A whale smashed the boat, you know. She is looking after him." Bald little sentences, such as one might use to a child, dropped foolishly from her lips. "Have you always been dumb?" she asked, suddenly.

His head moved in violent negation; he sat up, and began to make clumsy explanatory gestures.

"I see; it was the shock of the wreck. When you go back you will see a doctor. Probably another shock—or electrical treatment, or something——"

He shrugged his shoulders.

"Are you well off?" An ironic smile curved the fine weak mouth masked by the moustache. "I mean, have you means to live?—to support a wife?"

He shook his head; whether this was meant to indicate that he was poor, without means of existence, or that he could not remember, she was not sure.

"What are you going to do—take Sanchia with you?"

He sat staring at her, giving no sign; he seemed to want her advice. Miss Robbins, whose eyes were becoming accustomed to the gloom, made out that he was shivering; his clothes were very ragged; his hand, when she reached out to feel it, was icily damp.

"It seems a stupid thing to do; to take a woman away, without having anything to take her to. Have you got relatives—friends who would look after you?"

He put his hands to his head; clearly he could not remember.

"It's absurd!" cried Miss Robbins. "You and Sanchia like a couple of waifs—stranded—no one to take care of you—oh, I expect you think Sanchia would do that. How could she—what does she know of life in England—by the way, you're English, I suppose?"

He nodded, uncertainly.

"The ship will be here soon," said Miss Robbins, distinctly. "Until then you've got to hide. Do you understand?"

He let her see that he did.

"Do you want Sanchia to go with you?"

He remained still for a long time; then he shook his head. There was no indecision in the movement; he looked directly at Miss Robbins, and let her see that he knew what he was talking about.

"I suppose you remember what's happened—between you and Sanchia?" she said, sharply.

He nodded.

"But in spite of it," she persisted, "you don't want to— marry her, or anything?"

He shook his head quite violently.

"Well," said Miss Robbins at last. "I can't make out if you're a knave or a hero! I don't suppose it matters very much. I'll let her know I've seen you. You're getting food —I'll try and arrange for you to have more. You are being a dickens of a nuisance, you know. Why on earth you had to get mixed up with Sanchia I can't think. Of course, you may be neither—neither knave nor hero, I mean; you may be a perfectly honest, dull man, who went for a walk up the Peak to have a look at the scenery. Never mind. You'd better take a couple of these blankets; I can get some more from Maggie. I can't think how you found out I was here; but now you know we'll be able to keep in touch—if you're cautious. I might be able to arrange for Sanchia to see you. I don't promise.

"You'd better stay here until the moon sets. Lie down and get some sleep; I expect you can do with it. Get into bed. I'll——" She paused to think what she had better do; he was crawling stupidly on the bed; his movements were drenched with fatigue; in another few minutes he would be fast asleep. She waited until his heavy breathing proclaimed it, and then huddled her clothes about her and stepped out on the grey-black beach.

The boom of the breakers drowned the crunch of the shingle as the Reverend Smith returned from his errand of mercy without the pail, and started violently as he overtook her.

"I've got him. He's in my room."

"My dear Miss Robbins! This is very unwise."

"Of course. He's not going to stay there. How long before moonset?"

"Three hours at least."

"What a bore. Can I come and sit in your living-room? You needn't treat me as a visitor. I don't expect to be entertained, but I couldn't find my undervest, and the wind is cutting right through me."

"Certainly," said the Reverend Smith, stiffly; "I'm afraid I let the fire go out——"

"We'll light it," said Miss Robbins, promptly. "I'll make some soup, if you've got any cubes left——"

"Hush! You are raising your voice."

"He doesn't want to marry her, at any rate," whispered

Miss Robbins, as they tiptoed cautiously past the San-guinetti's cottage.

"Confound the fellow! He ought to!" spluttered the Reverend Smith, forgetting caution.

She smothered a burst of laughter in her cupped hands.

The little houses huddled under the bluff like sleeping animals; overhead soared the Peak, black as ink against the iron dark sky. Now and again, as the clouds that raced before the pale disk of the moon thinned, everything became visible in a curious twilight.

CHAPTER XIII

PITY, that dubious handmaiden to love, so overwhelmed
Sanchia in those long days of watching over Gregory that
the rancour and suspicion, the scorn and espionage to which
her every action was subjected, actually had no power to
penetrate to her inner consciousness. Cased in the thin but
impenetrable armour of her pitifulness, she went about her
duties, her ears quick to catch each inflection of the groaning
that went on day and night, her feet swift to bear her, at his
bidding, to perform some hopeless act that could not bring
an instant's intermission in the long agony that Gregory
endured from hour to hour. She was clumsy in her ministrations, for life had brought her few opportunities of attending
to the sick or injured. She became, during those long days
of spiritual twilight, aware, as she had never been, of the
up-springing strength of her own young body; and this
strange awareness served to illuminate the ruin of Gregory's
manhood. She, who was unaccustomed to acts or phrases
of tenderness, fought inarticulation on new ground; softly
reiterative as a bird, her lips formed over and over again,
as she stood by his side, her left hand mangled in his
clutch, her right employed in wiping away the sweat
that matted in his hair and beard: "Poor Gregory. Poor
Gregory."

No one but a man driven mad by jealousy or suspicion
could have credited her, at such a time, with ill will towards
the unconscious being at her mercy. Such a man was
Samson Jodrell, who never left his son's bedside, whose
bitterness increased like a salt sea, each time her name passed
Gregory's parched and purpling lips.

Yet, so relentless a grip had life upon Gregory Jodrell, that in a few weeks' time it became apparent that his minor injuries were healing. Calvary men are hard, like animals; death, when it comes, must battle against a formidable combination of rock and iron and stubborn will: rarely succeeds in its first onset, but recoils, to gather its mysterious forces for the final encounter. Temperate living, inherited hardiness, and the vigour of the islander, yoked with his will to live, pulled Gregory from the kindly arms of oblivion: cheated him of forgetfulness, and death of its victim.

Sanchia drew back, and drew breath. She continued to pity Gregory, in word and deed; but she had time to think. The stunning effect of calamity gradually withdrew from her mind. Gregory was going to live: and now—what? She began to understand how easy pity had been, in those days when everyone believed that Gregory was going to die: how simple a matter to devote herself, mind and body, to his service, when it seemed only for a little while; a few short weeks, in which to purchase ease of conscience and, at last, liberty! She was surprised to discover that she had a conscience; still more, that it had had power to govern her in the first shock of Gregory's helplessness. But now—how different, how difficult it was going to be: when she, a young, vigorous and desirous woman, who had already given herself to a lover, was forced to live on at his side: a wife, yet not a wife; a nurse, a drudge. Sitting by Gregory's bed, her hands idle in her lap, her lips compressed and her whole aspect so brooding that she affected those who watched her with a curious unease, Sanchia weighed the situation: measured it by her powers of endurance, looking down the long vista of years, past countless acts of drudgery, to her own old age. That was how it would be—if she remained with Gregory. A slow withering. She looked down upon her small, plump hands with the faintly gleaming nails that she tended to the best of her ability; in a few years' time the fine brown skin would become coarse and knotted, bunches of veins would rise as the flesh sank in between the bones, and blackened and broken nails spell the downfall of her pride. Half unconsciously she raised a hand to her head, and touched the fine silk of her hair above the ear; this too would change, would coarsen and blow in eldritch wisps of iron-grey about her hollowing temples: her lips, her teeth— a spasm of indrawn breath set them into her lower lip so sharply that minute spots of blood appeared along its rich outward curve.

And if she left Gregory for the dumb man? Something as cold and fearful as a wave lipped her: the dread of the unknown. To face it on the arm of one who could advise and protect her—that was one thing; to go into it blindly, one's feebleness enhanced by the burden of another living soul who depended upon her for everything, was another matter. How would the delicate fabric of love support the rough wear of such a situation? She had loved him enough to give herself to him; but how much of endurance was there in the gift? She had not set eyes upon him since the day of Gregory's accident: did not know if he were dead or alive. She wondered at her calmness in uncertainty. Could love endure such ignorance? Yet she was sure she loved him; a glow pervaded her whole being in remembering his embraces, and she knew that she had borne the whole brunt of her servitude in the belief that she would be locked in those arms again.

She continued to tend her husband faithfully; but the words "Poor Gregory" died upon her lips. It was a ghost that walked in Samson Jodrell's house: or the empty shell of a woman whose spirit walked the Peak with her lover.

Miss Robbins faced Samson Jodrell, squaring up to the old man like an enraged turkey hen. For the past fortnight she had striven vainly for a few words in secret with Sanchia; the girl seemed impervious or deliberately indifferent to her hints.

She invaded the bedroom where the sick man lay; no obstacle was placed in her way—indeed it was a common thing for seven or eight people to gather there: the women gloating rather ghoulishly over Gregory's half-conscious body, or men, who came and stood awkwardly, silently, filling the room with the stuffy reek of their clothes and their bodies, using up the air which the invalid needed; impeding the movements of Sanchia—whom they ignored—and departing with a clumsy act of respect to the old man propped up in his chair at the bedside.

Miss Robbins found Samson Jodrell with his beard grown nearly to waist-length, his eyes red-rimmed from lack of sleep, and many signs of neglect and exhaustion about his person.

"Some people might be sorry for you, Samson Jodrell," she said briskly. "I think you're an old fool. Why don't you go to bed?"

He blinked at her stupidly; his wits were numb with weariness; all that remained to him of consciousness was his suspicion of Sanchia, his dread of relinquishing Gregory to her ministrations, his determination to keep an eye on her movements. In a corner of the room was the pallet bed which Sanchia had mutely placed there for his use; rarely had he availed himself of it, for sleep came all too easily when one lay down, and in sleep what might come to Gregory? So he dozed in his chair, waking with a start each time that Sanchia performed some cautious movement to relieve Gregory's pain.

"What's that ye're giving him?"

"A little milk and water."

"Let's see ye drink some of it yersen."

Obediently, even meekly, without rancour or rebellion, she would raise the cup to her lips and take a draught; his eyes would strain to observe the swallowing movements of her throat.

"Sanchia!" the sick man would groan; and she, bend-

ing gently, pitifully, over the dishevelled bed: "Poor
Gregory."

"Sanchia must get out," said Miss Robbins.

"What's that ye say?" croaked Samson, his voice coming
raspingly from his throat, as though he had forgotten the
use of his vocal organs.

"She's not been out since Gregory had his accident. I've
come to take her for a walk."

The cunning glint in the old man's eyes did not escape
Miss Robbins, as she turned away. Old brute! He knows
everyone is watching her for him.

She met Sanchia in the doorway.

"Come for a walk along the beach with me, Sanchia."

She shook her head.

"Gregory might call."

"He's fast asleep; we'll not be more than ten minutes."

It seemed to the closely watching Miss Robbins as though
a faint light quivered for a moment across the still face of
the girl. After a moment of hesitation, Sanchia reached out
her hand for the black shawl, which, during the weeks of
Gregory's illness, had hung, unused, behind the door. With
her movement of untrained grace she flung it over her head;
beneath it her small face peeped out, a pale oval, like a nun's
beneath her hood. Weeks of indoor life had bleached
Sanchia's skin to almost the clear pallor of a pearl: such
trace of sunburn as remained lingered on its smooth surface
with the smooth grey gleam of an oyster shell. From her
woman's point of view Miss Robbins had never particularly
admired Sanchia's looks; to her Westernized mind there
was something rather negative than positive about the girl's
claim to beauty; but now, for the first time, as the sun smote
into Sanchia's face, faintly gilding it, she thought her lovely.
Confinement had thinned her, as well; there was something
elusive and delicate about her; Miss Robbins looked at her,
half-puzzled: she was of the island, yet not of the island.
Some strange between-world claimed her. Suppressing a
start, Miss Robbins recalled the creatures that she had seen

swarming upon the rock at sunset; Sanchia might be one of those, scaling the inaccessible, poising upon air, familiar of the El Secredo earth!

They walked silently down to the beach, Miss Robbins, with a defiant glance towards Atlantic View, slipping her arm through Sanchia's. There were plenty of people about; but it was singular how little notice they appeared to take of Sanchia and her companion. Even the few children, seeking beneath rocks for creatures left by the receding tide, nudged each other and ran a little farther away. Yet, behind their seeming indifference, Miss Robbins sensed a sharp vigilance, and wondered whether the girl was conscious of it. If so, she gave no sign; but walked in her accustomed fashion, with eyes cast downwards, withdrawn so far into her own thoughts that she seemed hardly to realize the contact of Miss Robbins's arm with her own.

"What is he doing now?" asked Sanchia, suddenly.

"Why, Sanchia!" Miss Robbins stood stock-still, in her astonishment at the abruptness of the question. "I thought," she said, huffily, for her irritation with Sanchia during the past weeks had risen to boiling-point, "I thought you weren't interested, as you snubbed me each time I tried to tell you anything."

"I had naught to think of then but Gregory," she answered, simply. "And it didn't matter, so long as I knew he was alive."

"But you didn't know as much as that!" cried Miss Robbins.

"I'd have known if he'd been dead," said Sanchia, with quiet certainty.

"He has been down to my shed two or three times, on dark nights," said Miss Robbins, feeling that it was useless to be huffy with Sanchia. "It's not very safe. He'll have to stay hidden until the ship comes. What are you going to do then?"

Sanchia remained silent; Miss Robbins chafed inwardly.

"Come, Sanchia; you must have thought about that.

You'll have to choose between Gregory and—and the stranger, won't you?"

"Maybe the island will choose for me," said Sanchia, oddly. "Maybe the wind will blow, this way or that, an' I'll find myself doing as it bids——"

"But haven't you any wishes of your own? Are you going to settle down here for the rest of your life"—in spite of herself a note of disparagement sounded in Miss Robbins's voice—"or are you going to take your chance of escape?"

Sanchia sat down suddenly upon a rock; she had withdrawn her arm from Miss Robbins's, and her shawl was folded tightly over her breast.

"An' I don't even know his name," she murmured, as though to herself.

"Oh, names don't matter," said Miss Robbins, impatiently. "Call him Smith, Brown or Robinson. What about it?"

"When next ye see him," said Sanchia, looking, not at Miss Robbins, but at the heaped waters that met the sky in a glittering line far out to eastward, "ye must tell him that I will come—some way—some night."

"For goodness' sake be cautious, Sanchia; they have you watched like a prisoner."

"Ay." She nodded. Miss Robbins noticed that many of the little, late-acquired refinements had slipped from her speech. "It will be hard."

"You'd better make up your mind to get away," said Miss Robbins, impulsively. "Your life won't be worth living if you stay here. They'll never forget, you know."

"I know. 'Twill be hard- -whether I go or stay."

"What do you mean?"

"Here they'll be hard on me, maybe——" She stopped suddenly, as though she were unable to follow her own thought to its conclusion. "Maybe I could look after him, if we went away together?"

Miss Robbins felt that an important part of what Sanchia had intended to say had been left out. It was like trying to piece together the scraps of a torn page. She felt it was her duty to point out to Sanchia the formidable difficulties that civilization presented to her and the dumb man. A choice between familiar and unfamiliar evils: that was the alternative that life presented to Sanchia Jodrell. How far would love mitigate the position? How much of love was there in it, anyhow? Was it not, rather, a matter of romance, the magnetism of the unknown? The ironic mind of Miss Robbins rapidly evoked such arguments as would be advanced by the Reverend Smith Prudhomme.

I ought to remind her that she is married to Gregory Jodrell; I ought to ask her how she proposes to face life with the incubus of a dumb man, to whom she is not legally married; I ought to remind her that she has no money, and no equipment for earning any save in the way she most dislikes—through domestic labour. . . . Imagination boggled at Sanchia, in cap and apron, opening people's front doors, answering a telephone, keeping a house in order.

"You see," said Sanchia, calmly, "I may be going to have a child."

"That settles it, then," said Miss Robbins, controlling her interest. "You'll have to go away."

"Maybe," said Sanchia. "Yet I think, maybe, if Gregory'd forgive me, an' take the baby for his own, I'd stay wi' him. I dunnot love Gregory: but I be mortal grieved for him."

"Sanchia!" cried Miss Robbins, in horror.

"The island—it will never let ye go," she said, fatalistically. "'Tis too late; I'm wed to Gregory Jodrell. 'Tis not as if he"—Miss Robbins understood that the pronoun did not refer to Gregory—"could look after me. How can a dumb man earn his living? An' what do I know o' work, save scouring floors an' bakin' bread? 'Twould be starvation for the pair o' us, an' for the baby as well. 'Tis safer to stay here, maybe."

"Sanchia," said Miss Robbins, in a low voice, "safety can be a very ignoble thing. But I know what you mean by the island—the way it holds you. I've felt it myself. Sometimes it seems as though it's got hold of me——"

"Nay!" cried Sanchia, with a ring almost of horror in her voice. "Ye must not let it! Ye must get away, as fast as ye can!"

"I've thought of staying," said Miss Robbins, rashly. "You wouldn't understand what makes me feel like that. I—I don't exactly love El Secredo: it's too terrifying for that. But I feel as if it wants me; and I'm willing for it to have me! Perhaps if I were to stay, Sanchia, it would let you go!"

She was checked by the stark look in the eyes of the girl.

"I said you wouldn't understand; but I mean it. El Secredo has got a kind of hold on me. It crushes me, and yet it draws me at the same time. I feel its awfulness, and yet I'm not afraid. The other night"—she hesitated—"I saw something. I don't know how to describe it to you; people—on the rock——"

Sanchia gave a cry and covered her face.

"Ye must go; ye must not stay here!"

"Have you seen them as well?"

"Nay; I've heard tell o' them. Old Betsy Barker used to talk o' them. Folks said she was mad; but she used to tell me tales o' the things she'd seen afore she got too old to climb among the rocks."

"But what are they, Sanchia? Are they ghosts? And why do they haunt the Point? Who died there?" persisted Miss Robbins.

But Sanchia would say no more; she crossed her arms on her bosom, and leaned forward, staring out to sea and rocking herself silently to and fro. At last she said:

"'The island keeps them as belong to it. I'll have to stay here—but you must go."

Miss Robbins, biting her nails in perturbation, inwardly cursed the fates that obstinately denied her the consolation of the heroic gesture. To have said to Sanchia: "Come with me, I'll see you through," was the logical, besides the heroic answer to Sanchia's pusillanimous mood. For all that problematical tenth that leavened her, Sanchia was nine parts an El Secredo woman; three generations intervened between her and mystery; and the island women are cautious.

Caution was a quality singularly repellent to Miss Robbins, who had had to live according to its dictates for the greater part of her life. Her first incautious act, on any generous scale, had been her setting out for El Secredo. With a mind tuned to adventure, she had by now practically decided that England held nothing for her but the petty inhibitions which lack of means forces upon would-be adventurers—outside of the extremely faint hope that her new book would command sufficient *réclame* to relieve her of pecuniary embarrassment for the rest of her life. Up to the age of thirty-five, every book she wrote, held, for Miss Robbins, its glittering possibility; at thirty-six she set dreams aside for a dogged determination to wring at least a means of livelihood from her pen.

What had she to offer Sanchia, if the pair of them went to England? There was no room in her flat for the island-bred girl—who, ten to one, would stifle in London air, before she was frozen out by the one or two relations who persisted in using the flat as a cheap hotel when they came to town. She was not the kind to make friends readily with her own sex; nor was she likely to command attentions—of a useful kind—from the other sex. The problem of finding her employment would interfere seriously with writing, and the responsibility of looking after her would limit mental output.

Yet, in relinquishing Sanchia—and a willing, or at least,

passive, Sanchia—to the grip of the island, Miss Robbins
had a sense of failure: of defeat from sources she had chosen
to consider negligible. She had been so sure that she had
established in Sanchia's mind the lure of the *beyond*. On the
face of things, it had seemed so logical that Sanchia should
quit the island. Miss Robbins, one of whose weaknesses
was a trick of dramatizing herself in connexion with the
characters she put into her novels, had seen herself as
Sanchia's deliverer, from a spiritual, if not from a material,
standpoint. Besides, there were actual, as well as intangible
reasons, for the girl to be got away. Supposing matters
should come to a head on the island; supposing that the
smothered ill-feeling should break out once again? A
singularly uncomfortable feeling stirred at the roots of Miss
Robbins's hair, as she meditated upon the disaster which she
and the Reverend Smith Prudhomme so narrowly averted.
Against her will she recalled the grim history of the woman
and her lover, who were bound face to face and flung over
Sail Point. It would not be like that, of course; civilization
on the island had advanced beyond communal murder. But
a hundred things might happen; what could be easier
than the staging of an "accident," some combination
of circumstances which should end fatally for Sanchia
herself?

Sedulously she had held the image of liberty before the
eyes of the girl. Having sown the seed, she had watched it
germinate, and the bitterness of the gardener, in the discovery that his cherished seedlings are withering, was hers,
in the pusillanimity of her protégée.

Sanchia returned to Gregory; Miss Robbins, in an
uneven mood, to her writing. Sanchia's message to the
dumb man: that must be delivered, she supposed; but to
what end? *Failure*, wrote Miss Robbins's pencil, some half
dozen times, on the margin of the block that held her disjointed notes—now in process of development into the
novel. Sanchia had decided for caution: that is to say, she

was giving the lie to all Miss Robbins's psychology: a psychology never very sound, depending more upon intuition than science, and always a little at the mercy of her dramatic sense. An annoying situation: doubly annoying because, while proving the weakness of Miss Robbins's psychology, it robbed her of that proud confidence in her subject without which no writer can hope to carry conviction to his public.

A few days later, Gregory Jodrell made an attempt to speak. Sanchia was sitting beside him; she laid down her sewing to bend over the bed, and old Samson twitched suspiciously forward to catch the faint echo of speech which passed his son's lips.

"Get me a drink, Sanchia; there's a thing I want to say to ye."

She obeyed, filling the cup from a ewer, under Samson's watchful eye; mechanically she put the cup to her own lips before offering it to Gregory. The action had become habitual, for the old man suspected each mouthful that she brought for Gregory's acceptance. Although she supported his head, much of the water ran down into his beard, now nearly as long as Samson's. She had made as though to cut it one day, but was imperiously checked by the old man.

"Let yon be! Gregory'll do it for himsen when th' time comes."

Useless to point out that the time would never come; she obeyed with that new meekness that was upon her. Through the curly, encroaching hair the sick man's flesh showed pale as cheese; his eyes had sunk far back under the bushy brows, and the grime had worn from hands thin and bloodless as parchment. He seemed not to see his father as he spoke, in that echo of a voice, for Sanchia's ears alone.

"Ye've been rarely good to me, Sanchia."

"Nay, I've done naught but what I should," she answered, awkwardly; a terror of what he might be going to

say stiffened her limbs; she had never expected him to speak
coherently again.

"Ye'd best not talk, Gregory; it'll harm ye."

"Nay, naught'll harm me. I'm not dying, Sanchia; the
Lord has seen fit to deliver me from the jaws o' death—
praised be His Name."

"Amen," came from Samson, edging himself nearer by
the aid of his stick; his voice quivered: "Gregory, my
son——"

"'Twas the mercy o' the Lord that spared me," whispered Gregory. "Else I'd ha' died wi' ungodliness in my
heart. The whale was the messenger o' the Lord, that He
sent as punishment for my sins."

Too jealous to share with her the agony in his mind,
Samson Jodrell believed, with Sanchia, that Gregory was
wandering. Both were relieved by the entrance of the
Reverend Smith, who came on his evening visit. Twice and
three times a day he had been coming in his capacity as
medical attendant, although painfully aware of his limitations in this direction. The usual purpose of his evening
visit was to give Gregory the sleeping draught; his attitude
to Sanchia was formally sympathetic, but he had ceased to
call her by her Christian name. As Mrs. Jodrell the appel-
lative was so unfamiliar to Sanchia that she did not always
realize that he was addressing her.

He stood by the bedside; the tall, gaunt figure of a man
himself in serious need of medical attention. His broken
ribs, clumsily set by John Robertson, under his own direction, were making a bad job of healing; he had almost forgotten what it felt like to draw a breath without pain; and
heroism, even of that obstinate kind indulged by the
Reverend Smith, had begun to lose its glamour. There were
many, however, who would have said that the Reverend
Smith, conscientiously pursuing his parochial duties, his left
arm hugged to his side to mitigate, as far as might be, the
continual throb of flesh in which the bone splinters still
festered, came closer to the heroic than ever before. His

voice, when he addressed Gregory, had lost its hearty note;
it was the voice of a tired man, clinging doggedly to that
hope which smouldered in every heart on Calvary—the
coming of the second ship.

"Well, Gregory, this is more encouraging."

"Ay, I'm not dying," gasped Gregory. "I'm getting well
—to testify to the glory of the Lord. I'm glad ye've come.
There's a thing I've got to say to Sanchia, an' maybe 'tis
seemly ye should hear it too."

The Reverend Smith's expression became non-committal,
as he shot a glance across the bed at Sanchia. Really, her
self-possession was indecent. Here was a woman who had
put herself outside the pale of respectable society: who
should, by rights, be embarrassed by the presence of a
minister of the church. . . . At this moment the Reverend
Smith's inimical eye caught the tremor of Sanchia's gown.
Beneath it—although the Reverend Smith was not to know
this—her knees shivered like aspen leaves. Her face,
pale and composed, the carriage of her head informed
with that monstrous dignity which had always so
incensed him against her, she was obliged, nevertheless,
to stretch out a hand and steady herself against the
wall.

"Ha! Nervous," thought the Reverend Smith. "Hrrum
—conscience-stricken—as well she may be!"

"There's been evil tongues on Calvary," Gregory was
whispering. "There's been a deal o' chatter an' uncharitable
talk; an' I think shame to myself I heeded it. Will ye forgive
me, Sanchia?"

Her lips became bluely pale, like skim milk; she had to
moisten them, and still no sound came through; she put a
hand to her constricted throat. The eyes of the Reverend
Smith popped, fishlike. Denunciation he had been prepared
for; he was ready, if occasion arose, to add the maledictions
of the church to those of a duped husband; he only wished
he felt less feverish, more clear-headed. It was difficult to
preserve one's sense of values when one's temperature

wobbled uncertainly round and about a hundred and one. But Sanchia's day of reckoning was overdue. She had warded it off cunningly enough, with her attendance on Gregory; she had taken cover longer than was reasonable behind the unconscious figure of her husband. Calvary was itching for reprisal; the girl, little as she appeared to heed it, was in actual danger of her life. They would have burnt the roof over her head, had it not been for Gregory; they would have howled their rage and resentment under her windows, had it not been for their respect for Samson Jodrell. With Gregory's restoration to health, danger grew a little nearer to Sanchia; she would have to be made to understand that her safety lay in her own hands.

But Gregory was not going to recover; how could a man with a broken spine recover? He would linger on and on, perhaps for several years, until he died; and then—well, it would be necessary to get Sanchia Jodrell off the island before that happened. In fact, the sooner she went, the better. Something must be arranged—quickly; Gregory must be made to understand that Sanchia's departure was imperative: she must be sent to a mission——

Rather incoherently, but with the rapidity of lightning flashes, these thoughts followed each other through the brain of the Reverend Smith: the while he stood aghast, listening to Gregory Jodrell asking pardon of the woman who had betrayed him. To send Sanchia to a mission: this would be to acknowledge defeat. An uneasy flush crawled up the Reverend Smith's cheekbone. To dismiss her would be tacitly to acknowledge the failure of his years of ministry, so far as Sanchia was concerned. Yet here was a woman whose stubbornness resisted all religious intervention: it was the devil victorious over the Holy Ghost! A terrible thought. The Reverend Smith, in complete confusion of mind, found himself divided into two individuals; the spectator, dispassionate and interested, and the minister of God.

Of the three who listened to Gregory's speech, the only one to retain his powers of speech and action was Samson Jodrell.

"Ye're mad!" he cried.   "This woman——"

The white light of Sanchia's gaze scorched him across the bed, so that he fell back, whimpering. Her fingers still at her throat she strove for speech, and none came.   The Reverend Smith stood, woodenly, seemingly impassive.

The sick man twisted his head, striving to catch a glimpse of Sanchia's face, which was lost in the shadow that cut midway across the room from the low-hung eaves that encroached upon the window space.

"Ye've been rarely faithful to me, Sanchia, an' we be husband an' wife. Time'll come when I'll be proper husband to ye; there's the house awaiting for ye—Samson Hawkins, he's fixed in the windows; an' there's a grand door I made ye, wi' his help, by way o' surprising ye. I thought to ha' taken ye down to look at it; but ye mun go alone, Sanchia. 'Tis grand wood, black an' heavy: 'twould keep th' Atlantic out!   An' I've chipped out the letters as stands for our names, Sanchia: S. and G. J., right on th' lintel, so's we'll walk under 'em each time we goes in an' out. 'Tis hard to be lyin' here, when I'd thought to take my bride to her own home. I know, my lass, it's not been too happy for ye here. My father's an old man, an' a good man, but he doesn't understand.   Maybe I'm not so good at understanding mysen. But ye've been a good wife to me, even times when things ha' been sore against ye; an' ye shall have your house, so soon as they'll lift me out o' here an' carry me down to th' beach.   An' there's a thing I have to ask ye—an' ye as well, minister.   Sanchia an' me's been a long while wed; an' before the Lord laid His hand on me, we was to have had our feast.   Maybe some folks will say 'tis a gloomy thing to have a sick man at a feast; but maybe there's others will overlook that. I say, let the feast be held, an' then some o' the lads can carry me into my own house an' let me get back my manhood agen, wi' Sanchia to look after me."

Dead silence followed the gasped out sentences. Samson's breath roaring in his throat, suddenly choked him, and he broke into a paroxysm of coughing. The Reverend Smith, inwardly execrating the situation, began perfunctorily:

"When you are stronger, Gregory, the matter——" and was checked by the glare shot upon him by Sanchia.

Had she and Gregory been alone, she would have made her confession, accepted her humiliation, borne his grief, and prayed his forgiveness on behalf of the consequences of her sin. She was certain, now, that she was going to have a child; certain, also, that escape from El Secredo would be madness. Her only hope was to remain, and purchase forgiveness by producing a female child for the island.

But all her pride was up in arms before the attitude of Samson Jodrell and the Reverend Smith Prudhomme. They liked to feel that she was at their mercy; that a word from them could blast Gregory's trust in her. They liked to torment her with their silence, biding their time until Gregory was fit to hear that his wife had betrayed him. And the queerest part of it was that they did not really know. Only their suspicions had led them to a conclusion which Sanchia might well have refuted for want of immediate proof. Only she could tell that the proof was there, within her, waiting to confound her. She had hoped, with simplicity, that her devoted attendance on Gregory would incline his heart to look kindly upon her and the child, and to afford them protection from the rancour of the islanders.

Now, stung by that leer of knowledge in both men's eyes, she hardened into a bold defiance. Let them accuse her if they chose. Instinct informed her that Gregory was in no mood to listen to accusations, unless she chose to accuse herself. If they opened their lips against her now, she would fling back the words in their teeth—and Gregory would believe her. Her instinct was to mark time, to achieve a temporary safety, to let the future look after itself, and, above all, to thwart the ill intention of Samson Jodrell and the minister.

She bent down, suddenly snatching Gregory's hand against her breast, and her eyes challenged the onlookers, as she answered:

"Ye shall have it as ye will, Gregory. We'll have the feast, an' them as doesn't want it can stop away."

The Reverend Smith made a curious noise in the back of his throat, as he jerked up his head and walked out of the room; Samson Jodrell staggered out of his chair, and supporting himself by the bed, limped to Sanchia's side.

"Ye may deceive my son, but me ye shall not deceive, ye loose woman!"

"Hold your tongue, old man," she answered, calmly. "Ye may say what ye please wi' that poisoned tongue o' yours, ye'll not come between us now." She wiped the sweat that had gathered at the roots of Gregory's hair—Gregory, who did not appear to hear or heed his father. His grasp tightened upon her hand.

"Ye're my true wife, Sanchia," he whispered, reiterating the words as though he wished to convince himself. "'Twas the devil as tempted me to think otherwise. 'Tis the devil as steals my father's wits. . . . We'll have the feast, Sanchia? There'll be a plenty fat geese to kill an' the sheeps' in fine condition. An' ye can tell Timothy Hawkins to be practising his tunes—th' folks'll be in fettle for dancing, after this long while——"

Her heart was touched by his childish planning; very soon exhaustion claimed him, and his eyes glazed with the sleep-like stupor which had alternated, through the last dreadful weeks, with his bouts of pain. Ignoring the old man, she went about some household task.

As she entered the kitchen, full of purple gloom, a figure sitting beside the table lifted its head. Although night was sweeping upon El Secredo with the swiftness of a black-winged bird, she knew the Reverend Smith Prudhomme. Her body stiffened to antagonism, she became the offended mistress of the house.

"I thought ye had gone," she said, coldly.

"Are you not ashamed of yourself, Sanchia Jodrell?" he asked; and, to do the man justice, there was something both wistful and pitiful in his voice.

"Ashamed?" She shrugged her shoulders.

"It is my duty to warn you that the people are likely to take very badly to this idea of a feast. You must be aware that you have—hrrum—offended the community, and that —hrrum—it is extremely unwise to challenge a demonstration at the present moment, when there is so much bitter feeling abroad."

"Ay, there is bitter feeling," she agreed, and, resting her hand upon the table, looked down at it: the young, plump hand. How much longer would it preserve its dimpled roundnesses? "An' ye have done your share in fostering it, no doubt. They may think ill o' me; their thinking's done me no harm this nineteen years. But they respect Gregory Jodrell. 'Tis for his sake the feast's being given; ye can mention that, when ye're telling of it. They'll not go against the wishes of a dying man, maybe? The feast is naught to me," she added, with a scornful gesture. "But 'tis surely no hardship to go through wi' what has been begun, to please Gregory?"

Once again her effrontery baffled him. He had waited, on purpose to administer some clerical reproof. In the privacy of his home, he had, on more than one occasion, walked the floor, thundering the Church's wrath on Sanchia Jodrell. His patience was at an end; even when he had been most long-suffering in his attitude towards her, the Reverend Smith now recognized, he had always detested Sanchia. An un-Christian state of mind; he had prayed against it, frequently. But he was a man of strong likes and dislikes; while flattering himself upon preserving a strict equity in his dealings with his parishioners, he had been totally unable to escape the very human foible of making pets of some, while disliking others—beneath the mantle of ministerial impartiality.   Sanchia, with her strong, implacable little fingers, had rent the mantle: he could not readily forgive her for that.

He made another attempt.

"You must see that Gregory is totally unfit for the excitement of a public gathering at present. Better to postpone it until he has recovered sufficiently to enter into discussion as to the—hrrum—wisdom of this—hrrum—rather marked step.   You fully understand," said the Reverend Smith, pulling himself together, "that unless you yourself make a clean breast of it to Gregory, it will be my unpleasant duty to inform him of the attitude of the people—of their resentment of his wife's conduct?"

"And what," she asked, calmly, "is the reason of their resentment?"

The Reverend Smith stared, open-mouthed.

"Come now, let's have this matter out," she said, boldly. "What are ye all saying of me? What have ye got, any of ye, to go on, but suspicion? An' what have ye ever been but suspicious of me, ever since I was a little child?"

"You will admit," said the Reverend Smith, coldly, "that appearances are against you; that your conduct, during the past months, has not been becoming to a virtuous woman and a faithful wife. Nevertheless," he added, with a sudden ray of hope penetrating the ugly darkness which clouded his mind and shadowed its peace, "if you will give me your assurance that you are innocent, Sanchia, of the sin which is laid against you, I will accept your word, and thankfully take steps to reinstate you in the eyes of this community; provided that you will undertake at the same time to order yourself in a proper manner in future."

He ended with a sigh, almost relieved to find that he

actually wanted Sanchia to say that she was innocent. His words sounded pompous and insincere, even in his own ears; he could not, for the life of him, alter his address to this insolent young woman, so patently indifferent to the opinions of those about her. A touch of humility, a hint of shame would have changed his tone; he was uncomfortably conscious of a lack of Christianity in his method of dealing with her. Passionately he recalled the words of the Nazarene, to the woman taken in adultery: "Go—and sin no more." How could one employ such words to one so flagrantly indifferent? Accustomed to repentant sinners, or to those who had the wit to appear repentant, he was nonplussed in his encounter with one who seemed to glory in her sin. Many he had frightened into confession, but he knew instinctively that Sanchia was not to be frightened.

"I have naught to say," answered Sanchia, quietly.

"It is to be hoped," said the Reverend Smith, his temper rising, "that the grace of God will move you to confess to Him that which you withhold from those who have a right to question your conduct. You understand, Sanchia, that I must refuse the sacrament to you, while you are in a state of sin?"

Sanchia laughed, softly.

"I have naught to say to that, either. I've not troubled church sin' Gregory was ill, maybe church 'll not trouble me either," she answered, and ended the conversation by passing into the outer kitchen, whence she heard the slam of the door which signalized the Reverend Smith's departure.

Miss Robbins came round an hour later, and called to Sanchia, outside the bedroom door.

"What's this about the feast?" she whispered, eagerly, as Sanchia came out, holding the door-handle behind her.

"What have you heard?" asked Sanchia, with caution.

"Well, so far as I can gather from the parson, who seems likely to have a seizure at any moment, Gregory has ordered the feast, and they're to go on getting ready; but half the stuff must have gone bad by now," said Miss Robbins, practically, "unless they've eaten it."

"Ay; Gregory wants the feast, so we're to have it."

"Good gracious, Sanchia, there'll be a riot among the people!"

"Maybe."

"You don't care!"

"'Tis naught to do wi' me," she said, in an indifferent way. "Gregory wants it, an' there's naught to be gained by going against him. I'll wear the taffety gown—if I can get hold of it."

The cool matter-of-factness of her acceptance of the situation rekindled Miss Robbins's enthusiasm for the girl in whom she had begun to be disappointed.

"It will be dark to-night, Sanchia; if you have anything to say to *him*—well, I should think he'll be about. Only for heaven's sake take care. You can say you're coming down to see me, if you like."

"That would be no use," answered Sanchia; her eyes, glinting in the candle-light, reminded Miss Robbins of a cat's. What a strange secretive creature she was! Never would any creature of her own sex know Sanchia. "But I'll find a way, maybe. I must give Gregory his supper now."

Miss Robbins hurried away; as she went she marked the lights in the houses, doors ajar, shadows dodging upon the blinds. Along Atlantic View groups came and went hurriedly, popping in and out of the houses, or lingering to chatter on the rough cobbled pathway facing the sea; several figures clumped in a black patch before a crimson curtain behind which stood a lamp, then dissolved into the darkness. She caught a hum of voices, and guessed—so fast does news travel on El Secredo—that they were discussing the Jodrells' feast. When she went into the

Robertsons' for her supper, Maggie met her, scarlet-cheeked.

"'Tis never the truth they're telling!"

"What about? The feast? I think so."

"Jodrells an' Mullyons 'll never abide it! 'Tis fair an outrage! She'll not have the impudence to go on wi' it!"

"Gregory wants it; that seems to be enough for her. And after all, Maggie, what do we know?—that Sanchia Jodrell went for a walk with the stranger and showed him the Peak. Poor evidence, isn't it?"

Maggie Robertson twitched her shoulder quickly away; charitable as she was, this was asking too much. Willingly and with good grace she had come to Sanchia's aid in her time of trouble; but to the islanders the wedding feast is nearly as sacred a matter as the ceremony itself, and her own resentment did no more than reflect the general feeling of the community, few of whom were likely to exercise her restraint.

Lights burnt late on El Secredo that night; with a constant coming and going, with flickering of lanterns and an occasional disquieting laugh, the subject was thrashed out from house to house. In only two houses was there silence and darkness; in the Mullyons', where the Reverend Smith Prudhomme sat and offered sympathy to two obdurate old people, refusing, granite-faced, to have part or parcel in the sacrilegious scheme; and in the Jodrells', where silence, torn by the stertorous breathing of Gregory and his father, ebbed and flowed about empty rooms.

Sheer chance—the chance of the minister's anger at Sanchia's summary dismissal—accounted for her finding, after his departure, the bottle with Gregory's sleeping draught on the kitchen table. Instantly her mind had grasped the opportunity which fate had put in her way. Gregory had his usual dose; Samson Jodrell, chewing his mess of potatoes and onions, failed to detect in the strongly flavoured food the taste of the drug that Sanchia mixed with it.

Choosing her moment, she slipped out into the darkness; her feet led her unerringly across the pasture. Under the trees of the orchard they clung together, each tremulously aware of the instinct that had led them to each other's arms.

CHAPTER XIV

FOR a week or more the island had lain under rain-clouds; an incessant depressing drizzle fell, and the summit of the Peak was veiled with cloudy vapour, through the rents of which appeared at intervals the blackened, shiny surface of the rock. Down the deep channels of the lava a multitude of rivulets churned their way down to the beach; the whole island echoed with the sound of running water, dominating the bourdon of the sea, which heaved with a heavy ground swell. Calvary fever made its appearance; asthma, rheumatism and lumbago played their old devilish pranks with the islanders, and kept the Reverend Smith and Miss Robbins, who had enlisted herself in his service on some impulse provokingly resembling compunction, busy with saltpetre, embrocations and thermogene. The two little Robertson girls went down with what Maggie called "the bad stomach," a natural outcome of poor and insufficient food. Martha was even dangerously ill, with a high temperature and symptoms suggesting dysentery. Isolation was impossible, and Maggie watched anxiously for the infection to spread to the other girl. Job Barker was bitten by a snoek fish, and the wound turned septic.

In the midst of it all, Miss Robbins found herself involved in a sentimental imbroglio.

When discussions upon the ever-fertile topic of sex agitated the circles to which she belonged, she had been in the habit of declaring that she had lived a life remarkably free from sex-consciousness. "Perhaps," she was wont to add, with a certain wry candour, "my writing would have profited if I hadn't." Such love affairs as had come her way—as come they will, unless a woman be abnormally unattractive to the opposite sex—had been a trifle *cérébrale* : having their inception, usually, in some temporary sense of kinship on literary subjects. At forty-eight Miss Robbins was a virgin: simply because none of the inducements to adventure held out to her had been sufficiently persuasive. An actual proposal of marriage had never come her way; if her pride regretted it, she found consolation of a sort in the construction of various mordant and slightly cynical proposals which brightened the pages of her novels. She had had a late ripening. Until well over thirty she had never, to her own knowledge, awakened desire in any man. One or two contemporaries had, casually, and with an air of accident, invited her to become their mistress. With an equal assumption of carelessness, and with no sense of moral resistance, she had refused—in most cases because the suggestion was inopportune. Once or twice she had seriously considered whether she had better acquiesce for the good of her work; but it is difficult to run a liaison hand in hand with conventional family connexions; and at one period at least, an anxious publisher, sniffing danger on the horizon, had gone out of his way to warn her that the public does not take kindly to moral peccadilloes on the part of its novelists.

"What about . . . ?" she had indiscreetly inquired; to be informed that so distinguished a personage was granted latitude, in the first place, because he was a male, and secondly, in acknowledgment of the services he had rendered literature: at which Miss Robbins, in whom the bump of veneration was imperfectly developed, sniffed her singularly independent and rebellious sniff.

At forty-eight, she distinctly told herself, the time had come to eschew amorous dalliance. Unless one happens to be a George Sand, a Sarah Bernhardt or a Ninon de Lenclos: in other words, unless one possesses tremendous intellectual force, inexhaustible sex vitality or imperishable beauty, the spectacle of a woman close on her fifties indulging a passion properly supposed to belong to the young and fair borders upon the ridiculous. For several years she had practised camaraderie with the opposite sex, and found it, on the whole, agreeable. She had reckoned, however, without Henry Martyn.

Being of an observant turn of mind, certainly less humble, and no less intuitive than the majority of her sex, it took Miss Robbins less than a fortnight to sum up the state of Henry Martyn's mind, so far as it concerned herself. It was extremely embarrassing, being loved by Henry Martyn. So far, Miss Robbins's swains had been of the talkative kind: prone to dissertations upon themselves, their subconsciousness, their achievements, their complexes, and—within reasonable limits—Miss Robbins herself. She was used to letting them talk, until the urge rose in her to assert herself; when she would begin, in a slow, purposeful, yet piercing voice, which sooner or later discouraged the monologuist, and ended by shattering his conception of Miss Robbins as the perfect listener.

Henry Martyn wooed her with monumental silences. She had become accustomed to his presence, usually at a discreet distance, when she took her evening walks abroad. Henry Martyn's cows supplied the greater part of the milk used on the island; after milking time, and the distribution of the milk to the few families which did not fetch it themselves from the Martyns' byre, he was free to dog Miss Robbins's footsteps. She bore with that; but found it more difficult to support his presence when he came and leaned upon the Robertsons' wall, apparently indifferent to his surroundings, socially at ease, and perfectly understood by the men of the family, who, although ordinarily on friendly terms, seemed to consider it a mark of courtesy to ignore his nightly visits. Miss Robbins was annoyed with herself for allowing herself to feel embarrassed, but it would indeed have been difficult to remain totally unselfconscious, with Betty and Martha giggling in corners, with bright eyes fixed on her, and the women, including Maggie, scrupulously avoiding her, so long as Henry Martyn continued to prop up the wall.

Determined at all costs to escape this sinister form of wooing for a while, Miss Robbins, wriggling irritably into her oilskin, caught sight of the Reverend Smith passing the gate, and thrusting Henry Martyn out of her way, ran out after the minister.

"Are you going for a walk? For goodness' sake, take me with you."

"I'm going to bathe Job Barker's hand," replied the Reverend Smith, exhibiting his bottle of permanganate.

"I'll go with you as far as his house. You simply must call Henry Martyn off, you know."

The Reverend Smith looked at her with an expression which Miss Robbins found extremely peculiar.

"Martyn is an excellent fellow," he said.

"What? Oh, you're mad!" gasped Miss Robbins.

"A most respectable family," elaborated the Reverend Smith.

"Do you understand he's courting me?"

"I hope he is perfectly respectful?" said the Reverend Smith, amazingly.

"So respectful he won't utter a word. It's ridiculous!"

The Reverend Smith halted in his stride and looked narrowly at Miss Robbins.

"You have several times intimated that you would like to remain on Calvary. Whether you are serious or not I have no means of judging. At any rate, you must see that you, an unmarried woman, can only remain here on certain conditions."

"But," gasped Miss Robbins, "you can't possibly suggest that I should marry Henry Martyn! He's young enough to be my son."

"I don't suggest anything," replied the Reverend Smith, primly. "I am merely trying to point out to you that it is quite impossible for you to remain here at all."

"You have a gift for setting people by the ears, haven't

you?" said Miss Robbins, softly. "I don't wonder Sanchia——"

"I do not deny," said the Reverend Smith, who did not wish to enter into any discussion of Sanchia, "that you have many qualities that fit you for our—hrrum—simple island existence. Courage, for instance, and considerable fortitude; together with a physical resilience which your appearance does not lead one to suspect. You have, no doubt, formed ties in England?"

Miss Robbins made a queer, inarticulate noise in her throat.

"Matrimony is a natural state for the healthy human being," said this incredible man. "As one grows older one becomes lonely . . . perhaps you have already discovered that. The—hrrum—affection of an honest man is a tribute of which any woman may be proud."

"But pride need not lead her so far as to the altar rails," said Miss Robbins, recovering her voice. "Do you know, I think you're a very little mad? Let's talk of something else. What about the feast?"

"The Mullyons have consented," he told her.

"What!"

"I have succeeded—very much against my convictions—in making them see that for the sake of preserving the peace of Calvary, we must try to bring some propriety to bear on this—hrrum—equivocal situation. In other words, if Gregory is prepared to overlook the past, it will certainly be more prudent for the rest of the community to appear to follow suit."

"And what has the rest of the community to say to that?"

"I have told you these people are like children. They have been accustomed, for generations, to take their cue from Jodrells and Mullyons. Certainly many of them are incensed still; among a few of the young men there seems to be an exceedingly bitter feeling. But we shall hope, as time goes on, that this will subside; although," added the

Reverend Smith, stiffly, "it is neither to be hoped nor desired that they should come to condone the conduct which has drawn their just and reasonable anger upon Sanchia Jodrell."

"What about forgiveness?"

"Although we are commanded to forgive," boomed the Reverend Smith, "neither forgetfulness nor condonement come within the Divine decree."

"I can imagine nothing more painful," said Miss Robbins, "than living in an atmosphere of forgiveness. Personally, I'd rather go reviled to the end of my days."

"Has Sanchia been seeing that—fellow?" said the Reverend Smith, suddenly.

"Why?"

"I do hope you are not encouraging her," he answered, fretfully. "Really, Miss Robbins, I cannot feel that you recognize our responsibility, as the enlightened members of this little community, towards those who look to us for precept and example."

"I'm not encouraging her. Sanchia doesn't confide in me any longer; I think she distrusts my friendship with you. Why do you think she is seeing him?"

"I cannot help remarking a very—hrrum—ominous brightness about her these days; she appears at times almost light-hearted. I don't wish to seem in any way sympathetic; she has earned whatever punishment comes her way. But, on the face of things, her life with the two Jodrells can't be very cheery just now!"

"I know. I dare say they've found a way to meet."

"Dear me! I must see the fellow. It's too bad. And really one must admit that her care of Gregory since the accident has been exemplary. That fellow has no business to disturb her again. I had relied on Samson's—er——"

"Espionage."

"An ugly word. How can you call a man a spy who defends the honour of his home? Whatever it is, it strikes me she is evading it. I have reasons—very un-

comfortable reasons—for thinking that she is getting out at
night——"

"How can she? Samson has taken to sleeping in the
living-room—if he sleeps at all. He generally prowls about
the house——"

"I happen to know that Samson has slept soundly, in
Gregory's room, for several nights now; and—I have lost a
bottle of sleeping mixture."

"Do you think she is doping them both?"

"One cannot be sure of anything. All I am certain of
is that I had the mixture on the night when Gregory
first spoke of the feast. I don't remember whether
or not I replaced it in my pocket, after measuring out
the dose; but it was not there when I took my coat off
at night."

"You dropped it somewhere!"

"That's impossible. Of course, I questioned Sanchia."

"And equally, of course, she denied any knowledge of it.
Well, well! I wonder whether she realizes the possibilities
of an overdose?"

"I am terrified of that," said the Reverend Smith, simply.
"Of course, she will tell me nothing; but I wondered if
you——?"

"She'll not tell me anything," said Miss Robbins, with
conviction. "You don't give Sanchia credit for the sharp-
ness of her wits. She's very simple, too. If she saw Gregory
in pain she would be quite likely to give him the rest of the
bottle, out of pity."

"God forbid! It is a very disturbing matter," said the
Reverend Smith, as he raised his hat absent-mindedly,
turning in at the Barkers' gate.

The drizzle blew into Miss Robbins's face, as she turned
to retrace her steps. Looming through the clouds of rain
and spray, blown almost horizontally along the foreshore,
came a sturdy figure, which resolved itself—without
surprise on Miss Robbins's part—into that of Henry
Martyn. In the midst of her irritation she was unable

to withhold a grudging admiration for the calmness and security of his bearing, as he came face to face with her.

"For goodness' sake, Henry Martyn, don't hang about my heels like that; it annoys me," she snapped, with a guilty sense of pettiness; fuss and fume seemed incommensurate with the calm that was Henry Martyn.

He was dressed in the hideous best of the islander; rage seized Miss Robbins at the thought of the witless conventionalist who exported to these sons of nature that most hideous sartorial production of the age, the bowler hat. No self-respecting islander will make his appearance in church without one; many of them are historic trophies, handed down from father to son. Of such was the greenish and obsolete specimen that crowned, uncomfortably, Henry Martyn's springy crop of dark hair, beaded with mist beneath its curling brim. An ill-cut suit, like a waiter's, strained across the various parts of his anatomy, and, to add the final touch of the ridiculous, his feet were thrust into native sandals of cow-hide, which the islanders make mostly to trade with the ships, but wear themselves, for best, in suitable weather. Every vestige of that natural dignity which is the islander's birthright had vanished beneath the grotesque get-up, which, thought Miss Robbins, would have fetched roars of laughter on the stage of a West-end music-hall. Yet he stood there, calmly, with an unconsciousness that commanded respect, even from a being so congenitally indisposed to respect her fellow men as Miss Robbins.

"Did you want anything?" she asked—and then cursed herself for affording him an opening.

"Ay," said Henry Martyn, slowly. "I been seeking a place to talk wi' ye."

"That's easy enough," she replied, nervousness lending asperity to her voice.

It cannot be denied that Miss Robbins, in her youth at least, had resembled the rest of her sex in dreaming about the proposals which (in those days) she had felt were bound to come her way. Originally these had been set among the lanes of her native Cotswolds; a somewhat stagy moon illuminated the scene, and the young man who proposed was a tall, dark charmer, who treated her with a romantic deference. As her taste for the masculine matured, Galahad was replaced by a middle-aged man of sophistication, deriving obscurely from Seymour Hicks, who made love headlong across a table at the Berkeley. Whatever forms her aspirant took during the progress of years, it is positive he had never assumed the character of an island savage, or the venue of the proposal the rain-swept shore of a South Sea island.

She gave a kind of mental shrug of the shoulders. Here it was—at last! At the age of forty-eight, Love—dared one name it as such?—had caught up with her, within a thousand miles of the South Pole; love of the kind that families call honourable, because it implies the offices of the Church and the wearing of a gold ring on one's fourth finger (what would Henry Martyn do about the ring?). Love, masquerading in an old bowler hat and cow-hide sandals, but love, in spite of everything. She had an absurd desire to cry. It was all so different; and for the last eight years she had succeeded in emancipating herself from all those tumultuous fleshly demands that a woman of imagination is bound to experience. The restlessness in her blood had died down naturally; she had accepted celibacy, and embraced its decencies. Now Henry Martyn was threatening her with a revival of things comfortably dead and laid aside; she felt poisoned with regret for all that had never been. It was like life's irony, to deprive her through the years of her youth of that crowning tribute of womanhood, her first proposal, only to offer it now, in her late middle-age, in this antic guise!

Her eyes stung with restrained tears; she felt that life mocked at her. For all her assurance, her truly deadly arrogance and aggressiveness of nature, Miss Robbins crumpled, in this poignant moment. Her small, thin fingers dug themselves into the pockets of her coat, as she flung at Henry Martyn the concluding words: "You see plenty of me at the Robertsons'—more than you should do," she added, virulently. "It's extremely inconvenient for Maggie to have you hanging round, when the girls are ill." Of course, she should have treated the whole matter lightly; should have informed Henry Martyn that she knew all about it, and dismissed the topic—for ever—with a laugh and a shrug. One might as effectively have shrugged one's shoulders in the scarred face of the Peak itself.

"Ay," answered Henry Martyn, "I were not minded to speak afore all on 'em, though they know well enough what I had to say to ye. We drawed lots, an'——"

"What!"

"'Twas I as won the right to speak the first," said Henry Martyn, coolly. "Will ye wed me? I've gotten the means to keep a wife, an' our farm is the richest on Calvary. If ye'll wed me we can have the feast at same time as the Jodrells' an' settle down right away."

Miss Robbins had a peculiar sensation as though some-one had both hands on her wind-pipe to strangle her. "This is ridiculous! This is absurd!" she kept whispering in her heart; but the words passed meaningless through the cross-weaving of thoughts that tangled in her brain.

Here before her stood Henry Martyn: symbolizing all that was most opposed to her customary way of living. A crude type; a "cave man." What would Alice Raye say if she could see him? How would her caustic tongue play with the event of Miss Robbins's marriage? "Lenox's grizzly bear," "Lenox's tame gorilla." There would be others, too; less playful in their scorn. "Good old sex! It's caught Robbins at last!" "My dear, a woman of *that* age! Positively shy-making!" Lenox's tame gorilla; a thing carved out of Calvary rock; to which the standards of Miss Robbins and her kind were a closed book. Granite and alkaline water: rock and kelp and sea-wrack: rain and wind and hail—and wind, wind, wind. Calvary. Calvary. The harsh syllables that had begun to fascinate her, as modern discords begin slowly to fascinate the mind educated to classic harmonies. Calvary, which she had begun to dread exchanging for civilization. For battle. For the ceaseless battle with little forces that humiliated in conquering one. The ceaseless struggle with petty things; the struggle to maintain one's place in the wage-market; the struggle to improve one's position a little; the struggle to pay one's income tax, and to keep "in the swim;" to meet the "people who mattered," to be "interesting," to impress agents and publishers and strangers who might be "useful;" to secure the right sort of publicity; to squeeze higher royalties from the reluctant hands of publishers; to find new plots, new angles of vision; to earn enough to keep up a petty kind of dignity. In such terms as these her past life presented itself to Miss Robbins, in contrast with life on the island.

Peace, quiet, time to digest the crowded impressions of close living; time to sort them out and reduce them to calm phrases, to some sort of philosophy. Freedom from the claims of society, leisure to meditate on new ideas, new plots. Life purged of the torturing element of money. Solitude which was not solitude, because she could share it at will with other human beings. Silence undisturbed by the little chatterings of people, like herself, anxious to impress themselves on an audience: apprehensive, greedy of praise, dreadfully anxious lest their epigrams and aphorisms should go unnoticed, jealous of each other's bit of success.

True, other teasing reflections crossed her mind at the same time; the isolation from the few friends whose existence made a difference to her own; the crudities of life on the island—she dismissed these as irrelevant; one could introduce one's own forms of civilization. The difficulty of disposing of one's literary output, or of keeping abreast of contemporary thought—did that matter so very much? If one discovered a new formula, fashions could go hang; and what so conducive to new formula as virgin soil? Life emptied of a thousand trivial torments; life of a large simplicity—which one could exchange at will for the complexities of western living; a matter of a long sea trip, a dipping into old wells, and—return! Often she had visualized it, in her little shed, apart from the creakings and chatterings of the Robertsons' household. But never, in this half-glimpsed Utopia of hers, had Miss Robbins included the limiting figure of a husband. Only latterly had she begun to pay attention—reluctantly—to the problem Henry Martyn and the Reverend Smith Prudhomme, together, had forced upon her notice. Life on the island, for an unmarried woman, was an impossibility; she read prohibition in the clear eyes of Maggie Robertson, in the intelligent gaze of Sanchia, in the sheepish attentions of the men and the disapproval of the minister. Would it really be worth while to purchase literary freedom at the cost of a husband? And would it, indeed, amount to freedom at all?

Miss Robbins turned with a start from her contemplation of the rain-pricked ocean to Henry Martyn, standing there with his hat upon his head and his great hirsute hands hanging by his sides, and came to her senses with a jolt. Domestic drudge to a labourer! How had she ever played with the thought? A strong physical repulsion to Henry Martyn blotted out all other reasoning. To deliver herself—her body—to such a one! Like an animal; only removed from the animal state by a narrow margin of intelligence. She became suddenly cool, mistress of herself, gently contemptuous towards Henry Martyn and that which he represented. Love, indeed! Romance, forsooth! She, who had been so sharp in her deprecations of Sanchia's marriage, ever to have fallen into the trap herself! She felt shamefully apologetic towards Sanchia.

To Henry Martyn I am hardly a woman; merely the

means whereby the Martyn stock may be perpetuated. A satisfaction of his desires: "Ugh!" said Miss Robbins, inwardly, and was about to return terse refusal of Henry Martyn's proposal, when she checked herself sharply.

There was Sanchia; the problem of her escape. From the beginning Miss Robbins had had small belief in the outcome of Sanchia's confession to Gregory. It was hardly thinkable that he would accept the stranger's child as his own; jealousy —the jealousy of a man cheated of his rightful heirs—would surely tip the balance against Sanchia, strangle any goodwill he might bear towards her personally. Sanchia and her lover had to be got off the island, in safety. Any day now the moment might come: the ship might arrive: and it would become necessary to smuggle those two on board, without the knowledge of the islanders. It would be difficult. The Reverend Smith Prudhomme, she had decided, was not to be relied upon; willing as he might be to further the departure of so turbulent a member of his flock, sheer physical inability would prevent his doing things that might need to be done. It might even be necessary to carry Sanchia and the dumb man aboard, concealed in a crate or a sack. One might not be able to rely on the captain; he might have scruples, he might fear trouble with the owners, if there was any hostile demonstration from the islanders; he might object to carrying passengers, without authorization from the firm—a hundred things might interfere with Sanchia's escape. It was essential that some able-bodied person should be at hand, to further the scheme, to stand between Sanchia and the violence of her enemies, or to protect the dumb man when he emerged from his hiding-place. If the ship left at nightfall it would be easier, of course; but there was little likelihood of that. Strangers to the dangerous waters about El Secredo were unlikely to risk navigation in the dark; she knew, from the Reverend Smith, that the ship did not make a long stay; two or three hours after the disembarkment of cargo, she set forth on her return

journey, glad to escape the vicinity of icebergs and the un-
charted waters of farther south.

Miss Robbins became feminine, serpentine in her attitude
to the guileless Henry Martyn.

"It is extremely nice of you," said Miss Robbins. "Thank
you very much for the compliment."

Henry Martyn stared; it was the first time he had heard a
proposal of marriage called a compliment, and he did not see
how it could be any such thing. It was not a compliment
when one went to barter butter for fat geese. One had to ask
a woman to marry one: how else could one set up a household of one's own and have children? In return for these
services one kept a woman; one fed and warmed her.
(Clothing was a matter that rested with the missionary.) There was no compliment about it, to his way of
thinking; it was a matter of business, of bald physical
necessity.

"You will understand that I couldn't possibly give
you an answer straight away, won't you?" asked Miss
Robbins, a trifle hysterically, because the whole matter
had suddenly become so ludicrous to her that she felt
capable, at any moment, of breaking into peals of
laughter, which would surely have hurt the feelings—well
layered in with Calvary rock as these might be—of Henry
Martyn.

"I can wait a bit," he said, gruffly.

"It might be some days," said Miss Robbins, hastily. "A
week, perhaps, or more."

"The Jodrells' feast is next week," he reminded her.

"Yes—Henry," said Miss Robbins, feeling more like a
siren with Caliban than she would have thought possible,
"I might be wanting you to do something for me. Would
you do it?"

"So long's it don't come in the way o' farm work,"
answered Henry Martyn, cautiously. He shot the islander's
look of cunning at her; it was unusual for the women to ask
favours of the men of the island, but he was prepared, up to

a point, to find unusual things about Miss Robbins. She
would settle down and become like the rest, eventually. It
was story-book-like business, this asking a fellow to do
something before she'd promise to marry him; a slow smile
broke through the dark growth of hair that covered his
face. Of course, she wrote story-books. Well, she'd not
find time for that, after they were married; there were
other things, more fitting, that a married woman had to
do.

"It won't interfere with the farm," said Miss Robbins,
thoughtfully. It had begun to dawn on her that, to accom-
plish her object, she would have to be extremely nice to
Henry Martyn, during the remainder of her stay on the
island. Flirtation was not her long suit; she decided with
relief that it was not likely to be Henry's either. She said,
painstakingly: "If it is fine to-morrow night we might
go for a little walk, and you might tell me about the
farm."

"There's naught to tell," said Henry Martyn, crushingly.

"There must be," gulped Miss Robbins, and fled. One
cannot think too harshly of her for burying her face in her
bedding and giving vent to her suppressed laughter. For
the best part of half an hour she whooped and gurgled into
her pillows; when it was over she sat up, dried her eyes,
and took stock of the situation. A slight feeling of panic had
superseded her hysteria; but she reminded herself that the
ship was due at any moment, and that there was really no
need to panic at all.

The epidemic of ailments which had attacked the island
confined itself for the most part to the men; the women continued stolidly about their labours, neglecting housework
for labour on the land. One or two, more intrepid than the
rest, volunteered to help John Robertson, whose fishing
fleet was depleted, and the fleet went out with women in
the boats. Gregory Jodrell continued very ill; his aches and
pains aggravated by the humidity of the air. Sanchia could

do little to ease him; he had ceased to call for her, but lay in patience, grateful for her services, and full of solicitude for her well-being.

"Ye must get out, Sanchia; there's naught ye can do here."

She stood by the window, staring out at the rain; the Reverend Smith Prudhomme had just taken his chill departure.

"The two Hawkinses are down wi' fever."

"'Tis poor-like weather for sickly folk. What's John Robertson doing?"

"Janet sailed wi' him yesterday."

"Maybe 'tis your turn to offer, lass."

"I cannot leave ye, Gregory." She would not tell him that she had offered, and that the men in Robertson's boat had gone on strike, rather than sail with her.

"Maggie'll have an eye to me; I dunnot care who 'tis—so long as it's not yon writing body. She's too full o' chatter—it makes my head turn."

"She's kindly-like."

"Ay, sure; but 'tisn't seemly for a woman's tongue to clack so fast. Ye'll make Jack the offer, Sanchia?"

"I cannot abide the boats," she snapped.

"Him an' me's always been good friends, an' 'tis naught but duty, lass. I'd not have them saying as my wife didn't do her duty. They'll take it kindly o' ye."

"I'm not saying aught."

He sighed.

"They can ask me if they want me," she added, defiantly.

"Ye might ha' told Jack I'd fain be wi' the lads. 'Tis unlucky, wi' all this sickness now. Seems as if the Lord's hand is laid on Calvary."

She crackled into irritation.

"Oh, you an' the Lord's hand!"

The rain was teeming down; for two nights she had not seen her lover; although she had threaded the downpour in blackness the night before, no figure awaited her beneath the fruit-trees; evidently he had thought the rain would keep her indoors.

"Some day ye'll feel it like I do," he answered, placidly. "Are they getting on wi' the feast, Sanchia?"

"Folks is busy these days," she answered, evasively. "When the men are about again, they'll get on wi' it."

"Has your mammy been to see ye?" Each day he put the question, hopefully. In his new-born love for Sanchia he could not bear that others should withhold their goodwill from her. He was puzzled by the absence of the women from the house; sickness as a rule draws the housewives of the island together. Some few came to visit him, but they went away quickly, not pausing to talk with Sanchia.

"Nay," she answered, in a hard voice; her upper lip twitched contemptuously.

"You'll be going to see her yoursen, likely?" persisted Gregory.

"What would I go to see her for?"

"'Tis your mammy," he repeated, stupidly. His sentimentality stiffened something inside her; she felt as remote as when she listened to the Reverend Smith's sermons. Remote, and rebellious because she knew that, as she hoped to wear the taffety dress at the feast, she would be obliged to go and ask Sophia Mullyon for it. After all, they had given their consent to the feast; and for the sake of Mullyon pride, a Mullyon woman must go fitly gowned on such an occasion. For the past week Sanchia had been wondering if Sophia would pocket her pride so far as to offer it; she knew now that her mother intended to humiliate her to the last.

That night, when Gregory slept—the Reverend Smith had called to administer the dose; he was now particularly careful to replace the bottle in his breast pocket, after measuring the liquid into the horn cup which Sanchia held to receive it—she went into the outer kitchen to brush her hair. A tiny square of looking-glass, that had once adorned

Mrs. Prudhomme's handbag, afforded her a glimpse of her features. Into it she smiled enigmatically, like a young Mona Lisa. How suspicious the old fool was! As she stood demurely, the cup in her two hands, he shot at her suddenly:

"You're *positive* you haven't seen the other bottle, Sanchia?"

She had lied proudly, certainly, with her eyes cast down; not because she feared to face him, or to betray herself, but because it was her habit to look downwards; had she looked him in the eye he must surely have suspected something! (In this she was more subtle than he, for, assured of her guilt as he was, the Reverend Smith accepted her disinclination to face him as proof positive.)

"It is very unfortunate; the slightest drop of an overdose would certainly prove fatal," he had uttered, distinctly.

The old fool! How wicked he believed her to be. She reflected ironically that it would be almost amusing to be as wicked as the Reverend Smith Prudhomme thought her to be.

Thoughtfully she set the pins of shell at an angle of coquetry in her sleek hair, and folded the black shawl primly over all. The rain had left off; a little wind went whispering along the beach, as she walked towards her parents' house.

The door was closed, but a lamp still burned in the window.

Sanchia lifted the latch and entered.

She was a little relieved to find that her mother was alone. Instant antagonism leapt out between the two women as Sophia Mullyon came from an inner room, and, resting her hands on her broad, flat hips—so much broader than her shoulders—stood, looking at her daughter. Her long, sheep-like face wore an expression of peevish ill-temper; to look at her one might well have wondered how she came to mother the slim, bold creature who faced her across the well-scoured floor.

"Now then?" said Sophia Mullyon.

"I've come for the taffety dress," said Sanchia, with no beating about the bush. "Ye promised it me—long ago— for my feast."

"Ha! Did I, then? Well, there's been naught but decent women has worn that dress sin' it were made. I'm having no trollops parading themselves in it."

"Ye promised it," repeated Sanchia, stamping her foot.

"Then I'm unpromising it now. That's the end o' it."

"That's the end, is it? Well, to be sure, I don't care." She swung on her heel, her chin went up, she looked as lovely and pagan as a Spanish dancer. "'Twas only for Gregory's sake I was wanting it. Jodrells like their women to look well. 'Tis naught to me if I dance at the feast in my old rags, though maybe Samson Jodrell 'll take it badly, an' say it's putting shame on 'em all. Eh, how they'll laugh at ye, Sophia Mullyon, for not affording your daughter a dress to dance in at her own feast!—an' I'll laugh too—loudest o' the lot! 'There's Sophia Mullyon, so church-mouse mean that though she's clothes a-plenty in her chest she'll not spare a bit o' taffety to her own daughter!'"

A dull, purplish flush suffused Sophia's face as she stood there, looking on at Sanchia, rocking with eldritch laughter.

"I'll box your ears, miss!"

"Nay, that you won't! I'm a married woman, same as you are yourself, an' ye can't maul me about any longer. I'll not trouble ye any more——" As Sanchia spoke, her bright eyes roved about the room. Ay, there it was, in the place where it had always hung. Once, as a child, she had stolen it, and had earned a thrashing so physically painful that never again had she attempted to explore the contents of her mother's ancient chest. The key, polished like the rest of Sophia's possessions, shot out little gleams of light like a knife-blade.

Under the window the chest stood, just where it had been placed by Mullyon grandparents, fifty years ago. It shone like wine, polished by the proud, covetous fingers of Sophia herself; in her grudging attempts at housewifery Sanchia had never been permitted to polish the chest; she used to bite her lip for the sole task in which she might have found pleasure. How much of Sophia's claim to supremacy among the island women was based upon the contents of the old sea-chest no one knew; merely to think of it jerked her head an inch higher, elevated her long, narrow nose, brought an ungodly sparkle into her dull eyes. On set occasions she went through its contents, sought viciously for moth, while the garments, unfolded from their creases, blew in the wind upon a line rigged out in the front of the house. It was the proudest day of Sophia Mullyon's year, when neighbours came to gloat upon that treasure of rusty velvet, quilted satin, and odds and ends of trimmings. Humbly they sued for her favours on state occasions: a wedding, a christening, or the missionary's birthday: and with what condescension she bestowed upon this one a little Empire bonnet, upon that a dolman, heavy with beaded trimming. Then she would press upon some selected victim a pair of tiny, square-toed slippers in satin, with low heels and a scrap of rotten elastic across the instep: just for the pleasure of hearing their mortified confession that they could not get their feet into them. Neither could Sophia Mullyon, but this embittered not at all her pleasure. When the goods were returned— with a suitable gift of a few eggs, or a little flour—Sophia would go over them, inch by inch, to find any damage; woe betide the guilty party, if any existed! Never again could she apply to Sophia for help in a sartorial crisis. It was said that she never spoke to Rose Sanguinetti's mother until the day of her death, because of a tea-stain discovered on the quilted satin petticoat—worn as a dress skirt on the occasion of Ellen Jodrell's wedding. And she never lent the taffety gown or the Paisley shawl, for these were reserved for Mullyon brides; she had worn them herself, on her marriage to Thomas Mullyon, and, as time went on, had forgotten, or chose to forget, that she held them only by virtue of her marriage. Sanchia had once infuriated her mother by crying, rudely:

"Silly old things! When they come to me I'll cut some of them up and give the rest away!" It was a case of sour grapes, because Sophia had forbidden her to dress up in them; but Sophia took the threat seriously and rated her daughter for a week, bemoaning that she had no one to inherit them but a worthless daughter. The girl successfully concealed from her mother her own passionate interest in the garments, her longing to wear them, her nigh-adoration for the old, beautiful materials and the out-moded patterns. To her, as to the rest of the island, they represented the pinnacle of fashion; such modern styles as came their way, in the vitiated form of illustrations to the religious magazines sent out to El Secredo, were voted poor things beside the Mullyon wardrobe. And so indeed they were; for it is a curious fact that the editors of such blameless journals seem unable to reconcile Christianity with the vogue in feminine fashion.

As Sanchia left her mother's house, her mind was made up. She would have the taffety gown, whatever it might cost her. A longing was upon her to deck herself out in beautiful materials; a longing purely feminine, for beauty for beauty's sake. Her lip curled upon the idea of dressing herself up for the island folk; what criterion had they, from which to judge her?

The only one for whom she would have cared to adorn herself was her lover, towards whom her swift feet now carried her. His hands fastened upon her in the darkness of their usual meeting place; silently they vanished into the rock crevice where once, with Miss Robbins, she had eluded her would-be captors.

She felt, as she always felt when she left him, soft and beautiful; the rain had ceased earlier in the evening; the perfume of replenished earth poured into her nostrils and an almost feline voluptuousness had succeeded her irritable mood of the day. Each night their meetings lengthened; she was aware of that. She knew that it was dangerous to stay so long: the sleeping-draught might lose its potency as their systems became accustomed to it, either Gregory or Samson was likely to awake, and discover her absence. She must be more discreet; but any day might bring the ship, and she was determined to wring the utmost drop of pleasure from these meetings. She thought of them as farewell to youth; when they were over she would become Gregory's domestic beast, and, presently, an old woman with a single exquisite memory hoarded in the secret places of her heart. Had she been of a morbid nature, or less capable of living fully in the pleasure of the moment, she might have embittered these hours with tears; instead, she clung more passionately, more greedily to her lover, as each too-short night brought them together. The mystery, which had at first been so all-enthralling, had declined a little; the pleasure she had in him was now almost entirely physical. He had taught her ready body the meaning of love, and as her powers of responsiveness grew, so waned, gradually, the curious spiritual tie which, at first, had bound her to him. She had even arrived at the point of realizing that she had no desire to link herself with him eternally. The limitations imposed by his dumbness had come to chafe her, save in those moments when passion had its way with them. She was too arrogant, too questing in her demands, to be satisfied with one who could feed only one side of her nature. In the moment of their meeting she had, invariably, a little cold thrill, as though a ghost laid its hand upon her. Save when passion transformed him, he was negative, while she was positive. In Gregory, even a maimed and broken Gregory, she sensed more of manhood than in this lover who swung so oddly between a feverish obsession with her body and wraithlike disassociation from everything which she had come to consider actual and permanent.

All these things her mind pondered, functioning clearly within her eased, contented body, as she retraced her steps to her parents' door.

Few of the islanders bolt their doors at night; there are no thieves on El Secredo, and, if here and there a nervous soul shivers in his bed, it is generally conceded that mere bolts and bars are unavailing against the things that walk the island in the night. As Sanchia had expected, the latch yielded easily and noiselessly to her fingers; she closed the door carefully behind her, for fear of occasioning a draught, and stood for a moment in the darkness, listening to her parents snoring. The grotesque noise almost made her giggle.

Presently she sought for a candle; she knew where they were kept. Sophia's store-room was as orderly as a grocer's shop. She struck a light cautiously, waited for the flame to steady itself, and took the key from its hook beside the fireplace.

The scent of old flowers, of cinnamon and myrrh swept up at her as she set the lid of the chest back against the window-sill. Eagerly she plunged her hands in among the hidden treasure: the stiff crustings of embroideries, the unmistakable lozenges of quilting, the bloom of velvet—ah! at last. At the very bottom, enshrined as the most precious of all, folded in India muslin softer than silk—the taffety gown!

She drew it out with many precautions against its rustling; with it, wrapped in its stiff folds, was the Paisley shawl—so fine it would go through a wedding ring.

She stood for a moment clutching them both to her bosom, savouring her triumph over her mother's ill-will. Presently she felt a drag upon the fringes of the shawl, and looking downwards caught sight of something sparkling. . . .

It was a necklace; a fabulous thing. Filigree and little polished shells, pearls and less recognizable jewels had gone to its making. In a dream Sanchia held it in her hand. Never had she heard of this before. Presently it lay on her bosom: a torque of golden lace, the points picked out with gems. As she stood in the candle-light, breathing quickly, veils stirred: the mystery of El Secredo pressed through the darkness towards her.

CHAPTER XV

Rose Sanguinetti's baby was a girl. The cottage on Atlantic View was besieged with congratulatory visitors, each bearing in hand the customary goodwill offering to the new-born child; mocassins, polished ox-horns, odds and ends of needlework, eggs, butter and milk. The elder women had delved into their hoards and produced bits of jewellery—an old-fashioned brooch or chain—which the parents pinned proudly into the baby's garment, or hung about its tiny red, wrinkled neck. It had come into the world on a little wailing wind, shortly before midnight. Across Rose's bed during her agony had fallen the red glare of flambeaux; according to island custom, the neighbours had kept watch, until Miss Robbins—nominally in charge of proceedings, but secretly much in awe of the brusque efficiency of the island women—came to the door, and looking extremely small and scared, announced the birth of a Sanguinetti girl. Then she hurriedly withdrew and was very sick, for the rough and ready obstetrics which she had just witnessed had come as a severe shock to a spinster, whose practical acquaintance with birth was limited to visiting nursing homes, at a discreet interval after the event, when she firmly discouraged any inclination on the part of the convalescent to enter into details. "After all," said Miss Robbins, "with twilight sleep and all that, having a baby is as unimportant as eating one's dinner." There was no twilight sleep on El Secredo, and Miss Robbins was indulging one of her periodic hates of the powers that arrange such matters, as she stood, unwillingly and ineptly handing flannels and basins to more experienced ministrants than herself.

Sanchia Jodrell came from her father-in-law's house, proudly, with her gift in her hand; not to have brought it would have been interpreted as a gratuitous insult to the Sanguinettis, but she was doubtful of its reception. The buzz of voices which filled the cottage was stilled at her entrance; thumbs and elbows enjoined silence as she marched into the room where her erstwhile school-mate lay, so soft and still, with the ugly little head on her arm.

"I've brought ye my gift, Rose. They tell me it's a girl."

Rose made embarrassed noises. She had been strictly enjoined by her husband to hold no converse with Sanchia, but lacked the will, or maybe the unkindliness, to thrust back the gift in the hand that offered.

"Ye'll be having one of your own afore long," she said, weakly; it was a mere formula of speech, the patronage of the mother to the childless; but the colour flew up Sanchia's pale cheeks until it seemed the very roots of her hair must take fire.

"I'd sooner kill it, if it were a girl, than let it grow up on El Secredo!"

Rose gave a little cry, and dropped the gift—a little shift of pink wool, in Sanchia's large, careless knitting. Someone rushed in, pushed Sanchia aside. She swaggered out, under staring eyes, her hands on her hips.

"Well, did ye ever?" Nell Barker was chattering: she held up the shift, mockingly. "Did ye ever see the like o' that? A fine gift for Jodrells to make! Don't ye fret, Rose—Samson'll do better by ye; he was al'ays friendly towards your mammy. An' all them silver spoons as was left Gregory by his mother—I suppose she'll not be sparing ye one? Ye'll not be putting a poor thing like yon on your baby's back, Rose?"

"You'd better hide it," whimpered Rose; "Harry'd

go at me properly if he knowed *she'd* brought it here."

"Ay, we'll pop it on the fire," said Nell Barker, venomously. "Sophia Mullyon's in a rare fanteeg this morning! I come here as fast's my feet 'ud carry me to tell ye about it— folks need cheering up wi' a bit o' clacketty when they're sickly, I says to myself. Ye'll know I popped round early, to mak' sure o' the quilted petticoat? Last year Janet Hawkins got in afore me, the mean trollop, an' I heerd she was countin' on it agen. Well, when Sophia opened the chest, the taffety gown was gone! Ye mind the taffety Sophia was wed in? Nay, now; ye wasn't born. Think o' that, now! I see Sophia, as though 'twas yesterday, strutting along the beach in that gown, not six months after she'd been wed to Stephen Horne in her own old print, wi' a hat the missionary's wife gave her, as made her look like an old bantam! She were homely, Sophia, always!"

"But where's the taffety gown?"

"Ay! Where is it?—wi' folks a-creeping about i' the night, when decent people is asleep. Sophia's gone up to Sanchia's about it; they'll just ha' missed each other, but Sophia'll wait for her—the baggage! Such a fanteeg I never did see: there's more to it than the taffety gown, or ye may call Nell Barker a noodle. *Close* Mullyon women have al'ays been, an' Sophia's closest o' the lot. I'd like rarely to ferret through yon chest for mysen; Sophia's that wily she'll never let ye get a-near it! Right on the far side o' room ye may set, and she'll open the lid an inch or two, and grope about till she finds what ye're asking for. I've heerd my granny tell rare tales o' the Mullyons' old chest. I've heerd her say——"

In the Jodrell living-room Sophia and Sanchia faced each other.

"Ye'll give me back the goods ye've stolen!"

"I've stolen naught. You promised me the dress an' the shawl, an' I've got a right to wear 'em. They don't belong to you. They're Mullyon stuff, an' they'll be mine one day, anyhow!"

"That they shan't, if I set fire to the lot o' them!"

"Ye'll not do that," said Sanchia, easily. "Ye're that set on the old rubbish—'twould be like burning yourself. Besides, gold an' pearls won't burn."

"Who's talking o' gold an' pearls?" whispered Sophia, hoarsely.

"I am; ye know I've gotten it—the fine necklace ye never even gave me sight on, all these years! No good to ye it was, an' ye was too jealous to let me wear it!"

A change had come over Sophia; a sickly pallor superseded the angry flush that patched her high cheekbones and long foolish chin; her hands, clasped across her waistband, clenched themselves so that the veins stood out like dark worms.

"'Twasn't jealousy," she muttered, and moistened her dry lips. "Afore you was born I swore to your granny I'd not let ye see it. I swore as I'd get rid o' the thing: throw it over the Point into the sea. 'Tis cursed gold—*pirates' gold.*"

Sanchia stared, as she asked, uncompromisingly:

"Why didn't ye keep your word?"

"I couldn't make up my mind to it," confessed Sophia. "When I was young an' vain I used to look at it, an' wonder how it would go round my neck; but I never durst put it on. 'Twas cursed—your granny telled me so."

"An' how did she come by it?"

Sophia twisted her fingers, her head jerked from side to side, like a fowl's, evading her daughter's imperious eyes.

"'Twas pirates' leavings—heathen stuff——"

"That's all very well; but how did Mullyons come by it? The soldiers went off wi' the treasure—ye've told me so, many a time."

"Ye're to give it back," muttered Sophia, weakly.

"Nay," said Sanchia, and her hand went to the neck of her gown; it came up to the base of her throat, as women's gowns are worn on El Secredo; but now Sophia noticed a disarrangement, a straining of the clumsy gathers about the neck. Her fingers flew to her trembling mouth.

"For pity's sake, Sanchia, ye're wearing it now!"

"Maybe 'tis pirates' gold," said Sanchia, "but what was Ralph Mullyon? No more Mullyon than yon rock! There *are* no Mullyons! The last Mullyon died in 1863, an' Ralph, him as they called Mullyon—he——"

With a thin cry of rage Sophia smote her daughter across the mouth. A red patch flamed, and a little drop of blood beaded Sanchia's lip, where her tooth had caught it.

"The woman wi' hair like flax on a spinning-wheel," went on Sanchia; she was smiling faintly, appeared unconscious of the blow. "Ask Nell Barker, who got it from her granny; 'twas she that wore this necklace; 'tis her blood as runs in my veins—no speck or spot o' Mullyon——"

With a whoop of hysteria Sophia Mullyon dragged open the door and rushed away. Sanchia laughed a little, and trembled, and pressed the golden torque closer into her flesh. When she saw Miss Robbins approaching the house, she had a woman's longing to display her treasure, to enjoy the other's admiration and envy; but second thoughts decided her to reserve her effect for the night of the feast.

Miss Robbins had arranged, on the previous evening, to help Sanchia to prepare her new home. It was a task in which, as a rule, the island women delighted: jesting slyly as they worked at the expense of the newly married couple. But none had come forward to offer their services to Sanchia; nor had she troubled herself, with the feast at hand. "Why should I get fretting about it? There's little enough to do."

Gregory had directed her attention to a couple of sea-chests, one on top of the other, that stood against their bedroom wall, on the night he had brought her home as bride.

"Them's full o' my mammy's things, as she gave me afore she died, Sanchia; there's a rare feather-bed as she made herself—for my wife, she told me!—an' a heap o' bedding, wi' some pictures she were fond of. Ye'll look 'em over one day?" She had brushed the subject aside, but the time had come for her to take stock of her resources. Some of the furniture was Gregory's as well; enough to furnish two rooms sparsely. Her mother had promised her more, but she was little likely to get that. Miss Robbins was much more elated at the prospect than Sanchia herself.

"Look here, Sanchia," she began, without preamble. "I've got myself into a nice pickle on account of you."

The girl's stare was almost insolently indifferent; no one on earth, thought Miss Robbins, was more unsatisfactory to help than Sanchia Jodrell; because it was by no means certain that she wished for help.

"I have got myself engaged, in a sort of way, to Henry Martyn."

"Engaged?"

"Betrothed, or whatever you call it. I——" Miss Robbins's confidences were interrupted by a ripple of laughter; up and down it went, like a bird's call, the lovely notes shaken like liquid gold from Sanchia's throat. Her shoulders shook, her hands pressed themselves to her bosom to control her panting breath.

"Whatever did ye do that for?"

"I think you're very ungracious," pointed out Miss Robbins, coldly. "You don't suppose it is amusing to be betrothed to Henry Martyn?"

"Ye'll never wed him?" gurgled Sanchia.

"And why not, pray?"

"Ye're too old," stated Sanchia, coolly. "An' he's but a lad!"

At the words' unconsciously wounding, the colour ran up Miss Robbins's weather-beaten cheek.

"You are extremely rude!"

"Is truth rude?" asked Sanchia, innocently.

"Truth is nearly always rude," snapped Miss Robbins. "If I take you to England with me, Sanchia, I shall insist on your not telling the truth."

"Who says I'm going to England?"

"Oh, stop laughing, and I'll explain. I suppose you think that getting off this island is going to be as simple as walking into the sea?"

"I'm not leaving the island," said Sanchia.

"Perhaps you are, perhaps you aren't. It depends on Gregory. You haven't told him yet, I suppose?"

She shook her head slowly.

"The sooner you do, the better; then we shall know where we are. If Gregory turns you out, the island isn't the place for you."

"What is?" she asked, simply.

"You'll have to come to England with me."

"Is Henry Martyn going to England with you?"

"Don't be silly. Henry Martyn is part of my plan for getting you away."

"Why?"

Miss Robbins explained, as far as possible in words of one syllable; Sanchia regarded her fingers thoughtfully.

"Shall I have to marry the dumb man?" was her surprising query.

"Certainly not. If it comes to that, he isn't at all anxious to marry you."

"Then I don't mind going," said Sanchia, looking up.

"Sanchia; do you love anything or anybody but yourself?" demanded Miss Robbins, abruptly.

"Ay; I love him. But I don't want to wed him. I want to wed someone I can talk to, someone who can tell me things——"

"Then if he recovered his voice——?"

She shook her head again.

"Nay; we're not made that way. Not for marrying. The world's big; there must be others . . . I'll tell Gregory, after the feast."

"But the ship may be here any day now?"

"Then I'll tell him when the ship comes."

"I believe you really want the feast, after all!"

"I want to wear the taffety gown," said Sanchia.

It is customary on the island for the bride-to-be, some days before her feast, to call upon each family, formally inviting them to the festivities. Generally she performs this slightly embarrassing duty on the arm of her future husband; dressed in their best, the young couple proceed solemnly from house to house, on their superfluous errand: superfluous because, since every man, woman and child on El Secredo has done his or her share in preparation, exclusiveness is out of the question. Enemies are invited as effusively as friends, friends as stiffly as enemies. Exhausted with their labours of goodwill, people sit at home, waiting for "the askings," which take place about sunset, when the day's work is done. At each house a meal is spread, and the visitors invited to partake; by the time the "askings" are over the bride is generally bilious and the groom torpid with indigestion. Everything is carried out according to strict tradition, and with the most scrupulous formality.

"I'm grieved ye'll have to do the askings by yoursen, Sanchia," said Gregory.

She started; for some reason or other this formidable ceremony had escaped her reckonings.

"'Tis foolish to have the askings," she said, stubbornly. "We're wed already, an' they all know to come, wi'out my going round from door to door."

For some reason or other Gregory was adamant; it appeared that to omit "the askings" would be sorely to offend the majority of his friends.

"If ye're timid at going by yoursen, I'll ask my father to go wi' ye," he said, persuasively.

"I'll go," said Sanchia. It was not fear that held her back, but her proud disinclination to eat the bread of people whom she felt hated her. She let it be known, through Miss Robbins, that she intended to do "the askings," and prepared herself for the ordeal. When she had washed, and rearranged her hair, she found a clean print gown. It was hardly the weather yet for flimsy stuffs, but the old brown was patched out of decency; over it, after a moment's consideration, she draped the Paisley shawl.

Her first call, in accordance with tradition, was at the mission. The Reverend Smith, opening his door in person, was taken aback by the vision of a slim beauty silhouetted against the golden evening sky; here and there, from the Paisley shawl, glowed like jewels a ruby red, a fierce emerald, that, with the shifting of the light, merged themselves inexplicably once more into the soft autumnal web that draped Sanchia's shoulders. She dropped her curtsy, by no means unaware of the effect she had made.

"I have come, on behalf of Gregory an' me, to ask you to our feast," she said, demurely, having supplemented the time-honoured formula by the introduction of Gregory's name.

"Dear me, Sanchia!" said the Reverend Smith. "Dear me—hrrum! I hardly knew you at first. I shall be delighted to come, of course"—the note of Christian forbearance which sounded, in spite of himself, in his voice brought a warning flash to Sanchia's eye—"I have been—hrrum—extremely busy all to-day, and I'm afraid there is not much to eat; but you will take a cup of tea with me?" Etiquette allowed of no less, but he was acutely embarrassed as she stepped across his threshold, with the air of a young queen, and, seating herself by his table, allowed him to wait upon her.

It was trying to discover that Sanchia by no means shared

his embarrassment. Her manner was composed, quiet, and she neither attempted to make conversation, nor was discountenanced by his silence. Having drunk her tea, she rose, dropped her curtsy, thanked him kindly, and swam out like a dark young cygnet upon the evening twilight. At the Robertsons' she found them prepared for her; John and Maggie, Jack and Jed, with Timothy, Seth and Barnabas Jodrell, young Betty and young Martha—both a little tallowy and black-eyed, after their sickness: Miss Robbins, and, inevitably, Henry Martyn—all in their Sunday best, painfully clean and tidy, the men in their Sunday suits, the women as smart as they could manage to be. The palms of Sanchia's hands felt damp, but a little tingle of elation ran along her spine, as she approached, conscious of their eyes, and conscious, too, that, whatever might have been their attitude towards her in the past, they were constrained to civility, if not to deference, in the present instance. She made her curtsy, spoke her little speech, and waited; it was for the head of the household to respond. They all stood, staring at her, stupidly, like oxen; solemn their faces were, as though each one of them considered whether she was worthy of their courtesy. Maggie poked her husband in the ribs, and John Robertson spoke heavily, gracelessly:

"Ay, we'll all be there—to cheer Gregory up."

The equivocal speech was covered by Miss Robbins, who rushed forward a little nervously and embraced Sanchia, glad of the opportunity to hide her face for a moment against the girl's cool cheek.

"I'm looking forward to it most awfully," she whispered, and withdrew, somewhat chilled by Sanchia's calm reception of her greeting.

"Ye'll come an' eat, Sanchia," Maggie was saying. "Sit ye down there—atween Jed an' Henry Martyn."

The long table was lavishly furnished; the little girls slipped into their seats with covert squeaks and giggles, and eyes for none but Sanchia. Miss Robbins was placed on the farther side of Henry Martyn, whom presently she nudged, during a pause in the conversation.

"Speak to Sanchia!"

"Why should I? I've naught to say to her."

"Tell her she looks nice in that shawl."

Henry Martyn stared at Miss Robbins as though he imagined that she had taken leave of her senses. She bent forward impatiently and spoke the words for herself:

"That shawl's marvellous, Sanchia!"

All eyes focused solemnly upon Sanchia; with jaws masticating their food, the household looked more than ever like creatures in their byre.

"You look wonderful in it!" persisted Miss Robbins. Young Martha choked in her tea-cup, and was vociferously scolded by her mother; silence fell again, broken only by the sound of mastication and the men sucking the tea out of their saucers. Betty Robertson broke out explosively:

"Mammy's made twenty tarts for ye, Sanchia!"

"That's kindly," said Sanchia, with a semi-royal inclination of her proud head. Jed Robertson gave a guffaw, which he hastily repressed as his sister had done. Seth essayed a mild jeer, to show that he, at least, was not overawed by this strange, adorned Sanchia; but they were all exquisitely uncomfortable, and, save for these hysterical manifestations of their discomfort, well-behaved. The only one who appeared to act naturally was Sanchia herself, who ate with a young, healthy appetite of the food provided by Maggie, and, presently, with none of the awkwardness which Miss Robbins had seen among more civilized society, rose, wished them good day, and withdrew. Her going left a silence; each glanced furtively at his *vis-à-vis*, unwilling to take the responsibility of a first opinion. Maggie, as behoved the mistress of the house, spoke characteristically:

"Sanchia looks right bonny. I'd not be surprised if she don't settle down rarely, once her an' Gregory's truly wed."

A sceptical grunt from John was the only dissentient sound.

So Sanchia passed from house to house; meeting, if no definite welcome, at least no demonstration of ill-will. Tradition holds fast on El Secredo, and for the sake of the Mullyons they stifled their dislike and received her with the stiff, ambiguous courtesy of the occasion. Her visit to the Hawkins's was the most uneasy; it was difficult, even for Sanchia, to sit unmoved beneath the frosty politeness of Janet, the thinly veiled mockery of young Jim, and Samson's heavy obliviousness of her presence. She sighed with relief when she left their table for the Barkers'; the false amiability of Nell was easier to withstand than the stately honesty of Janet, who had always hated her: who hated her more on account of her first-born, Samson.

She came back to Gregory with her mission accomplished, to find him in the throes of his agony; the bedding was soaked with sweat and old Samson doing his well-meaning best. Flinging off her hat she cast one glance at the bed.

"Ye should ha' fetched the minister. Go on now, as fast as ye can; 'tis morphia he needs."

He was too far gone to be told the result of her visiting; she did the only thing she could—held fast by his hand, until the Reverend Smith arrived. It seemed to her that she had never seen him in such pain; her own body cringed with the imaginative reflex of Gregory's suffering.

The immediate result of "the askings" was a change of attitude towards Sanchia. With relief the people, tired of a feud that led nowhere, sank their malice in childish enjoyment of preparation: now they worked differently. Whereas each had laboured glumly, deferring to Sophia Mullyon, but secretly, as regards each other, and with a sense of disassociation, they now consulted Sanchia, went to her, naturally, for praise, approval or criticism, as would have been the case had they been living in amity before. She received their overtures—unselfconscious as they were: so

far, at least, the Reverend Smith was right in his estimation
of their childishness—with dignity, dismissing the past yet
not denying it. Courteous she was willing to be; but not
friendly. There was nothing odd about that; they had never
known her otherwise. At her best she had tolerated them;
more frequently she had moved in their midst, ignoring
their existence. They came to her a little shyly, but unconscious of any awkwardness in the situation: if they chose to
forget the past, why should not Sanchia do likewise? The
few who were inclined to patronize were disarmed by
Sanchia's cool demeanour: found their services accepted as
her due—the due of any young married woman of the island
—the question of favour dismissed.

Everyone felt the lifting of the cloud of malice which had
threatened to rob them of full enjoyment of their rare
festivity. The Reverend Smith's geniality reappeared like
the full-orbed sun from behind a cloud-bank; a joyous sense
of justification radiated through his depleted energies, and
would have made him unbearable, at any rate to Miss
Robbins, if that lady had not experienced also a thawing of
her icily critical spirit. Even when he rashly indulged in "I
told you so's," she mercifully withheld comment which
might have betrayed her own growing apprehension and
clouded the summer of his new-born delight in his islanders.
"You see, I was right; these people are like children. An
appeal to their childishness is the solution of all difficulty,"
crowed the Reverend Smith like an amiable bantam.

A group of school children was passing the mission, their
arms laden with grasses and the few struggling flowers that
spring was bringing to the island; they were on their way to
decorate Sanchia's new house. They sang and chattered, like
ordinary, pleasant children; taking the cue from their
parents, they had sunk their whispering and giggling. The
somewhat unhealthy interest which had centred in Sanchia
as a "bad woman" was replaced by joyous apprehension of
the coming feast. . . . And a knot of young men, led by
Job Barker, vanished up into the mountain, shortly before

nightfall; fortunately for them, the Reverend Smith did not observe their departure.

A great pooling of resources had taken place. Although the islanders were starving for the practical necessities of life, there were few households that could not boast a little secret store, of jam, or flour, or sugar, jealously hoarded for the Christmas junketing that coincides with the island's mid-summer. Janet Hawkins had a dozen jars of bottled cran-berries, and parted with them sourly, a prey to island tradition, which brooks no niggardliness on such occasions; as she dispatched them to the Mullyons' cottage, her eye rested with passionate resentment upon her son Samson. He had grown dour and silent, and his temper was like gun-powder. Harry Sanguinetti sheepishly produced, at Rose's bidding, an enormous side of bacon. The lack of salt and the lack of soap were the most difficult obstacles to over-come; garments and household linen lay out on the beach, weighted with heavy stones, to bleach in the wind and sun-shine: a fitful scurry of rain brought anxious housewives to the rescue of their finery, a brief blaze of sun sent them forth once more. There was no shortage of geese, or mutton: fish, sea-birds and their eggs: potato puddings, and the butter which each housewife managed to save from her milk ration. Twenty-four hours before the feast was to begin, all was ready: the ovens built, firing collected, meat dressed and potatoes peeled. El Secredo retired to its rest, in blissful consciousness of duty done and merriment ahead.

The Reverend Smith Prudhomme left the Jodrells' house carolling his favourite hymn, *Onward, Christian Soldiers*; he could not carol very loudly, because breathing was still a painful matter, but he achieved a militant humming, which continued while he scanned the horizon for the expected ship. It would be a fine, triumphant touch if she elected to arrive during the festival proceedings. Pray heaven there would be a doctor on board; Gregory Jodrell had had a terrible day. A day so bad that the Reverend Smith had been obliged to postpone his own suggestion—that the feast should begin with a short service in the mission: a few hymns, a portion from the Bible, and a brief admonition to the islanders on the subject of moderation and abstemiousness, even in feasting. Gluttony, he hoped to point out, was as revolting a sin as drunkenness—his heart quickened a beat; what about the illicit still in the mountains? He prayed, urgently and sincerely, that he might not be brought into contact with Calvary beer. He had kept a sharp look out during the past weeks, and was tolerably satisfied that all was well: yet uneasiness stirred in his brain. He had frequently denied the secretiveness of the islanders, because to acknowledge it seemed to reflect upon his own influence.

Samson Jodrell, to whom he mentioned the matter, favoured the mission service; Sanchia, who had stood at his elbow during the brief conversation, at least withheld irony. Gregory would like it, she averred, without committing herself to personal opinion.

"Then I may look forward to seeing you there, Sanchia?" pressed the Reverend Smith, rather rashly.

"'Twill depend on Gregory," she replied. "If he's sick I'll not be able to leave him."

On impulse, the Reverend Smith laid his hand upon her sleeve.

"You have been very good to Gregory," he said. She looked surprised, and Samson resentful.

"'Twas her duty," he muttered.

"Ay, Samson: and if we all did our duty, we should build Eden on Calvary, eh?" said the Reverend Smith, and departed in an atmosphere of Christianity.

Samson turned upon his son's wife; she stood calmly, with her hands folded.

"I don't trust ye," he flung at her, suddenly.

"Nay, I know that," she responded.

"Why should ye cherish him nowadays—when ye refused to be a wife to him afore?"

"I'm wed to him, aren't I?"

"What have ye done wi' yer fancy man?"

"If ye speak o' the dumb fellow, 'tis for the rest o' ye to answer that—not I."

"He'll ha' died by now!"

"Maybe."

He glowered at her from deeply suspicious eyes, before turning and stumping away into the house.

CHAPTER XVI

DAWN was at hand: with a rustling of grasses, with grey in the sky, with a quickening of the surfaces of the kelp, with a crying of sea-birds. It was still too dark to read a page of print; indoors the shadows were scarcely disturbed. An icy coldness, as from a wind that has cooled itself among the bergs of the Antarctic, penetrated through hide and tarpaulin, and brought to sleepers their first consciousness of the coming day.

Sanchia flung aside the bed-coverings, offering her body, moistly warm from her slumbers, to the morbid chill that filled the room: a chill of unopened windows, of stale air. A quivering excitement, a sense of climax, drove her from uneasy sleep to activity. It was her feast day; but it was more than that.

She allowed the rumpled nightgown to slide to her feet, and sat, looking down at the pale lines of her own body. Her glance focused on the smooth curve of her abdomen; was it her fancy, or had its roundness already faintly increased? It would increase and increase: like a great vase . . . until one day, it would lie flat, concave, small and shrivelled: perhaps the stretched skin would wrinkle; and then she would know she was old. To-day was her festival: the festival of her farewell to youth. Afterwards, Gregory must be told.

She had a strange reluctance, that was not fear, to telling Gregory. She neither feared his wrath, nor was ashamed of her confession. The whole thing seemed to her inevitable. The impersonality of her feeling towards Gregory robbed her of a sense of betrayal. She had simply fulfilled herself as a woman; it was a kind of accident that it had not been Gregory who had helped her to do it. She had not felt "that way" towards Gregory; sex had not stirred in her until the coming of the dumb man. The rest had been natural: she could see it was natural. No one could make her feel wicked about it. The mistake had been in her own weak adherence to her promise, whose recognized folly had scared her into insistence upon its immediate redemption on the night the mission was burnt down.

She began to wonder what the child would be like; the stranger in her womb—something to do with the touch of the dumb man's mouth on her own and the quick soft caresses of his hands. She had no conventional feelings of motherhood towards it: rather, a philosophical acceptance of this, the logical outcome of her infidelity to Gregory. Her mind groped among dim conjecturings upon heredity, for some clue to the result of this curious mingling of blood: Sanchia, so-called Mullyon, and the unknown: El Secredo and western civilization. A soft, half-melancholy pity stirred in her, a brief compunction for her own share in the act that brought another child to El Secredo.

She had persuaded herself almost completely of Gregory's forgiveness, by now; yet she shrank from telling him. His helplessness had made her tender towards him: the cessation of his demands on her womanhood had made it easy for her to feel gently to him. She had begun to realize that all her anger and enmity had arisen from that physical love for her which she was so far from returning. She wondered how many other island women had felt the same for their husbands, and had smothered their dislike, either for the man's sake, or from a sense of the hopelessness of it all.

She must tell Gregory. In some way or other, the arrival of the feast had crystallized her determination. If only Gregory could have a fairly painless day. The drug that she had stolen was finished; otherwise she might have given him a little dose, which, together with the Reverend Smith's

morphia needle, would have ensured several hours' freedom
from pain. When should she tell him? Perhaps early;
before old Samson had taken up his station by the bed. No;
second thoughts suggested that it would be better when
they were alone: when Henry Martyn and Samson Hawkins
had carried him down to the new house. After the guests
were gone: at night: immediately after they had given him
his sleeping draught.

Then the ship might come as fast as it pleased: and her
lover would escape: and relinquish her to the island and old
age.

It did not seem odd to Sanchia's curiously detached and
objective mind that she should thus part with the man who
was the father of her child. No speck or spot of sentimentality flawed the clear metallic outline of her intellectual
make-up. She knew, unmistakably, that she had exhausted
the possibilities of her lover. He had served her to the
limit of his capacity, and now it was time for them to part.
Her future belonged to the island, and to Gregory Jodrell.
Perhaps she had had some obscure warning that in that
outer world to which she had longed to escape lay disillusionment: failure. In common with many untrained
minds, Sanchia's was crowded, sometimes, with a confusion
of intuitions and fancies that eluded all attempt at formula-
tion or expression. She was a creature of instinct. Hating
El Secredo, she was bound to it in such a fashion that it
required some stronger wrench than the dumb man, or Miss
Robbins, in her different way, could supply to induce her to
exchange certainty for nebulæ. And, for all her somewhat
melodramatic "farewell to youth," she was still young: and
in the young, hope dies hard. The coming of every ship
would bring hope to Sanchia, until the river of her blood
slowed into middle-age. She was willing to set forth, but
she required a fellow traveller, a crutch to her hand. Had
Miss Robbins offered some certain support, Sanchia would
have accompanied her: but the girl's natural shrewdness
apprehended the precariousness of trusting to one of her

own sex, and the knowledge of her own deficiencies made her distrust her own strength.

Her fingers, wandering up her uncovered arm, felt the goose-flesh prickling the surface of her skin. From head to foot she was icy cold.

She pulled a blanket about her, and went, barefooted, to look in through the open door of Gregory's room. Usually, at this hour, he was awake, and she took him a drink. No answer came to her whispered query: Samson was breathing heavily on his pallet in the corner. To-night, thought Sanchia, we shall have a place to ourselves: away from that old man. Standing there, in the darkened room, she thought of the many times when he had sought to humiliate and to drive her: and with the bitter remembrance came instantly the gentler memory of Gregory's protection, which had not failed her when she had been too proud to sue for it. Now, for the first time, she was going to throw herself upon that mercy.

She returned, tiptoe, to her room. Not for another hour would the island be astir. Dawn broadened in the sky. She took the sudden determination to go over to The Rescue and bathe. The weather was still cold, and bitter at this hour of the morning, but Sanchia was hardy, and accustomed as a child, in all weathers, to the water of the bathing pool.

She slipped on the rough serge dress over her naked body, twisted her hair into its knot, and flung a towel about her shoulders. It was difficult to unlock the door without making a sound, but she succeeded, after pushing a little goose-grease into the keyhole, and ran along the shore in the teeth of the freshening wind.

The top of the Peak was already silvered with the dawn when she reached The Rescue. Here a ring of rocks kept at bay the encroaching kelp, and formed a series of pools, most of which were brackish, save the largest and deepest one, which, fed by a stream, showed, clear as glass, the sandy bottom layered with small shells and pebbles. It was a little more than ten feet in depth, and twenty yards across: a puerile effort for a swimmer. She ran a little along the shore, shedding her dress as she ran: then dived, like a young porpoise, into the breath-taking chill of the water. For a few seconds she swam wildly, exerting herself to set the circulation running in her limbs. Always the water struck icily at her body, the flung drops spattered like hail from the sweep of her arm. Suddenly the sky began to blush: rose-red lay upon the ocean. Sanchia leapt from the water, and began to scour herself with the towel; presently she stood upright, an ivory statue, dyed to blush rose by sunrise. She glowed from head to foot, and, reluctant to resume her harsh garment, stood looking out to sea, balanced upon a rock, on which her white toes curled as a gull's feet curl. And, at that very moment, with Sanchia balanced like a lone siren of El Secredo, a trail of smoke, fine as a thread of frayed-out grey silk, appeared on the horizon.

"You could hardly have arrived at a more opportune moment," said the Reverend Smith Prudhomme, as he grasped the hand of the captain of the visiting ship, almost before that worthy had set foot on the beach. Behind the Reverend Smith was ranged the entire grinning population of El Secredo, in Sunday best: for even the arrival of the steamer had not driven from their minds that this was the day of the feast. Starched white cotton dresses took the place of drab serge gowns: old and young alike among the female population of the island flew to starch as the ultimate expression of fashion, and the wind, catching hold of voluminous skirts, cracked them like flags. Miss Robbins, whose use of the needle stopped short at sewing on a button, or darning—extremely badly—a pair of stockings, had accepted Maggie Robertson's offer to run her up a gown out of one of Mrs. Prudhomme's sheets. She stood at the Reverend Smith Prudhomme's elbow, ready to clutch at his arm, for the wind, getting under the hem of the skirt, which Maggie had artlessly fashioned by the simple expedient of joining the ends of a long strip of the heavy linen, and gathering the waist in a bulky frill, threatened at any moment to carry her up in the air, a human balloon, and float her out over the Atlantic.

"That so?" said the captain, and proceeded to wring Miss Robbins's hand, under the erroneous impression that here was the missionary's wife. "I'm afraid you've been through a patch o' dirty weather, ma'am."

"This is Miss Robbins," said the Reverend Smith, hastily. "A—hrrum—famous novelist, Captain——"

"Beecham," said the captain, while Miss Robbins was recovering her breath from this unexpected tribute.

"She has been extremely heroic; we shall be very sorry to say farewell to her," added the Reverend Smith, making it instantly clear that he expected to get rid of Miss Robbins at the first possible opportunity. "A most opportune visit, Captain Beecham! I hope you will be able to prolong your stay sufficiently to join in one of our island festivities. The wedding feast of a most worthy young couple, the Jodrells; the man, poor fellow, has met with a sad accident, while whaling: his young wife has tended him with the most exemplary fidelity——"

Miss Robbins drew another strangled breath, and found Henry Martyn at her elbow. He wore again the antic costume in which he had made his proposal of marriage.

"I want to talk wi' ye."

"They'll be unloading the boats in a minute: you'll want to be there," she pointed out. Her eye flew round the assembly for Sanchia, who was not to be seen. Was she now making her confession to Gregory? What was to be done?

The large hand of Henry Martyn descended upon her arm and drew her irresistibly aside.

"'Tis time I had my answer. If ye'll give me the word we can join in the feast as a betrothed couple."

"Henry," whispered Miss Robbins, looking about her like a hunted hare. "Do you remember me telling you there was something I wanted you to do for me?"

"Ay. Tell me what ye're wanting, an' I'll do it," he answered, forgetting, in his urgency, to be cautious.

The clattering, white-gowned throng had gathered round the boats, the men, many of them, had run to their houses to exchange their decent clothes for rough daily wear. The sailors were unshipping the crates, and the captain, with the Reverend Smith Prudhomme, was wandering up towards the mission.

Miss Robbins came a little closer to Henry Martyn.

"Do you know what's happened to the dumb man?"

He shot a suspicious glance at her before replying.

"He's dead, likely," he muttered, ungraciously.

"No, he's not," contradicted Miss Robbins. "He's alive —very much so: and we've got to get him off the island."

In the following silence Miss Robbins became very conscious of her ridiculous appearance. One could hardly, she reflected wryly, play the Delilah in a costume made of a linen sheet. Then she remembered that to the eyes of Henry Martyn she probably appeared to be dressed in the height of fashion.

"I'll ha' naught to do wi' that," stated Henry Martyn, roundly.

"Look here," said Miss Robbins, "it's no use keeping him here. He'll only die. He's no use. You may as well get rid of him in a less brutal fashion."

"Ay," drawled Henry Martyn, "that's all right. But the chaps here be mortal down on him. Like as not they'll shoot him, if they set eyes on him coming down from the Peak."

"Exactly; and that's why I want you to help us to get him off safely."

"Nay," he answered, shaking his head. "They'd just as soon go for me, if they was to see me helping him."

"But they *won't* see," pointed out Miss Robbins. "Oh, do listen to what I'm trying to tell you. Sanchia's got to be got away, too."

"Eh?" said Henry Martyn, stupefaction appearing on his face.

"She thinks Gregory's going to forgive her, but he won't, of course," babbled Miss Robbins, incoherently. "He'll turn her out—and there'll be nowhere for her to go, and——"

"'Tis a bit too much for me," confessed Henry Martyn. "What's Gregory's wife got to do wi' this business?"

"She's going to have a baby," said Miss Robbins, pushing the wind-blown wisps of grey hair out of her eyes. "Not Gregory's of course; she can't have it here—I'll——" She stopped, suddenly remembering that she could not, at this juncture, inform Henry Martyn that she proposed to take Sanchia with her to England. But the slow wariness of the islander lightened in his eye, and Miss Robbins, cowering inwardly, felt as though a lump of rock was about to fall on her, as he stooped towards her.

"An' ye? An' ye? What's all this got to do wi' ye, I'm asking? Are ye wedding me, or are ye not?"

"Oh, Henry," cried Miss Robbins, weakly, "we can't stop to talk about our own affairs just now."

"Maybe we'll talk o' them when ye're out i' mid-ocean, an' I'm standin' here, eh? Is that your game, my lass? Ye're tricking me, are ye? I'll have my answer, yea or nay, now, whiles I got ye here."

"Oh, and if it is nay?" gasped Miss Robbins. She caught at Henry's hairy hand. "It would never do, Henry! You must see it would never do. We lead different lives; you'd hate mine, and I—I couldn't put up with yours. I thought perhaps I might—I *like* the island: it scares me and it attracts me. I like the spaciousness of life out here. But space isn't everything. I can't marry you, Henry. I must go home. I must——"

He made a queer noise, shook her hand from his wrist and turned his back to her.

"Henry; won't you help me over Sanchia?" Her voice sounded thin and futile, the plaything of the wind; but it brought him swinging round to sneer at her.

"I'll ha' naught to do wi' that. What have ye got to do wi' Gregory's wife? She's an island woman, an' she mun take what the island brings her, good an' ill."

"Henry——" She hesitated, baffled; then a memory from her brief talks with him, when he led her, sheepishly, over his farm buildings, gave her a clue. "You want a new reaper: I'll send you one from England."

"Buyin' yerself free, are ye?" He gave a short laugh. "Nay, there's no need o' that. Some chaps might force ye— ye've led me a gay dance, haven't ye?—just to get me to fall in wi' yer plans. I'm havin' none o' them, an' none o' you. 'Tis finished. Ye can go to England, but ye'll let Sanchia Jodrell alone."

She understood that further pleading was vain, and stood, twisting a fold of her ridiculous skirt, biting her lip and wondering what to say. As he began to move away from her, she pulled her wits together, and ran a few steps after him.

"You'll not tell anyone, will you?"

"Eh, haven't ye quit yer pestering?" he rejoined, rudely.

"But you *must* promise! You'll ruin us all if you say anything."

"'Tis no affair o' mine," muttered Henry Martyn; and with this she had to be content. Left alone at The Rescue— for all the others had gone over to the missionary's house with the crates, and a lively bartering, under the direction of Samson Jodrell and Thomas Mullyon, was in progress— Miss Robbins felt a fool. Honesty obliged her to confess that she had made the situation worse, so far as Sanchia was concerned; neither could she persuade herself that her conduct towards Henry Martyn was in any way creditable. She sat down, rather forlornly, in the billows of her linen skirts, and looked hopelessly out over the Atlantic. In another couple of months all this would be a memory; dismissing the thought of Henry Martyn, her mind clutched avidly at each detail of her surroundings. It was yet early morning: the sky as delicate as turquoise arched above the menacing Peak; a family of penguins waddled down upon the beach, and sought pensively among the rocky pools for fish stranded by the sinking tide. Sail Point jutted out, in a froth of foam and spray, every inch of the rock white with sea-birds. Nature was in one of its rare beneficent moods; the island had decked itself in sunshine for Sanchia's feast.

"Lenox Robbins, you are simply a fool," she apostrophized herself. "Why on earth couldn't you let well alone? Why on earth had you to start mixing yourself up with the lives of these people?"

Henry Martyn did not want her; so much the better. Sanchia did not want her; that was folly on Sanchia's part, of course. But was she to be blamed? As Miss Robbins put this poignant question to herself a gust of wind came rooting along the shore, flinging the sea spray against Miss Robbins's face—an acrid reminder of the island in less benevolent mood. Words of Sanchia came back to her mind: "'Tis queer, the wind on El Secredo. It seems like as if it governs us. Ye mean to do a thing, an' the wind says ye nay. Ye don't mean to do a thing, an' the wind bids ye do it." Had the wind bidden her resign herself? And to what? What fearfulness awaited Sanchia, when Gregory knew all?

She was on her feet, running, running towards the Jodrells' house. She must see Sanchia, and know: and when she knew, there were things to be done—she had her own odds and ends to collect—not much they amounted to—a brush and comb of Mrs. Prudhomme's, her old knitted suit, her precious manuscript. And she must be on the look-out for the dumb man, and warn the sailors, and——

Miss Robbins fell clumsily over the embankment, having hooked her skirt on the top of it. The doors of the Hawkins's and the Mullyons' houses stood ajar: their occupants were at the bartering. Samson Jodrell's door stood wide: she knocked upon it timidly.

Sanchia's voice answered her, softly, from within: the girl appeared, finger to lip, a shawl thrown about her. Pale, gentle, cautious, she came from the indoor twilight into the sun.

"He's just fallen asleep," she whispered. "A rare bad bout he's had—'tis a blessing he's sleeping now."

"Haven't you told him?"

She shook her head, smiling.

"But, for heaven's sake, Sanchia, the boat's in!"

"Ay. We're not going to bother about the boat," said Sanchia. "I'm stopping wi' Gregory, ye know. 'Twill be best, anyhow. Things'll shape themselves, somehow. I'll write an' tell ye, when it's over."

"But Sanchia——!" A weakness slackened Miss Robbins's limbs, and her eyes grew misty. She could not bring herself to remind the girl of the scene from which she had been rescued, on the day of Gregory's accident—if indeed it had passed from her memory. "I can't leave you to it!" burst out Miss Robbins.

Sanchia's eyes became saucer-like with surprise.

"Eh! I can see to myself." Her glance wandered to the Peak, to the vultures that circled in the turquoise arch. "The island'll have its way. Pity's a grand thing," said Sanchia, thoughtfully. "I'm that sorry for Gregory I could nearly care for him; an' the baby'll keep me busy—poor misery! I wish it had come—I'd ha' given it ye to take away, for El Secredo's a poor place for children. Maybe I'll find a way to get rid o' it—maybe someone 'ull come in another boat as will take it away an' save it from growing up here."

"Then there's nothing for me to do," said Miss Robbins, with a sense of flatness.

"Naught," replied Sanchia. "Except ye'll see to *him* getting off, won't ye?"

"Shall you miss me?" asked Miss Robbins, foolishly.

"Ay," responded Sanchia, and smiled her beautiful, rare smile. "It's been fine to talk wi' ye. Maybe ye'll write, an' send me some pictures now an' again? I'll be thinking often o' London an' England an' taxi-cabs! The mails come out twice a year now; 'tis a great convenience."

"Oh, yes, I'll write," said Miss Robbins, and fled, with a sense of rising hysteria.

She realized, as she bundled her possessions together, that a great experience had passed her by, and that she had not known how to make the most of it. Is it possible, she thought, shuffling through her fingers the sheets of her manuscript, that one can be plunged in the Atlantic, saved from death, and brought into contact with a strange and simple folk, and gain nothing thereby? Can one travel to the very bounds of eternity, and return, and be just the same—no better, no wiser; prey to the same old vanities, the same cravings, the same pettiness? If so, what is the use of it? Caprice, or Divine direction—which is responsible?

Half-absently she was reading through a few pages of her novel: the novel that was to raise her from literary obscurity to distinction: the book that was to show the lettered world that she, Lenox Robbins, was a power to be reckoned with. Now and again she smiled over a paragraph: more frequently her brow contracted over some cheap, snappy phrase that detracted from the value of what she had to say.

In a moment of self-assertiveness fostered by the unusually swift exhaustion of a second edition, Miss Robbins had laid down the law to her publisher—a man who, having learnt infinite patience in dealing with woman novelists, allowed at times a speculative glint to lighten in his eye when conversing with Miss Robbins. Lenox Robbins: she had never really made good. Yet one never knew: one saw rather too much of that kind of thing—publishers turning down their old clients, only to send them to another firm with a best-seller in their hands. One might almost think they did it on purpose. At any rate, it was wiser to keep Robbins in the lists for a little longer; better to entertain her —mercifully at lengthy intervals—with China tea and sweet biscuits, cigarettes and a tactful and seemingly receptive ear —until one was quite sure.

"For every second-rate book that is forced upon the public, the chance is minimized for the conscientious writer," Miss Robbins had stated, secure in temporary success.

He made a pooh-poohing gesture through the tobacco wreaths that floated above the desk.

"Value always finds its way to the top."

"That's the theory, of course; it depends what one considers the top. Succès d'estime is all very well if one has a pocket to support it. Material success is equally valuable because it relieves financial anxiety, and liberates the mind for its true purpose—the creative."

"What about *Orlando? The Galaxy? Cimarron?*" He spoke at random. "All of 'em best-sellers, and all the real stuff. No amount of rubbish could choke books of that sort; they rise naturally, of their own purity, as the scum sinks."

"Oh, yes; and what about——" She ran off a list of books, each excellent of its kind, that had failed to reach the level of best-sellers. "What about those? Do you remember what St. John Ervine said about Dennis Hughes's last? It's only been out three months, but you can't find a copy anywhere now. Publicity, I know—Fuller Bannerman's never advertise things properly; but time has a lot to do with it. The English reading public isn't naturally selective; neither are the libraries. If they choke their shelves with rubbish, how is the reader going to find time to struggle through the welter, in search of the few worth-while books? Most people read because they are bored, or sleepy, or want to forget something; they are literary gourmands, not epicures, and anything will do to slake their appetites. Even the reviews don't help much: the papers get lost, or one hasn't a pencil at hand to make out one's list—it is so much easier to go to the girl at the library desk and ask her to recommend something, and she generally has her own axe to grind: a book by a friend, or an influential subscriber——"

"Possibly you're right," he answered, smiling in an annoying, masculine way. "But one mustn't criticize, you know, without offering an amendment. What do you propose to do about it?"

Miss Robbins held her tongue, nonplussed for once.

"Perhaps you would advocate a round robin, requesting all novelists who have sold less than—say, ten editions of their last work, to refrain from production?"

Under the silky phrases Miss Robbins felt the stab of mockery. Who was she to suggest such a course? Yet she knew that she was right. Part of her income was derived from her labours as second reader to a firm of publishers; she knew all about the welter of typescript that finds its way into a publisher's office: the almost impossibility of weeding the grain from the chaff; she knew all about wire-pulling, influence, expensive publicity. Her own small successes had been gained on her own merits—she thanked heaven for it; no rich uncle had financed her publications, she had no relations in the publishing world. These were matters to which one did not refer, face to face with one's own publisher: but she knew they existed, and knew, to a nicety, how far they influenced the big, lazy, easy-going public.

To read her own works gave Miss Robbins a sense of sleek pleasure; she had a certain slickness of style, a feeling for the balance of a sentence, was not sensitive to the importation of foreign phrases—secretly, in a dark corner of her heart, she had a snobbish liking for the neat row of italics which picked out some idiom, demonstrating her familiarity with other tongues. She was well aware that a couple of lines in Italian flattered a good many of her readers.

She read from page to page, smiling, often, with appreciation, at the turning of a phrase, at a jaunty interpolation . . . Gradually the smile died from the corners of her mouth, her brow knit itself; she read with more absorption—and with more misgiving.

As she laid down the concluding pages of the first eleven chapters, Miss Robbins recognized, humbly, that she was not, and never would be, a great writer. Half-stunned by the discovery, she had begun to understand that it is not sufficient to have great material put into one's hand: one must be able to handle it. That without dignity of treatment, even great subjects become commonplace. That flippancy and the cynicism of modern life are like dirty thumb-marks upon the fair surface of idealism. That drama, wrongly treated, too easily becomes melodrama. And that the frivolity that modern convention brings to bear upon the most serious topics had corroded her writing, as it had corroded her mind.

Here and there a bit of portraiture stood out, brilliant, photographic in its fidelity: that was "clever," she supposed. No one had ever denied that her books were "clever." But it takes something more than "cleverness" to raise light fiction to the level of literature.

Heaven knew, she had not intended to mock at the islanders: yet a vein of badinage ran from line to line. Again and again she found herself flippant, where she had intended to be serious. Her characters were caricatures—or puppets twitched out of simple human semblance into gross extravagance of action and speech. The forced note of melodrama sounded again and again, harsh as tympani in an orchestra.

A miracle had happened: Miss Robbins had discovered a literary conscience. She sat there, with the sheets of her last chapter in her hands, and wondered, for the first time, whether she was justified in contributing to an overcrowded market. She saw, in imagination, the work of some new writer being crowded out in favour of her own more familiar name. And she recalled some rather snobbish advice she had once delivered, gratis, to a niece with a talent for scribbling and a thirst for print.

"Unless one is convinced one has done one's very best, and that one means every word one has written, no one has a right to publish anything at all."

Very slowly, with a feeling of rending at the heart, Miss Robbins began to tear into strips the sheets of her manuscript.

The Reverend Smith Prudhomme, genially arm-in-arm with Captain Beecham, popped a roguish head in at the door.

Miss Robbins sat upright on the edge of her bed, with the palms of her hands pressed tightly together. She was doing all in her power not to cry. She looked almost nun-like, in the stiff white linen folds of her gown.

"All ready for departure, Miss Robbins?" called the Reverend Smith, cheerily; Miss Robbins, in her normal mind, would have found something tactless in such cheeriness. "No hurry—no hurry, of course; our good Captain Beecham is giving us the pleasure of his company and that of his sailor lads at our merry-making to-night, so Sanchia will have a gay party indeed! We must have some hornpipes, eh, Captain? I once danced the hornpipe myself, and remember the steps quite well. But I am forgetting my errand. Our good friend Maggie Robertson sent me to tell you that among the goods the women are unpacking is some female apparel which she seemed to think might interest you. I do not know if you are equipped for a sea-voyage? The dress you are wearing, although eminently becoming, would probably be a little draughty aboard ship."

Miss Robbins rose from her bed somewhat as a somnambulist may move.

"You must not forget any of your belongings," admonished the Reverend Smith, looking round the little shed. He managed to stifle a sigh of relief. After all, she had been helpful—according to her lights. He had been quite glad of her, since his accident. The ship's doctor was coming over presently: that was a good thing. He dropped his voice to a note of caution. "I have managed to get a word in with our good Captain—about our—hrrum—unfortunate friend in the mountains. The sailors will look after him when he makes his appearance. He is no doubt aware the ship has arrived?"

"No doubt," said Miss Robbins, dully.

"Your—hrrum—domicile will, I presume, be the rendezvous? You will instruct your men to be on the look-out after nightfall, Captain?"

"That's right," said Captain Beecham. "'S' a matter o' fact I've got a kind o' notion who the fellow may be, from your description of him. It sounds mightily as if it's a sort o' relative o' the owner—not as there's been any partic'lar hue an' cry after him, as you might say: a bit of a ne'er-do-weel. They shipped him off for the trip to get him out of a bit o' trouble in Cape Town."

"Then he's not dumb?" came explosively from Miss Robbins.

"Dumb, ma'am? I should say not—not in them days, anyhow. 'S a matter o' fact, it was his tongue as got him into trouble. Too good at fairy tales, he was—if it's the chap I mean. Thin, mingy-looking sort o' chap—no stamina, if you get my meaning."

"Well, well," cried the Reverend Smith, heartily. "The poor fellow's identity makes no difference to us, though we are glad to know he has people who will receive and succour him. The service will be at eleven, Miss Robbins: I have put it an hour later, to give the people time to finish their bartering and tidy themselves up. Then, hey for our merry-making! You, Miss Robbins, will foot it featly, I am sure! A happy memory to take with you, when you return to old England—to write."

"I am returning to England—to think," said Miss Robbins, slowly.

CHAPTER XVII

Between the Jodrell house and the new cottage, clapped on to the end of Atlantic View, which Gregory had built for his bride, stands Samson Jodrell's barn, a building always in requisition for island festivities. It is packed from wall to wall for the dance which forms the invariable climax to such entertainments. The men, still gorged from their midday meal, make, as a rule, phlegmatic partners; the women, for once in the ascendant, pinch, tease and buffet their unwilling attendants into activity.

Above the heads of the throng, precariously perched on the long rafter which spans the barn midway, sits Timothy Hawkins, with his fiddle. On the rafter beside him are cans of refreshment—of a kind that offers no menace to his balance: a sickly sweet fruit cordial, made from cranberries, fresh or bottled, according to season, and freshened with sprigs of mint; tea, brewed black in an open copper over the fire in the lean-to, is the alternative drink, and, being more potent, is much in request.

Up among the shadows and the cobwebs Timothy tunes his instrument; amid the blackness of the beams sparkle like pin-pricks the watchful eyes of the large, voracious Calvary rats, resentful of Timothy's invasion of their premises. Black smoke rises upward from the flambeaux clamped mediævally to the sides of the barn: Timothy is wreathed in it—before the night is over his shining, sweaty face will be black as a negro's. The smoke pours out into the night through the vast gap of an improvised chimney, above which appears a blue silken rectangle of night sky with great, low, blazing stars.

Tunes long forgotten fall wistfully from above, delicate as rain on sweating brows; tunes that came to the island with Jebusa Horne and his followers titivate the feet to a dancing measure: it must have been the womenfolk who remembered these tunes, and crooned them over the cradles, when their menfolk were out of the way; for Jebusa never lifted his great voice, save in hymn tunes of the most lugubrious, and there was no dancing in his reign. *Pretty Polly Perkins of Paddington Green, Vilikens and his Dinah, Come, Lasses and Lads*—these are rare lilting airs for the feet to trip to.

At the beginning of the evening, a certain stiffness controlled the proceedings; men and women, a trifle self-conscious, uncertain of their steps, went cautiously, their faces set in grim lines of concentration and anxiety: teeth were set, nails dug into brawny arms, ribs cracked under remorseless and purposeful grips. The sailors made a difference to all that: better fed, and therefore less gluttonous than the islanders, they had not gorged their wits away on the potato puddings, the fat geese, the hastily improvised sweetmeats of the dinner hour. Again, at midnight, the revellers would sit down, to eat again of the same fare; the men would overeat themselves, go outside to vomit, and return to the tables, grimly determined to make the most of their opportunities.

"Clear the floor!" shouted the Reverend Smith, peremptorily. "Now, my friends! Lancers! Six sets at a time, and the rest of you must sit out and wait your turns. Now, Captain, you must set the ball rolling by choosing your partner!"

Running a finger round the edge of his wilting collar, the captain stood in the middle of the floor, smiling lazily. His roving eye explored the ranks.

Rose Sanguinetti giggled. With the recuperative powers of her kind, she had left her bed, and come, baby in arms, to join the company. She was very pale, transparent and pretty, with the bright light of excitement burning in her eyes.

Harry's mother had made a rare fuss about her coming: "'Twas enough to be the death of her," she had said. Did they think she was going to forgo the chance of appearing in Mrs. Prudhomme's best gown? She tossed her pretty head invitingly, and laid the baby in Harry's arms, as a signal that she expected to be asked. But Captain Beecham's eye wandered idly over her head, and she flushed with mortification.

"'Tis Sanchia he's looking for!" she cried shrilly. She wasn't going to be overlooked for anyone but Sanchia. After all, it was her feast, and she had a right to dance with the captain.

"Where's Sanchia?" shrilled a chorus of female voices: they grudged her the honour, but were too mistrustful of their own powers to volunteer to fill her place. One or two of the elder women began edging their way to the background.

The captain nodded approval; it was Sanchia he wanted. She had caught his eye in church, and afterwards, at the dinner, he could scarcely look away from her. Captain Beecham, a lady-killer by nature and opportunity, had experienced a sinking at heart, after his first glance at the island women.

But Sanchia—she was not pretty: she was better than that. There was something provocative about her: if she would only lift her head and pay a bit of attention to a fellow. He'd see if he couldn't waken her up when she danced with him.

"Sanchia's putting her gown on!"

It was Maggie Robertson's Martha that volunteered the explanation: Martha, who, thrilled out of her usual stolid puddingishness, looked really pretty as she seized her mother's skirts and jumped up and down.

"Hold your noise!" said Maggie, bestowing a slap, not unkindly, but in order to vindicate her own authority in the eyes of the onlookers. But Martha was beyond the bounds of parental control: she and Betty had been for the last ten

minutes out in the darkness, with their noses glued to a
window-pane of the Jodrell house; and while they clung
there, gasping and thrilling, their elder brother Jed had
come by, asked what they were "peeking" at and, when
told, took a "peek" for himself and laughed; then he had
pulled Martha's plait—she was his favourite, and offered her
a drink out of a can: and she had taken a gulp and nearly
choked: the tears had filled her eyes and the burning liquid
had run out of her mouth down the front of her clean pina-
fore.   Jed had laughed even more at that, and told her to
"Hold her tongue" and not tell anybody; and presently,
when her mouth had ceased to burn, a wonderful feeling
came over Martha, of gaiety and courage, so that, in spite of
being a rather stodgy and self-conscious little girl, she had
run into the barn and told her mother, before them all, that
Sanchia was changing her gown!

"An' Miss Robbins is a-helping her—an' they've got
cangles—twenty cangles—an' she's shinin'—an' she'll be
here soon!"

They all heard the piercing proclamation, and a few of the
women looked with disfavour upon Martha's apple cheeks,
that fairly glittered to-night with excitement and the drink
Jed had given her.

"That child'll have the bad stomach to-morrow," said
Janet Hawkins, sourly: she had never been able quite to
forgive Maggie Robertson for having two girls.

A buzz of anticipation filled the room: a vague excitement spread itself among the people. At the far end, on a
platform built of salvaged planks, sat the principal characters
at this feast: in the midst of them, propped up on a tilted
trestle bed, like the corpse at a wake, lay Gregory. He had
insisted upon being carried into the barn for an hour. His
face was the colour of the spotless, unbleached sheets; his
lips smiled stiffly over his teeth. He had allowed Sanchia to
clip his beard and moustache, so that he looked less wild;
but in some way the loss of the covering accentuated his
look of fragility, made it unearthly; Miss Robbins had shud-

dered; she was reminded of an early Italian painting of the
Christ being lifted into the sepulchre.

On Gregory's left sat Samson Jodrell: on his right
Thomas and Sophia Mullyon—the latter incredibly stiff in
rusty satin, with multiple bows and ruchings; the skirt,
intended to be worn over a crinoline, fell voluminously
about her broad hips and knees: she had to hold it up in
both hands when she walked. Her watchful eye glinted
here and there, keeping guard over her belongings: Nell
Barker, in the quilted petticoat, which, worn with a pleated
bodice and lace yoke, gave her the appearance of having
wrapped her lower extremities hastily in an eiderdown. An
air of children's masquerade hung over the party; odd
sartorial compositions, in which a dolman trimmed with
moth-eaten fur partnered the sprigged summer print of the
island. Like a hawk Sophia Mullyon's eye swooped upon
Ellen Barker, who trailed about in the puce sarsanet, a cup
of tea in her hand.

"Put it down—set it down this minute, Ellen!" shrilled
Sophia. As Ellen tossed her head, but turned to obey,
the barn door swung open, and Miss Robbins came in
hurriedly.

"Here's Sanchia," she announced, in a breathless voice.
All heads turned towards the door.

A young goddess swam in among them. Every inch of
the narrow fringe that looped and bordered the flounces of
the taffety gown rippled with her movement, as a field of
corn ripples with the passing of the wind; the light from the
lanterns flowed down the winy folds like orange fountains;
her hands clasped at waist-level, with an instinctive primness
that derived from the lovely gown, were lost in the triple
fringe of wide belled sleeves. She wore her secret, downcast
look: as though the audience were nothing to the fine company of her own thoughts. Secret, dark, reserved she was:
neither humble nor proud. The Paisley shawl hung behind
her, as Miss Robbins had draped it over her forearms. And
from the pearly base of her throat the silken bodice was

tucked away, so that all could behold the gleam and flash of the golden torque.

Sophia Mullyon's face flushed purplish, and she caught her lower lip in her teeth. In the awkward moment, while breath was held, and eyes slipped sidelong to glean opinions of this unforeseen spectacle, Captain Beecham stepped up to Sanchia and made a low bow.

"Mrs. Jodrell, ma'am," he began, and stammered a little, for all his hardihood, as Sanchia's eyes lifted themselves to the level of his own, "will you favour me——?"

She was about to lay her hand on his arm, when an inspiration came to her, of her new-born consideration for Gregory. Her head turned sharply across her shoulder towards the pale, corpse-like figure on the platform, and she tugged her hand from the captain's ready clasp, and ran to her husband.

"I'll sit wi' ye, Gregory, if ye'd rather?" she said, quickly.

"Nay, lass—I'd like fine to see ye dancing in your pretty gown," whispered Gregory. "I'll not be staying long—it's starting again—the pain: but I'd like fine to see ye in one dance, afore they carry me home."

His eyes travelled lovingly up the young curve of her bosom to the soft uncovered space where the gold torque shone.

"Yon's grand finery; I never knowed ye'd got it. Ye look rare kindly to-night, Sanchia; 'tis burning shame ye've got no husband to tender ye."

"You're all I want, Gregory," she whispered, pantingly.

"Ye're uncovered," snarled Thomas Mullyon, snatching at her arm as she passed him.

"Let go o' me, Father!"

"Cover your neck, ye hussy!"

She dragged herself away with a laugh, and ran out on the floor.

"Begin!" she cried, and extended her hand to the captain, who placed himself, with a leap, at her side.

The fiddle chirped: the heavy tramp of feet began— set to partners—set to corners—ladies in the centre. The Reverend Smith's stentorian roar governed the dancers. As Sanchia's feet, and the taffety gown, and the dancing fringes flew out, Miss Robbins tweaked the missionary's sleeve.

"I'll just run over and see if he's come down yet," she whispered. "While they're dancing will be a grand opportunity to get him on to the ship."

The Reverend Smith nodded. Everything was going his way. Here were his islanders, enjoying life in the innocent and childlike fashion natural to them. Their time of tribulation over, they celebrated the new era of plenty. Friendliness and goodwill in every eye. Troublesome elements eliminated—in an hour, at least, the most troublesome would be safely off the island, aboard the ship. Pleasant to see that Sanchia was unaffected by his going—perhaps they had misjudged her, after all? One must be careful, charitable in one's judgments. It had been difficult to view things coolly, in a time of universal stress. A young, high-spirited thing; it was now all right between her and Gregory. God moves in a mysterious way His wonders to perform. Gregory praying for Sanchia to be brought to the way of righteousness. Poor fellow, poor fellow; he couldn't last long. . . . This was a teasing thought, and the Reverend Smith thrust it hurriedly aside; he had had enough, for the present, of Sanchia's matrimonial complications. Miss Robbins: an excellent woman, but subversive to authority: too adventurous a mind. She too would be removed; her fretful criticisms would cease to worry him. And the ship's doctor had paid attention to his ribs, so that he was tolerably comfortable. Sad that nothing could be done for Gregory Jodrell. The Lord's will be done. The Reverend Smith metaphorically stretched out arms of welcome to the new peace that had come upon Calvary.

The dancers were out of breath; shrieking, panting, clutching each other, laughing with an abandon foreign to their usual selves. And a few young men passed out into the darkness.

In the boisterous clasp of Captain Beecham Sanchia whirled like a butterfly on a branch. As Timothy Hawkins brought the dance to an end, with a grand roulade on the fiddle, she broke away with her hand to her side; she stood there, laughing like a mænad—like a mad thing, said the disapproving few—her hair had become unpinned, and rolled down her back in a heavy curl, warm with lantern-light. Those who had been sitting out stampeded on to the floor to take their turn; slipping like an eel between them, she evaded Captain Beecham's hungry clutch and made her way to Gregory. A glance showed her that things went badly with him: she sobered instantly, and cried above the clamour of voices:

"Samson Hawkins—Henry Martyn! Where are ye? Gregory is ready to be carried home."

The dancers halted impatiently, repeating the names after Sanchia. Neither Samson nor Henry made their appearance. At a groan from Gregory, Sanchia cast herself down beside him.

"Oh—find them—quick! He's poorly—we must get him away."

Someone ran out into the dark; Timothy Hawkins peered down at the sick man, suspending his bow; the crowd pressed in towards Gregory's couch. "Give him air! Stand back!" cried the Reverend Smith, thrusting his way to the front. "Courage, Gregory, my man; we'll have you out in a minute. Very rash to have brought him there," he muttered aside to Samson Jodrell.

"Ay," said the old man, sourly. "She would have it. She'll not be content till she's killed him."

"You've no right to say that," retorted the Reverend Smith. "Well, George, my lad?"—George Hawkins had come panting through the crowd to the edge of the platform.

"We canna find Samson—no more Henry Martyn;

they've gone—the two o' them," gasped the lad, his eyes fixed on Gregory's fearful face.

So heavy was Gregory that no other two had been judged strong enough to move him; now Sanchia cast a despairing glance about the circle.

Captain Beecham stepped forward; he had discarded his ruined collar, and the sweat rolled in thick drops from the corners of his jaws into the vast hairy recesses of his chest.

"I can give ye a hand, ma'am; if there's another fellow can help me," he began, when someone cried——

"Here's Samson Hawkins!"

The red-headed giant came rolling towards them; the few inches of flesh that showed above his beard were crimson as raspberries, and his eyes blinked in the lantern light. A gasp which went up from the assembled people escaped the Reverend Smith Prudhomme, who was occupied in thrusting the morphia needle into Gregory's uncovered arm.

"Are you there, Samson, my good fellow?—it's an occasion for haste, I'm afraid—but gently, gently: don't jar him more than you can help."

Samson lurched forward, stumbling against the Reverend Smith as he did so. The missionary was jerked aside. Samson's great arms went round Gregory's shoulders, and, as they did so, Gregory gave a scream and fainted away.

"Just as well," muttered Captain Beecham, raising the poor limp legs. "We couldn't ha' avoided hurting him a bit. Heave-ho, my hearty! Where now, ma'am?"

Sanchia's eyes, wide with rage and horror, were fixed on Samson Hawkins, who lurched off the platform with a movement which must have agonized Gregory, had he been conscious.

"Samson Hawkins!" she screamed, and flew at him like a wild cat. "Put Gregory down!"

"Eh?" grunted Samson, smiling foolishly.

"Ye're not fit to carry an empty bucket!" shrieked Sanchia. "You're drunk, Samson Hawkins!—drunk on Calvary beer!"

He gave a chuckle; a sort of strangled exclamation went up from the mob; one of the sailors elbowed his way to Samson's side, and managed to get his arms round Gregory.

"'Ere, let go, mate," he cried, warningly.

Samson's irascible temper flamed up, he tightened his own grip; as though unaware that it was a living thing he carried, he gave the body a wrench away from the helper. Rose Sanguinetti squealed like an animal—and a horrible thing happened; between them, they let Gregory fall to the ground.

Sanchia, like a mad thing, flew at Samson; her nails hooked in his beard, she was tearing, tearing: the blood ran down among the red hairs: she struck upwards at the foolish, bleary eyes. Janet Hawkins flew to the rescue of her son; she grabbed at Sanchia's loosened hair, she tore out handfuls and battered with her fists on Sanchia's shoulders. Above chaos the voice of the Reverend Smith piped like a gull——

"You fools! You fools! You are trampling on him—cease your folly!"

And as they dropped back, panting, Captain Beecham, with a glance at the pale and distraught face of the missionary, stooped and lifted Gregory's senseless body in his arms. His bellow rang in Sanchia's ear—"Lead on, ma'am; I'll see him out o' this."

She dragged her hair from Janet's restraining hand; the taffety dress was torn, the Paisley shawl hung from one shoulder and was trampled underfoot. Her way was blocked by red, bemused faces—she struck out at them with the palms of her hands—and the reek of Calvary beer was in her unaccustomed nostrils. Jed Robertson, propped up by his brother Jack; the younger Jodrell boys, giggling foolishly, too unsteady to trust each other's support, clinging by the door-post; Henry Martyn, sullenly drunk, querying her right to pass; they had all come in out of the night, and she saw in them enemies to Gregory and herself. The ship's doctor—where was the ship's doctor? She had noticed him at the dinner—a thin, youngish man, with a complexion which, had she known it, meant malaria, and tell-tale pouches under his eyes: just the sort of medical man one would look for on a ship of that class; a derelict of his profession. Not that Sanchia realized that: she sought him wildly among the crowd that gave way at their passing. Ah —there at last! She was about to open her mouth, to summon him, when she saw that he was clinging for support to Job Barker's shoulder; his mouth hung open, dribbling, his eyes were glazed. Sanchia knew a drunken man when she saw him; her hope died in her breast. "Wha's'a ma'er?" he was stammering stupidly.

"Get on!" breathed Sanchia in the captain's ear. He too had seen, and an angry flush climbed up the back of his bull-neck.

"Too bad, by gad, ma'am!" he muttered. "Have ye far to go?"

"Only a few yards."

They passed out into the roar of the incoming tide; at their heels went, mutely, the Reverend Smith Prudhomme, his cup of happiness dashed from his lips. Samson Jodrell and the two Mullyons came silently in the rear; and Maggie Robertson's Martha, dimly apprehending what all the excitement was about, but feeling, oh, so gay and beautifully dizzy, with the lights of the lanterns turning round in cartwheels before her enchanted eyes, lifted her petticoats up to heights undreamt of in respectable society and kicked her happy legs in their calico knickers—until her mother's outraged scream penetrated her ears, just a second in advance of the horny hand that clouted sensibility into her fuddled brain. Poor howling Martha! Never again was she to be allowed to forget her lapse from decency. It lay like a blot of ink upon her adolescent years. "We've seen Martha Robertson's drawers!" the small boys chanted. . . .

They laid Gregory on his bed in the little newly-finished house. A black stain of blood ran from the corner of his mouth to his jaw. There seemed nothing to be done; the six watchers stood stiffly, their shadows patching the walls;

Captain Beecham, awkwardly conscious of intrusion, twirled the buttons of his open waistcoat, wondering how he was to get out without thrusting Sophia Mullyon aside. Presently the Reverend Smith prayed, briefly. When the amens had died away, they stood, looking at each other; there was nowhere to sit down.

"I think we had better leave you, Sanchia," said the Reverend Smith faintly. "I shall be within earshot, if you call."

"Ay, go," she answered, without raising her head; she was on her knees at the bedside, her face only a few inches from Gregory's; she seemed to be willing him to return to her.

The Reverend Smith laid a paternal hand upon her shoulder.

"Do not distress yourself, my child, it is no doubt the best way. He is not likely to know any of us again."

"He's not dead," she retorted, stubbornly.

"No," said the Reverend Smith, and was nudged by Captain Beecham.

"I'll come along with you," he said, hoarsely. "If there's anything further you want, ma'am——?" It looked mightily as though this attractive young person was going to be a widow in an hour or two: the captain cast a frowning look of deliberation upon the still figure on the bed. If that were so—it might be early days to speak, but circumstances altered cases. He should stand as good a chance as any of these hairy-faced Calvary fellows. They were due to sail at four in the morning: Gregory Jodrell had better be getting on with his dying—if he meant to die, poor chap.

"Take them all with you," said Sanchia, suddenly, without changing her position. "Let me be—let me alone wi' Gregory."

The Mullyons turned swiftly, and walked out; Samson Jodrell stood his ground. The missionary touched him on the shoulder.

"Come, Samson; we have work to do for the Lord. I shall need your support in recalling our people to righteousness." The Reverend Smith's voice broke. "The first time, during my ministry, that we have been faced with that cursed beer."

The uproar from the barn reached them, even in the little closed-in room. "Come, Samson." The three men passed out together, leaving Sanchia alone with Gregory.

She moved stiffly, tripping, as she attempted to stand, in a loosened loop of the fringe. Swiftly she whipped her hair into its coil; she set the window wide, and lit another candle. A sense of possession animated her movements; she looked about her, at the blue-washed walls, at the clean print counterpane and freshly scrubbed boards; at the bunches of grasses that the school-children had thrust into jam jars on the window ledge. The room was empty save for the big, luxurious bed, that Gregory's mother had left for her son and his bride. There were but the two rooms—this and a living-room, the latter supplemented by a shed, built on at the back, which served as cookhouse. Two unframed oleographs of Edward VII and his queen, hung on the walls by tacks; the exquisite, unblemished face of Alexandra looked calmly at Sanchia across the pearl dog-collar.

Cautious steps came tip-toeing across the outer room; Miss Robbins appeared in the doorway.

"What has happened, Sanchia?"

"They're all drunk with Calvary beer; Samson Hawkins dropped Gregory," she answered, briefly.

Miss Robbins winced.

"He's not dead?"

"Nay; he swooned when they lifted him."

"Sanchia, I've got him!" Miss Robbins's excitement dismissed, a little crudely, the topic of the unconscious Gregory. "The sailors are ready to take him to the boat. It's dangerous, but it's the best way: we daren't wait until daylight."

Sanchia nodded.

"He wants to say good-bye to you; will you come?"

She stood still, with her hands clenched lightly at her sides. Had the light been stronger, Miss Robbins might have observed a whitening about her lips. It was a moment more poignant than Sanchia had expected; deliberately, during the last few days, she had set away from her the thought of parting from her lover. The finer substance of love was withered: but its baser element persists long after its beauty has departed. A kind of slow shuddering shook Sanchia's limbs, and she had a sensation as of death—as though her soul parted from her body. The physical aspect of her love presented itself to her with a frightful vividness. She battled with it as with a serpent. Again and again it reared its head and confronted her. And beside it rose another phantom, her own old age, taunting her with forgone opportunity.

"Will you come, Sanchia?"

". . . No."

"I think you are wise," said Miss Robbins, after a moment's pause, and went as quietly as she came.

It was not easy to shake her head at the weak, wild face that showed in the candle-light of her little shed. She spoke tersely, revoking her half-formed intention of inventing some farewell message to cover Sanchia's deficiency.

"She thought it wisest not to come; Gregory has had an accident." He shrugged his shoulders, and pity passed from her heart. She went behind them, as they stumbled down the beach in the darkness. A feeble thing, like straw; no more actual than a ghost, or a bad thought that had troubled several minds. Worthless, and imperilling lives more worthy than its own. It was no simple task to row out through unknown waters, to the spot where the ship's lights rode, beyond the farthest islands. But the sailors had been warned to keep southward, in a wide crescent, and only turn the boat inwards when almost on a line with the ship. She could hear them swearing at the kelp, as they plunged waist-deep in the water, heaving and thrusting. One at least of them had partaken of Calvary beer, and was fuddled: the others were sober enough. "Good-bye, miss," came a hoarse voice through the dark. "Till to-morrow morning!"

Till to-morrow morning—when the Peak should dwindle behind them into a speck on the horizon, and fade from sight with the curving of the earth's surface. For the last time she stood there, alone in the blackness, and heard the surge and thunder of eternal seas about the coasts of Calvary.

"Oh, Gregory, don't—don't suffer so!" She breathed it like a prayer. For nearly an hour she had gripped his hands, until her own were cramped with the strain; she wiped the sweat from her brow with her forearm. Her body was racked with his agony. To check the awful sound of his cries she pressed her brow again and again to his lips. Once or twice people had come, had looked in on her, and withdrawn; her absorption excluded them, there was nothing they could do. Twice, unavailingly, the Reverend Smith Prudhomme had hurried in and administered morphia; then, with a despairing gesture, had hurried out again, to attend to equally pressing matters. The islanders were out of hand: mysteriously the fatal cup had passed from hand to hand; the majority of the young people, now, were drunk: Rose Sanguinetti was dancing like a maniac with one of the sailors—her mother-in-law had snatched the sleeping child and rushed for safety to her own house and locked the door. Timothy Hawkins, drunk as a lord, had tumbled from his perch and broken a leg; his cousin George, a less skilled performer, had seized the instrument, and went capering about, shouting the melodies he had not the art to play. A fine, Hogarthian Walpurgis Night was being enacted in the barn, not the least piquant feature of which was the group on the platform, formed by Samson Jodrell, the Mullyons, Maggie Robertson—poor Maggie! It was a night of humiliation for her! John had succumbed, and sat propped up against the wall by his two sons—and one or two of the older couples of the island; with tears rolling down their furrowed faces they stood there and sang hymns. It seemed the best they could do. Calvary beer makes men dangerous, as well as light-hearted. The sailors, to whom the discovery of Calvary beer had been the one event of a tedious voyage, were attempting liberties with the women, and not being repulsed as they should have been. The Reverend Smith had experimented in turn in threats and exhortations, bellowed from the platform, or shouted in the ears of individuals; all without avail. It was Samson Jodrell who turned to him drearily, and roared above the tumult: "There's naught to do, seem'ly, but beseech the Lord." So distracted was the mind of the Reverend Prudhomme, that he actually started "Eternal Father," blind to its inappositeness. They took it up solemnly, and the grave stanzas rose now and again, faintly, in counterpoint to the dancers' lilt. A sailor pulled a whistle from his pocket, another tried to dance a hornpipe, lost his balance, and was trampled underfoot.

"Oh, Gregory," groaned Sanchia. She drew back a little, looking down on the dreadful face on the pillow; she had not known that pain could so disfigure the human countenance.

Slowly, painfully, she loosened her clasp upon his hands. Another shriek was coming: she saw the set jaw loosen itself—and quick as thought, she snatched the pillow from beneath Gregory's head. The head fell helplessly back on the bolster; she thrust the pillow over the staring eyes, the gaping mouth, and pressed, and pressed. Her own breath came in sobs. There was a very little struggle—no more than something very young and weak could make, beneath her thrusting hands. "It's better like this, Gregory!" she panted. "It's better—much, much better——!"

The struggle ceased; her head twisted across her shoulder, she watched with terror for someone to come in; the blood drummed in her ears. Or was it the thunder of the sea?

When she took the pillow away it was finished.

With an almost steady hand Sanchia composed the eyes, and set the bed in order. She passed her handkerchief over her lips, and stood for a moment, collecting her thoughts.

A footfall sounded in the outer room. She went instinctively to the door, to check the incomer. It was the Reverend Smith Prudhomme.

"He's gone," said Sanchia, briefly.

He stared at her as though he did not at first understand. She stood aside, and indicated the bed with a movement of her hand. The Reverend Smith hastily inclined his head, and remained a moment silent, in deference to the dead. Then he held out his hand to Sanchia. "My poor young girl——"

She thrust her hands into the belled openings of her fringed sleeves. Actually a smile flickered about the corners of her lips. He felt an impulse of recoil. Never did Sanchia produce sentiments becoming to the situation. It was very unseemly to smile with the yet warm body of one's husband within arm's-length. The Reverend Smith frowned, and withdrew his hand.

"I will send Maggie Robertson to you at once." To Maggie fell the duty of laying out all the dead of the island. "You had better let me take you to your mother's."

"What time does the ship sail?" asked Sanchia, with apparent irrelevance.

"Eh? Ah—presumably at four." The Reverend Smith, drawn by curiosity, no less than by the instinct to close those dreadfully protuberant eyes of the thing that had been Gregory, had approached the bedside. His heart gave a great leap in his bosom. The eyes—the tongue—the blackened contusion of the features. . . . Nature leaves none of these grim signs, nor does innocent death so brand its victims. . . . And, besides, Sanchia had actually not remembered to replace the pillow. It lay crumpled against the foot of the bed.

"Sanchia!" said the Reverend Smith. And again—"Sanchia."

She showed no signs of discomfiture, but looked down

upon the bed with a strange, vague smile, pushing the hair from her temple with her two hands.

"'Tis queer, what pity makes ye do," she offered.

"For Christ's sake—Sanchia!"

"He were in such pain. An' he were weak. It wasn't very hard."

The Reverend Smith Prudhomme felt such a weakening at the knees that it was impossible to remain standing upright. He sat down, on the only place that offered—the foot of Gregory's bed. He felt as though she had taken him by the shoulders, and swung him out, like a harpy, over a gulf in which dissolved the whole material of his accepted moral and religious life. To put it plainly, Sanchia had committed murder, and proffered an excuse. As though there could be any excuse for the mortal sin of taking human life. His obvious duty was to denounce her to the community. . . . Stay: was the course of duty so plain after all? To denounce her was to deliver her to the island's justice. The Reverend Smith, who had an inward shrinking from all forms of physical cruelty, shuddered. Over the Point—or out to sea in a punctured coracle. An eye for an eye, a tooth for a tooth. Crude Mosaic justice. "Far too much symbolism has arisen in the interpretation of the Divine Law: moral cowardice and physical sloth have brought about latter-day adaptations which sooner or later will challenge the jurisdiction of the Church Militant . . . the narrow and painful path of the literal . . ." A voice crying in the wilderness, his own voice, echoing from the pulpit, sounded thinly in his ears. "If I were a Jesuit . . ." he pondered wistfully: and forgot to be shocked at himself for the heretical thought. To shelter Sanchia was called—what was it called? Compounding a felony. Unthinkable for a minister of the English Church.

Why did she ask me about the sailing of the ship? Was it possible that she did this thing deliberately, in order to make her escape with her lover? Did she cloak that ineffable sin beneath the virtuous mask of pity?

His eyes pierced the shifting candle-light suspiciously; she stood there, her shadow flickering across the body of the dead man. In the calm immobility of her face he read neither shame nor apprehension. To be so calmly certain of the right! Bitterly he envied her—many things; her youth, her simplicity, her paganism, her directness and lack of sentimentality. He felt sick, helpless, dazed, as he had done on the night when she forced him to marry her to Gregory Jodrell. A sense of littleness, of unwisdom, tortured him. His resentment revived, that she, an ignorant woman of the people, should have power to reduce him to insignificance, his principles to ashes. Her air of a Romish saint irritated him against her; his Protestantism was of the narrow and militant order; the Roman churches were to him places of abomination; sightseeing, reluctantly, on his Italian honeymoon, he had been obliged to dig his nails into the flesh of his palms, not to reach out and dash the gilded saints from their pedestals; the same mad impulse seized him now, to crash his fist into the calm, aloof face of Sanchia, which regarded him with the same gentle certitude as the Paduan Virgins. She stood there quiet, safe as in a niche, safe in her own certainty of rectitude. She had everything that he had not; she had the best thing of all—supreme belief in herself and her judgments. Convention, even the moral law itself, slipped off her lightly, like rain. Her vision pierced the close weaving of accepted forms, and found clarity, somewhere—somewhere the other side of religion.

For the first time he found himself tremulously reviewing the possibility of a Beyond that transcended the formula invented by Church and society for the preservation of their own solidarities. For the first time he glimpsed a virtue which concerned itself not at all with adultery, with the supposed sacredness of human life, with a supposed Divine law, interpreted through generations of human misunderstanding and misrepresentation. Had his call to Calvary been planned for this?—to give him opportunity to shed the outworn mantle of the religious teaching he had absorbed and in his turn disseminated in his pastorate?

Black and white he had always accepted as the symbolic colours of human conduct; the grey of compromise he had disclaimed with a sturdy self-righteousness which blinded him to the many occasions when he had called upon its useful aid to tide him over an awkward or unpleasant situation: his favourite form being the shifting of responsibility to other shoulders. With the true self-deception common to many religious individuals, he had called this shifting of responsibility by a more euphemistic name: as humility, a frank confession of his own inability, it satisfied his conscience, and he, paradoxically, prided himself upon his meekness.

Here life had trapped him; here he was faced with a responsibility that could neither be shared nor shelved: a secret of deadly import, that lay between Sanchia and himself. It was for him to determine whether she had acted in innocence or with guilty intention: for him to bear the onus, henceforward, of liberating a murderess upon the community, or of sending her to her judgment. The burden of her life lay upon his reluctant shoulders; his duty to God, to Sanchia, to the islanders. . . . He bowed his head.

Sanchia waited. She thought:

I have killed Gregory. It was I—with these hands that will wither and warp, though they are so firm now—who pushed the pillow over his face and held it there, while he was struggling and his chest was heaving, until the breath was driven back in his lungs and he choked to death. A little pain for a long peace. Gregory, you know that now. You will thank me for it, Gregory. No more pain. No more pain. For ever and ever, amen. And now I can be happy, too, because I haven't to bear Gregory's pain any longer; the pain that crept and creaked here in my stomach until I thought I'd go mad with it. I killed Gregory. That's what they do with animals that are sick; they put them out of their pain. We're all animals. It's right to put us out of our pain. I've taken life, and by and by I'm going to create life. I shall have a child. The Lord He gave and the Lord He has taken away. I have done those same things. In me is power.

That's like finishing a chapter. The chapter of Gregory is done, and the chapter of the dumb man is done, and the chapter of El Secredo is done. Three chapters; three mistakes. Now we begin again. Everything must be new. New like the new-born babe in my womb. We wait—we both wait to see what is going to happen to us. This bald-headed man who is not even as wise as I is going to decide. If we die, that will be new, and if we live, that will be in a new way. He is praying to God, and he won't even understand when the answer comes; he does not know that I am as clever as God. But we must wait and see. When he has finished his For Jesus Christ's sakes and his Amens we shall know. He only has two words to say: *Death* or *Life*. But he is not brave enough to say *Death*, because he is afraid of Calvary ghosts, and because he knows I have not sinned. He *knows*. I did it for Gregory, not for myself. In me is power, and he is weak, and frightened of things. Frightened of life, frightened of death, frightened of God. I put my hand in God's and say, "I have done as You have done, because I am brave and I am not frightened of living or dying."

If he is much longer people will come. I ought to close your eyes and bind up your mouth, Gregory, but I don't want to touch you again. I'm not afraid of you, because you know why I did it, and you are thanking me. But I don't *want* to touch you. You don't belong to me now; you belong to El Secredo, you belong to the earth where they will put you; and by and by grass will grow and men will cut it with scythes and the grass will be you, Gregory; and the cattle will feed on it, and the cattle will be you, Gregory. And maybe you will call to me one day with a young bull's voice, and I won't hear you, because I'll be across the sea; and you'll go lowing, lowing over the island, Gregory, wanting to thank me, and I'll hear you—somewhere—in a room, all shut in, with motor-cars running along the streets alongside, and lights all up and down the houses. I'll hear you because when you were sick I grew friendly to you; for I know you were good, and that you loved me as well as my body. My body that was another's. Bodies talk as lips do, and yours was always dumb to me, Gregory; dumb, for all your wanting. But you were kind to me, and because you were kind, and didn't let folks torment me more than you could help, I did this for you. That was fair, wasn't it, Gregory? I did it because I was friendly to you, and because my body ached with all your pain.

Steps sounded along the cobblestones outside. Her eyes turned anxiously to the Reverend Smith. Had he heard? The decision must be taken, the answer given.

The pillow lay, crumpled against the foot of the bed, within reach of his hand. The pillow, of goose-feathers and coarse, unbleached calico, that had suffocated Gregory. There was a little patch of damp, of saliva, in the middle of it. He bent to recover it, and, still only partly conscious of his actions, he raised the head of the dead man and laid the pillow in its place. Swiftly his thumb pressed down upon the staring eyelids; quickly he twitched the sheet upwards to cover the unseemly features of the dead.

A soft sigh broke from Sanchia; instinctively she placed her hands over her abdomen, as though to reassure the child within. Miss Robbins was in the room; she had changed into her woollen suit; a little bundle of odds and ends was tucked under her left arm. She stood still, staring at the sheeted figure on the bed; swiftly she moved to Sanchia's side, gripping the girl's hand in a warm clasp.

The Reverend Smith walked to the window, looking with an experienced eye upon the faintly lightening sky.

"You are ready for departure?"

"Yes." She hesitated, speaking, at last, in the hushed voice which people assume in the presence of the dead. "Sanchia had better come with me, hadn't she?"

"I have many things to do," said the Reverend Smith, vacantly. "I find that I have builded a house upon sand, and I must set to and begin all over again. You can both pray for me—I wish you God speed; yes, Sanchia had better go with you. . . . "